Dawn's End

Ashram Stormrider Book 1

Syd Nault

To Dave,
Thanks for buying my book and supporting my dream of being an author. I hope you enjoy it.

Paperback ISBN: 978-1-0694761-0-4

Ebook ISBN: 978-1-0694761-1-1

Acknowledgements

To my wonderful wife—your unwavering encouragement, thoughtful insight, and editorial eye have been invaluable throughout this journey. Your belief in me breathed life into every page.

To my father and step-daughter, thank you for reading my book with care and offering your constructive feedback and editorial assistance.

And to all my family and friends who stood by me with words of support and moments of kindness—know that your encouragement carried me farther than you may ever realize. I am deeply grateful.

Prologue

The door creaked on its hinges as Malakar pushed it open, the sound reverberating down the empty corridor behind him. The room beyond was shrouded in darkness, but to his kind, light held no meaning. His eyes—those remnants of a once-living body—were little more than hollow vessels, empty and devoid of life, yet still capable of seeing. His vision, if it could be called that, had transcended the limitations of mere sight. It was a supernatural awareness of light's subtle variances, a sense of the world that defied logical explanation, a power not fully understood but intimately familiar.

He shuffled across the room, the hem of his long black robes trailing across the cold stone floor with a whisper of the fabric. The obsidian table loomed in the center of the chamber with its surface dark and polished like the void itself. Malakar rounded the table and sank into a wooden chair opposite the door. He leaned forward, while resting his skeletal hands upon the table. For a moment, his gaze fell on those hands—bare bone, the skin stretched taut over them like an afterthought. Beneath the thin membrane, little remained of the flesh that had once covered them. The absence of life was not just evident in his hands, but in the very air he breathed. What had he become?

The thought lingered in his mind, as it always did in moments like these. His hands, once capable of wielding power through flesh and bone, were now nothing more than dry remnants of a dead man. Yet his mind, that sharp and calculating part of him, clung to the idea that he was still alive—though in what way, he could not say. His body, he knew, had died long ago. The essence of life that had once animated it was long gone, leaving behind only a semblance of motion, a shadow of what he had been.

The early years had been the worst, when the stench of decay clung to him like a second skin, a constant reminder of his unnatural state. Those were the years of pain, of struggle. But as time wore on and his body dried and withered, it became easier. His reliance on physical senses had waned, replaced by a growing connection to the dark powers that now sustained him. The stench of decay had faded, and with it, the last remnants of his humanity.

Footsteps echoed down the hallway, faint at first, but growing louder. Malakar's senses sharpened instinctively. He knew who it was. The others were coming. It was time to discuss the matter at hand concerning the monk and his proposition. Malakar had tried to warn them, tried to persuade them to prepare for contingencies, but they were placing far too much faith in the young monk's abilities. His promises were fragile, built on the ambitions of youth. Malakar felt that they had invested too much in him, far more than the monk could ever deliver.

Two figures entered the open door, their black robes flowing around them like shadows given form. They seated themselves at the table, each one pulling back their hood to reveal the faces that lay hidden beneath. Malakar suppressed the urge to recoil, though it was an instinct that he had long suppressed. Each time their faces were exposed, it struck him with a visceral shock. The skin was drawn tight over their skulls, thin and translucent, like parchment stretched too thin. Their eyes, hollow and dark, gazed back with an emptiness that felt like staring into the abyss itself. Their lips were drawn back, revealing teeth that had long since decayed into sharp, jagged remnants of what they once were.

Malakar knew well the horror of his own reflection, the abomination that he had become. But it was a price he had chosen to pay, a price he had been willing to accept. The power they wielded, the dominion over death itself, came with a cost. And that cost had been steep. Immortality, once seen as a gift, had become nothing more than a curse. They had become bound to the endless cycle of decay. But there was this power that they had all embraced, a power that bound them in their shared fate.

He glanced once more at the two who had joined him, their unspoken presence a reminder of what they had all become. The world had fallen silent around them, and it was in this silence that the true weight of their existence settled upon his shoulders.

Valrath was the first to break the silence, his voice scraping through the still air like the desperate scurrying of a thousand beetles beneath dry earth. The sound was grating, like something long dead, struggling to force its way out. “The monk has presented us with a new opportunity,” he said, the words thick with bitter disdain, each one laced with the weight of contempt. “It may prove to be a poor outcome, but I believe it is one we should explore.” He ended his statement with a coughing fit, the sound harsh and ragged, tearing at the fragile remnants of his throat. Even the simple act of speaking seemed to drain the last vestiges of life from him, as if the very process threatened to strip away the shreds of what little humanity remained.

Thal’gorath, the youngest of the trio—though age, in his case, was a deeply misleading term—responded with calm, his voice smooth and thoughtful as he tapped one long, clawed fingernail against the dark obsidian surface of the table. “You are too quick to leap, Valrath,” he murmured. “This monk may make grand promises, but what of his ability to deliver on them? He speaks of power, but we cannot yet be certain he is capable of seeing his plans through. What if we invest in him only to watch him fail?" There was a quiet authority in his tone, despite the irritation that underlay it. With a sense of caution, he spoke. "We need a alternative plan, should this not unfold as we hope."

Valrath's grip tightened on the edge of the table as he leaned forward, his eyes narrowing, the faintest tremor of impatience creeping into his voice. "I have watched him. He shows great potential. With our guidance, he will succeed," Valrath said, the words laced with certainty, his belief unwavering. "There is no one in his homeland who could challenge him. These powers are foreign to them. He will be a storm they never see coming."

Thal'gorath allowed himself a moment of reluctant agreement. The eastern lands, with their comforts and complacency, seemed far too preoccupied with the maintenance of their fragile, easy lives to investigate the deeper mysteries of the world. It was entirely possible that this monk, unopposed by any true force, could slip into their midst, work his will undisturbed, and see his plan unfold as he hoped. Even so, Thal'gorath could not shake his reservations. He was unwilling to place all their hopes into a single figure, regardless of his apparent promise. They needed to prepare for the possibility that things would not unfold as expected. This monk, for all his potential, might yet prove to be a disappointment.

"I will go along with this plan, Valrath,"

Thal'gorath conceded, his voice barely more than a hiss, a faint whisper as his lips parted. "But know this: I do not trust in putting all our faith in this one monk. If he fails, we lose the opportunity to expand our powers. It could also be a solution to the decay of our own forms." His words carried a dangerous undercurrent, the desire for power, for control, palpable in the air.

Valrath hesitated, the weight of Thal'gorath's caution sinking into his thoughts. Yet, his resolve remained firm. "You will reap the rewards of his success, as will I," he said with growing conviction, his voice steady now. "Wait and see."

Malakar's voice cut through the exchange, deep and authoritative, dragging the focus back to him with a force that could not be ignored. "Then it is settled." His words were brief, but they held the finality of a decision already made, a command issued from a place of quiet authority.

For most of their discussions, Malakar was more an observer than a participant, his presence felt only in the occasional murmur of agreement or sharp look, as though he were merely a shadow among them. And yet, despite the apparent aloofness, Malakar held dominion over this gathering of minds. He ruled not by force of personality, but through a subtle manipulation of influence, a careful game of subtlety. He cared little for the superficial struggles for dominance between Valrath and Thal'gorath; his gaze remained focused on the larger game, one they had not yet fully understood. But they would—eventually.

The room settled into an eerie quiet once more, the weight of their decisions hanging thick in the air. The tension between them, however unspoken, was palpable. Malakar's gaze lingered on his companions, his thoughts distant, already calculating the next move in a game that was far from over.

There was no need for further words. The other two liches stood in unison, their movements fluid, almost rehearsed. Malakar gave a brief, sharp nod to acknowledge their compliance before watching them turn and make their way toward the door. The sounds of their footsteps faded into the distant hall, leaving Malakar alone with his thoughts.

His companions, ever hungry for more power, were consumed by an endless thirst for dominance. Yet, for all their desire, Malakar could not help but wonder: to what end? They already wielded vast power—far more than most could ever dream of—and yet, they squandered it in petty contests. Each one vied for superiority, each struggle a futile attempt to prove who could do more with the gifts they had been granted. A competition that had no clear victor, no resolution, only an endless cycle of ambition and envy.

Malakar, however, saw a different path. A possibility that stretched beyond the reach of their narrow aspirations, one that no doubt would be dismissed as madness if he were to voice it aloud. It was a vision that stood in stark contrast to the ceaseless bickering of his companions. While they fought over the spoils of their power, Malakar envisioned something far greater—a goal that transcended their petty squabbles. But to reveal this would be to risk the very foundation of their alliance. To speak it would invite suspicion, or worse, mockery, and so he kept the thought to himself, buried deep within the recesses of his mind.

Malakar had no illusions about his authority. He knew well enough that neither Valrath nor Thal'gorath could challenge him—not truly. They had their strengths, their cunning, but they were both too ensnared by their own egos to ever pose a real threat. Even so, Malakar was not eager to provoke a conflict that would tear apart the fragile alliance they had forged. There was no need to upset the balance, to bring down the weight of his considerable power upon them just yet. Not when their cooperation still served his long-term goals. He had no doubt that when the time came, he would do whatever was necessary—however ruthless—to achieve his ultimate aims. But that moment had not arrived. Not yet.

For now, he would wait and see how this all progressed. He would continue watching his companions fight among themselves while he quietly worked toward his own end. The game, he knew, was far from over. And when the pieces finally fell into place, he would make sure that he was the one who would end up on top. It would not be Valrath or Thal'gorath who would dictate the terms of their success.

Malakar let a growl of frustration escape his throat, low and guttural, as he stood from his seat. The chair scraped across the stone floor with an unpleasant screech, a sound that seemed to reverberate through the stillness of the room, an echo of his own internal unrest. Malakar stretched, feeling the ancient stiffness of his bones—a reminder of just how long he had existed in this form. Time, it seemed, moved differently for one such as him.

He moved to the center of the room, his thoughts sharp and focused. He would have to act soon. He could feel the creeping weight of inevitability, the pressure of the decisions that loomed ahead. There would come a time in the future when he would eventually have to put either Valrath or Thal'gorath in their place. He would have to remind them of their subservient role in their uneasy alliance. But for now, there was no need to rush. Patience, after all, was a virtue that had served Malakar well over the centuries.

He would continue to work alongside them, for the moment at least, and continue down the path he had set. His end goal was still distant, but it was within reach. And when the time came, when he had laid the foundation for his ultimate purpose, he would claim what was rightfully his. There was nothing that could stop him now.

Chapter 1:
The Maiden's Haven

Ash stood at the window of his private chambers, his gaze fixed on the monastery courtyard below. The morning sun spilled its pale, golden light over the grounds, illuminating the cobblestone paths and casting long, angular shadows that clung to the edges of the buildings like unspoken secrets. A gentle breeze stirred the leaves of the ancient trees scattered across the yard, their rustling a soft counterpoint to the faint crunch of gravel underfoot. Two monks emerged from a building to the left, their robes trailing behind them as they made their way toward the meditation hall. Routine had dictated their steps, as it did for most at this hour.

Ash lingered in the golden stillness, his longing left unspoken. The sun's warmth, he imagined, would feel good on his face, but he doubted it could penetrate the chill that had settled deep within him. It was a cold not born of the room's air, nor the faint draft that slipped through the open window, but of something more insidious—a dream that had wrenched him from sleep and now coiled tightly around his thoughts.

The dream. It lingered like a phantom on the edges of his consciousness, refusing to dissipate. Not since his days as a wanderer had he experienced something so vivid, so urgent. A face he had not seen, not even thought of, in over twenty years had surfaced in the haze of sleep. And with it, a warning. Its words, though ephemeral as smoke, had carried the burden of reality, too vivid to dismiss as mere nocturnal imaginings.

Ash frowned, his hands moving mechanically to the pitcher of steaming water left on the table by a novice. He poured the water into a basin beneath the window. Wisps of steam rose, curling and twisting in the sunlight like strands of ghostly hair. For a moment, he watched their dance—a passing interplay of life and death, a mirror to the balance he had tried to maintain the last few years of his life while living here in the walls of this monastery.

He dipped his hands into the basin, letting the warmth bleed into his palms before bringing it to his face. The heat was a welcome balm, washing away the sweat clinging to his skin, a relic of the dream's grip. His hands lingered there for a moment before slipping to the long, white strands of hair that framed his face. He gathered them back, tying the locks into place with a strip of worn leather pulled from the folds of his robe.

Leaning over the basin, he stared into the now-still surface of the water. His reflection stared back, almost ageless yet marked, a stranger wearing the face of the man he used to be. The eyes that met his gaze were fathomless, piercing brown eyes etched onto the pallid canvas of his weathered face. Though the gifted powers of the Divine Mother whom his order served with unwavering devotion—had stayed some of the years carved upon his soul. The immensity of a life hard-lived lingered still, its presence whispered in every ache and scar.

Years of relentless training and meditative devotion had been required to master the sacred power bestowed by the Divine Mother. To wield such supernatural force was the ultimate aspiration of the monks, the zenith of their practice. Yet for Ash, the weight of those years now felt hollow, as if all that effort had been squandered on a mission that no longer resonated.

Once, Ash had revered the gift, embracing it as divine affirmation of his devotion—a sacred testament to the path he had chosen. But as the years unfurled, the glances of unease and veiled revulsion became ever more frequent. The blessing began to weigh heavy, like a brand seared into his very being. To strangers, it marked him not as a guardian or healer, but as something to be distrusted.

A sigh escaped his lips, soft and bitter. He had walked the Divine Mother's path to bring solace to those in need, yet how often had his efforts been met with recoiling gazes and trembling hands? Too often. Some would rather die than accept the help from a man who bore the Divine Mother's touch.

The water in the basin rippled as his hands tightened against its edge, his reflection warping and twisting with the motion. For a brief moment, the dream's warning surfaced again in his thoughts, sharp and unrelenting. He closed his eyes, willing the vision to fade, but its weight remained, coiled within him like a predator waiting to strike.

He straightened, his movements deliberate as he stepped away from the window. Whatever the dream's meaning, it would not release its hold on him so easily. It was a herald of change, and Ash could feel its shadow falling over his quiet life like a storm building on the horizon.

Turning from the golden warmth spilling through the open window, Ash approached the heavy oaken door of his chambers. His hand lingered on the cool brass handle as he paused, the moment stretching longer than it should. A choice hung in the air, unspoken but palpable. Step through the door and follow the rhythm of his daily routine, or remain in the quiet solitude of his room, lost in the labyrinth of thoughts his restless mind endlessly conjured.

A faint sigh escaped his lips, and with it, his hesitation. The door creaked faintly as he pulled it open and stepped into the dim hallway beyond.

His bare feet whispered against the cold stone floor,

a subtle shuffling that barely disturbed the silence of the monastery. Along the corridor, a young acolyte in simple robes tended to the candles nestled in wall sconces. She turned at the sound of his approach, her movements hesitant. Her head dipped in a bow—whether in reverence or to avoid his penetrating gaze, Ash couldn't be certain.

"Good morning, Brother," she said softly, her voice barely more than a whisper, fragile as glass.

Ash paused, his dark, unyielding gaze locking onto hers. Her eyes—bright and unblemished by the passage of years—stirred a pang deep within him. They were a painful reminder of a time when he, too, had carried such untainted innocence. A shadow of sorrow flickered across his thoughts, unbidden yet impossible to ignore.

He realized too late that his silence had unsettled her, and she seemed poised to retreat. Ash softened his expression, offering her a warm smile that felt practised but sincere enough.

"My apologies, young Sister," he said, inclining his head. "Good morning to you as well."

The tension in her shoulders eased, and her lips curved into a faint smile before she returned to her task. Ash resumed his journey, his steps carrying him toward the ornate double doors at the end of the hall.

Pushing through the heavy doors, he was met with a wave of sunlight so bright that he squinted against its brilliance. For a moment, he stood still, letting the light wash over him, allowing its warmth to caress his face. It was tender, almost comforting, though it failed to dispel the cold knot of unease that lingered deep within him.

The sound of the door closing behind him jolted him into motion. He descended the short stone steps into the courtyard, his feet meeting the cool cobblestones of the winding path. The morning air was crisp, and the monastery grounds were quiet save for the faint rustle of leaves stirred by a gentle breeze.

With a destination in mind, Ash veered off the path, heading toward the meditation hall. Its imposing structure loomed ahead, solemn and silent, but he had no intention of entering today. He knew the agitation in his mind would not allow the stillness he sought.

Instead, his eyes turned to the gardens flanking the entrance to the hall. Neatly arranged beds of flowers and herbs had begun to show signs of neglect—a stray weed here, a patch of soil turned dry and cracked. It wasn't much, but it was enough to give him an excuse.

Ash knelt by one of the beds, his hands moving instinctively to pull at the offending weeds and loosen the hardened soil. To the casual observer, he might seem engaged in diligent service, tending to the grounds as any devoted monk might. But in truth, this was his refuge, a way to isolate himself from the watchful eyes of his brothers and sisters. Here, amidst the quiet rustle of leaves and the earthy scent of soil, he could lose himself—if only for a while and stave off the questions he was not ready to face.

The scent of lavender drew Ash to this quiet corner of the monastery grounds, a place where time seemed to still and the world softened. The fragrance stirred something deep within him—a memory not fully formed, a shadow of a thought. It eluded his mind's grasp, slipping away like smoke, but left behind a feeling as warm and fleeting as a long-forgotten embrace.

His fingers moved along the stems, tracing their delicate curve, dragging upward to the velvety bloom that crowned each stalk. As he brushed the lavender, the flowers released their aromatic essence, a soft, intoxicating perfume that filled the air. It teased his senses into a quiet bliss, and, without thinking, the corners of his mouth lifted into a faint smile.

Here, amidst the earth and fragrance, there was peace—fragile, fleeting, but real. For all its trials, this monastery had offered him moments of solace, shards of serenity among the storms of his mind. Ash held onto that thought for a moment longer, breathing deeply as if the scent alone could root him in the present.

The spell broke with the creak of wood cutting through the stillness. It was distant but persistent, the rhythmic groan of strained wheels. Ash turned, his dark eyes scanning the courtyard. Across the grounds, a young man trudged along, pulling a wooden cart piled high with crates of produce.

Ash's stomach responded with a low, insistent grumble, a sharp reminder of his morning fast. He realized he hadn't eaten since the previous afternoon. Perhaps the cart held something simple—a ripe fruit, a handful of nuts, or a few seeds to stave off the growing hunger.

He rose from the garden, brushing dirt from his robes, and set off toward the kitchens, his steps carrying a subtle vigour now that his hunger gave him meaning. Along the way, monks passed him, moving to and fro about their morning tasks. He returned their greetings with quiet nods, his gaze fixed ahead.

By the time he reached the back entrance of the kitchen, the cart stood abandoned near the slightly ajar, moss-streaked door. Ash glanced over the crates packed within the wagon. Squash and peppers gleamed under the sunlight, cobs of corn sat stacked neatly, and a crate of earthy-smelling potatoes rounded out the haul. Yet none of it piqued his appetite, none of it stirred the faint hope for something to break his fast.

Then it came—the unmistakable aroma of fresh-baked bread drifting through the open doorway. The scent wrapped around him like an old friend, warm and inviting. A smile returned to his face, unbidden, as his stomach growled once more in eager agreement.

With a quiet chuckle to himself, Ash pushed open the door and stepped inside, the promise of simple pleasures guiding him forward.

The air in the kitchen was thick, weighted by the radiating heat of wood-fueled ovens that lined the walls like silent sentinels. The warmth clung to Ash's skin, amplified by the faint smell of charred wood and baked flour. At the room's center, a broad wooden table dominated the space, its surface laden with overflowing crates of fresh produce and streaked with the powdered remnants of the morning's baking. From the rafters above, an assortment of tools dangled within easy reach, gleaming faintly in the golden light filtering through the high, narrow windows.

Ash's eyes darted over the crates, his stomach rumbling as he searched for the prize his senses craved. The scent of freshly baked bread lingered in the air, tantalizing and maddening. "Where are you?" he muttered to himself, rounding the table as if stalking prey.

A booming voice cut through the quiet. "Now, Daelon, you're letting your imaginations get the better of you. Really?"

The sudden sound jolted Ash, and he straightened instinctively, his composure returning in an instant. A large woman stepped into the room, her apron dusted with flour and her movements brisk. The figure trailing behind her collided squarely with her back as she stopped, nearly toppling over before catching his balance with an awkward shuffle.

"Beggin' your pardon, master monk," the woman said hurriedly, her cheeks flushing as she began brushing the flour from her apron in vain. Ash nearly chuckled at the gesture—it was like trying to dry a rain-soaked cloak with bare hands. "I didn't see ya slip into me kitchen. I meant no offence." She offered a bow so deep that Ash half-expected her to tumble forward.

"No need to apologize, my lady," Ash replied, his voice a soothing melody as he softened his smile. The tension in her frame melted away, and her expression brightened. "It is I who've intruded on your sanctuary, and for that, I should apologize to you."

He stepped forward, extending a hand in greeting. Her grip was plump but soft, her touch surprisingly delicate for someone who worked in the heat and labour of a kitchen. As Ash withdrew, a wiry arm snaked out from behind her, its owner stepping into view—a man with dirt-streaked clothes and the unmistakable scent of freshly tilled earth clinging to him.

"I'm Daelon," the man said quickly, pumping Ash's hand with an enthusiasm that bordered on excessive. "I bring the produce from the village below." His nods came in rapid succession, as if punctuating his every word. The woman shot him a sharp elbow to the ribs, earning a muffled grunt.

"No need to pester the brother," she chided, her tone firm but affectionate. She glanced back at Ash with an apologetic smile. "I'm sure he's got more important things to tend to than your chatter."

Ash offered her a reassuring nod before turning his attention back to the table. His eyes settled on a golden-brown loaf of bread nestled among the crates, its aroma practically calling his name. "Would it trouble you if I stole the end of this loaf? My belly would be most grateful."

The woman's face lit up. "Oh, please, sir, it'd be me honour. Let me cut a bit for ya—maybe some fresh butter to go with it? That'd be nice, eh?" She manoeuvred around him with surprising agility for her size, though not without narrowly avoiding bumping him into the table.

"No need for butter," Ash replied with a gentle smile. "Your baking is perfection on its own." He offered a slight bow, a gesture of gratitude that brought a pleased chuckle from the woman as she carved off a generous slice of bread.

While she worked, Daelon had already dragged a stool over and plopped himself down with a grin, earning a disapproving glare from the baker. Ash paid him little mind until the man leaned forward, elbows on knees, his eyes glinting with excitement.

"Perhaps, Heddy, the brother monk would like to hear my story?" Daelon asked, his voice brimming with anticipation. He glanced at the woman, seeking her approval like a child awaiting permission to speak.

"Oh no, the brother doesn't need to hear your ramblings," the baker snapped, her voice sharp as the glare she shot Daelon. "Keep your tall tales of dead men walkin' about to yourself."

The scolding quieted Daelon, but only served to pique Ash's interest. He turned, fixing Daelon with a gaze that could strip the truth from a liar's lips. The man shrank under the scrutiny, sliding halfway off his stool like a child caught in mischief.

"I just mean..." Daelon stammered, his words tripping over one another in a desperate bid to escape. "You're the one they talk about, ain't ya? The one who spent his life hunting such abominations?" He looked ready to bolt, his hands gripping the edges of the stool as though preparing to flee.

"Stay seated," Ash commanded, his voice low but firm. He pulled another stool from beneath the table and sat. Behind him, the baker fell silent, her presence palpable in the sudden stillness of the room.

"This tale of the undead," Ash said, leaning forward slightly. "Is it truth, or are you spinning yarn?"

Daelon swallowed hard, his Adam's apple bobbing

like a buoy in a storm. "As far as I know, it's as true as can be. I swear on the name of each of the gods." He hesitated, glancing at Ash with wide, pleading eyes, as if awaiting permission to continue.

Ash let out a low grunt, a sound that could mean anything, then gave the man a single nod.

The words poured out of Daelon in a rush, tumbling over one another like a flood breaking through a dam. "Last night, I was down at the inn, having a few pints. Not too much, mind you—I knew I had to be up early for the fields. Anyway, in bursts this man I'd never seen before, going on about some dead feller running through the streets of Farrow's Point." He paused, his face twisting in an awkward smile. "That's the village over yonder, if ya didn't know."

Ash frowned, his lips pressing into a thin line. Daelon must have noticed, for he hurried on.

"Yes, well, anyway… I thought maybe the man was just drunk outta his mind, spewing nonsense. But he looked… I don't know, terrified."

"Hey, I told you that the lad was probably drunk outta his mind, you buffoon," the baker cut in from behind Ash, her voice sharp and accusing. "You were going on like this fellow was preaching the truth." She froze when Ash turned his head slightly, then retreated back into silence, content to glower from her post by the table.

"Whatever," Daelon said with a dismissive wave of his hand. "The man was clearly scared. He half expected the room to rise up and march to his little village's aid. Instead, everyone laughed at him. The minstrel picked up her pipe, the dancing started again, and that was that." He paused, lowering his voice as though sharing a secret.

"But I stopped him as he was about to storm out. Asked him straight up if his words were true. He looked me dead in the eye and swore on his momma's grave that they were." Daelon shrugged, his shoulders rising and falling with an air of detachment, as if to say he wasn't sure what to believe himself.

Ash leaned back on the stool, exhaling a long, tired sigh. He didn't say a word, his mind turning over the man's story like a stream over a stone. Perhaps the claim was honest—a kernel of truth buried in a field of drunken exaggeration. Or perhaps it was nothing more than the imaginings of a man too deep in his cups, passed along by someone who wasn't far behind him.

Either way, Ash felt the weight of it settling on his shoulders, heavier than it should've been. He rubbed a hand across his brow, feeling the years pressing in, and thought—not for the first time—that he was getting too old for this kind of thing.

Ash turned back to the table, his fingers closing around the slice of bread Heddy had cut for him. He thumbed off a corner and tossed it into his mouth. The taste was divine—a perfect union of crust and crumb, rich and hearty. The flavour ignited his senses, flooding him with a rare and simple joy. For a fleeting moment, he allowed himself to bask in it. This was the life he wanted. A life of quiet pleasures, unburdened by the weight of monstrosities and the endless chase that had defined his past.

He sighed, breaking off another piece. His thoughts drifted, like smoke curling from a dying flame, only to be interrupted by the groan of wood. A creak sounded beside him. Ash turned to find Daelon leaning on the table, his expression a blend of curiosity and expectation.

The monk considered the deliveryman's tale, turning it over in his mind like a stone, feeling its rough edges, weighing its truth—or lack thereof. At last, he exhaled, a sound of resignation and resolve. "I'll take your story to the Headmaster," he said, rising from the stool.

Daelon shot to his feet so quickly that his stool wobbled, nearly toppling. "If you'd like, I'd be happy to come with you," he offered, his words tumbling out in a rush. "I could retell the story myself, straight to your master. It'd be no trouble, none at all."

Ash raised a hand, palm out, a subtle yet unmistakable gesture of stillness. "That won't be necessary," he said, his tone sharp, and his gaze steady. Then, nodding toward the half-empty wagon visible through the doorway, he added, "Besides, it seems you've still got duties to attend to."

Daelon hesitated, his mouth opening as if to argue, but Ash's calm authority stilled him. Whatever protest the man had been about to voice faded, replaced by a sheepish nod.

With a faint lift of his brow, Ash turned and made his way to the open door. The cool air greeted him as he stepped outside, a welcome reprieve from the oven's heat. Behind him, the clatter of Daelon shifting his crates signaled the man had returned to his work.

Ash set off down the cobblestone path, his bare feet producing a quiet, yet steady rhythm against the stones. The path wound through the monastery's grounds, bordered by carefully tended gardens and the occasional murmured conversation of passing monks. But Ash paid them no mind.

He was heading to the Headmaster's quarters—a destination he would have preferred to avoid. Not because he doubted the truth of Daelon's story, but because of what might come next. He could already hear the Headmaster's calm yet unwavering voice urging him to venture beyond the sanctuary of these walls, back into the chaos of the outside world.

Ash clenched his jaw, his thoughts heavy as he

neared the simple wooden door of the quarters. The taste of the bread still lingered on his tongue, a reminder of the peace he had found here. But peace, he knew, was a fragile thing. And fragile things never lasted.

Chapter 2: The Headmaster's Chamber

Ash stood before the ornate door, the brass plaque gleaming in the dim light. The word *Headmaster* was etched into the metal in bold strokes. He flexed his hands, squeezing them open and closed, the motion calming his nerves. After a moment's pause, he rapped on the door, the sound sharp, and urgent.

"Enter," came a voice from within—muffled, yet resonant, with a quiet authority that seemed to fill the hallway.

Ash pushed the door open, and the familiar scents of old parchment and earthy incense washed over him like a wave. Inside, the room was dimly lit by a single lantern, its glow casting long shadows over the towering shelves of tomes and scrolls that lined the walls. Behind a massive oaken desk sat an elderly man in simple brown robes. His quill hovered above an unmarked sheet of parchment, his expression a blend of concentration and faint frustration. At the sight of Ash, the man's features softened. He set the quill down, offering a faint but warm smile.

"Ah, Brother Ashram," the Headmaster said, his voice rich with affection. "It has been some time since you've graced me with your presence."

Ash felt the weight of those words settle over him like a shroud. Beneath Mandor's warmth lingered a quiet sadness—subtle, yet undeniable. Once, Mandor had been more than a mentor to him, more than a teacher; he had been a father in all but name. In those days, Ash had craved that connection with a desperate intensity. Now, though, he found himself avoiding the man, almost unconsciously. It was a feeling he neither fully understood nor could bring himself to justify.

"Master Mandor," Ash replied, inclining his head in a respectful bow. He fought to keep his expression neutral, lest shame reveal itself. "I intended to see you sooner, but, as you know, the duties of a monk never seem to cease."

It was a lie, and Ash despised himself for telling it. The truth was far more difficult to confront: lingering too long in Mandor's presence stirred an ache in him, a yearning for what once had been—a time when the world seemed simpler, untouched by the horrors that had since carved away his innocence. Back then, under Mandor's guidance, life had been a cycle of training and meditation, a pursuit of mastery and purpose. But that simplicity had been devoured by the grim reality of his calling—a life spent battling nightmares most would never even know existed.

Mandor waved a hand, brushing the words aside. "No need for apologies, my young friend," he said, his tone as forgiving as ever. That single word—*young*—struck a strange chord in Ash, lingering in his thoughts. *Young*. A word only someone like Mandor, with nearly a century behind him, could wield so casually. Ash suppressed a smile at the thought.

Mandor leaned back in his chair, his movements slow and deliberate. He stretched his arms behind his head, a soft groan escaping him as his joints cracked audibly. "So," he said, his tone casual but edged with curiosity, "what brings you here this morning?"

Ash stepped inside, gently closing the door behind him. He approached the desk, noting the faint etching of wrinkles on Mandor's face. They were subtle, but they hadn't been there before. The Divine Mother's touch slowed time's toll on those within the Order, but not indefinitely. Few monks bore the markings of age to this degree, yet Mandor now wore them like a faint map, etched into his skin.

When Ash had first arrived at the monastery, Mandor had seemed ancient, a figure weathered by time beyond comprehension. Now that he thinks about it, the man probably was no older than he was now. These days, Ash couldn't even hazard a guess at the man's true age. Perhaps a little less than a century had passed since Mandor's birth, though he bore the appearance of someone decades younger. His vitality defied the years. It felt like a lifetime ago when Ash himself had been naïve enough to make such assumptions, when youth had coloured his perception of the world.

Mandor's gaze remained fixed on him, patient but expectant. Realizing he had lingered too long in silence, Ash exhaled a quiet sigh and began. He relayed the deliveryman's tale, lacking the fervour Daelon had poured into it. Still, he tried to convey the young man's sincerity, the legitimate fear that had gripped him.

When Ash finished, Mandor leaned forward, his brow creased in silent contemplation. His fingers moved absently over the desk's surface, tracing the faint outline of a shallow groove. The mark so subtle it was nearly imperceptible, yet Mandor's touch lingered there as if the flaw held some deeper meaning. At last, his hand stilled, and with a decisive tap of his fingers against the wood, he seemed to reach a conclusion.

"It's probably just the ramblings of a drunkard itching for attention," Mandor said at last, his voice breaking the silence. He leaned back again, but not before pointing a finger at Ash. "But you wouldn't have brought this hearsay to me unless you thought there was more to it. So tell me—what's on your mind, my friend?"

Ash hesitated. The dream. He hadn't spoken of it to anyone. Part of him wanted to dismiss it as a figment of his own restless mind, a phantom conjured by memories he'd rather forget. But the timing gnawed at him. He sighed, shrugged, and began to recount what he could remember of the dream, his voice low and steady.

Mandor listened in silence, his expression unreadable, but Ash could see the weight of his words settling over the Headmaster like a shadow.

"Before I came to live here at Maiden's Haven, I resided at Dawn's End Monastery," Ash began, his tone steady but carrying the weight of memory. "Far to the north, deep in the mountains. I was quite young then. Just a boy, in truth." He lingered a moment too long on the word *young*, as though trying to convince himself as much as Mandor.

"During my time there," he continued, "I became close friends with another novice who had just joined the Order. His name was Kael." The name seemed to catch in his throat, foreign after so many years unspoken. He paused, the sound of it hanging in the air like a ghost. Over thirty years had passed since he had last said that name aloud, and now it felt strange, almost wrong.

Ash's gaze dropped to the floor. "I hadn't thought of Kael in a long time—not since I moved here to Maiden's Haven. In truth, I'd even forgotten what he looked like." A flicker of sorrow touched his voice, the kind that comes with realizing how much time has stripped away. "But this morning, I was jolted awake from a dream. A dream of battle. And there he was, his face vivid in my mind—not as the young man I once knew, but as an older monk, one who had served as many years as I."

Mandor leaned forward slightly, his expression expectant. He didn't speak, but the subtle tilt of his head urged Ash to continue.

Ash hesitated. The words felt heavy, as if speaking them would give the dream too much power. Still, he pressed on. "In the dream, Kael wasn't my friend—not anymore. He was something else, something darker. He led an army of the dead, sweeping across the land, leaving nothing but ruin in their wake." Ash closed his eyes, as though trying to pull the memory of the dream into sharper focus. "It felt… real. Too real. I haven't had dreams like this since my days hunting the ghouls of this world."

His hands had begun to rub together unconsciously, betraying his unease. Noticing, Ash quickly dropped them to his sides, forcing a calm he didn't entirely feel. "Something about it doesn't sit right with me. I can't put my finger on it, but… it feels wrong." He allowed himself a bitter chuckle, trying to shake off the importance of his confession. "Reluctantly, my life had greater meaning when I was out there, fighting instead of sitting behind these walls with my hands buried in the dirt of the gardens."

Mandor's lips curved into a faint smile, his eyes

crinkling with a trace of amusement. "Well," the Headmaster said, his tone warm yet edged with the weight of authority, "Farrow's Point is only half a day's walk from here. Perhaps a bit of wandering would do you some good. Get out of these walls for a few days. See for yourself if these claims hold any truth." He leaned back slightly, his gaze sharpening as it settled on Ash. "If nothing else, it might help you clear your head." A wry smile tugged at the corners of Mandor's mouth as he gestured toward Ash with a knowing glint in his eye. "And who knows? It might even bring a little life back to that tired gaze of yours."

Ash winced, the weight of the suggestion settling on him even before Mandor spoke it aloud. He had no desire to return to the business of adventuring, not now, perhaps not ever. Ash felt that travelling the world was a young man's game. But, of course, Ash knew that Mandor would suggest it. That was the way of things. For a fleeting moment, Ash considered deflecting, offering that another monk might take his place. The thought, however, withered before it took shape; he knew it would make no difference.

Mandor's gaze remained fixed on him, calm but unyielding, his faint smile underscored by quiet resolve. The older monk leaned back slightly, one brow arching in a wordless challenge, daring Ash to refuse.

With a resigned sigh, Ash nodded. "I'll prepare to

leave at first light," he said, his voice steady, though a storm brewed behind his eyes.

Mandor's smile widened, a glimmer of satisfaction in his expression. "Good. The journey will do you well, my friend."

"But before you set off on this little adventure," the Headmaster began, a faint glimmer of amusement sparking in his eyes, "I'd like you to take a young monk with you—Kiran. She's eager and more than capable, one of the most skilled fighters of her class. But she could use some experience beyond the safety of these walls, a chance to temper her training in the real world." Mandor's gaze sharpened, the weight of his authority underscoring his next words. "And who better to guide her than you?"

Ash tensed, the protest forming on his tongue before he could stop it. He preferred to work alone—always had. He knew better though, than to argue with Mandor. The Headmaster's calm expression, the slight upward tilt of his brow, told Ash the decision was already final.

Mandor caught the flicker of resistance in Ash's eyes and responded with a knowing smile. "Good, then," he said smoothly, his tone leaving no room for argument. He cast a cursory glance around the room, as if expecting a window that wasn't there, before reaching for a scrap of parchment. With brisk, deliberate strokes, he scrawled a note, the sharp scratch of the quill punctuating the silence. "You'll find

Kiran in the training grounds," Mandor continued, sliding the note across the desk. "Hand this to Brother Faiden—it will excuse her from her lessons without question or fuss."

Ash took the parchment without looking at it, tucking it into the folds of his robes. As he turned to leave, something compelled him to pause at the door. He glanced back at Mandor, whose eyes were already on him. "It was good to see you again, Mandor," Ash said, his voice quiet but sincere.

Mandor's smile softened, and he waved Ash off with a dismissive flick of his hand, as if shooing away sentiment. Ash nodded once and stepped out, pulling the door closed behind him.

The crisp air of the monastery grounds greeted him as he walked the familiar paths toward the rear, where the fighting rings were located. Even before rounding the last of the sandstone buildings, he could hear the sharp clack of wooden staffs striking against each other. The sound stirred memories—days spent sweating under the sun, bruises earned in endless practice, the thrill of learning to control his body as an extension of will.

The open training yard came into view, alive with movement. Groups of young monks danced through synchronized drills, their steps precise, almost elegant. Others clashed in sparring matches, their focus intent. Ash couldn't help but notice how few students there were compared to his own training days.

At the edge of the yard, a monk paced the perimeter, his hands clasped behind his back. Ash's eyes lingered on him for a moment. That must be Brother Faiden. Though Ash had never been introduced to the man, he recognized the commanding presence of a seasoned veteran. Ash had avoided mingling with most of the monks since returning to the monastery a few years ago, preferring solitude to camaraderie.

For a moment, Ash stood quietly, observing. The rhythmic movements of the students, the sharp discipline of their strikes, brought a flicker of something close to nostalgia. A few of the younger monks had noticed him now. Their gazes lingered, hushed whispers spreading through the group. Ash knew what they saw: not a monk seeking peace, but a figure draped in old stories and faded glories. A hero of sorts, though Ash loathed the title.

Faiden must have caught sight of him because the older monk changed course, striding toward Ash with the steady assurance of someone accustomed to command. As he approached, Ash noted the scar that ran the length of the man's face, a pale groove that cut deep into his features. But it wasn't the scar that struck Ash—it was the man's eyes. They carried a weight, a depth that Ash recognized immediately. He'd seen that same depth in his own reflection on more than one sleepless night.

"Brother Ashram," Faiden said, his tone both curious and formal. "It's not often we see you in this part of the monastery. What brings you to the training grounds this morning?"

Ash didn't respond right away. Instead, he reached into his robes and produced the folded note. He offered it to Faiden without a word. The other monk took it, unfolding the parchment and scanning its contents.

Faiden's gaze shifted back to the group of young monks, now standing silent and still, their practice halted as they watched the exchange between the two elder monks.

Ash stood quietly, waiting. He could feel the weight of their stares, the unspoken awe and curiosity of the younger generation. It wasn't admiration that made him uncomfortable—it was the distance it created. The pedestal they placed him on was built from legends he no longer wanted to carry.

Faiden's expression didn't change as he folded the note and tucked it into his own robes. "I'll fetch her for you," he said simply, before turning toward the group. He entered a small grouping of young students before returning.

Brother Faiden wove his way through a cluster of young students, pausing only briefly before turning back toward Ash. Behind him, a young woman followed. Ash's gaze lingered on her longer than he intended, drawn to the sharp precision of her features. Her long black hair was tied back neatly, and her piercing blue eyes seemed to catch and hold the light, as if they themselves radiated it.

Those eyes, Ash thought grimly, would one day lose their brilliance, swallowed by the same encroaching darkness that had overtaken his own. The thought coiled within him like a bitter serpent, leaving a taste of ash and regret in its wake.

She greeted him with a bright smile, her cheeks flushed from exertion, her chest rising and falling as she caught her breath. Despite the obvious fatigue from her morning drills, she radiated an almost unsettling energy. With a fluid motion, she clasped her hands behind her back and straightened into a posture of readiness, nodding respectfully to Ash.

"Brother Ashram, this is Sister Kiran," Faiden said, gesturing toward her with a flick of his hand. Without another word, Faiden turned away, his focus already shifting back to the training grounds. With a sharp whirl of his hand in the air, the young monks resumed their drills, the clatter of wooden staffs echoing once more.

Ash barely noticed. His focus remained on the young woman standing before him, brimming with expectation. He let out a quiet sigh, trying to keep it subtle, though he doubted it went unnoticed. Too much sparkle, too much unbridled enthusiasm. How in all the realms was he supposed to survive this? He could already picture Mandor sitting in his office, grinning ear to ear at the thought of this mismatched pairing.

"Head back to your quarters," Ash said at last, his tone firm but not unkind. "Wash up, gather your staff, and pack whatever essentials you think you'll need. Meet me at the front gates when you're ready."

The joy on her face faltered, replaced by confusion. She blinked at him, hesitating. "I'm… leaving?" she asked, her voice tinged with disbelief. "Have I… have I displeased my trainers?" She glanced over her shoulder at the other students, her brows furrowing in worry. "If it's something I've done, I can correct it! I swear. Please, don't send me away."

Ash raised a hand, his voice softer this time. "You're not being sent away. You're not in trouble." He paused, searching for the right words to calm her. "This is a mission. The Headmaster wants you to join me on a trek beyond the monastery grounds."

Her face transformed in an instant. Confusion melted into radiant excitement, her smile returning with an almost blinding intensity. "A mission?" she exclaimed, her voice rising with childlike enthusiasm. "Yes, sir! I'll prepare right away!" She spun on her heel and took off down the path, nearly tripping over her own feet in her eagerness to obey.

Ash watched her retreat, the faint echoes of her hurried footsteps fading as she left. He shook his head, running a hand over his face. It had to be a joke. Mandor had to be laughing himself breathless somewhere, picturing this scene.

With a resigned sigh, Ash followed the path after her, his pace slower, his thoughts already dreading the boundless energy he would have to contend with.

Chapter 3:
The Nargrim & The Fallen Monk

Ash approached the front gate, his quarterstaff in hand and a bag slung over one shoulder. Ahead, Kiran waited, her youthful energy evident in the slight bounce to her step. She practically radiated enthusiasm, and though Ash had already resigned himself to the day ahead, he couldn't help but sigh inwardly at the sight. Shaking his head, he continued down the path toward her.

"Do you have everything you'll need?" he asked as he stopped beside her.

"Yes, sir! Brother Ashram, I'm ready to go," she said, her voice bright and eager, her excitement utterly unrestrained.

Ash arched a brow, the corner of his mouth tightening ever so slightly. "First off," he said, his voice low and firm, "just call me Ash. Not 'Brother Ash.' Definitely not 'Brother Ashram.'" His tone left no room for argument. "If we're going to work together, treat me like your companion, not some revered elder."

The chastisement hung in the air, but Kiran didn't flinch. Instead, her eyes lit up like she'd just been handed the greatest gift imaginable. Ash winced inwardly. That look was going to get old fast.

"Secondly," he continued, turning toward the path that wound its way down the hill toward the village below, "we're heading to Farrow's Point, east of here. There's been a report of an undead man wandering their streets."

He expected her enthusiasm to falter at the mention of the undead, but instead, she matched his stride with an excited spring, her energy as relentless as ever.

Ash grunted to himself. "I did say an undead man?", he said.

"You did." she said, glancing up at him with an innocent smile.

"Doesn't the idea of possibly encountering a nárgrim worry you even a little?" he asked, his curiosity genuine now.

Kiran hesitated before speaking, her brow furrowed in thought. "Nárgrim?" she asked, testing the unfamiliar word on her tongue. The uncertainty in her voice told Ash that she had never heard the term before. He wasn't surprised. Unless one had spent time scouring the crumbling remains of the Ancients' civilization, few would ever encounter one.

"They are believed to be the corpses of the Ancients," Ash said, choosing his words carefully. "Most of the time, they are just that—lifeless remnants, long abandoned to time." He glanced at Kiran, noting the way she hung on his every word, the unspoken questions in her gaze. “You usually only find them within the ruins, the places where the Ancients once lived and died.”

She was listening intently now, her focus locked on him. He exhaled and continued. “But sometimes… some do not rest as they should. Some remain tethered, haunting the bodies they once inhabited.” He frowned, knowing his explanation was lacking, inadequate in ways he couldn’t quite name. He was no scholar, no teacher of scriptures like the elders at the monastery. “They are nothing more than shades of what they were—no true life remains, only a hollow, lingering presence. A ghost confined to rotted flesh, lost and confused. They are driven by primitive hunger rather than reason.”

It was the best way he could describe them. One day, Kiran would see one with her own eyes, and when that day came, it wouldn’t be the threat that unsettled her—it would be the sheer wrongness of it, the unnaturalness. It would be a thing that should not be, a body that was not alive, nor truly dead.

His lips curled into the faintest smirk, though his voice remained even. “Now that you understand that, does it worry you a little more?” He watched her closely, searching for any flicker of doubt in her expression.

"Not at all." she replied, the word crisp and matter-of-fact. Then, with a grin, she added, "I’m with Brother Ashram Stormrider, the greatest slayer of abominations the world has ever seen." She stopped abruptly, her cheeks flushing as she realized her mistake. "Sorry—Brother Ash… I mean, Ash."

Ash paused, his eyes narrowing slightly as he studied her. She was entirely unshaken, her grin already returning. Shaking his head, he started walking again, deciding against telling her to tone down the accolades. What would be the point? She wouldn't listen anyway.

The path from the monastery snaked down the hillside, flanked on either side by a dense assembly of ash, oak, maple, and birch trees. Their branches formed a shifting canopy, dappling the ground with fragments of light and shadow. The trail itself was a mix of loose sand and scattered stones, the latter an occasional hazard for the unwary, waiting to catch the careless step of those not watching their footing.

The hills gradually levelled as they descended, revealing glimpses of the village through breaks in the trees. Thatched roofs and weathered stone chimneys rose above the greenery, their silhouettes softened by the haze of smoke curling lazily skyward. The path widened as it merged with a narrow side street, its well-worn surface leading toward the heart of the town.

At the heart of the village stood a weathered stone well, where a woman worked heedlessly, drawing up a container of fresh water. Ash cast a glance over his shoulder at Kiran. “We’ll rest here,” he said, his voice low as he adjusted the strap of his pack. The sun bore down with relentless intensity, and the dry rasp in his throat made the thought of cool water all the more enticing.

Kiran nodded and hurried to the well ahead of him, already pulling up a bucket of fresh water by the time he reached her. She offered him the first drink with a smile, and he accepted with a quiet nod of thanks. After he drank, she took the bucket and brought it to her lips, taking a few refreshing gulps before setting it down.

She perched herself on the edge of the well, her bright eyes scanning the streets. Villagers passed by with quiet purpose, their faces carefully neutral. Ash knew the look all too well—studied indifference, born of distrust. Most of them wouldn’t meet his gaze, wouldn’t dare approach. Monks like him carried a reputation that walked ahead of them, a reputation the common folk neither understood nor cared to understand.

Kiran let out a small sigh, her gaze shifting back to him. "Do you ever get used to it?" she asked softly. "The way they avoid looking at you, I mean."

Ash met her eyes, the honesty of her question catching him off guard. He thought for a moment, running the edge of his hand along the stubble on his cheek. "You just… learn to become dull inside," he said at last, his voice quiet. "You tell yourself it doesn’t matter."

"But it does, doesn't it?" she pressed, her voice almost a whisper. "It does bother you."

Ash inhaled deeply, as if preparing to offer her some profound wisdom. Instead, he simply nodded, his gaze shifting away. She deserved better than this life, he thought. Better than the burden of being invisible, of being a ghost among the living.

"Why do they treat us so differently?", Kiran asked, looking up at him with a touch of sadness in her eyes.

"People do not like things that are different than themselves, especially if that something somehow makes them seem inferior in anyway.", Ash said trying to sound as compassionate as possible. "We learn to harness the ability to manifest the Divine Mother's power which can be unsettling to someone who does not understand it."

What more could he say? That was just the nature of people. She seemed to understand what he was saying because she nodded to him then stared off into the hills behind them.

"Come on," he said abruptly, pulling his pack over his shoulder again. "Let's walk."

Kiran hopped off the well's edge without another word, falling into step beside him. Whatever thoughts lingered in her mind, she kept them to herself, her expression calm but thoughtful as they made their way toward the heart of the village.

They had barely passed two houses when a sharp scream split the air, cutting through the village's midday commotion. Ash and Kiran stopped in their tracks, their eyes darting toward the source of the cry. The sound echoed off the stone walls, bouncing between the narrow alleys, before a woman burst into view from between two houses. Her face was twisted in terror, her breath coming in ragged gasps as she fled.

Two figures lurched after her, their movements disjointed and unnervingly erratic. Their tattered clothing hung in strips, revealing patches of skin beneath—grey, leathery, and stretched taut over unwholesome frames. Ash's eyes narrowed, his jaw tightening as recognition settled in. He knew that gait, that unmistakable visage. He had seen it before. Too many times.

Without a word, he dropped his pack and broke into a sprint. The woman was barely ahead of her pursuers. One of them lunged, seizing her by the back of her dress and dragging her down. She screamed, clawing at the ground as the second figure loomed over her.

Ash reached them in moments, moving with a speed that belied his years. His quarterstaff came down in a sharp arc, smashing into the side of the first creature's head. The skull caved in with a sickening crunch, and something foul spilled out, the stench making his stomach churn.

The second nárgrim turned toward him, its lifeless

eyes fixing on its new prey. The woman scrambled beneath it, her fingers tearing at the dirt as she tried to crawl away. Her screams rattled in his ears, but Ash's focus remained on the creature before him.

A sharp kick to its temple sent it sprawling, and before it could rise, Ash drove his staff down with brutal precision. The butted end crushing its skull, silencing it for good.

The woman was gone before he could offer reassurance, her panic driving her to flee in the opposite direction. Ash barely spared her a glance as he stepped back, his eyes scanning the street.

Two bodies lay at his feet, still and broken. But instinct prickled at the back of his neck—this wasn't over.

"Kiran."

He whirled, his heart pounding as he searched for her. Then he saw her, back by the well where they'd stopped earlier. She was locked in a fight of her own, her quarterstaff spinning as she held her ground against one of the undead.

Ash's muscles coiled, ready to sprint to her aid, but a sudden movement to his left caught his attention. Three more of the creatures poured out from between the buildings, their vacant eyes fixed on the panicked villagers scattering in all directions.

For a brief moment, Ash stood frozen, his mind

calculating. His instincts screamed to protect Kiran, but the chaos unfolding around him demanded his attention. He tightened his grip on his staff, forcing his focus to steady.

There would be no room for hesitation now.

The three figures that had wandered into the street turned, their hollow eyes fixing on Ash in unison. Without hesitation, they charged, their staggered gaits betraying an unnatural coordination. Ash set his stance, his grip firm on the worn wood of his staff.

The first of the creatures closed in fast. Ash sidestepped sharply, twisting low and driving the end of his staff in a sweeping arc. It cracked hard against the creature's knees, sending it crumpling to the ground with a guttural moan. He didn't wait for it to recover. The other two were already upon him.

Ash pivoted smoothly, centering himself between his new opponents. With practised precision, his quarterstaff became a whirlwind of motion—a rapid succession of strikes that landed with satisfying cracks. Bone splintered, and flesh gave way. Within moments, the pair collapsed, motionless, to the dirt.

A rasping groan drew his attention back to the first creature, still writhing on the ground. It reached for his ankle with clawing fingers. Ash's response was swift and merciless: he brought his staff down in a crushing blow, ending the threat.

Straightening, Ash surveyed the carnage, his chest rising and falling in steady breaths. Movement at the edge of his vision drew his attention, and he turned to see Kiran sprinting toward him. Her hair was a chaotic cascade, her robes dusted with grime, but her opponent lay sprawled behind her. A second figure—no doubt another adversary—was motionless a few paces away.

Kiran skidded to a halt in front of him, her breaths coming fast and shallow, though her face betrayed no fear. A faint smile tugged at her lips, one born of adrenaline rather than relief. She'll have to temper that, Ash thought grimly. Excitement in battle leads to recklessness. But there was time for her to learn—plenty of time.

"Any injuries?" he asked, his gaze sweeping her for signs of blood or broken flesh. "Some of these things carry diseases. Their corruption isn't always immediate, but it will kill you eventually."

Kiran's expression sobered. She shook her head quickly, though Ash couldn't tell if it was reassurance or simply a reaction to his words. Either way, he grunted his acknowledgement and turned back to the street, his thoughts already moving ahead.

"We need to get these people out of—" His words died on his lips.

A figure stepped into view at the far end of the street. Ash froze, his eyes narrowing. This one was different.

Its gait was the same—clumsy, unnatural—but the robes it wore were unmistakable: monk's robes. His breath caught as he noted the empty black orbs where its eyes should have been.

"Stay behind me," he said, his voice low but firm.

Ash's mind raced as he moved forward. A monk? No. It wasn't possible. The Order's burial rites ensured that their dead didn't rise again. Yet, as he closed the distance, the truth became undeniable. The gouges across its face, the gaping wound that stretched from jaw to collarbone—no living being could endure such injuries. Its mouth twisted into something resembling a grin, revealing blackened teeth and rotting flesh.

This wouldn't be a simple fight.

Ash's steps slowed as he felt Kiran's presence falter behind him. He turned, catching the fear that had finally surfaced in her wide eyes. Gone was the youthful exuberance she'd carried into the village. Now, she stood rooted in place, her trembling hand gripping her staff like a lifeline.

"Stay here," Ash said, his voice softer but no less commanding. "Be ready in case others come out of the shadows."

He turned back to the creature, his grip tightening on his quarterstaff. Kiran wasn't ready for this, not yet. Perhaps the Headmaster had erred in sending her along. Or perhaps Ash had erred in agreeing to it. Either way, there was no time to dwell on regret. The thing before him—this grotesque mockery of a monk—had to be dealt with.

Ash shifted his stance, stepping forward with sureness. Every movement carried the influence of experience, his muscles coiled and ready for the inevitable clash.

The creature advanced, an aura of preternatural darkness rolling off it in waves, devouring the light and leaving the air thick with unease. Its fists clenched and flexed with a grotesque animation, a vile parody of life. Ash's eyes narrowed. This wasn't the shambling, thoughtless dead he had fought before. There was an unsettling motive in the way it moved—a predator's awareness, its actions tinged with a shadow of the life it had once known.

Tightening his grip on the staff, Ash stepped into the fray. Instinct took over, years of training guiding his movements with unerring accuracy. The staff became an extension of his will, spinning and striking with the fluid grace of a seasoned warrior. But the creature was no mindless foe. It blocked and countered with uncanny accuracy, each move purposeful and calculated.

The dance of combat intensified. Ash weaved through its strikes, every motion thoughtful, every response a measure of discipline honed over decades. Then, in a blur of motion, the creature spun—a powerful kick connecting with Ash's chest, sending him skidding across the dirt. He landed hard, the impact rattling his ribs.

Pain flared, sharp and immediate, a visceral reminder of his mortality. Gritting his teeth, Ash pushed himself upright. His gaze locked on the creature, expecting it to charge. But it didn't. Instead, it stood still, its blackened eyes fixed on him with a disquieting patience.

Thin tendrils of dark ooze coiled and writhed along its arms, struggling to manifest into something tangible but failing. Ash's breath hitched as he watched. *What was it trying to summon?* The question cut through his mind like a blade, urgency coiling in his chest. Whatever power it sought, Ash knew he couldn't allow it to succeed.

But this wasn't a mindless corpse to be smashed into submission. This was a warrior—a fallen comrade turned against the light. And warriors demanded respect, even when no mercy could be afforded.

Drawing a deep breath, Ash reached inward, calling upon the Divine Mother. Her power answered swiftly, surging through him like a river of fire. It climbed his spine, filling his chest with searing vitality before igniting in his brow, illuminating his mind with divine clarity.

Blue flames erupted along his arms, flickering and twisting like living serpents. Their brilliance cut through the gloom, bathing the battlefield in otherworldly light. Ash moved then, faster than the eye could follow, his quarterstaff a blur of motion. Each strike was precise, relentless, a symphony of destruction designed to overwhelm.

The creature faltered beneath the onslaught, its dark energy unravelling with every blow. Finally, it crumpled, collapsing into a lifeless heap.

Ash stood over the fallen foe, his chest heaving with exertion. Slowly, he allowed the Divine Mother's energy to recede, the flames extinguishing as they seeped back into the earth. The tension in his body unwound, his breaths slowing as the divine fire faded.

He lowered his staff, the truth of what he had just faced settling over him. Another battle fought, another shadow defeated. But the questions lingered, gnawing at the edges of his mind. *What power had it been reaching for? And how many more would come seeking the same?*

Turning, he found Kiran standing frozen, her staff forgotten in her hand. Her eyes were wide, her jaw slack, as she stared at him like a child witnessing a god. She had never seen the Divine Mother's gift wielded before. Few had at the monastery. Even among monks, those who witnessed its true power often stood in awe.

"Welcome to the truth of a monk's life," Ash said, his voice steady, cutting through the silence like a blade. The words pulled her from her daze.

"What was that?" she asked, her voice trembling with equal parts fear and excitement. "Will I be able to do that someday?"

Ash expected the question. He'd asked it himself the first time he'd seen such power unleashed. But this wasn't the time for that conversation. There were still people to save.

"Gather as many townsfolk as you can find," he said, his tone firm, his words carrying the weight of command. "We need to get them to the safety of the monastery."

Disappointment flickered across her face, but she nodded. He softened his expression, offering a faint smile. "We'll talk about it later—when everyone is safe. Until then, we have work to do."

Her resolve returned in an instant. She was off like a hare, her voice ringing out through the streets as she called for the townsfolk to gather.

Ash turned back to the fallen creature, his gaze lingering on the robes it wore. There had been a time when this man—if he could still be called that—had followed the same calling as Ash. What had happened? What foul force had twisted him into this monstrosity? Kneeling, Ash began rummaging through the creature's robes, his thoughts clouded with questions and an unfamiliar heaviness in his heart.

Beneath the creature's tattered robes, Ash's fingers brushed against cold brass. He pulled free the pendant every monk carried, an identifier etched with the sigil of their Order. The medallion swung loosely on its frayed cord as Ash turned it over in his palm. His breath hitched as the markings came into view—lines and curves unmistakably forming the symbol of Dawn's End.

For a moment, the weight of the pendant seemed to double in his hand. Dawn's End. The monastery that had once been his home, his sanctuary. The place where he had learned to wield the quarterstaff now resting in his grasp. And now, it had given rise to this—a monk twisted into a grotesque parody of what they had once been. Ash clenched his jaw, the metallic tang of old grief rising in his throat. He hadn't been surprised, not truly, but the confirmation carved a hollow ache in his chest. Too many questions. Not enough answers.

He wrapped the frayed cord of the pendant around the brass medallion and slipped it into the folds of his robes. The creature's vacant, decayed face stared up at him, unmoving, offering no explanation. Just another riddle in a nightmare without end.

Chapter 4:
The Veil Of Sanctuary

The sound of hurried footsteps pulled Ash from his reverie. He turned to find Kiran returning, a small group of townsfolk in tow. Others had already started their ascent up the hill, moving toward the safety of the monastery. Relief flickered in his chest, tempered by the urgency of the moment.

"We need to get them up the hill quickly," he said, his voice steady despite the storm of emotions beneath. He placed a reassuring hand on her shoulder, his grip firm but not overbearing. "I fear there may be more of these abominations nearby."

She nodded, her expression resolute, and began barking orders to the villagers. Her voice rang with authority, cutting through the lingering fear that clung to the air. The townsfolk obeyed without hesitation, their steps quick and determined as they followed the path Ash and Kiran had descended earlier.

Ash watched her for a moment, his gaze thoughtful. She moved with intention, her commands sharp and clear, her presence steady even in the chaos. Perhaps he had been too hasty in judging her readiness. Beneath her youth and inexperience, there was a spark of true leadership. With the right guidance, she could grow into more than just a capable monk. She could become a force to be reckoned with.

Falling in behind the last of the townsfolk, Ash let the isolation of his position wrap around him. Most of the villagers avoided his gaze, hurrying ahead as though his presence worried them. He didn't mind. The solitude offered him a brief reprieve—a moment to reflect.

But it didn't last. Kiran wove her way back through the throng, her slender form slipping past heads and shoulders until she fell into step beside him. She matched his pace, silent but present. Ash could feel the weight of her unspoken questions, the tension in her shoulders betraying her curiosity. She glanced up at him now and then, her expression caught somewhere between admiration and uncertainty.

Ash didn't like such attention. It reminded him of the gap between them, a gap he preferred to keep unacknowledged. He had never sought admiration, never needed it. Yet he understood that for her, this was part of the journey—part of becoming. In time, the awe would fade. One day, they would walk as equals. Until then, he would endure her quiet admiration.

"They call it the Divine Mother's Grace," Ash said at last. The words brought a flicker of a smile to Kiran's face, though he could see the unspoken questions lingering in her eyes. She would want more than a simple name.

"We monks train our bodies intensely," he continued, his gaze steady on hers, "so they become weapons as deadly as any blade. But it is through meditation that we cultivate the focus and stillness required to embrace the Divine Mother's power." He paused, searching her face for signs of understanding before pressing on.

"This power," Ash said, lifting a hand and clenching it into a fist as if to grasp an invisible force, "is not something you can seize by sheer will. It's not a thing to be taken. You must empty yourself—empty *of* yourself. Free yourself from the identity you cling to, the personality you call *yourself*."

He let the words hang for a moment, searching for the right phrasing to convey what was so difficult to articulate. "Within the depths of your being, you must create a void. Only then will the Divine Mother fill that void with her essence, and that essence *is* the power."

Kiran nodded slowly, her expression thoughtful, though Ash could tell she hadn't fully grasped the concept. He couldn't blame her. It wasn't something easily put into words. No one had ever explained it to him either; it had simply... happened. He had meditated endlessly, following his teachers' cryptic instructions until, over time, the void within him emerged, and the power of the Divine Mother flowed into its place. When he'd asked his masters for clarity, they had only nodded and said, "That is how it is meant to be."

"You will learn to channel it in your own way," Ash said, breaking the silence that had stretched between them. "Each monk uses the Divine Mother's power differently. Its expression is unique to the individual—guided, it seems, by her will through intuition."

He watched her carefully, noting the questions still clinging to her lips. Yet, he felt his own frustration growing, knowing he could not explain it in a way that would truly satisfy. Finally, he relented with a sigh.

"Focus on your meditation," he said, his tone softening. "When it comes, it will come. And when it does, I'll be here to help guide you through it."

With that, Ash let the matter rest. Some truths, he knew, could only be understood through experience, not words.

"Let's keep moving," he said, his voice soft but firm. And together, they climbed up the hill, leaving the fallen monk, its denizens—and the questions it posed—behind.

A cluster of monks stood guarding the open gates with curiosity written on their faces. With disciplined movements they ushered the frightened villagers through the entrance with efficiency, all the while maintaining a watchful guard on the surrounding wilderness. As Ash approached the monk coordinating the crowd, he wasted no time recounting the grim events in the village below. His voice was steady, but the weight of what he described seemed to seep into the air around him.

"I don't believe anyone else remains behind," Ash concluded, his tone leaving no room for argument. "Close the gate, but keep watch for any stragglers, alive or dead. It's unlikely, but we can't afford carelessness."

The monk nodded, his expression grim, and Ash didn't linger. Without another word, he pushed through the throng and strode onto the cobblestone path that led deeper into the monastery grounds. Kiran followed in his wake, her silence a mirror of his own. The two moved in tandem, their steps echoing faintly against the ancient stones as they approached the building Ash had visited that very morning.

But this time, the headmaster was waiting. He stood framed in the doorway, his aged face drawn tight with concern. The lines around his mouth deepened as his gaze settled on Ash and Kiran.

"Ashram. Kiran. You've returned," Mandor greeted them, his voice heavy with a compassion that carried an undercurrent of expectation. "Come inside. We need to talk."

Ash and Kiran followed Mandor into the monastery's main hall, its dimly lit corridor cloaked in a hush that contrasted sharply with the chaos outside. They walked in silence until they reached the headmaster's private quarters. Mandor opened the door and stepped aside, gesturing for them to enter. Ash paused, allowing Kiran to step in first before closing the door behind them with finality.

"Quite the commotion out there," Mandor began, his tone mild but probing as he moved to his seat. "I trust you have an explanation for why the entire village has migrated within our walls."

He lowered himself into a chair with the ease of someone accustomed to carrying the weight of others' burdens. His gesture to the two monks was subtle but clear: sit. Ash took the wooden chair across from Mandor without hesitation, his posture loose but composed. Kiran, by contrast, perched on the edge of her seat, her back ramrod straight. She looked out of place here, and she knew it. Ash could tell by the way her fingers fidgeted with the hem of her robes, though her face remained stoic.

Mandor raised a hand, inviting Ash to speak. Ash cleared his throat and began his account, laying out the events with a precision honed by years of disciplined storytelling. He detailed their diversion to the nearby village, the attack, and the horrors they encountered there. Mandor listened with the calm of a man used to bad news, his expression unchanging. That was, until Ash spoke of the battle with the transformed monk. At that, Mandor's brows knit ever so slightly, and he leaned forward in his chair.

"At first, I thought the monk was trying to reach for the Divine Mother's power," Ash said, his voice low but steady. His gaze shifted as if replaying the memory, the image burned into his mind. "But... something else answered the call. Something dark. It was like living vines of darkness, seeping from his flesh."

He paused, gauging Mandor's reaction. The older monk's expression remained composed, though there was a glint in his eyes—an acknowledgement, perhaps, or something deeper. Ash couldn't tell. But the lack of surprise was unsettling.

Had Mandor seen this before? The thought took root in Ash's mind, twisting with possibilities.

There was still more to address—another discovery that lingered in Ash's mind like a shadow. Reaching into the folds of his robes, he retrieved the pendant he'd taken from the fallen monk. It rested heavy in his palm, its weight both physical and symbolic.

"This," he said, locking eyes with Mandor, his voice edged with gravity, "needs answers as well."

The dull brass surface caught the faint flicker of candlelight, its sheen muted and ominous. When Ash placed it on the desk and slid it forward, the atmosphere seemed to shift, a subtle tension creeping into the air. Mandor's expression hardened, the easy warmth in his features giving way to something more guarded.

His fingers closed around the medallion with care, lifting it for inspection. The sigil etched into its surface—Dawn's End monastery, unmistakable—drew his attention immediately. His eyes narrowed as he traced the lines with a capable gaze, the silence between them thick with unspoken meaning.

"Dawn's End," Mandor murmured, almost to himself. There was no mistaking the hint of unease in his tone. His thumb brushed the edge of the pendant absently, a reflexive gesture as his mind worked through the implications.

Ash reached out, his finger pointing to the medallion. "Turn it over," he said, his voice steady but weighted.

Mandor shot him a questioning glance but complied. As he flipped the pendant, his breath caught, the faintest intake of air betraying his surprise. The blank surface on the reverse, meant to be unmarked, now bore an unfamiliar engraving—a symbol neither Mandor nor most monks in the Order would recognize.

Mandor's eyes flicked up to Ash, his expression shifting from curiosity to realization. "You've seen this mark before, haven't you?" The words were spoken, but Ash had already seen the question in his mentor's gaze.

Ash didn't answer immediately. He held Mandor's

gaze, letting the silence stretch. When he finally spoke, his voice was quiet but firm, a low rumble of certainty. "I have."

Mandor's lips pressed into a thin line as he set the pendant down carefully, almost reverently, on the desk between them. The weight of what had been revealed hung heavy in the room, thick as the air before a storm.

"Please," the headmaster said, his tone calm but insistent—a clear cue for Ash to continue.

Ash shifted in his seat, maintaining his composure as he spoke. "It's the mark of an old friend." His words carried a weight that filled the room, though he did not say the name aloud. He didn't need to. The recognition was already there, reflected in Mandor's narrowing eyes: Kael. Just that morning, Ash had recounted the dream—frantic, vivid—of a time long past, a time shared with the man whose mark now tainted the sacred pendant.

"He used to leave that symbol on everything he made," Ash continued, gesturing toward the crude sigil etched into the medallion's surface. "Whether it was a trinket carved from wood or a line of poetry on parchment, that mark was his signature. His calling card." Ash let his words hang in the air, choosing to leave the rest of his thoughts unsaid. Some truths were too tangled to unravel here.

Mandor's thumb brushed against the pendant as if

seeking some hidden meaning in its cold, metallic surface. He shook his head, the confusion etched into his features. For a moment, it seemed he might speak, but he stopped himself, setting the medallion down on the desk with a quiet clink. He leaned back in his chair, the flickering candlelight deepening the lines of contemplation on his face.

The room remained silent. Kiran sat rigid, her gaze locked on the floor as though it might offer her some anchor. Ash reached out and rested a hand on her arm, a gesture of reassurance. She looked up, and when she saw the faint smile tugging at the corner of his lips, her own tension seemed to ease. She sat back slightly, her posture softening.

"I'm not sure what this means," Mandor finally said, breaking the quiet. His voice carried the weight of uncertainty, but also resolve. The sound drew Kiran's attention immediately, her body snapping back into readiness. "What is clear," Mandor continued, "is that we'll need to send an envoy north to Dawn's End. Perhaps we'll find answers there."

Ash suppressed the sigh that threatened to escape him. He had known these words were coming; the inevitability of them felt like a stone settling in his chest.

"Rest while you can, young friend," Mandor said, his tone carrying an air of finality. "I want you to lead this mission yourself." He reached for a quill and a piece of parchment, his movements deliberate. "I'll assign a few of your brothers and sisters to accompany you. You leave at first light."

As Mandor began to scrawl his instructions, Ash leaned forward, his voice steady but carrying an edge of insistence. "I'd like Kiran to join us."

The words seemed to startle Kiran more than anyone. Her head snapped toward him, her eyes wide with disbelief. Ash met her gaze, his expression calm, steady. "If she's willing," he added, his tone softening. "I believe she would benefit from continuing her journey alongside me."

Even Mandor appeared momentarily surprised by the request, but he quickly masked it. Ash pressed on. "She's proven herself to be a promising student. There's work yet to be done, of course, but under my guidance, I believe she could become a formidable ally."

As Ash spoke, he saw the shift in Kiran's demeanour. The shock gave way to something else—a glimmer of pride. The faintest flush of colour rose to her cheeks, and her shoulders straightened, as though bracing herself for the responsibility she had not yet accepted.

Mandor's gaze shifted between the two before settling on Ash. "If she chooses to go, she will be in your care. She will be your responsibility." The weight of those words hung heavily in the air.

"Understood," Ash replied, his tone firm. He glanced at Kiran and offered her a reassuring nod. Her nervousness was still evident in the way she fidgeted with her robes, but there was also a spark of determination in her eyes. "You'll be fine," he whispered, his voice low enough that only she could hear.

Mandor clapped his hands together, a sharp sound that seemed to punctuate the discussion. "Very well, it's decided. I'll have supplies prepared for you and your party. Be ready by first light. I won't be there to see you off, but you have my gratitude—and my prayers."

With that, Mandor rose, signalling the end of the meeting. Ash and Kiran stood as well, following the headmaster to the hallway. The door closed softly behind them, leaving the two alone in the dim corridor.

Kiran's stance remained stiff, her hands tugging at the fabric of her robes as though trying to smooth away her uncertainty. Ash regarded her for a moment before speaking.

"Relax," he said, his voice carrying a quiet confidence. "You're ready for this. This is why you came here. You'll make an excellent monk—I'll see to that."

His words, punctuated by a small but sincere smile, seemed to ease the tension in her shoulders. She returned his smile, albeit hesitantly, and nodded. Together, they turned and walked down the hall, their steps falling in sync as they headed toward the courtyard and the challenges that awaited them beyond.

Chapter 5:
New Companions

A sharp knock shattered the lingering haze of Ash's restless sleep. He jolted awake, the remnants of yet another battle-haunted dream fading into the corners of his mind. He rubbed at his temples, cursing the return of those visions. They'd left him in peace for years, only to resurface now, vivid and relentless. With a groan, he swung his legs over the edge of the bed and ran a hand through his hair, the pale strands coarse under his fingers.

"Enter," he called, his voice hoarse from disuse.

The door creaked open just enough for a young novice to peek in, his eyes darting up nervously before fixing on the floor. *Barely more than a boy*, Ash thought. The lad's timid voice quivered as he spoke.

"Sir, you requested a morning wake-up."

Ash offered the boy a faint smile, an effort to ease his unease. "Thank you," he said with a nod. The novice bobbed his head in response, quickly retreating and shutting the door behind him.

With a sigh, Ash rose, his muscles protesting with a stiffness he hadn't felt this strongly the day before. Too long without proper exertion, he thought bitterly. Memories of younger days crept into his mind: battles fought in the western wars, the endless pursuit of meeting his monastic duties, and the rough justice he'd delivered to grave robbers and worse. His body was weary, but his spirit still craved the call of the road—despite knowing it might kill him sooner than later.

He dressed quickly, tugging on trousers and fastening his robe tightly with a rope belt. Crossing to the window, he pressed his palm to the cool glass and gazed out, but the predawn darkness offered little beyond his own reflection. The man staring back at him was unfamiliar, his once sunlit hair now completely white, the shadows under his eyes carved deep by years of hardship.

Is this what the Divine Mother intended for me? he wondered, tilting his head upward as though to catch some whisper from above. But the silence that met him was as familiar as it was absolute. Fastening his hair back, he turned towards the door.

Grabbing his quarterstaff from where it rested against the wall, he stepped into the hallway. Darkness greeted him. The lanterns and candles had yet to be lit, leaving the corridor eerily still. Only the faintest brush of his robes against the floorboards disturbed the quiet. Ahead, a thin line of light seeped under the heavy door to the outside—a beacon in the black. Ash let it guide him, his staff tapping lightly against the floor as he moved, cautious of unseen obstacles.

The air inside was cool, heavy with the promise of a morning yet to be born, and Ash couldn't help but feel that this day would bring with it more burdens than relief.

Ash pushed the door at the end of the hall open and was immediately greeted by a shroud of dense fog, a wall of white-grey that clung to the world beyond. The cool droplets kissed his face as he stepped into the quiet embrace of the early morning. The cobblestones crunched softly beneath his boots, each step a measured cadence in the stillness. Overhead, the faintest blush of dawn streaked the horizon, barely breaking the veil of darkness.

His footsteps echoed in the hush, an intrusion upon the tranquil solitude. Each step made him acutely aware of the next, a rhythmic awareness he welcomed. Rounding the corner of the monastery's outer buildings, the fog began to thin, and the looming outline of the front gates materialized ahead.

Two figures stood motionless on either side of the sturdy wooden barrier, their forms swallowed by the faint shadow of the walls. At the base of the gate, four more moved about, their silhouettes shifting in and out of view like spectres in the mist. One of them caught sight of Ash and broke away from the group, striding forward to meet him.

"The Divine Mother's blessings upon you, Brother Ash," said the man, his voice deep and warm, accompanied by a respectful incline of his head. He was tall, with short-cropped hair and a beard peppered with grey at its edges. "I am Brother Rowan," he continued, his tone earnest. "I've been tasked to follow your lead on this expedition."

Ash inclined his head in acknowledgement, his expression unreadable. Rowan gestured toward the others with a sweep of his arm, inviting Ash to follow. "Come," Rowan said, a faint smile curving his lips, though his dark eyes held an unfathomable depth. "Let me introduce the rest of the party."

As they drew nearer, Rowan raised a hand toward a stout woman standing just within the lantern's muted glow. Her compact, muscular frame conveyed a readiness that required no adornment, her arms crossed in an unspoken challenge. The dim light caught the sharp angles of her face, but it was her eyes—piercing violet, like shards of amethyst—that held Ash's attention. They seemed to see more than what the moment revealed.

"This is Sister Celest," Rowan said, his voice touched with pride. "A fighter of rare talent. We've been through a few scrapes together, and I've seen her hold her own against odds that would leave most trembling." He turned his gaze to the group, the confidence in his words unwavering. "I trust her with my life. You'd be wise to do the same—she'll serve us well."

Rowan moved with intent, resting a firm hand on

the shoulder of a young monk standing near a heap of travel-worn packs. The youth was lean but well-built, his movements carrying the poised confidence of someone who had earned his scars through years of discipline. "This is Brother Seanne, my protégé," Rowan said, his voice infused with pride. "Young, yes, but don't let that mislead you. He's been with me through more trials than most twice his age, and he's never faltered. I trust him completely."

Seanne's dark eyes locked onto Ash's with a steady, unyielding focus. His shaggy brown hair fell over his brow in untamed strands, and he absently brushed it aside, revealing a thin scar tracing the line of his jaw. It wasn't just a mark—it was a story, though one the young monk didn't seem eager to share.

Ash nodded in quiet acknowledgement, his gaze lingering on Seanne. He saw the raw strength in the youth's frame, but more importantly, he noted the quiet intensity etched into his features—the mark of someone who had already faced the kind of trials that carve men into warriors.

Finally, Rowan stopped behind a crouched figure—a young woman with long, dark hair draped over her face, who was deeply engrossed in rummaging through the contents of her pack. "And we are all aware that you know this curious young creature, Sister Kiran" Rowan said, his voice laced with amusement.

At the sound of her name, Kiran shot to her feet

with startling speed, narrowly missing Rowan's chin with the top of her head. She stood tall, brushing her robes with an air of nervous energy.

"It seems that she's made quite the impression around the monastery," Rowan remarked, a knowing grin spreading across his face. "Word around the monastery is that the legendary Brother Ashram has finally taken on a student—and a junior acolyte, no less."

Rowan's words hung in the air, as his gaze settled on Ash, expectant but patient. Ash, however, had no intention of elaborating. His thoughts were still muddled from sleep, and the prospect of conversation felt more burdensome than the packs they were preparing to carry. His expression remained inscrutable, offering nothing more than the faintest smile directed at Kiran.

She glanced up, meeting his eyes briefly before returning to her task, her focus shifting back to her pack with the quiet confidence of someone who found reassurance in his silence.

"Headmaster Mandor has placed her under my guidance. She's young, yes, but I believe it's time for her to gain some real-world experience." This was all he would offer as an explanation.

Rowan studied Kiran for a moment longer, then stepped back to Ash's side, the curiosity in his gaze unvoiced but unmistakable. Without pressing the matter further, he turned toward the gate, falling in step with Ash as they moved to review the details of their impending journey.

"Celest and Seanne were briefed on the essentials last night when I approached them for the task," Rowan said, his voice carrying the efficiency of a man used to action. "Both were eager to join the expedition, though I assumed it was because it was an opportunity to get out of this place. A true traveller does not like to stick around any place too long, am I right?"

Ash let the comment linger in the silence. He could feel the call of the roads as well. He enjoyed the peace of the sanctuary's seclusion, but the daily ritual of monastery living had been slowly wearing down his enthusiasm for solitude. Ash nodded in agreement to the elder monk which earned Ash a smile from the middle-aged man.

Rowan turned from Ash's gaze and gestured to the travel packs neatly stacked on the ground. "Master Mandor was thorough, as always. It seems he had these prepared well in advance." Rowan gave a nod, his smile faint but reassuring. "We're ready to move as soon as you give the word."

Ash's gaze lingered on the packs before shifting back to Rowan. "And Farrow's Point?" he asked, his voice low with concern. It had been their original destination, before events had forced him and Kiran back to the monastery.

"What of the people there?"

Rowan's expression flickered with recognition. "I heard the headmaster sent a small group of monks to assist." His tone sharpened, curiosity edged with unease, "Were they… nárgrim?"Ash knew that Rowan was no stranger to the undead of these parts.

Ash nodded. "They were," he confirmed.

Rowan exhaled sharply, his brow furrowing. "Nárgrim this far south? That's... unusual. There aren't any ruins within a days walk from here." He trailed off, his eyes narrowing in thought before settling back on Ash. "What do you make of it?"

"I don't know," Ash admitted, his voice steady but weighed with frustration. "There's more to this than you've been told. I'll explain when we stop to rest. But for now, we need to get moving."

Without waiting for a response, Ash grabbed one of the travel packs and slung it over his shoulder, the weight a familiar burden. He stepped toward the gates, leaving Rowan standing there, questions burning behind his eyes. Ash felt the tension but offered no answers. Not yet. He didn't have them. His mind was still unravelling the impossibility of what they had faced—the undead monk, the pendant, the dream that haunted him. It was all fragments, pieces of a puzzle he couldn't yet solve.

The guards at the gates moved into position, the

groan of the heavy wooden barriers breaking the silence as they swung open to reveal the path ahead. Ash stepped through, feeling the frost-hardened dirt underfoot. He caught sight of Kiran to his left, trudging forward with her pack strapped tightly to her back. She moved with a youthful determination that bordered on eagerness, as if this were a childhood adventure and not a journey into the unknown.

A flicker of doubt stirred in Ash's chest. Was she too young for this? The thought gnawed at him, unwelcome but persistent. He'd seen her potential, but potential didn't always mean readiness. Then there was the dream—the part he hadn't shared with Mandor, the part he hadn't fully remembered until he first laid eyes on her. The images whispered of significance, of Kiran playing a role he couldn't yet discern.

Ash shook his head, forcing the thoughts aside. They would have to wait. For now, there was only the road ahead.

As they began their trek down the winding path, Seanne jogged up beside Kiran, his breath steady despite the pace. "So, you're the young one now," he teased, his tone light with amusement. "I mean no offense," he added quickly, raising his hands in a conciliatory gesture. "It's just… I'm usually the one considered the youngster on these expeditions."

Kiran met his playful grin with a small smile of her own. Ash, walking a few steps ahead, observed the exchange. He understood the weight of being the youngest in a group of seasoned monks—he'd carried that mantle once, as had every monk at some point. Everyone started as the new recruit.

"I have noticed you around the monastery.", Kiran said to Seanne then blushing, obviously aware of what the implications of the statement might be misunderstood to mean. "I mean, you caught my eye." Her face now a bright red that could just be made out in the dim light rising over the tree tops. She shook her head in clear frustration. "You look a lot like my brother, Tavian. He was tall like you and kept his hair messy as well."

This time it was Seanne who blushed a little. "Messy. This hair style is all the fashion these days, or at least it should be." Seanne said with a hearty laugh. This made Kiran smile a bit.

"You speak of your brother in the past tense. Does that mean he is no longer with us?" Seanne spoke with a touch of compassion in his voice. He kept his gaze on the young woman and nearly stumbled over a stone protruding from the edge of the path.

"I don't know." she responded. She looked away from Seanne and turned her head to the ground that passed beneath her feet. "I was quite young when he left. I heard him get in a fight with my mother about wanting a better life in the city of Vaelthorne. It was the last time I ever saw him. He stormed out of the house and never returned."

A silence hung in the air between them for a moment and Seanne left the young women to her thoughts. Ash watched as Kiran walked in silent reflection for a moment, no doubt she was soaking in the bulk of her memories before continuing.

"We owned a farm in those days. It was small but it sustained us. Then my father passed away. He succumbed to an injury he sustained while working on the farm." Ash could see her eyes water a bit as she spoke. "My brother became the primary labourer of our little farm. Now that I am older, I understand that it was too much for someone so young. My mother tried to help, but when my brother left we could no longer keep up the farm duties. That is when we moved to the monastery. My mother got a job in the laundry rooms."

"Watching the monks in training at such a young age, I just naturally grew up wanting to be like them." she said, offering up a small smile to lighten her mood. "As soon as I was allowed, I began my studies."

Ash watched Seanne give the young woman a gentle pat on her shoulder. She seemed to appreciate the gesture as he watched her look up at the older monk and gave him a smile. Ash realized that everyone had their own story to tell, very few without tragedy or hardship.

"Can I ask you a question?" Kiran's expression turned thoughtful as she looked at Seanne. "Have you experienced the Divine Mother's powers yet?" she asked.

Seanne nodded. "I have."

"How long were you a monk before it happened?" she pressed. "Ash hasn't shared much about his first experience with me."

"That's probably because it was so long ago the old man can't remember," Rowan quipped as he fell into stride with them, delivering a light clap to Ash's shoulder.

"I heard he first felt it when he was only four years old," Celest chimed in with a laugh from the rear of the group, her tone laced with mischief.

Ash chuckled, shaking his head. "Not four," he corrected. "I was brought to the monastery at eight. But I was young when it happened—maybe fourteen or fifteen. Though, I had started my training earlier than most." His voice trailed off, tinged with the faint memory of a long-distant past.

Seanne finally had his chance to answer. "I was on my second expedition outside the monastery when it happened," he said, his voice quieter now, as though sharing something sacred. "I must have been nineteen at the time."

Rowan laughed. "The lad makes it sound like he's

trying to recall a dream," he said. "But we all remember our first time. It's unforgettable—a reward for all the years of devotion and discipline."

Even Celest nodded at that. "I remember mine as if it were yesterday," she said. "I was a late bloomer, though. I was probably twenty-one. My tutor and I were sent to investigate a ruin, preparing for an expedition team to recover artifacts. A group of thieves caught me off guard, and I barely held my ground. It wasn't until the Divine Mother gifted me her strength that I managed to hold them off long enough for my tutor to arrive."

"The Divine Mother always answers her devotees when they're in need," Rowan said, his voice steady with conviction. The group nodded in agreement, even Ash, though he kept his own story locked away, unwilling to share it with the others.

"And you, Rowan?" Kiran asked, her curiosity undeterred. She peeked around Ash to catch Rowan's eye. "If everyone remembers their first time, what about you?"

"Our times were different from what you enjoy now," Rowan began, gesturing toward Ash and himself. "We were part of the monastery during the war with the Western Expanse. By the time I was in my seventeenth year, I was sent to join the military and fight the invading armies." He glanced at Ash, as if inviting him to add something, but Ash remained silent, his expression impassive. Rowan pressed on.

"Not long after I joined the troops, we were attacked in the dead of night," Rowan continued, his voice steady but edged with the memory of tension. "A band of mercenaries hit our camp. It was chaos—we were caught completely off guard. I was sure I wouldn't make it." He paused, the weight of that moment lingering in the air. "But that's when I felt it—the Divine Mother's power. It was like she enveloped me, filled me with a strength I didn't know I had. I fought through the night. We lost so many, but for reasons I still don't understand, I survived." Rowan gave a small nod, as though cementing the memory into the conversation.

"Exactly," Ash said, breaking his silence. "Everyone's experience is different. It comes when you need it, and when it does, you have to embrace it. No two moments are the same." He turned to Kiran with a small, knowing smile. "I'm just not as eloquent as Rowan or Celest when it comes to explaining these things." He chuckled, drawing laughter from the others as well.

As they continued down the darkened path, Seanne twirled his quarterstaff absently, letting the butt end thud against the ground every so often, the sound breaking the quiet rhythm of their march.

"If you don't mind, *young* fellow," Celest said, putting an ironic emphasis on the word *young*, "we'd rather continue in silence." She jabbed him lightly on the shoulder, her grin betraying her jest.

"Sorry," Seanne said sheepishly. "It's just something I do when I'm nervous… or thinking." He shrugged, trying to dismiss the habit. "I was just remembering all the times I've walked through the monastery gates on assignments, wondering what I'd encounter. I guess it's the anxiety of facing the unknown."

"We all feel that way," Celest replied, her voice warm with understanding. "Leaving the monastery walls always comes with a mix of nerves and anticipation."

Ash listened quietly, the younger monks' words stirring faint memories of his own early days. It had been years since he felt that nervous edge. Now, when he left the monastery, he rarely expected anything new—only the familiar challenges that needed dealing with. And deal with them he did.

The five monks moved in silence, their steps cautious on the uneven path. They watched their footing carefully, wary of loose stones and fallen branches hidden in the gloom. Shadows clung to the trees around them. Every so often, the crunch of a dry leaf broke the stillness, the sound sharp and fleeting.

Ash walked at the front, his staff lightly tapping the ground with each step, more out of habit than necessity. The darkness pressed around them, but he could feel the faint promise of dawn on the horizon. Soon, the sun would break through the night's veil, chasing the shadows away. Until then, silence was their only companion.

Chapter 6: Darkness Rising

A heavy hand slammed down on the makeshift table. Echoes reverberating through the hollow, stone chambers stretching beyond the massive hall Kael had claimed as his workshop. Dust drifted from the ceiling in faint streams, caught in the weak light of the brazier's flickering flames. Kael stepped back, running a hand through the tangled mess of his hair, revealing a face carved by battles and etched with bitterness.

"I'm missing something," he muttered, pacing back to the ancient tome spread open before him. Its brittle pages whispered against the air as his finger traced the faded script. His voice dropped to a frustrated whisper. "The process was perfect. Where is the flaw?"

He emerged from behind the table, leaving the responsibility of the forgotten knowledge in his wake. His footsteps fell lightly against the cold stone, the sound swallowed by the vast silence of the chamber. At the bottom of the steps, he halted, his gaze locking onto the stone slab that loomed at the room's heart. Upon it lay a corpse—not of flesh and blood, but of dust and time itself. The remains were withered beyond recognition, the skin like brittle parchment, drawn tight over a skeletal frame that seemed ready to crumble at the whisper of a breath.

He moved slowly, circling the slab, his eyes tracing the ruin of what had once been a body. The remnants of its clothing clung to the wasted form in fragile, threadbare shrouds, so decayed they seemed woven from shadow and memory rather than cloth. What remained of the skin was cracked and desiccated, a network of fissures splitting its surface like dry riverbeds in a wasteland. The bones beneath pressed starkly against the withered hide, greyed with age, brittle with the slow erosion of centuries. It had not simply died—it had been abandoned to the ages, left to be claimed by the silence of eternity.

"Who were you?" he mused aloud, his voice low, almost reverent. "Warriors, thinkers… creators of wonders lost to the world. Now forgotten, your names erased by time." A faint smirk tugged at the corner of his mouth. "No matter. Your role is no longer yours to decide."

Kael's fingers hovered above the corpse's chest before brushing lightly against the hardened flesh. His touch was almost tender, mocking the words that followed. "You will serve as my weapon, my sword unsheathed against this wretched world." He pressed the cold metal of the pendant beneath his robes against his chest, feeling its familiar weight—a cruel comfort.

The faint echo of footsteps coming from down the hall reached his ears, drawing him from his thoughts. His hand dropped, and he stepped away from the slab, letting the façade of indifference settle back over him. He moved toward the table and began flipping through the tome again, though his thoughts churned with frustration. It must be the translation, he thought. Even with his fluency in the language of the Ancients, subtle misinterpretations could unravel the entire process. He clenched his jaw and rubbed his knuckles against the table's rough surface, the pain a small distraction from his irritation.

The figure emerged from the shadowed hallway, his footfalls unhurried. Kael straightened, his piercing gaze meeting the man's—eyes as black as polished onyx, reflecting the same cold darkness that resided in his own. A comrade, one of the rare few who had followed him from the monastery, into the depths of the underworld. The man halted before him, his posture shifting, unwinding slightly beneath Kael's unspoken recognition. He was a hulking figure, his hair cropped short, his face set with a sternness that bled into the very air around him—an unsettling presence that clung to him like a second skin.

"What news from the search parties?" Kael asked, his tone curt as he returned to the tome. He reached for a smaller, newer book—*The Languages and Culture of an Ancient Race*—and opened it beside the brittle pages of the older text. He began comparing the two text for any sign of error on his part.

“There is word of a ruin to the north,” the man began. His voice carried a faint edge of anticipation. “Our team has broken through the entrance and discovered a series of chambers. Bodies, many of them, scattered throughout the site. However, they’ve encountered a barrier—a steel door blocks further exploration. They’re working to decipher the mechanism.”

Kael nodded absently, his eyes still tracing the worn lines of text before him, though his thoughts drifted elsewhere. “And Thane?” he asked, his voice steady, yet laced with a thread of unease he couldn’t quite mask. He had sent the monk south days ago, charged with investigating whispers of a ruin beyond the hills. Since then—nothing. Only silence.

The creature—Kael's own bitter term for what remained of Thane—had met his end in an ambush, the nárgrim descending in a relentless tide of decayed flesh and lifeless hunger. Their assault had been swift, merciless, leaving no room for strategy, no chance to reclaim the upper hand. Kael had attempted to bring him back, weaving the dark threads of necromancy to pull the monk from death’s grip. And it had worked—after a fashion. The body had risen, and the mind... most of it, at least. But something was missing. A hollow echo lingered in Thane now, an emptiness that gnawed at the edges of his being. Any with the senses to perceive it would know—what had returned was not the man who had left. Not entirely.

"Still no word," the man murmured, his voice carrying a hint of frustration. "He was due back yesterday... perhaps today?" He shifted uneasily, brushing invisible wrinkles from his robes, an awkward gesture betraying his discomfort in delivering the report. He need not have worried, for the message was clear. "His group was delayed, but there has been no indication of trouble."

Kael's brow furrowed. He knew better than to dismiss the unease that gnawed at him. He had probably been too reckless, sending Thane and his nárgrim party so close to The Maiden's Haven monastery. The risk of their discovery by a wandering monk was a gamble, one with consequences far more dangerous than most realized. Yet, the temptation of finding more nárgrim to command—of controlling that power—had proven too great to resist.

Kael exhaled, his fingers pausing over the page. “Our numbers are sufficient, but I’d prefer another third before we move out.” He turned his gaze toward the man, sharp and unyielding. “Go north. Oversee the new dig. Animate the bodies. I want them ready to march as soon as possible.”

The man bowed slightly, a motion born of respect and pragmatism, before turning to leave. Kael watched him retreat into the shadows, his thoughts drifting to Thane. A useful asset, even with half his face ruined from that encounter with the nárgrim. Kael's lips curved in a faint, humourless smile. The resurrection had been a success, he mused. Thane retained more than just obedience; there was understanding there—a spark of will that might prove invaluable.

"Progress," Kael murmured to the silence around him, his gaze flicking back to the corpse on the slab. "Even death has its uses."

Kael stood before the table, its surface laden with ancient tomes cracked and faded by centuries. His gaze lingered on the oldest of them, its inked glyphs a labyrinth of secrets. Slowly, carefully, he extended his right hand. Dark threads oozed from his skin like liquid night, curling around his fingers and coiling up his arm. The air thickened with their taint, whispering promises of power. He felt their hunger, a wicked presence pressing against the edges of his mind, eager to consume even as it granted. He did not resist.

"You vile darkness," he murmured, his voice a reverent hush. "What secrets do you still withhold?"

The gloomy darkness slid through his fingers, weaving and unwinding in an unholy dance. He felt their despair, a keening ache woven into their essence. They longed for freedom—but freedom from what? From where? He didn't know.

The questions clawed at him, persistent as the dark

tendrils themselves. Where had they come from? Did the Ancients forge this power, or had they merely uncovered it, another forbidden secret wrenched from the unknown? The tome before him—a find of years past—hinted at much but revealed little. The incantations it held allowed him to draw upon the void threads, but their true nature remained a mystery, veiled in riddles he had yet to untangle.

Kael clenched his hand, feeling the power's potential writhe beneath his grasp. It was immense, limitless, yet constrained—as though a dam existed between him and its source. He wanted more. He needed more. But the darkness held back, tantalizing him with their refusal.

"Someday," he vowed, his voice low with conviction. "Someday, you will be mine."

Releasing his hold, he watched the black threads seep back into his skin, retreating like an obedient tide. His lips curled into a smirk. "Once I uncover the truth beneath Dawn's End, your secrets will be laid bare. And then, I will ascend. I will become what I was destined to be."

He moved around the table, his boots echoing against the stone as he approached the slab at the room's center. The corpse of a nárgrim lay there, its desiccated form still as death. Kael's smile darkened. "Until then," he said, placing a hand on the creature's chest, "you will suffice."

Closing his eyes, Kael reached for the darkness

again. They answered, rushing into him like a flood of despair, filling him with the same vicious essence that had long replaced the bliss he once knew. The Divine Mother's light had been a pale comfort in comparison to this intoxicating darkness. He would make the trade a thousand times over.

Tendrils of black erupted from his body, swirling around him in a storm of writhing obsidian threads. He directed his will into the nárgrim beneath his hand, and the weaves obeyed, flowing down his arm like venom into the lifeless corpse.

The blackness seeped into the creature, disappearing into its withered flesh. Kael stepped back, watching as the nárgrim stirred. Its limbs twitched, then jerked into motion. The thing sat up, its hollow eyes staring into the void.

Kael's grin widened. He had seen this moment a thousand times, and yet, it still thrilled him. This was creation—his creation. He was a god, breathing life into death.

"Rise, my soldier," he commanded, his voice ringing with authority. "Rise, and serve your master."

The words tasted sweet, a litany of power he never tired of. Soon, he thought as the nárgrim climbed from the slab, its movements stiff but obedient. Soon, there would be no need for these rituals. With but a thought, he would raise legions. And they would kneel before him.

"Follow me, my dark child," Kael intoned, his voice soft yet resonant with authority. He turned from the slab, his robes brushing against the cold stone as he moved toward the far door. "Come and meet your destiny."

The nárgrim stirred, its movements halting and awkward, as if its limbs were uncertain of their function. It stumbled after him, its gait uneven, feet dragging across the stone. Kael listened to the faint groans that escaped its desiccated throat—muted protests against its fate, a futile struggle drowned beneath the bindings he had imposed. It would obey. It must obey.

Kael had mastered the ritual bindings through bitter necessity. Early failures had taught him the danger of unbound creations—mindless predators driven by hunger, indiscriminate in their wrath. But now, his command was absolute. The nárgrim moved not by its own will but by Kael's, as if his intentions had been fused to its flesh. He would allow it to feast soon enough. Hunger made them sharper.

They walked together through the chamber, Kael's steps orderly, while the nárgrim's came uneven. The corridor ahead stretched into shadow, twisting around a bend before opening into a smaller room, barren but for a single torch sputtering weakly on the wall. The flame cast feeble light, trembling in the grip of the stale air. Kael pressed on, his shadow stretching long behind him, the nárgrim shuffling in his wake.

The passage beyond was narrow, the walls close, until it spilled into a wider hall that seemed to stretch endlessly toward the glow of natural light. The brightness at the far end stung Kael's eyes even at a distance, an unwelcome intrusion. He raised a hand to shield his gaze as he approached, blinking against the glare.

When they crossed the threshold, the world beyond the ruins unfolded before him. Kael paused in the stone archway, his dark figure framed against the light. A hill sloped downward, its grass scorched and dry, and below, a field populated with the restless dead. Thousands of nárgrim stood swaying in place, their forms grotesque and contorted, their lifeless eyes fixed on nothing.

Kael felt a swell of satisfaction as he surveyed the throng. His army. A sea of darkness bound to his will, a force poised to shatter the light of Dawn's End and beyond.

"Go now," he commanded the nárgrim beside him, his tone unyielding. "Join your brothers in arms."

The creature lurched forward, its uneven steps carrying it down the hill toward the waiting horde. Kael watched it descend, his gaze sharp, his thoughts darker still. He could feel the hunger emanating from them, the unquenchable thirst of the shadows that animated their forms. Death and ruin—they craved it with every fibre of their existence. Soon, he would give it to them. Dawn's End would fall. And then? The world.

But for now, there was still much to do. Kael turned away from the light, back into the ruin's suffocating darkness. The void welcomed him, its cold embrace familiar and comforting. More secrets lay buried here, veiled in shadow. Secrets that might yet strengthen his hand.

With a faint smile, Kael stepped deeper into the gloom, leaving behind the ruins' threshold and the field of waiting death. The light at his back dimmed, swallowed by the encroaching dark.

Chapter 7:
A Revelation

The monastery's silhouette had long faded into the horizon as the group of monks trudged along the winding dirt road. The village they'd passed earlier now seemed like a distant memory, a ghost fading into the hills. Shortly after navigating through the ravaged streets, they had veered northward onto the trade route. Rowan led the way with meaningful strides, his presence a steadfast anchor for the group. Ash, walking behind, welcomed the reprieve from taking point. It gave him space to wrestle with his thoughts, though the weight of them was no less burdensome.

At some point, he would need to share everything with his companions—the grim details he had yet to fully process himself. The image of the undead monk lingered in his mind, like a dark stain he couldn't scrub away. The dead rising was no new phenomenon to him; his life had been one of hunting and purging such abominations. Usually, these lost souls were driven by unresolved longings or oblivious to their own deaths. But this monk was different. His resurrection bore an objective, premeditated and thought-out, and Ash could sense another's hand in it. That realization disturbed him deeply.

A soft nudge on his elbow snapped him from his

reverie. Kiran, quiet and observant all morning, walked beside him. She glanced up without speaking, her expression offering quiet support, as though she understood the storm raging in his mind.

Ash smiled at her, his voice kind. "How are you holding up?"

"I'm fine," she replied in a whisper, though her tone hinted at exhaustion. "My belly's starting to ache, though…" She cast a glance over her shoulder at the others trailing behind before leaning closer. "…and I really, *really* need to pee." A sly grin spread across her face, punctuated by a playful lift of her eyebrows.

Ash chuckled, the sound light and authentic. "I see," he said.

The sun hung high in the sky now, its golden rays cutting through the canopy above. Ash slowed his pace and called out to Rowan, who had slipped ahead by a good twenty paces. "Rowan! Perhaps we could take a short break."

Rowan paused, turning back to meet Ash's gaze. His brow furrowed with mild displeasure, though not enough to argue. Before the veteran monk could voice his thoughts, Ash added, "I think it's time I shared the rest of the story." That earned a sharp, inquisitive look—and a nod of approval.

Rowan gestured for the group to halt, and the

monks gathered beneath the shade of a sprawling tree. Kiran disappeared into the bushes, her retreat met with a smirk from Ash. Each monk rummaged through their packs, pulling out morsels of food or taking long draughts from their waterskins. The weight of the morning eased, if only slightly, as they settled into the momentary calm.

Ash waited, giving them time to rest and collect themselves. When Kiran returned, she perched atop a nearby boulder, brushing her robes into place as she sat. All eyes turned toward Ash, anticipation flickering in their gazes. He stepped forward, his hand brushing the pendant at his neck as he sought the right words.

He cleared his throat, meeting each of their gazes in turn. It was time.

Ash decided to start from the beginning. He spoke of the young deliveryman's tale of the terrified man who barged into the inn and the headmaster's command to investigate Farrow's Point for any evidence of truth to the deliveryman's story. His words wove through the events like a steady tide, recounting his and Kiran's skirmish with the nárgrim in the ravaged village below. Their numbers seemed to raise eyebrows among the monks. As seasoned adepts, they knew the rarity of nárgrim venturing so far from the ancient ruins they typically haunted. The notion that so many had emerged from one of the Ancients' forgotten sites seemed improbable, even impossible.

Ash paused when he reached the part of the story involving the monk, unsure as to where to continue his telling of the events. He could feel the weight of their attention pressing on him now, their gazes unwavering. A few even leaned forward slightly, their postures betraying their intrigue. He glanced at Kiran, who sat frozen mid-bite, a piece of bread pinched just before her open mouth. She already knew how the story ended, yet it seemed as though she, too, was bracing herself for the reactions she knew would follow. And follow they would.

Ash continued his account, his voice thoughtful but edged with something darker—something that unsettled the others. He spoke of the encounter with the monk, once a brother of their Order, once a servant of the Divine Mother's light. Now, he was something twisted, something far less.

As Ash's words filled the space between them, he watched confusion take root in their faces, saw the flicker of disbelief in their eyes. He told them of the monk's gaze—his eyes, once filled with life, now black as polished onyx, empty and cold. Shadows coiled around his arms, slithering and writhing in unsettling contrast to the blue flames of the Divine Mother's blessing. Where once there had been grace, now there was only a creeping darkness.

Their eyes flicked between Ash and each other, uncertainty tightening their expressions, furrowed brows betraying the weight of their thoughts. For a fleeting moment, silence held them in its grip—then it shattered. Questions spilled forth in a chaotic rush, voices rising and overlapping, a torrent of words colliding in the tight space between them.

Ash stood unmoved, his gaze steady, his silence a quiet command. He would not indulge their frenzy.

Gradually, the clamour ebbed, tapering off into uneasy murmurs before fading entirely. They were left in the hush of their own restraint, their unspoken questions pressing heavy in the air. Ash let the moment stretch, ensuring they understood—he would speak when they were ready to listen.

"I assume the monk bore the mark of Dawn's End," Rowan said at last, his voice steady but edged with unease. "That explains our current destination."

Ash nodded in confirmation.

"Have we any word of the monastery's state?" Rowan pressed on, his voice growing quieter with each word, as if dreading the answer. "Has it been… compromised? Or even fallen?"

The final question lingered in the air like smoke. Rowan's gaze drifted, his thoughts clearly spiralling into darker possibilities.

Ash noted how Seanne and Celest exchanged uneasy glances at the suggestion, their composure faltering.

Even Kiran looked stricken by the idea, as if it hadn't occurred to her until now. Ash himself had been wrestling with the implications ever since he found the pendant bearing Dawn's End's sigil on the corpse of the dead monk.

"We know nothing for certain," Ash said, his voice cutting through the tension. "That's why we're being sent out, to find the answers."

The group fell into silence again, their minds clearly churning. Seanne, younger and less seasoned, turned his gaze to his mentor as if searching for some reassurance. But even the older monk seemed lost in his own thoughts, his eyes distant. For the remainder of the break, the companions sat in quiet reflection, each grappling with their own visions of what might await them.

The stillness was broken by Rowan's voice, sharp and commanding. "Come," he said. "We need to move if we're to cover good ground before nightfall."

One by one, they rose, repacking their gear, grabbing their staves, and shaking off the quiet weight that had settled over them. Each fell into stride as Rowan resumed his place at the front of the group, leading them down the road with a renewed pace.

Kiran fell into step beside Ash once more, her presence light but steady. The group moved in relative silence now, the road stretching endlessly before them. The air seemed heavier, the journey more solemn, as they drew closer to whatever awaited them at Dawn's End.

The party trudged along the dirt road in silence, their mood heavier than the air around them. Ash let his attention drift to the soft murmur of conversation behind him, catching only fragments of Celest and Seanne's whispered words before they faded entirely. He assumed they had intentionally lagged behind, perhaps to shield themselves from Ash's reprisal should they press him for more answers. He understood their curiosity. They all wanted to know more about the road ahead, even if the answers wouldn't bring them comfort.

Up ahead, Rowan maintained his steady pace, lost in his own thoughts, the gap between him and the others widening with each step. Ash's gaze followed him briefly before he felt the gentle touch of Kiran's hand on his own. It was subtle, but enough to draw his attention.

"I couldn't help but notice," she began, her voice low but laced with curiosity, "you didn't mention the second sigil on the back of the pendant." Her dark eyes studied him, searching for more than the surface of his answer.

Ash exhaled, returning his gaze to the road ahead. "Some information only invites more questions," he said. "They've got plenty to keep their minds occupied as it is."

But he knew Kiran wouldn't let it rest there. True to form, she pressed on, her voice quieter this time, her question carrying the weight of something personal. “He was your friend, wasn’t he?”

Ash nodded, his silence heavy with unspoken words. He could feel her waiting, her presence beside him unwavering, unwilling to let the question fade. With a resigned sigh, he began.

“I had just arrived at the monastery back then,” he said, his voice steady but distant, as if pulling the memories from a fog. “Some come to Dawn’s End by choice. I didn’t have that luxury. My path was... inevitable.”

He paused, drawing a slow breath, sifting through the weight of memory before speaking again. “My father died not long after I was born. Drafted into the first war with the western kingdoms—sent to the front when they invaded Vaelthorne’s borders. That war consumed everything it touched and left little for those of us who endured it.”

His gaze drifted to Kiran. She listened in silence, her face carefully blank, though curiosity flickered beneath the surface. To her, the war was nothing more than a distant echo, a story told and retold long after the blood had dried and the dust had settled. But still, she clung to his words, as if by understanding them, she could grasp something of the world that had come before her.

“My mother, my sister, and I lived on a farm,” Ash went on, his voice softening. “It wasn’t much, but we made do. Then my sister came of age and ran off with some young fool who thought the world of himself. She left my mother and me to fend for ourselves. I was barely twelve winters old."

The memories stirred in his mind, vivid yet distant, like glimpses of a dream. Ash paused again, the silence stretching just long enough for Kiran to notice, though she didn't push him. She waited, patient as always.

"It wasn't long after that my mother passed," he said at last. "The cough took her. I was too young to understand what was happening, too helpless to stop it." His voice carried no sorrow, only a quiet detachment. Some wounds, he thought, were so old they no longer felt like his own.

"I tried to find my sister," he continued, "thinking she could help. But she was gone—lost to me. I don't know if she would help even if she could. Either way, I was alone." His words trailed off, leaving the question of his sister unanswered, her absence an unresolved shadow in his tale.

"For a while, I tried to survive on my own," he said. "But I was just a boy, and the world doesn't have much mercy for young, lost boys." His voice grew quieter. "I was losing the battle."

Kiran's gaze softened as he spoke, her expression full of questions she didn't voice. Ash pressed on, his tone unwavering. "Two monks found me on the roadside. I was starving, dehydrated—barely alive. They took me in to their care, fed me, nursed me back to health. By the time I could walk again, we'd reached the gates of Dawn's End." He gestured to the distant mountains, their jagged peaks visible on the horizon, as if to emphasize the significance of that moment. "They gave me a home when I had none."

"Shortly after, I became an acolyte," he continued. "It wasn't long after that before I met him. Kael." The name hung in the air between them. "He'd been there for less than a year when I arrived. Just a boy, a few winters older than me, but he was... different."

Ash's voice grew quieter, as though he were speaking more to himself now than to Kiran. "At first, he was just another novice monk. But he had this way of pulling others into his orbit. He wasn't like the rest of us." He shook his head, a shadow of regret flickering across his face. "Looking back now, I wonder if that difference was always there, waiting for the right moment to emerge."

Kiran said nothing, but her silence spoke volumes. Ash could feel the weight of her gaze as the memory of Kael loomed large in his mind. Somewhere ahead, the mountains beckoned, and with them, the truth waiting to be uncovered.

"We hit it off instantly," Ash began, a faint smile tugging at his lips. "I suppose we had to, being the only two students at the monastery in our age group. Others came, but at that time there was just be the two of us." His smile turned wry. "Maybe if there had been others my age, I wouldn't have stuck with Kael for so long."

Kiran stayed silent but attentive, her eyes fixed on him with quiet encouragement to continue. He glanced at her, gauging her interest, and, reassured by her smile, pressed on.

"Kael was always... curious. Inquisitive to a fault. He devoured every scrap of knowledge he could get his hands on, spent hours buried in the tomes of the library. He was sharp—brilliant, really. I have to give him that." Ash paused, his gaze drifting to the road ahead as the memories stirred like leaves in the wind. "But it wasn't until we became full-fledged monks that I started noticing the changes in him."

He shifted his footing, the weight of the recollection heavy on his shoulders. "It started the day he returned from one of his expeditions. He'd gone to explore some ruins higher up in the mountains. When he came back, he had the old remains of a book with him."

Ash's tone grew quieter, as if the memory itself demanded consideration. "The book was unlike anything I'd ever seen. The cover was crafted from aged leather, intricately etched with patterns that seemed both decorative and... significant. The metal bindings were heavy, almost ceremonial. Inside, the pages were intact but so brittle they felt like they might crumble under the slightest touch." He ran a hand through his hair, trying to dislodge a gnat that had become tangled in its strands.

"Kael became obsessed with it," Ash continued. "He started copying the pages into a new book almost immediately, afraid the original might not survive the passage of time. He admitted to me that he understood very little of the text, but the fragments he could decipher seemed important to him—vital, even."

Ash rubbed his temple, as though massaging loose the tangled threads of the past. "For years, that book consumed him. Every free moment was spent studying it, copying it, preserving it. It became his child, in a way—the kind of child that some parents dream of. Perfect. All-consuming." He shook his head, a shadow passing over his features. "That book took him from me. Whatever bond we'd shared was... gone, swallowed up by his obsession."

Ash's voice grew sharper, tinged with regret. "Others noticed it too. Some of the monks began questioning him about the book, asking what it was and why it mattered so much. But Kael... he became defensive. Hostile, even. He pushed everyone away."

He paused, his jaw tightening as old memories stirred, unwelcome but relentless. "It was only a few seasons after he finished transcribing the text that Kael vanished.

He took a handful of younger monks with him—those who had fallen under his influence, drawn in by the secrets he whispered from that damned book."

Kiran blinked, caught off guard. Ash could see the surprise in her eyes—she'd been expecting a different ending, perhaps something more dramatic, more definitive. Behind them, Celest and Seanne had drawn closer, their footsteps quieter now, their attention fully on Ash's words. He could not guess how long they had been there.

"We didn't send out search parties," Ash continued, his voice even, though tinged with bitterness. "He took everything with him—his notes, his belongings. It was clear he'd left of his own volition. There was no foul play. No sign of coercion. He was just... gone." Ash let the weight of that word settle in the air. "And that was the last I saw or heard of him. Until just the other day when we found that pendant."

"The monk's pendant? The one that marked him as one of Dawn's End?" Seanne asked, his voice low as he slipped up beside Kiran.

Ash gave a curt nod. "We found it on him," he said, his tone weighted with meaning. "And on the back of the amulet—Kael's sigil." He let the words sink in, the unspoken implication heavy between them. "His mark. The same one he used when he was still one of us."

The silence that followed was broken only by the

soft crunch of boots on dirt. Kiran's face was a mix of curiosity and sympathy. Ash could see the unspoken questions lingering there, but she said nothing. Instead, she simply nodded, allowing him the space to continue if he chose.

Ash did, though with less fervour now. "A few years later, the headmaster caught word that the Maiden's Haven was looking for boarders. Their numbers were dwindling, recruitment drying up. I volunteered." He smiled faintly, almost to himself. "I needed a change. The cold of the highlands was wearing on me, and honestly, I didn't want to keep walking the same halls where everything reminded me of Kael, and the things I had lost. So I left."

His words trailed off, and for a moment, the road stretched ahead of them in silence. Kiran seemed content with his explanation. She offered him a quiet "Thank you" and fell into her own thoughts, leaving Ash to his.

As the mountains loomed closer, Ash's mind wandered to the present. Kael was gone—but his shadow had returned, darkening their path ahead.

Chapter 8:
The Merchant

The road stretched ahead, cloaked in the golden light of the afternoon. The monks' spirits had lifted, and laughter occasionally rang out among the group. Their earlier silence had given way to lighthearted chatter, punctuated by Rowan's rare wanderings back from the front to share a tale or two of his own past adventures. The camaraderie among them felt almost like a balm, masking the unease that lingered in the back of their minds.

The dry path stretched before them, dust rising in faint, sunlit swirls with each step. The monastery lay behind them now, a silence settled between them. Kiran still carried a smile from their earlier conversation, and at the front of the group, Celest walked close to Rowan, their voices punctuated by occasional laughter.

Seanne drifted forward from the rear, his pace matching Ash and Kiran's. He didn't speak at first, but Ash sensed the hesitation, the unspoken words forming behind the young man's eyes. Seanne had something on his mind, something that pressed against his usual easygoing nature. When he finally spoke, the words came out carefully chosen, as if he was testing them for weight before offering them fully.

"I don't regret my time at the monastery," he said, glancing between them, though his question was clearly meant for Ash. "But I was relieved to leave it behind, too. Does that make sense?"

Kiran remained silent. She had known little else but the monastery's walls since childhood. This was Seanne's question, directed at someone who had known both confinement and the freedom beyond it.

He exhaled, looking up at the canopy overhead, where the light broke through in scattered, shifting shapes. "I had everything I could need there. A warm bed, hot meals, a place to belong. But the longer I stayed, the more it felt like a cage. I thought I would enjoy settling in somewhere, finally having a place to stop and breathe, but all I wanted was to be out on the road again."

Ash understood the feeling all too well. He had returned to the monastery only briefly, yet a part of him had already begun to itch for the road once more. There was something about movement, about the unknown, that settled deeper into a man's bones than stillness ever could. Once the world had opened itself to you, how could you willingly shut yourself away again?

"It gets into your blood," Ash said after a moment, his voice carrying the weight of experience. "At first, travel is a disruption—something new, something uncertain. But after a while, it becomes the familiar thing. Standing still feels unnatural, like a weight pressing down on you. When you're in motion, you're free."

Seanne gave a slow nod, but there was something unreadable in his eyes, something unresolved. Ash had seen that look before—the quiet turmoil of a man not yet certain of what he was searching for.

Seanne didn't push the conversation further. Instead, he spun his quarterstaff once, then let the butt of it strike the dirt in rhythm with his steps. The conversation faded into the sound of their boots against the earth, and the road stretched on ahead, waiting to see where it would take them next.

It was nearing midday when a merchant's cart came into view, wobbling along the uneven road and kicking up a plume of dry dust that hung in the air like a shroud. The cart creaked to a halt a few paces ahead of the monks. An aged man held the reins with practised ease, his face weathered by years of travel under the sun. Beside him sat a younger man, a bow resting across his lap and an arrow notched loosely in place. His posture was tense, his eyes scanning the monks with cautious curiosity.

Rowan and Ash stepped forward, their movements unrushed, a subtle reassurance to the travellers. Rowan spoke first, his tone warm. "Greetings. The Mother's Blessings to you both."

The elder of the pair offered a curt nod in return,

dismissing the blessing with a casual wave of his hand. "What can I do for you, monks?" he rasped, his voice jagged as though it had been worn thin by too many harsh winters.

"We seek news of the roads to the north," Rowan replied, his gaze steady on the older man. He couldn't help but notice the younger one shifting restlessly in his seat, as if eager to speak but restrained by some unspoken command.

The old man scratched at the stubble on his cheek, his eyes narrowing in thought. "Strange you should ask," he muttered, his voice like gravel rolling in his throat. "Been travellin' this road for years, see. Rarely cross paths with anyone worth mentionin'. But yesterday…" He trailed off, his tone uncertain, almost reluctant. The old man looked around as though expecting something to jump out at him.

The younger man leaned forward, his grip on the bow tightening. Ash caught the flicker of unease in his eyes, but the boy held his tongue.

"Yesterday," the old man resumed, his tone more deliberate now, "we passed near some old ruins, just beyond the village up ahead. Nothin' special about the place—just some stones stickin' out of the dirt, far as I ever cared to notice. But there was a commotion. Diggin'. Noise comin' outta the woods."

The old man paused, his weathered face tightening

as though he was chewing on the memory itself. "Curious, you know? Been up and down this road long enough to know it ain't common to hear that sorta racket in a place like that. Thought maybe someone was layin' a foundation for a new building or somethin'." He gestured with a shrug, but his tone betrayed unease. "So I sent Connol here to check it out. Boy's got better legs than me, and I ain't gettin' any younger. Can't be getting up an' down this ol' wagon all the time, you know?"

Ash's eyes shifted to the younger man, Connol, whose jaw tightened at the mention of his name. He was sitting stiffly now, his gaze darting between the monks as though weighing whether to speak, while also looking back over his shoulder at some unseen pursuer.

"He wasn't gone long," the old man continued, bobbing his head slightly as he spoke. "Maybe a minute, maybe less. Then he came runnin' back like his boots were on fire, shoutin' for me to get the cart movin'. Thought for sure there was a wolf pack on his heels, the way he was carryin' on. But when I looked, there wasn't nothin' behind him. Did as I was told, boy barely made the leap back up to his seat."

Connol's knuckles whitened on the bow. Ash could see the fear etched on the younger man's face, the kind of fear that left a mark far deeper than a fleeting scare. The old man lowered his voice, his words now more hesitant.

"Wasn't till we were far down the road, and it was clear nothin' trailed behind us, that Connol here told me what he saw. Said there were... dead folk. Workin' the ruins."

"Dead folk?" Rowan echoed, his tone skeptical.

"That's what he said," the merchant affirmed, his face darkening. "Folk who should've been lyin' still in the earth, movin' about like they had business to tend to. He said none of 'em noticed him, and none followed us. But still..." He trailed off, his words heavy with unspoken dread.

Ash and Rowan exchanged a look. There was no need for words; they both knew what this meant. The air between them seemed to thicken with unspoken resolve.

"I appreciate the warning," Rowan said, his tone calm but edged with steel. "We'll be sure to investigate when we reach the ruins."

"What of the village to the north?" Seanne's voice cut through the air from behind the gathered monks. His gaze lingered on the younger man clutching the bow. "You would've passed through there. Did anyone mention... anything unusual?"

The old man leaned forward in his seat, the creak of worn leather punctuating his words. "Stopped in this morning. Still too early for most folk to be up and about." He shrugged. "Ran into a few folks wantin' to trade, though. Told 'em what my boy saw out there, and they looked proper spooked. Walkin' dead ain't exactly somethin' they hear about every day." A grin tugged at the corner of his mouth, weathered and amused. "Can't say I blame 'em. I would be pretty spooked to if I had heard such a tale."

"They didn't do anything, though." The younger man's voice wavered, his grip on the bow tightening. "I don't think they believed us."

The old man shot him a glare and raised a gnarled hand, half warning, half habit. "Quiet, boy. I'll do the talkin'." He shifted his weight in the saddle. "But he's right. Ain't seen the like of undead 'round these parts before. Probably thought we were spinnin' tales to lighten their pockets." He nodded to himself, as if settling the thought. "Didn't much like the talk, though. Just traded quick and went their way."

Rowan stepped forward, tapping his knuckles against the wagon's side. "Not surprising. People who haven't seen the horrors of this world refuse to believe them until they're staring straight into the abyss."

The old man's head bobbed in agreement, his expression grim.

Ash folded his arms, eyes narrowing on the distant road. "Your road south should be clear." He met the merchant's gaze. "We've had trouble to the west, but it's being dealt with. You shouldn't run into anything...

unnatural."

The merchant grunted and offered a stiff nod. "You folks take care. There's a dark feelin' in the air these days." His grip on the reins tightened. "Hate to see good folk get hurt."

With a flick of his wrist, the cart groaned into motion. The monks stepped aside, watching as the wagon trundled down the road, kicking up a lazy plume of dust that swallowed them whole within moments.

Ash lingered a moment longer, watching the trail settle. Dark times indeed.

As the monks resumed their march, Ash felt the weight of the merchant's tale settle over the group. The laughter and lightheartedness of earlier were gone, replaced by a quiet tension. Ahead, the ruins awaited, and with them, the truth of whatever lay stirring in the shadows.

"I don't like the sound of nárgrim stirring in so many places," Celest said, her voice cutting through the uneasy quiet.

Seanne nodded, his brows drawn in thought. "I haven't been a full monk for long, but I've yet to cross paths with a nárgrim myself. Now we've heard of two sightings in as many days." He twirled his staff absently, the polished wood whispering against the air. "Doesn't sit right with me."

Kiran glanced over her shoulder at Seanne,

searching for reassurance. He met her gaze with a lopsided grin and a wink. "Don't worry, little sis. We've got this. Just gotta keep an eye on the old folks—make sure they don't slow us down."

Laughter rippled through the group, and even Ash allowed himself a small smile. Rowan chuckled, his voice rich with years of hard-won experience. "You won't be laughing when us old folks haul you out of trouble, boy."

Ash watched Rowan with a quiet sense of relief. It was good to hear this old companion laugh a little. They needed these moments, however fleeting, to stave off the creeping darkness that seemed to press closer with each step.

"I've seen nárgrim before," Celest said, turning to Kiran. "Mindless things, really. Keep your distance, strike hard. Aim for the head." She nodded, offering a small, knowing smile. Ash caught the subtle shift in Kiran's stance, the way her shoulders eased, her gait loosening.

Seanne barked a laugh. "Sounds simple enough."

Ash tapped Kiran lightly on the arm, drawing her attention. "You've already learned that Celest is correct." he said, his voice steady. "Just remember, go for the head and try to be quick. They're slow, which means you'll have the advantage—if you don't let them get too close."

Rowan squinted up at the darkening sky. "We're not reaching the ruins today." His tone carried the weight of experience. "Navigating them at night? Bad idea. Nárgrim don't need eyes to find you. They move by... other means."

Ash nodded. He'd seen it firsthand, and he was certain Rowan had too. It was a challenge even seasoned monks didn't take lightly. With Kiran and Seanne in tow, it wasn't a risk worth taking.

"The village the merchants spoke of should be close now," Rowan continued. "We'll stop there for the night. A warm meal will do us good before whatever tomorrow brings."

Ash didn't miss the flicker of unease on Kiran's face at the notion of battle. Even Seanne, for all his bravado, lacked enthusiasm for the prospect. Ash's gaze shifted to Celest. As always, her face betrayed nothing—an expression honed by a lifetime of experience. Whatever tomorrow held, she would face it with the same unshakable calm.

Soon evening draped the horizon in hues of amber and indigo as the group crested a hill, revealing the modest village below. The five monks descended toward it, crossing a wooden bridge that arched gracefully over a rushing creek. The sound of water tumbling over rocks filled the air, a soothing counterpoint to the day's march. Ash glanced at Kiran, who had paused mid-bridge, leaning over the railing to peer into the swirling current below. Whatever she saw seemed to satisfy her, and she returned silently to his side.

As they entered the village, the locals took notice. Farmers tending to their yards and children playing in the narrow dirt streets stopped to gawk, some whispering amongst themselves, others bold enough to point. The monks pressed on, heading toward a larger structure at the heart of the village—a weathered building that Rowan had identified as the local inn. It promised a meal and beds for the night, simple comforts that felt luxurious after a long day on the road.

Rowan reached the door first and held it open as the others filed in. The air inside hit Ash like a blow—thick with the mingling scents of ale, smoke, and the faint tang of unwashed bodies. Kiran raised a hand to her nose, her expression twisting in discomfort. Ash couldn't blame her. The room was dimly lit, its walls stained with years of soot from the hearth at its far end. A heavy wooden bar dominated one side of the room, while scattered tables filled the remaining space. They found one near the door, the largest available, and settled into their seats.

Seanne's distaste was clear, his voice a low murmur as his eyes scanned the grimy interior. "This place is a hovel," he muttered, his lips curling as if he'd just bitten into something foul.

Celest, ever the pragmatist, shrugged nonchalantly. "I've stayed in worse." Ash doubted she was exaggerating. He'd stayed in far worse himself—nights spent drenched on the open ground beneath a drizzling sky, or huddled beneath a jagged rock face as snow lashed him from all sides. Travellers took what they could get, he thought, a silent acknowledgement of their shared fate.

Kiran remained quiet, her hand wiping absentmindedly at the table's splintered surface. Ash wasn't sure if she was actually trying to clean the grime off or if she was simply avoiding the awkward conversation. She had likely never known discomfort in such forms. Even the barest living quarters at the monastery had been an unspoken luxury in comparison. But she said nothing, her eyes downcast, focused on the table rather than the company around her.

Ash's gaze swept over the room. There was only one other patron—an overweight man, flushed red with drink, his attention fixed on the barmaid, whom he was attempting to woo with fumbling words and drunken gestures. The woman, clearly accustomed to such advances, disentangled herself with practised ease the moment she noticed the monks. Her expression was neutral as she approached their table.

"What'll it be?" she asked, her voice raspy but not unkind. Her eyes flicked over each of them, sizing them up, assessing whether they were worth her time.

Rowan didn't hesitate. "We'll take a hot meal and some ales." He glanced around the table for objections, but none came. Even Ash felt the pull of the promise of warmth in his belly. "And rooms for the night," Rowan added, his voice firm.

The barmaid nodded, wiping her hands down the front of her grimy apron, her face unreadable. "Right, then." Without another word, she turned on her heel and disappeared through a door behind the bar.

The monks lapsed into light conversation while they waited, though the weariness of travel dulled their usual camaraderie. Soon, the barmaid returned, her arms laden with mugs of frothy ale, which she placed in front of each monk before vanishing again through a door at the back of the room.

Each of them grabbed their mugs, and with a quick glance between them, they took their first swig. Ash couldn't help but notice Seanne, though, carefully wiping the rim of his mug with his sleeve before bringing it to his lips. He hadn't seen whether the mug was truly dirty, but he wouldn't have been surprised if it was.

The ale slid down Ash's throat. It wasn't the finest he'd ever tasted, but it certainly wasn't the worst either. He thought he heard Rowan mutter something under his breath, comparing the ale to something far less pleasant—something that sounded uncomfortably close to warm piss.

Minutes later, the barmaid returned, this time accompanied by a burly man carrying trays loaded with steaming bowls of stew. Without ceremony, they placed the bowls before the monks, some spilling onto the table as they landed.

"Your rooms are ready," the barmaid said, jerking a thumb toward the back of the inn. "Last three doors on the left." She watched the man shuffle back to his post without a word, the silence hanging in the air between them.

Rowan offered a brief word of thanks, and with a silent nod from Ash, paid the price for their stay. Ash knew they had likely paid more than the place warranted, but he wasn't about to argue over the cost. It was still better than sleeping under the stars. The barmaid pocketed the coins and left just as swiftly, her presence slipping away like water down a drain.

The monks ate in near silence, the clatter of spoons against bowls the only sound to break the stillness. The stew was hearty enough to stave off hunger, though the taste left much to be desired. Ash couldn't bring himself to think too hard on the source of the meat, instead focusing on the fresh vegetables that, for a moment, made the meal tolerable. It was far from satisfying, but hunger made even mediocre fare feel like a small victory. By the time the bowls were empty, each monk looked a little more at ease, a little more content.

One by one, they pushed back their chairs, rising with the faint creak of old wood beneath them. Packs and staves were gathered up, and they made their way down the hallway the barmaid had pointed out. Celest and Kiran took the first room, Rowan and Seanne the second. The third room was left for Ash. He entered, closed the door behind him. What little noise came from beyond the door, faded to a distant hum.

Dropping his pack to the floor, Ash sank onto the edge of the bed. He tugged off his boots, letting them fall haphazardly beside him. He considered undressing, but the weight of exhaustion settled on him like a heavy blanket. Sleep's pull was undeniable. With a quiet sigh, he rolled onto the bed still clothed, and within moments, his eyes slipped shut, the dark quiet of the room swallowing him whole.

Chapter 9:
Into The Ruins

A heavy knock at the door jolted Ash awake. He sat up with a groan, rubbing sleep from his eyes as he squinted toward the small window. Through the warped glass, faint hues of violet and indigo brushed the horizon, heralding the arrival of dawn.

"One moment," he called out, his voice rough with sleep. He waited until the soft shuffle of footsteps retreated down the hall before swinging his legs over the edge of the bed. His joints protested the sudden movement, a dull ache reminding him of the miles they had travelled the day before.

Ash pulled his hair back, tying it loosely at the nape of his neck. A brush would have been a luxury on a journey like this, but necessity had taught him to make do with what he had. Smoothing the worst of the wrinkles from his robes, he slung his pack over one shoulder and took up his staff. He spared a final glance around the room before stepping out into the dimly lit hallway.

The common room glowed faintly ahead, lit by the pale firelight left smouldering from the night before. Sound of Ash's steps echoed softly as he approached, his staff tapping a rhythm against the wooden floor.

Inside, the others had already gathered. Seanne sat slouched in a chair, legs outstretched and eyes heavy with the remnants of sleep. Celest knelt beside him, rummaging through her pack with quiet efficiency. Across the table, Kiran rubbed at her eyes. When she saw Ash, her face brightened with a sleepy smile, the warmth of it cutting through the early morning haze. He returned the gesture with a small nod.

Ash's gaze drifted to Rowan, who stood at the bar speaking to the innkeeper. The woman, still clad in her nightclothes, wore an expression that teetered between irritation and disinterest. Ash watched as Rowan tossed a few extra coins onto the counter, coaxing a reluctant smile from her. With a curt nod, she vanished through the door behind the bar.

"Boiled oats and sliced fruit," Rowan announced as he returned to the table. He clapped Ash on the shoulder in greeting. "That's all she could manage for breakfast. I hope no one was expecting a feast."

Ash slid into a seat beside him, offering a faint smirk in response. Across from him, Kiran leaned forward slightly, her gaze settling on him. "How was your sleep?" he asked quietly, making an effort at idle conversation before the day's burdens inevitably intruded.

"It was fine," she replied, her tone light. "Celest and I tried meditating before bed. I think it helped—I drifted off almost immediately."

Celest and Rowan were already deep in discussion about the road ahead, their voices weaving together in quiet consideration. Seanne, meanwhile, seemed lost in his own thoughts, though his occasional glance at the pair suggested he was half-listening. Kiran, too, had turned her attention to the ongoing conversation, her expression reflective. Ash let the thread of small talk drop, settling back into his seat. He already knew what the day would hold; the plans might as well have been etched into the marrow of his bones after years of similar ventures. Orders, at this point, felt more like a well-rehearsed tale than actual preparation.

The low murmur of voices blended into a hum as Ash turned inward, his thoughts drifting. It wasn't until the sound of a bowl being set in front of him broke through the haze that he returned to the moment. He glanced up at the innkeeper, who had returned with their breakfast. Offering her a polite nod of thanks, he looked down at his meal—a viscous, grey porridge crowned with uneven wedges of apple.

Ash stifled a laugh, the corners of his mouth twitching. The meal was almost comical in its presentation, a far cry from anything appetizing. For a moment, he considered forgoing it altogether in favour of the dried rations in his pack. But it was warm, he reminded himself. With the probability of only cold meals ahead, warmth was no small comfort.

He scooped a spoonful of the paste, steeling himself before taking a bite. The faint sweetness of the apple slice barely masked the grainy texture and blandness beneath, but it was enough to keep his stomach from protesting. Around him, the others ate in silence, the soft scrape of spoons against bowls the only sound save for the occasional grunt of discontent. No one spoke; there was nothing worth saying. They had eaten worse and they had survived it.

The group rose from the table. Packs were slung over shoulders, staffs grasped in calloused hands. Without a word, they filed out of the inn and onto the quiet street. The path ahead stretched into the dim pre-dawn light, broken only by the soft glow of a lantern swaying gently from a nearby porch canopy.

Each companion fell into the positions they'd assumed the previous day, silence reigning over them save for the occasional cough from one of the rearward monks.

It was shortly after the sun had breached the horizon, painting the treetops in gold, that Rowan raised a hand to halt the group. "We're close," he said, his voice low but clear. "The place the merchant spoke of."

Following his lead, they shrugged off their packs and stashed them among the low brush just off the road, taking care to conceal them from any passing eyes. Then, one by one, they moved into the treeline, crouching low. Each monk moved with discretion of motion born of necessity.

Roughly a hundred paces in, Rowan raised a fist and dropped into a crouch behind the moss-covered trunk of a fallen tree. The others followed suit, sinking behind the natural cover and peering over the rotting wood to the clearing beyond.

True to the merchant's word, ruins jutted from the earth—ancient walls and jagged stone pillars that looked more like the work of time and weather than the hands of a skilled mason. In the center of the clearing, where the earth dipped into a shallow depression, an opening gaped like a wound in the ground. Two figures stood sentinel on either side of the entrance, their twisted forms unmistakably nárgrim. The tattered remnants of their garments shifting slightly in the breeze, and their unnatural stillness made the air around them feel heavier, colder.

Rowan turned to the group, his expression grim, his voice barely above a whisper. "Ash and I will circle around and take them out. Quickly and quietly. The rest of you, stay here and be on the ready."

Without waiting for acknowledgement, he began to move, crouching low as he circled the perimeter of the clearing. Ash followed without hesitation, his staff held loosely in one hand as his eyes scanned the ground for anything that might betray their presence—a brittle twig, or a dry leaf. He stepped lightly, careful not to disturb the silence that hung between them and their quarry.

They came in wide, creeping behind the nárgrim, who swayed faintly as if simply standing upright was a struggle for their decaying forms. Rowan stopped and gestured sharply with his hand, signalling that he would take the one on the right. Ash nodded his understanding, setting his staff down in the grass with the utmost care to avoid any sound.

The two advanced in unison, their movements slow and silent until the moment came to strike. At Rowan's nod, Ash surged forward like a coiled spring unleashed. He slammed into the nárgrim, the force of his momentum sending the creature sprawling to the ground beneath him. With a firm grip, Ash seized its head and twisted sharply. The thing's neck gave a sickening crack, its struggles ceasing instantly.

Ash rose to his feet, brushing dirt from his robes as he scanned the clearing for any signs of movement. Finding none, he retrieved his staff and turned back toward the others, who were already moving out from their hiding place.

Rowan stood near the opening in the earth, his gaze fixed on the shadowed interior. He crouched and leaned in cautiously, his hand gripping the edge of the stone for balance. After a moment, he nodded, signalling that the way was clear.

Ash stepped in after Rowan, the heels of his boots dragging against the worn stone steps as he descended into the narrow passage. The air was thick, heavy with the scent of damp earth and something older—something forgotten. Kiran followed close behind, only the quiet rustle of her robes could be heard in the silence.

"Stay close," Ash murmured, his voice low, steady—an edge of command tempered by an unexpected softness.

Kiran nodded, her expression a mixture of fear and trust. Ash glanced back at her, something stirring in him that he hadn't felt in years—a protectiveness he hadn't thought himself capable of. He caught himself wondering when he'd begun to think of her as something more than a companion. Like a father to a daughter, the thought whispered, startling him.

He pushed the feeling aside. There would be time to reflect later, once they were clear of this place and whatever dangers lay waiting in its depths. For now, his focus was on the task ahead.

The corridor ahead was dimly illuminated by torches mounted on iron brackets, spaced about fifty feet apart. Their weak flames flickered against the damp stone walls, casting restless shadows. A thick layer of dust carpeted the floor, save for a narrow, disturbed path where previous visitors had tread. Ash welcomed the presence of the dust, it provided a muted cushion beneath their step.

The group moved with stealth, pausing only to glance into side chambers, their eyes scanning for any sign of movement. The silence was unrelenting, broken only by the faint rhythm of their own breaths. When they reached the end of the corridor, Rowan raised a clenched fist, halting the party. He leaned carefully around the corner, his body pressed close to the wall as he peered down the new hallway.

The passage turned left and sloped downward, its incline steep but manageable. Rowan motioned for them to follow, and the group fell in behind him. The slope descended a good fifteen feet before levelling off into a straight path that stretched twenty feet farther to a wide stone archway.

Ash held back with the others as Rowan crept forward to inspect the room beyond. The monk's movements were methodical, his gaze sweeping the space ahead with clear consideration that spoke of long years of experience. Ash waited, his grip tightening around his staff as he watched Rowan's gestures. Finally, a backhanded wave signaled the all-clear, and the group advanced cautiously into the chamber.

The room was larger than Ash had anticipated, its

high ceiling supported by a series of ornately carved stone pillars that stretched twelve feet into the air. The torches along the walls barely illuminated the space, leaving deep shadows to pool in the far corners. Stone slabs lined the walls, each bearing the decaying remnants of forgotten treasures—rusted trinkets, shattered urns, and tarnished jewellery, their former lustre dulled by time.

Kiran wandered to one of the slabs, her curiosity overriding her caution. She leaned in, examining the artifacts with wide-eyed wonder. Before she could reach out, Ash made a sharp, disapproving noise, drawing her attention. She turned, abashed, and returned to his side.

"Touch nothing," he whispered, his tone low but firm. "There are dangers here that can't be seen—wards, curses, traps. Be vigilant. We cannot afford a mistake." His words were more stern than he intended, and the hurt in Kiran's eyes gave him pause. He softened his tone as he added, "Your safety is worth more than anything in this place."

The moment passed quickly as the group gathered near the far end of the chamber, where another descending hallway awaited. Rowan nodded silently and led the way, his careful movement soundless as they began their descent deeper into the ruins.

At the base of the stairs, Rowan came to an abrupt stop, raising a fist once again. The others froze in place, tension tightening their postures as they waited for his assessment. After a few moments, Rowan pressed himself back against the wall and slid into the shadows, returning to the group with careful steps.

"Five nárgrim," he murmured, his voice barely above a whisper. He crouched and began sketching in the dust at their feet. "Two stand on either side of a doorway at the far end of the room. Another guards this entrance—just to the right." He marked a dot on the crude map. "The last two patrol the space, moving in a predictable pattern." He drew two sweeping lines across the center of the diagram.

Rowan leaned back on his heels and looked at the group. "We'll move when the two patrolling nárgrim split apart. Seanne and I will head straight for the guards at the far side of the room. That should draw the others into motion." He turned to Kiran, his expression questioning. "If you can tackle the one guarding the doorway, it'll give Ash and Celest the opening they need to intercept the patrolling nárgrim."

Kiran nodded, though hesitation flickered across her face. Ash placed a hand on hers, the warmth of his touch steadying her. She glanced at him, and he offered a subtle nod of reassurance. Her posture straightened, a quiet assurance replacing the doubt in her expression.

Seanne gave Kiran a light clap on the shoulder, a sly grin tugging at the corner of his mouth. "You've got this, little sis," he said, a wink following his words. Kiran's smile in return was small but pure, and Ash noted the subtle shift in her stance—the faint edge of doubt easing from her shoulders.

Rowan glanced around the group, ensuring everyone understood their roles. Each gave a small nod of acknowledgement. Without another word, Rowan and Seanne dropped into low crouches, creeping toward the entrance to the room. When they were in position, they lunged forward in a coordinated sprint, their advance all but swallowed by the shadows around them. The fight had begun.

Kiran sprang into action, fulfilling her role without hesitation. She lunged at the sentinel as it broke from the doorway to pursue the charging monks. Her momentum pulled the creature off-balance, and they both tumbled to the ground in a heap. The nárgrim twisted and rolled, but her weight kept it pinned long enough to deny it any advantage.

Ash's instincts screamed for him to stay and ensure her safety, but Celest darted past him, forcing him back to focus on the task at hand. He fell into stride, resuming his charge toward the center of the room.

Ash struggled to match Celest's powerful stride, his eyes drawn to the effortless skill with which she wielded her quarterstaff. Each movement was a fluid blur, a controlled whirlwind of strikes and counters. There was no wasted motion, no hesitation—only the honed efficiency of years of relentless training.

The nárgrim ahead of him, distracted by Seanne and Rowan's approach, presented Ash with the perfect opening. It had turned its back to him, oblivious to the danger closing in from behind. He capitalized on the opportunity, closing the distance with proficient speed.

With a sharp snap of his fist, Ash drove a punishing blow into the creature's spine. The impact sent it crumpling to the ground, its limbs jerking in a futile attempt to recover. Ash wasted no time. With brutal force, he seized the creature's head and, with a twist and a surge of strength, tore it clean from its shoulders.

Rising to his full height, Ash scanned the room. Kiran had already dispatched her foe, her lithe form cutting through the air as she ran to assist the others. The skirmish, swift and silent, had ended before it could truly begin.

"I knew you had this," Seanne called from across the room, a grin tugging at the corner of his mouth. He lifted his quarterstaff in a mock salute, the gesture laced with easy confidence.

Ash straightened, pride flickering across his face. Across the room, Rowan caught his gaze and offered a rare, approving smile. The brief moment of triumph, however, was shattered as another nárgrim entered the chamber.

Seanne was on it in an instant, his speed and veracity unmatched. His strike connected squarely with the nárgrim's face, sending it stumbling backward into Rowan's waiting grasp. With fluid efficiency, Rowan finished it off, ending the threat as quickly as it had appeared.

"Hey, save some of these wretches for me, will you?" Celest quipped, clapping Seanne on the back with a playful thud. "Can't have you hogging all the glory." Her laughter was rich, the kind that cut through the tension like a knife.

The companions regrouped, retrieved their staves, and pressed on. Beyond the chamber, the hallway stretched forward before splitting at a fork. Ash and Rowan exchanged a glance, silently deliberating their next move, when faint voices echoed from the left corridor. The decision was made for them. They advanced together, returning to their silent movements.

As they neared the end of the hallway, light spilled toward them, flickering and unsteady. The voices they had heard had proved to be one, echoing through the chamber. It came as a loud, guttural roar that barked commands and curses. Whoever—or whatever—it was, the nárgrim seemed to pay it little mind, because the orders repeated over and over.

Rowan crept to the edge of the entryway and stole a glance inside. He pulled back quickly, pressing his back to the wall. "Too many," he muttered, almost to himself.

"How many?" Ash's voice was calm, unconcerned. The nárgrim had proven themselves weak and predictable. It was the owner of that voice, the mastermind behind the resurrection, who demanded caution. A thinking enemy was far more dangerous than mindless thralls.

"At least fifteen," Rowan answered grimly. "This must be where they are being resurrected. But if we all embrace the Divine Mother's power before entering, they won't stand a chance."

The group exchanged resolute nods, falling into silent focus. Each monk closed their eyes, grounding themselves in the energy of the Divine Mother. Within moments, their forms shimmered with ethereal power—wisps of blue flame danced along their bodies, curling around the staves they held with deadly intent.

Ash turned to Kiran, whose connection to the Divine Mother had yet to manifest. He placed a firm hand on her shoulder. "You'll stay here," he said, his voice low but steady. "Guard the door from the shadows. Engage only if you're approached." Relief softened her features, and she nodded her understanding.

"We can't risk any getting away," Ash said, his tone firm, though a part of him wondered if it was the truth—or just an excuse to keep his novice sheltered and out of harm's reach.

The monks stood together, their combined presence radiating power. The blue flames licked higher, a testament to their focus and resolve. Without another word, a series of sharp nods signaled the charge.

The four monks surged forward, breaking through the doorway like a tide of vengeance.

Ash surged to the left, his staff gripped tightly, the air around him heavy with the stench of the undead. Three nárgrim intercepted him, their clawed hands and crude weapons reaching out with singular, mindless intent. His staff whirled in a deadly arc, deflecting their strikes with fluid precision before slamming back into their bodies with bone-crushing force. The impact sent them staggering, but their tenacity drove them forward, unfazed by pain or logic.

He moved with the grace of a lifetime's discipline, weaving through their attacks with practised ease. As their strikes faltered, Ash slipped behind their ranks, his movements a seamless blur. With unrelenting speed, he struck the nearest nárgrim repeatedly across its spine. The creature buckled under the assault, collapsing to the ground in a spasmodic heap.

One of the nárgrim lunged, its jagged weapon slicing across his thigh. Pain flared, warm blood soaking his leg. Ash grimaced but did not falter. He turned, his eyes cold with disapproval, and drove the butt of his staff into the creature's face. The blow sent it reeling, shards of decayed bone splintering as it stumbled backward.

A sudden weight enveloped him as the third nárgrim seized him from behind. Its rotting arms locked around his torso, and its teeth snapped hungrily at his shoulder. Ash gasped in pain, his breath hissing through clenched teeth as its gnarled bite scraped at his skin. He threw his head back with brutal force, smashing it into the creature's skull. The nárgrim loosened its grip just enough for Ash to dip forward, flipping the creature's weight on to his back. With a sharp grunt of effort, he hurled both their bodies backwards to the ground, his weight crushing it beneath him.

Ash rolled free and scrambled to his feet. The nárgrim, now sprawled and disoriented, clawed at the ground to rise. Before it could recover, Ash delivered a swift, punishing kick to its head, snapping its neck and sending it lifelessly back to the floor.

The brief reprieve was interrupted as another body slammed into him from behind. He staggered, his boots scraping against the stone as he struggled to regain his footing. Clawed hands raked at his chest, tearing into his robes. Snarling, Ash shifted his weight and drove the creature into the nearest wall with a resounding crack. It clung to him with unnatural strength, forcing him to slam it again—and again—into the unyielding stone. On the third impact, its grip faltered, and it fell away.

Ash turned, his focus now on another nárgrim lunging at him. He met its attack head-on, pivoting with feline grace to avoid its claws. He lashed out with his foot, striking the creature's jaw with such force that its head snapped back, a sickening crack echoing through the room.

As the nárgrim collapsed, Ash spun to face his final foe. It charged, its decayed face twisted in a grotesque snarl. His arms blurred as he parried its wild strikes, his movements a study in accuracy and control. With a sharp upward knee, he drove his strike into its ribs, sending the creature sprawling.

Before it could recover, Ash closed the distance. He tackled the nárgrim to the ground, his hands locking onto its head. With a savage twist, he wrenched its neck until the vertebrae gave way, the creature falling limp beneath him.

Rising to his feet, his chest heaved with laboured breaths. Ash surveyed the room, his sharp eyes scanning his companions. Each held their ground with the skill and focus expected of their training. None required his aid.

Satisfied, he turned his gaze to the doorway where Kiran lingered in the shadows. Her wide eyes locked on him as if silently assessing his every move. But before he could call to her, movement caught his attention. A figure—human, robed—darted from the far corner of the room toward the entrance.

"Kiran!" Ash bellowed, his voice cutting through

the stillness like a blade.

The warning came too late. The man reached her, his arm snapping around her chest in a vice-like grip. He yanked her close, one hand pressing against her head, ready to snap her neck with a single motion. Kiran struggled, her fists hammering against him, but he deflected her blows with maddening ease.

"Stop!" the man roared, his voice a thunderclap that froze Ash mid-stride. "Move another muscle, and I'll break her neck."

Ash halted, his fists tightening until his knuckles whitened. His mind raced, calculating options, but the man's grip on Kiran was unyielding. She fought against him, her struggles fierce but futile.

The man began to retreat, dragging Kiran with him. Step by step, he backed down the hall, his face a mask of cold malice. When he had gained enough distance, he shoved her forward with a vicious kick. Kiran stumbled and sprawled onto the stone floor, gasping for breath.

The man turned and fled down the corridor as Rowan and Celest bolted past Kiran in pursuit, their forms disappearing into the shadows.

Ash rushed to Kiran's side, helping her to her feet. His hands lingered on her shoulders, his eyes scanning her for any signs of injury. She appeared unharmed, but the tension in her frame betrayed her shaken state.

"Are you hurt?" Seanne asked, his voice low, threaded with quiet concern as he stepped beside his companions.

Kiran shook her head, her breathing ragged. "I'm fine," she managed, though her voice quivered.

Ash exhaled, his worry easing only slightly. His gaze lingered on the darkened hall where Rowan and Celest had vanished. A storm brewed behind his eyes—a promise that the man who dared to harm her would not escape unscathed.

"I'm sorry," Kiran said, her voice tinged with remorse. She lowered her head, her posture heavy with shame. "I should have been more attentive."

Ash stepped forward without hesitation and wrapped her in a brief, instinctive embrace. The gesture was over as quickly as it began. The realization of the bond they had formed between them, dawned on both of them. Her wide eyes met his, surprise mirrored in her expression.

Ash placed his hands on her shoulders, holding her at arm's length. His tone was firm yet kind. "There's no need to apologize. Consider this a lesson—training, if you will. Be grateful you're unharmed. That's what matters."

He offered her a small, reassuring smile before turning his attention back to the center of the room. Seanne was finishing off the last of his opponents, the final nárgrim collapsing in a heap at his feet.

Ash's gaze settled on a stone slab pushed against the far wall, its surface lost beneath a sprawl of brittle parchments, ink-stained and worn with age. A single lantern, its oil nearly spent, flickered at the slab's far edge, casting restless shadows that slithered over the disordered pages. The shifting light made the words seem to move, as though the ink itself recoiled from his scrutiny.

He stepped closer, careful not to disturb the precarious stacks of parchment. The scent of old paper, tinged with something metallic—blood, perhaps—hung heavy in the air. His fingers hovered over the pages, skimming the fractured lines of text scrawled in a language he barely recognized. Fragments of maps, hastily drawn symbols, and annotations crowded the margins. Half-formed ideas, abandoned calculations, whispers of plans not yet realized.

He frowned, eyes narrowing as he searched for something—anything—that would give him a glimpse into their intent. The way the pages were arranged, scattered rather than discarded, suggested urgency, desperation even. These were not idle scribblings; they were pieces of a puzzle still in the making.

Sifting through the scattered papers, Ash's eyes caught on one in particular. A sigil stamped in the bottom corner snagged his attention—a mark he recognized instantly. Kael's. His jaw tightened as he picked up the note and scanned it silently.

The letter contained orders—directed, no doubt, at the man who had fled moments earlier. It detailed a directive to return to their headquarters and begin preparations for an assault on Dawn's End Monastery. Ash frowned. The monastery, perched in the icy solitude of the mountains, was an ancient relic, rarely visited. What could Kael possibly want there?

His eyes moved further down the page, and the answer revealed itself. The letter spoke of a city—hidden beneath the foundations of the monastery. Kael's words practically dripped with eagerness to begin his invasion, intent on reaching whatever secrets the buried city held.

A city beneath Dawn's End? Ash's brow furrowed, his mind racing. What was Kael searching for? And how far would he go to claim it? Folding the letter, Ash tucked it into the folds of his robes.

When he turned, Kiran and Seanne were already standing nearby, their faces expectant. Before Ash could speak, Rowan and Celest burst into the room, their breathing heavy, their expressions grim.

Ash shot Rowan a questioning look, and the man answered with a shake of his head. "We lost him in the trees," Rowan admitted, frustration clear in his voice. "We searched, but… there was no trace."

Ash nodded silently, his face unreadable as he

retrieved the letter from his robes and handed it to Rowan. The elder monk scanned the note quickly, his brow darkening with each line. By the time he finished, despair flickered in his eyes.

"We have to get there immediately," Rowan said, his voice steady but weighted with urgency. "They need to be warned. If Kael's forces reach the monastery unopposed, we'll lose any chance to stop them."

Ash inclined his head in agreement, already turning toward the exit. On the way out, he picked up his staff, his movements reflecting his intention. The others fell into step behind him, their silence underscored by exhaustion and the gravity of the situation.

They made a quick stop to retrieve their belongings from where they had dropped them. The road ahead was long, but time was not on their side. Every moment wasted brought Kael closer to his goal. With bags secured and resolve solidified, they set their course north.

Haste was their only ally now. If they were to reach Dawn's End in time to prepare, they could not afford any delays.

Chapter 10:
The Coming Storm

The small band of monks trudged along the winding path, the mountains looming ever closer with each step. On either side of the road, the forest thickened. Towering oaks, maples, and birches gave way to an advancing army of evergreens, their sharp, resinous scent mixing with the crisp air. The woodland buzzed with life—squirrels darting up trunks, the rustle of unseen creatures in the undergrowth, and the songbirds weaving intricate melodies above. Yet, for all the vibrancy of their surroundings, the group remained cloaked in a palpable gloom.

Ash walked at the rear, his gaze fixed on the trail ahead, though his mind was elsewhere. The silence among them wasn't born of peace but of shared reflection. Each seemed caught in their own labyrinth of thought, weighed down by the morning's encounter or the grim anticipation of what lay ahead. Exhaustion tugged at their shoulders—not just the physical strain of battle, but the heavy awareness of the storm gathering both within and without.

He tilted his head toward the sky. The clouds, once scattered, now coalesced in the late-morning light, dark and brooding. The scent of rain mingled with the forest air, and the leaves above them quivered in the sharp coolness of a descending breeze. It wasn't only the weather that spoke of impending conflict. The air itself seemed to hum with foreboding.

It was Rowan who finally broke the silence, his voice low but firm. "Let's stop for lunch," he suggested. No one protested.

Celest, ever eager, shrugged off her pack and staff with little regard for care, letting them fall unceremoniously to the ground. She dropped beside them, sprawled in relief, before dragging the pack closer to rummage for food. Seanne followed suit. He pulled out an apple, its glossy surface catching a glint of muted light, and bit into it with the enthusiasm of a man who hadn't eaten in days.

Ash found a fallen log and sank onto it, resting his bag between his boots. Hunger didn't gnaw at him, but he knew better than to forgo the energy food could provide. Reaching into his pack, he retrieved an apple of his own and took a bite, chewing slowly as he watched the others settle.

Kiran dropped down beside Ash, a strip of jerky clenched between her teeth as she struggled to tear a piece free. The stubborn meat resisted, forcing her to gnaw at it with growing irritation. Finally, it gave way, and she tore off a bite with a frustrated grunt. She chewed slowly, her jaw working as if the act itself might somehow settle the thoughts tumbling inside her head.

The silence stretched between them, the distant rustle of leaves and the occasional snap of a twig the only sounds filling the space. When she finally spoke, her voice was low, almost hesitant, carrying the importance of something she had been holding back.

"I'm afraid of what's coming," she admitted. The words lingered in the air, raw and unguarded, before she took a breath and pressed forward. "I've never seen anything like that battle. Watching you—fighting so many at once—it shook me." She dropped her gaze to her boots, as if the dirt beneath them might somehow offer reassurance. "I've only ever trained one-on-one. Sparring matches in the monastery courtyard, controlled fights with rules and a clear end. This..." she exhaled sharply, shaking her head, "this is something else entirely."

Her confession settled between them, a stark contrast to the light chatter of birds in the branches above. It was a truth spoken without pretense, one she likely wouldn't have dared voice in the presence of the others.

Seanne, who had been reclining against the twisted roots of a nearby tree, pushed himself up and eased down beside her. He stretched out his legs, rolling one shoulder as if working out a knot, his usual casual demeanour momentarily subdued. For a moment, it seemed as though he might say something, offer words of wisdom or comfort.

But instead, he remained silent.

Without a word, he placed a hand on her knee—not firm, not forceful, just steady. When she finally met his gaze, he offered her nothing but a small, knowing smile and a nod, as if to say, *You're not alone in this.*

Ash turned to her, his expression softening as he considered his response. He didn't want to dismiss her fears—they were valid. Instead, he leaned into the truth, offering what reassurance he could muster. "You're young," he began, his voice even, "but your skill surpasses your years. You've trained among the best fighters the monastery has ever seen. You have nothing to prove." He paused, weighing his next words carefully. "Stay close. Be mindful of your opponents. Trust in your training. That's all any of us can do."

It wasn't a promise of safety—he couldn't offer her that. He couldn't even promise it to himself or the others. All he could do was give her the confidence to stand firm in the storm that was barrelling toward them. Whether it would be enough, only time would tell.

Ash took another bite of his apple, the crunch breaking the momentary quiet. The storm clouds above grew heavier, casting the forest in an ever-deepening grey. The air seemed to press down on them, a silent herald of what awaited in the mountains ahead.

Ash's gaze drifted to Rowan, who sat across the

road, lost in his own quiet thoughts. The man gnawed on something unrecognizable in the dim light, his face shadowed by the growing storm overhead. Ash waited for him to finish his meal, the rustling of leaves and distant hum of thunder filling the silence, before raising his voice to break it.

"If those clouds above decide to let loose," Ash called out, his voice steady but carrying, "we'll have no choice but to take shelter until it passes."

The others stirred at the sound, their heads turning toward Ash as if snapping out of a collective daze. Rowan rose, brushing dust from his travel-worn cloak, and crossed the muddy path to stand before him. He glanced up at the ominous sky, his brow furrowed as he considered Ash's words.

"I'd prefer to cover as much ground as we can before the storm forces us to stop," Rowan said, his tone practical but firm. "Still…" His gaze lingered on the churning clouds above, their grey bellies heavy with promise. "You're right. This doesn't look like something we'll be able to outrun. There's a village not far ahead, just down the road. We can take shelter there—perhaps even grab a warm meal while we wait it out."

The suggestion was met with a noticeable shift in the group's energy. Celest gave a subtle nod of agreement, her usual reserve cracking just slightly, while Seanne thrust a fist into the air with exaggerated enthusiasm. His silent gesture of triumph drew a chuckle from Ash despite himself.

"Reasonable enough," Ash replied, though his tone carried the weight of reluctant approval. The thought of trudging through rain and cold didn't appeal to him any more than it did the others. Better to endure a detour than press on soaked and miserable.

Rising from his perch, he slung his pack over one shoulder and took hold of his quarterstaff, which leaned against the twisted tree beside him. The simple act was all the signal the group needed. One by one, they followed suit, adjusting straps, tightening belts, and shaking off their weariness.

They set off at a renewed pace, this time with a noticeable lightness to their steps. The prospect of shelter and warm food had a way of lifting even the heaviest of spirits. Bits of conversation broke out among them, a welcome reprieve from the sombre silence that had accompanied their earlier march.

But the reprieve was short-lived. As the minutes stretched on, the wind picked up, slicing through the trees and carrying with it the sharp chill of impending rain. The first drops came as a warning, cold pinpricks against their skin, quickly escalating into a steady mist that clung to their robes.

They paused only long enough to retrieve their heavy travel cloaks from their packs, bundling them tightly around their shoulders. The wind, merciless and relentless, whipped at the edges of their garments, forcing them to clutch at the fabric in a futile attempt to stave off the cold and wet. Before long, the mist turned to rain, falling in earnest, soaking through even the heaviest layers of cloth.

What began as misery soon turned to hope as the forest thinned, revealing the outskirts of a village nestled among the trees. Relief rippled through the group as they quickened their pace, boots splashing through the thickening muck of the road. Ahead, a large building with a wraparound porch and an overhanging canopy stood like a beacon against the storm, promising refuge.

Reaching the shelter, they stumbled beneath the canopy, their breaths coming in heavy gasps. One by one, they tore free of their drenched cloaks, shaking them out to shed as much water as possible. The rain fell in sheets now, its relentless rhythm punctuated by cracks of lightning that illuminated the darkened sky. Thunder followed, a deep, guttural roar that rattled the building's windows.

For a moment, none of them spoke. They stood in silence, watching the rain pound against the earth and cascade in shimmering waves from the edges of the canopy. The storm had found them, but for now, they had a reprieve.

"Shall we?" Celest asked, her voice cutting through the sound of the storm as she gestured toward the wooden door, its weathered surface a silent promise of warmth and a hot meal. The group exchanged tired but grateful nods before following her lead. Celest pushed the door open, ushering them inside.

The inn was alive with the sounds of laughter, clinking mugs, and the delicate melody of a lute. A roaring fire dominated the hearth at the far end of the room, casting flickering shadows that danced across the wooden beams of the ceiling. Patrons crowded around tables, tankards raised high as they cheered a minstrel seated in the corner. Her fingers plucked the strings of her lute with experienced grace, her haunting tune wrapping itself around the room like a spell.

Kiran stopped short, her face lighting up as the minstrel's voice rose in a bittersweet ballad of love and loss. "Her voice… it's beautiful," she whispered, her tone one of awe as she looked to Ash for confirmation. He gave her a subtle nod, silently acknowledging the skill woven into the woman's song. Even Ash, who rarely found himself moved by such things, could not deny the power in her voice or the elegance of her playing.

"Oh, goodness!" A warm, lilting voice drew their attention. A plump, middle-aged woman bustled out from behind the bar, her apron dusted with flour and her cheeks flushed by the heat of the fire. "Come in, come in—let's get you out of that dreadful rain!" she exclaimed, her tone motherly as she waved them forward. "We'll warm you up and soothe your souls, I promise."

She gestured toward the hearth. "Hang your cloaks by the fire to dry. Go on, now. I'll have you seated and bring some hot stew to fill your bellies. And," she added with a conspiratorial grin, "there's a fresh-baked apple dessert cooling on the counter in the back."

Ash blinked, momentarily caught off guard by her kindness. Such warmth was a rarity in his life, and he felt a flicker of gratitude as he nodded to her. It seemed monks like him and his companions weren't an uncommon sight to the woman. Offering a rare, genuine smile, he followed her lead toward a large table near the fire.

The group moved in sync, their wet cloaks dripping as they hung them on pegs protruding from the wall. The fire's heat was an immediate balm, seeping into their cold, aching limbs. Ash took his seat, the sturdy wooden chair creaking beneath him. Around him, his companions settled in—Celest and Seanne breaking into lighthearted chatter, while Kiran remained silent, her attention fixed on the minstrel.

"I've never heard a bard play before," Kiran said softly, her voice barely audible over the music. Her gaze stayed locked on the woman in the corner, her expression a mix of wonder and nostalgia. "I had an uncle who played the pipe once… but it was terrible," she added with a laugh, a smile stretching across her face.

Ash didn't reply, letting her words hang in the air. His eyes lingered on her as the minstrel's mournful song filled the room. Kiran swayed slightly to the rhythm, her usually tense demeanour softened by the music. For the first time since they'd met, he saw a flicker of peace in her expression—a glimpse of innocence long thought lost. The sight stirred something deep within him, a warmth that mirrored the fire crackling nearby.

The moment was interrupted by the arrival of the innkeeper, who returned with two young women trailing behind her. Each carried bowls of steaming stew, their contents sloshing slightly as they placed them carefully on the table. Ash's stomach growled at the aroma that wafted up—a tantalizing mix of rich spices, tender vegetables, and the unmistakable scent of roasted lamb.

As a bowl was set before him, Ash closed his eyes, inhaling deeply. The fragrance alone was enough to make his mouth water. He resisted the urge to dive in immediately, though others at the table were not so restrained. Celest let out a delighted hum, while Seanne was already shovelling spoonfuls into his mouth with reckless abandon. The sight of this made Kiran laugh.

"I'll have one of my daughters bring out some fresh

bread and butter," the innkeeper said with a smile, gesturing to the young women beside her. The mere mention of bread drew audible sighs from Celest and Seanne, their expressions bordering on reverence.

Ash chuckled quietly at their reactions, lifting his spoon and savouring the first bite of stew. The warmth of the meal spread through him, chasing away the last vestiges of cold and exhaustion. For the first time in what felt like days, the storm outside no longer seemed so pressing. Here, in the glow of the fire and the hum of life, there was comfort—if only for a little while.

The meal had been a small reprieve from the storm, a sanctuary of warmth and flavour that momentarily banished the weariness of the day. The stew had been hearty and satisfying, but the apple dessert—fresh from the oven and fragrant with spices—was a revelation. Each bite was a symphony of sweetness and seasoning, and the expressions of pure joy on their faces said more than words ever could. The innkeeper, smiling with quiet satisfaction, simply said, "I'm glad you enjoyed the dessert. One of my late mum's recipes."

For a while, they sat back in their chairs, letting the food settle and allowing the music to weave through the room, softening the edges of their thoughts. The fire crackled in the hearth, the minstrel's fingers plucked a soft ballad, and for the first time in days, the monks seemed to relax.

The minstrel's tune shifted to something faster, a jaunty rhythm that sent waves of recognition rippling through the room. The patrons, half-drunk and unbothered by their lack of vocal talent, erupted into a cacophony of attempted harmony, belting out lyrics in slurred unison. Seanne's face lit up in recognition. Rising from his chair, he strode toward Kiran and whispered in her ear. "Come, we need to dance.", he said. She nodded, her cheeks flushed with a mixture of embarrassment and excitement, and followed him to the center of the room.

What followed could only loosely be called a dance. Their feet stumbled in an unpolished sequence, hands flailing in improvised gestures that bore only a passing resemblance to choreography. Ash had never seen the steps before, though the pair seemed to enjoy their shared fumbling as much as the execution. Laughter spilled from their lips with every misstep, and the other patrons, clapping to the beat, cheered them on despite the chaos.

Soon, a young couple joined them on the impromptu dance floor, their movements no more coordinated but just as spirited. Laughter and applause filled the room, and even the gruffest of patrons were approving. Ash allowed himself a small smile. It was a moment of levity—a rare balm for their troubled hearts.

Rowan leaned over Ash's shoulder. "I'm stepping

outside for some air," he said, his voice low enough to be drowned by the roar of the crowd. Ash gave a quick nod and watched his companion slip through the door. The elder monk had carried a heavy weight all day, and Ash decided to let him have his solitude. There were burdens best left unspoken.

The minstrel transitioned seamlessly into another tune, equally upbeat, ensuring the dancers stayed on the floor. Seanne and Kiran remained, their laughter mingling with the lively cheers of the room. Even Celest, who had initially rolled her eyes at the antics, found herself coaxed onto the floor by an elderly man with an infectious grin and surprising agility. The room swayed with joy, a much-needed respite.

Eventually, Ash pushed back from the table, rising from his chair. The din of the tavern felt unbearable now, too loud and too full. He slipped outside, the cold air biting his skin as he left the warm haven behind. He cursed himself for not bringing his cloak but dismissed the thought as he spotted Rowan leaning against the porch rail, staring down the road that stretched to the north. Rain still fell in a steady rhythm, though it had softened from its earlier deluge.

Ash approached silently, his steps muffled by the patter of rain. He joined Rowan at the railing, his gaze following the other monk's toward the road. For a time, neither spoke, the only sounds the rain's percussion and the muffled laughter filtering through the walls of the inn.

"It doesn't look like it's going to let up anytime soon," Rowan said at last, breaking the silence.

"No, it doesn't," Ash replied simply. He didn't need to ask what was on Rowan's mind. The elder monk's frustration was palpable, his desire to push forward evident in the tense set of his shoulders. But Ash knew better than to indulge that impulse.

"Even if it did stop," Ash added after a moment, "dusk is upon us. We'd be forced to find shelter for the night regardless. A wet, muddy camp would do us no favours, not after finally finding warmth and food." His words hung in the air, punctuated only by the rain and the faint echoes of revelry from inside.

Rowan sighed, the tension in his shoulders easing ever so slightly. "I know," he admitted, though his voice carried the weight of disappointment. "You're right. A handful of lost hours won't change anything."

Ash offered a reassuring smile, though Rowan's gaze remained fixed on the road. "Get us rooms for the night," Ash suggested. "We'll be better off for it in the morning."

Rowan gave a curt nod and turned toward the door. "I'll see to it," he said before stepping back inside, leaving Ash alone with the rain and his thoughts.

Ash lingered outside for a moment longer, his gaze

fixed on a drenched cat huddling across the street. The creature, sleek and desperate, stalked a small mouse that darted just out of reach with remarkable precision. Again and again, the cat swiped, only to be thwarted by the rodent's quick reflexes. Finally, the feline conceded defeat, slinking off down the road in search of shelter from the relentless rain.

A sigh escaped Ash's lips, his breath a faint wisp in the cool night air. The chill creeping into his bones was an unmistakable herald of their approach to the mountains. The nights were growing colder—a silent warning that winter loomed just over the horizon.

He turned and stepped back into the inn, warmth enveloping him like an old, familiar blanket. The smell of stew and wood-smoke filled his senses as the door shut behind him. The dancing monks had returned to their table, their cheeks flushed with exertion and laughter. Across the room, Rowan stood by the bar, speaking with the innkeeper, whose face lit up as a handful of coins passed into his palm. The exchange ended with hearty nods and an exaggerated smile from the jovial man behind the counter.

Ash made his way to the table, settling into a seat closer to the fire this time. Seanne said something that sent Kiran into peals of laughter, her face bright and her eyes wet with tears of mirth. When she caught Ash's gaze, he smiled—genuine and warm. "You're enjoying yourself," he said, his voice soft amidst the noise of the common room. "It's good to see."

Before she could respond, Rowan returned, dropping into the chair across from Ash. His voice cut through the din, steady but raised just enough to be heard. "The innkeeper only had one room left, but he and his wife assumed we'd need a place to stay. They've gone out of their way to prepare an attic room for us. It's mostly used for storage, but they laid out mattresses and warm blankets."

The mention of sleep seemed to summon it. Ash yawned, wide and unrestrained, his jaw cracking audibly. He quickly covered his mouth, shaking his head with an embarrassed chuckle. "Apologies," he said, offering a sheepish grin as Kiran tried—and failed—to stifle her amusement. "It seems sleep has taken notice of me. I'd better find my way to a bed before I pass out here at the table."

The others laughed, their merriment adding to the general warmth of the room. Rowan nodded toward him. "The lone room with two beds is for the women," he said, gesturing down the hall. "Our place is at the end—there's a staircase leading to the attic. You'll find it easily enough." Rowan leaned back in his chair, a small smirk curling his lips. "I ordered ales for us, but I suppose yours won't go to waste."

Ash pushed back from the table, offering a quick nod to the group. "Goodnight," he said simply, turning toward the hall. His footsteps barely audible against the worn wooden planks as he moved past dimly lit sconces that cast flickering shadows along the narrow passageway. At the end, he found the stairs Rowan had described, bathed in faint light. They groaned under his weight as he ascended, each creak echoing faintly in the quiet above. The stairs turned sharply to a second, shorter flight that ended at a simple wooden door.

He pushed it open to reveal the attic room. A lantern burned low at the far end, illuminating three makeshift beds spread out on the floor. The air smelled faintly of dust and old wood, the corners of the room stacked with crates and boxes cloaked in cobwebs. The sparse light cast long shadows over the forgotten storage, but Ash barely noticed. Fatigue pressed down on him like a heavy hand.

He shrugged off his gear and outer garments, letting them drop haphazardly to the floor. The bed nearest the wall beckoned, and he dropped onto it with a sigh, facing the rough planks of the room's interior. Above him, the rain continued its steady rhythm, a soothing counterpoint to the muffled revelry below.

Within moments, his eyes grew heavy, and sleep claimed him. It carried him into a realm where the rain faded, replaced by shadows and dreams waiting to unfold.

Chapter 11:
Visions Of The Past

The scene unfolded before Ash like a fable brought to life, rich with strange detail and hidden meaning. He found himself standing in a room unfamiliar yet captivating. Its thick air had a scent that clung to the carved stone, a staleness that assaulted the senses. The light from ornate wall sconces bathed the chamber in a soft, flickering glow, illuminating the walls adorned with treasures beyond reckoning.

A table nearby shimmered with crystalline artifacts, each as long as a man's hand, their surfaces encrusted with jewels and gold filigree. They were arranged with ritual care, as though meant for some sacred offering. Across the room, a series of towering wooden bookshelves stretched along the far wall, crammed with books whose spines were worn and faded. Their titles, no matter how Ash strained to read them, eluded him like whispers lost to the wind.

At the room's center stood another table, atop which lay a map of staggering intricacy. Painted in vibrant hues, it depicted a world that seemed vaguely familiar yet wholly alien, its contours bending to a logic Ash couldn't quite grasp. He leaned closer, tracing the unfamiliar geography with his eyes, but before he could piece together its meaning, muffled voices broke through his concentration.

Turning toward the sound, Ash drifted—no, floated—toward the doorway. His feet made no sound, his steps not his own. It felt less like walking and more like being carried, as though the dream itself pulled him forward. The hallway beyond mirrored the previous room, its walls adorned with more golden sconces casting their pale light upon the polished floors. The voices grew louder as he moved, guiding him toward a vast opening at the corridor's end.

Ash moved cautiously down the corridor, the scent of incense thick in the air, clinging to his senses like a veil. The dim glow of braziers cast wavering shadows along the stone walls, giving the passage an otherworldly quality, as if reality itself had frayed at the edges. However, instinct urged him to press against the wall, to avoid the gaze of whatever unseen presence might lurk beyond the flickering torchlight. Yet another part—calmer, colder—reminded him that none of this was real.

It was a dream. A fabrication of the mind, no more tangible than mist. He could walk these halls unseen, unbound by the laws of the waking world. And yet, the stress of unseen eyes prickled against his skin, unsettling in a way he could not ignore.

When he stepped through, his breath caught in his

chest. The chamber beyond dwarfed anything he'd seen before. Its sheer scale was overwhelming, the vaulted ceiling stretching high above, held aloft by pillars carved with exquisite detail. Marble statues stood solemnly along the walls, their once-pristine forms now faintly worn by time, while golden lattice glittered like frozen sunlight against the surface of the walls.

At the chamber's center, a massive sphere of black sludge churned and writhed, its form a tangled mass of inky strands that seemed alive. The sphere pulsed, radiating an unnatural energy that Ash could feel in his core—a presence that clawed at his being. Around it, six figures stood in a circle, garbed in vibrant robes of emerald, crimson, and cobalt. Their arms were outstretched, their bodies tense as though straining to hold the malevolent force in place.

The orb hung suspended at the center of the chamber, a wound in the fabric of reality itself. It did not simply emit darkness—it consumed the light around it, devouring it utterly, swallowing every flicker of warmth until only a malevolent void remained. The air hummed with a sorrow that pressed against Ash's chest, and though his mind whispered that this was only a dream, the reality of it was too certain. His vision blurred. A sharp throb pulsed through his skull, radiating behind his eyes. His legs trembled. His body urged him to collapse, to scream—to do anything to expel the agony washing over him.

You do not belong here.

The voice did not come from the six figures gathered around the orb. Ash knew that with certainty. The words coiled through his thoughts like a viper, a presence slithering through his mind. The orb was speaking to him.

I see. You are bound to me now.

Ash clenched his jaw and shook his head, desperate to free himself from the invasive presence. It was in his thoughts, pressing in on him, probing, prying into the deepest recesses of his being. He willed himself forward, yet each step brought him closer to the suffocating pull of the darkness.

Tendrils of black threads coiled from the orb, stretching outward—not drifting aimlessly, but reaching with intent. Hunting. They slithered through the air toward him, drawn to his presence, their movements too precise, too aware. His breath caught in his throat. This was a dream, wasn't it? How could he feel them creeping toward him, drawn by something unseen that pulsed within his core?

The power you fear is already inside you. Let me show you.

The voice, rich and velvety, echoed inside his skull. A pressure built behind his ears, pushing outward, as if his very bones could not contain the weight of the words. He clenched his teeth against the agony, but the strain was unbearable.

The swirling void in the orb shifted, its writhing mass contorting, shaping itself into something recognizable—a face emerging from the ink, sculpted from the living blackness. A woman. Ash could make out the sharp contours of a jawline, the hollowed cheeks, the cold, piercing gaze that locked onto him as if she saw through every layer of his soul. He did not recognize her, but he knew—somehow, impossibly—that she recognized him.

You cannot fight what you are. Come to me.

Ash tore his gaze from the orb, his chest heaving, only to realize he had fallen to his knees. His hands clutched his head, fingers digging into his scalp, his entire body wracked with trembling. His throat constricted, his voice caught somewhere between a gasp and a whisper. He could not speak, could not answer.

And then, just as suddenly as it had come upon him, the darkness withdrew. The tendrils retreated, slithering back into the orb, and the woman's face smoothed away, dissolving into a churning void once more. Ash exhaled a shuddering breath as he forced himself to stand. His muscles felt drained, as though the mere act of resisting had siphoned something vital from him.

The chamber came into sharper focus. Gilded walls glimmered faintly under the dim glow of sconces. Towering marble statues lined the perimeter, their carved expressions cold and impassive, silent sentinels to whatever unholy ritual had unfolded here. Oil paintings, their rich hues dulled with age, hung in ornate golden frames, each depicting a scene Ash could not quite comprehend. The room was lavish yet hollow, as though time had stolen its warmth.

At the far end of the chamber, Ash saw two more figures who stood apart from the six robed figures encircling the orb. Their posture was rigid, their voices sharp, issuing commands with an urgency that made Ash's skin crawl. One of them—a man draped in layered silk, his robes embroidered with sigils unfamiliar to Ash—held an open book before him, his fingers trembling as he read. The words, though foreign, carried an unmistakable weight of desperation.

A pull deep within his chest urged him forward. Whether it was curiosity or something darker, he could not say, but his feet moved of their own accord. He felt untethered, a phantom drifting through the dream, unable to alter its course. The closer he drew to the orb, the more his limbs ached, his very essence seeming to unravel as the void beckoned him in.

A tremor rippled through the chamber. One of the six robed figures faltered, his knees striking the stone floor as he let out a choked cry. Another staggered, then another, each one collapsing beneath the unseen burden pressing down upon them. Their ritual was failing. The balance was shifting. Panic flickered through the group, their desperate whispers rising in urgency. And then it happened.

The sphere of vile darkness detonated with a force beyond comprehension, a wave of searing energy ripping through the chamber. Instinct took hold—Ash raised hands that were no longer his, shielding a face that no longer existed. The blast devoured everything in its path. Marble statues fractured and collapsed in showers of dust and stone, while gilded wall decor liquefied into molten streams that dripped and pooled like the lifeblood of the room itself. Paintings, once proud testaments to wealth and power, blackened and disintegrated, their frames sagging under the heat before crumbling into soot.

When the maelstrom subsided, the chamber lay in utter ruin—its grandeur stripped away, leaving only charred remnants and smouldering wreckage. The walls, once pristine, were now cloaked in a thick, oily residue that looked like wet soot but seemed like something far worse. Ash could sense it—an oppressive weight acting against the stone, sinking into the very bones of the place. The darkness did not dissipate; it lingered, creeping into the cracks and crevices, as if the room itself was drinking it in.

Ash lowered his gaze and surveyed the devastation before him. The eight figures lay crumpled on the ground, their vibrant robes now charred rags clinging to scorched flesh. The air reeked of smoke and burnt flesh, and Ash felt an ache deep in his chest—a hollow, gnawing pain that went beyond the destruction surrounding him. It was as though something vital had been ripped away, leaving behind a void he couldn't name.

He stepped forward—or perhaps he willed himself forward—toward one of the fallen figures. The body lay motionless, its features obscured by the dim light and lingering shadows. Yet, as Ash drew closer, the face came into view, and he recoiled in horror.

The visage was unmistakable: the grey, decayed flesh, the hollowed eyes, the twisted grimace of death. Staring back at him was the face of a nárgrim, similar to all the ones he had encountered before. These people here were the Ancients.

Ash's heart—or whatever semblance of one existed in this dream—lurched within him. The question echoed through his mind, sharp and unrelenting. *What was that thing?* He had never witnessed power wielded with such raw, unrestrained force. Not even the sorcerers of the city of Vaelthorne, with all their arcane mastery, had ever displayed anything close to it. This was something *else,* something that did not belong to the world he knew.

The realization gnawed at him, a festering wound in his thoughts. It felt like a truth he should have understood, an answer that hovered just beyond his grasp, slipping through his fingers like water. The force he had seen—it wasn't merely foreign; it was wrong. A presence from *beyond,* ancient and unknowable, left an ache in his mind that refused to fade.

The awareness struck Ash, driving him to flee the chamber in terror. The devastation lingered in every shadow, haunting him as he soared down the endless corridors. He passed over bodies burned and broken, their charred forms silent witnesses to a horror beyond reckoning. There was no direction, no clear path—only the overwhelming need to escape, to free himself from the suffocating confines of those cursed walls.

Hallways stretched endlessly, twisting and turning like a labyrinth designed to trap him. Each passage led to another, each doorway spilling into more corridors that seemed to stretch on forever. Ash's panic mounted, his thoughts spiralling as he fought against the unending maze. Just as despair began to claw at him, he stumbled into a vast chamber, its stone floor framed by towering pillars. Bodies littered the floor all around him.

Ahead, massive double doors, each twice the height of a man, hung ajar on shattered hinges. Beyond them, the unmistakable light of the outside world beckoned like a promise of salvation. Ash didn't hesitate. He bolted for the opening, throwing himself into the pale light and collapsing to the scorched ground outside.

Ash lifted his head, his vision swimming as he forced his eyes open. The world around him pulsed in shades of shadow and ruin. The ground, once solid stone, was now marred by a creeping black char that clung to the surface like a living thing, writhing in slow, intentional movements. The corruption was not content to remain on the surface; it slithered into the cracks and fissures of the earth, burrowing deep, as if searching for something to root itself into—like water seeping into the veins of the land, poisoning it from within.

His breath came ragged and uneven, misting before him in thin, ghostly trails. He exhaled again, watching the vapour curl and dissipate. The air was thin, crisp—but not as frigid as it should have been. That realization settled uneasily in his chest. He was high in the mountains; he could feel the altitude in the strain of his breathing, in the faint pressure behind his eyes. But the cold did not bite as it should.

Mountains. The word echoed through his sluggish thoughts. Yes, he was in the mountains. But which mountains? Where? His memory was a tangle of disjointed images—shadows shifting, voices calling to him, an orb of endless night swallowing the light around it. Had he walked here? Had he been carried? The answers danced just beyond his grasp, slipping through his fingers like grains of sand.

He steadied himself, willing his senses to sharpen.

The land stretched out before him, vast and alien in its silence. And still, that infernal blackness crept through the stone, a sickness burrowing deep, tainting everything in its reach.

Gone were the rolling hills adorned with emerald forests and the glistening rivers that carved their way through the landscape. What lay before him now was desolation. A wasteland of ash and ruin stretched as far as his eyes could see. The earth itself seemed wounded, scarred by unimaginable destruction. Blackened plains spread like a cancer, broken only by the occasional remnants of trees—burnt-out husks clawing at the sky in silent agony.

Ash stood motionless, the weight of the scene pressing against his spirit. He let the cold wind whip around him, trying to anchor himself in the present moment. And then, like a whisper on that same wind, a feeling of familiarity crept into his mind.

He turned, his gaze sweeping over the desolate expanse once more. The landscape—scarred and broken—held a familiarity he couldn't dismiss. He had stood here before. Or somewhere close enough that the memory pressed against the edges of his mind, insistent and unyielding. It was like staring at a warped reflection of a place he had once known, a scenic painting defiled by an unseen hand.

His lips parted, the words slipping out before he

could stop them. “This place... I know this place.”

Recognition struck him like a thunderclap. He was standing on the very ground where Dawn’s End once stood—or rather, where it *would* stand in the future. The realization sent a fresh wave of dread coursing through him. The devastation he beheld wasn’t some distant land or alternate world. This was home.

The revelation jolted Ash awake. He sat upright, his chest heaving as though he’d been running for miles. Sweat clung to his brow, and his heart pounded violently in his chest. He dragged in deep breaths, grounding himself in the present, the nightmare’s grip slowly loosening.

The dim light of the attic room surrounded him. His companions, Seanne and Rowan, lay nestled in their makeshift beds, their snores filling the silence like a comforting lullaby. The sight steadied him, calming his frayed nerves.

Ash dragged a hand through his damp hair, exhaling a lengthy breath. The dream—if that’s what it was—clung to him with a weight that felt anything but ordinary. It had been too vivid, too raw to be cast aside as mere illusion. The memory of it pulsed in his mind, heavy and unrelenting, like something ancient and inevitable demanding recognition.

As he lay back down, pulling the covers over him, his thoughts refused to settle. What kind of dream was this?

he wondered. No, it was no mere dream. He knew that much. This was something more—a revelation, a warning. It demanded to be spoken of, though to whom or when, he did not yet know.

For now, he let the rhythm of his companions' snores guide him back into a tentative calm. But even as sleep crept over him once more, the image of that ruined world lingered in the back of his mind like a shadow he couldn't shake.

Chapter 12:
Recognition Of Failure

Kael's attention drifted from the ancient texts sprawled across the scarred wooden table, their brittle pages whispering secrets long entombed. Voices echoed down the corridor, low and urgent, pulling him from his study.

He looked up in time to see the entrance darkened as two figures stepped inside, their argument cutting short the moment they crossed the threshold. Samdon, ever the sentinel, halted first. The hulking monk moved to the side of the archway, his arms clasped behind his back in a stance of rigid readiness, eyes cast downward in quiet obedience.

Tyland followed, his steps slower, more hesitant. Kael studied him in silence, fingers resting lightly on the edge of an open tome. Tyland had proven himself over the years—quick to learn, adept in the manipulation of shadow, yet too eager to wield destruction when patience would have yielded better results. That flaw grated on Kael more than he cared to admit.

Pausing just inside, Tyland glanced over his shoulder, clearly noting that Samdon did not follow him. He turned, eyes seeking his companion's gaze but finding the other monk stared only at the cold stone floor instead. Kael watched the hesitation, the way Tyland's gaze flickered briefly to him before lowering. Even after all these years, the man knew his place. They all did.

Kael let the silence stretch, savouring it, pretending to be absorbed in the faded ink before him. Tyland shifted but held his tongue. He had learned that much, at least.

Finally, Kael shut the fragile book with meticulous care and fixed his gaze on the man. "This had better be worth my time, Tyland. Both it and my patience grow thin." His voice was low, a blade sliding from its sheath. He leaned forward, eyes dark and probing, enjoying the subtle discomfort that crept into Tyland's stance.

Tyland swallowed, his voice rough, as though the words themselves were an effort. "Sir… our station at the ruins north of the village has been attacked." He shifted uneasily, gaze returning to the ground, hands nervously shaking at his sides.

Kael's jaw tightened, and his fingers flexed into a slow, tight fist. He had anticipated attention—digging so close to the village was a necessary risk—but an attack? Unlikely. The road heading north saw little military traffic; the soldiers preferred the safer, more established routes to the east and west. This was something else. Something unexpected. And Kael despised the unexpected.

"Who attacked you?" Kael's voice demanding an answer. Being so near the road he was not surprised that they had been discovered. But who would have the courage to attack a group of undead within the confines of an underground ruin? Soldiers perhaps? What would soldiers be doing taking that road this time of year?

Tyland shifted, the tension rolling off him in waves. "A small band of monks," he admitted, his voice tight. The admission tasted bitter, Kael could see it in the way his jaw clenched. Tyland was formidable—perhaps even Kael's equal in raw martial skill—but power? That was another matter entirely. Kael's command over the darkness set him apart, and they all knew it. They feared it. Tyland most of all.

Kael leaned back, his expression indecipherable. "I assume you didn't overcome them. Otherwise, you wouldn't be standing here wasting my time." His voice held an edge now, cold and rising. This was a complication he could ill afford. What would it cost him? How far would the ripples spread? He exhaled slowly through his nose. "Tell me you left no evidence of our work."

A heartbeat passed. Tyland swallowed hard. "I fled," he said, and though he tried to steady his voice, it cracked. His posture stiffened, rigid as stone. "I… I thought it best to report back—"

Kael cut him off with a look, a slow, withering thing that coiled around the room like a noose. Fled. The word hung there, a disgrace, a weakness. Kael flexed his fingers, feeling the familiar stir of dark power curling beneath his skin, itching for release.

"You thought," Kael murmured, his tone like a whisper of shadow. "I don't pay you to think, Tyland. I want you to follow orders."

Kael roared a curse that echoed through the hall, his fury punctuated by the violent sweep of his arm. The table's contents scattered across the floor in a chaotic spray of parchment, ink, and shattered glass. A ceramic inkwell shattered against the stone, its black contents bleeding across the ground. The debris missed the monk by mere inches, though the man dared not flinch.

Kael tightened his grasp at his sides, his body trembling with restrained rage. He wanted nothing more than to wring the life from the cowering fool before him, but deep down, he knew this wasn't entirely the monk's fault. Circumstance, not incompetence, had conspired against them. With a sharp exhale, he clasped his hands behind his head and paced before the scattered remnants of the table, his boots grinding against loose shards of broken glass.

On the scarred wood surface of the table, the open translation of the ancient text still lay undisturbed, surrounded by scattered pages that had miraculously avoided his outburst. Kael stopped suddenly, placing both hands on the edge of the table, his fingers digging into the wood as though to tether his fraying composure.

"How did they find you?" he spoke, his voice low but edged with menace. The question was more for himself than the monk standing near him, but the words slipped past his lips with little care.

The monk, still standing a short distance away, stammered. "I—I don't know, sir. It couldn't have been accidental. Their attack was… swift, exact. It had to be premeditated. They clearly knew we were there before hand." He hesitated to continue while under Kael's piercing glare, dropping his gaze to the floor as if searching for refuge there.

"Pick up this mess," Kael growled at the monk, waving at the scattered parchment as if the sight of it offended him. The monk immediately bent down, gathering the loose sheets with trembling hands.

"How many monks were there?" Kael asked, his tone quieter now but no less dangerous. He forced himself to sound calm, though inside he seethed. This was a setback—a costly one.

"Six," the monk replied quickly, though his uncertainty was clear. "Wait, no—five… No, six. Yes, six. But there may have been more in the side corridors. I only saw the ones engaging us directly." He placed the gathered papers at the edge of the table, his voice dropping to a near whisper.

Kael closed his eyes and exhaled, leaning heavily on

his hands. The silence in the room stretched as his mind raced through contingencies and calculations.

"Our masters within the Order of the Dark Witness will not be pleased if we suffer more setbacks," Kael said at last, his voice cold and clear-cut. Tyland flinched at the mention of their shadowy benefactors, his retreat subtle but telling—one step back from the table, as he nervously played with a scratch on the back of his hand. Kael watched with grim satisfaction. Fear was a useful thing. Let him dread the consequences of his failure.

Not that Kael himself was immune to such thoughts. The Veil of Shadows—those nameless figures who cloaked themselves in secrecy and whispers—were not men to be trifled with. When he first encountered them, he had dismissed them as relics, ancient fools spinning tales of the Void Weave, their knowledge little more than scraps he could scavenge and discard. He had thought to use them, bleed them dry of their secrets, and cast them aside.

But the truth had been far more troubling. They *knew* things—things that had eluded him despite years of study, of toil, of sacrifice. In their whispers, Kael had found answers to questions he had only begun to ask. And worse, they dangled more before him, always just out of reach. Their knowledge was a hook sunk deep, and they wielded it well, offering just enough to keep him in their grasp. He despised the leverage they held over him, despised that he *needed* them.

But he would endure it. He would play their game—until he learned enough to no longer require their charity. Until their power was his to wield. For now, he had no choice.

Kael's lips curled in the barest hint of a smirk, dark and humourless. "We cannot afford another failure, Tyland. Not when the cost will be measured in more than just our blood."

"Samdon." Kael said, summoning the towering monk from his silent vigil by the door. Samdon lumbered across the floor, his expression carved from stone. He took his place beside Tyland, the contrast between them stark—Samdon standing a full head taller, his presence casting a long shadow over his companion.

Kael didn't look up from the open tome before him. His mind churned with uncertainties. Time, once a tool he wielded with patience, now pressed against him with unwelcome urgency. Events had conspired to force his hand.

"How many nárgrim are ready?" he asked, his voice low, controlled.

Samdon inclined his head in a brief bow, his deep baritone unwavering. "Close to two thousand, sir. Perhaps more. Their numbers have been growing daily."

Kael acknowledged the report with a slow nod,

though the answer brought him little comfort. Samdon was a man of exactitude—succinct, disciplined, and devoid of embellishment. A quality Kael valued.

"Numbers alone won't ensure victory," Kael murmured, more to himself than to the others. His fingers drummed against the table in a slow rhythm. "If those monks send word to the monastery before we strike, we'll lose our advantage. Surprise is our greatest weapon." His gaze lifted, sharp and penetrating, pinning both men in place.

He allowed a beat of silence to pass before speaking again. "We must assume Thane is lost." The words carried no emotion, only cold practicality. The fool should have returned by now. Kael's jaw tightened at the thought. The mindless wretch had likely strayed too close to the monastery at Maiden's Haven and been cut down or captured. *That's how they knew,* Kael thought darkly. His plans, once so meticulously laid, were unravelling at the edges.

"The idiot was of little worth," Kael continued, his tone dismissive, though irritation simmered beneath the surface. "But the nárgrim he uncovered might have been useful." A wasted asset, one not quickly forgotten.

He straightened, pacing the length of the chamber. "Regardless, our intentions are known now," he said, the importance of it settling over him like a shroud. "Those monks will have already figured out that they need to send word to Dawn's End."

The thought clawed at him, but Kael forced his expression to remain impassive. He would not show doubt, not before these men. Strength, after all, was not just a matter of power—but the illusion of it.

"Tyland." Kael's tone was sharp, echoing against the walls. "Gather a force of nárgrim. Hunt down those monks before they have a chance to get word to the monastery."

If they moved swiftly, they might yet reclaim the advantage of surprise. And if that failed? Then Kael would ensure the monks were caught off balance—striking before they could muster a proper defence.

Kael turned to face Samdon, his expression as unyielding as stone. "We move now. The monastery won't expect an attack so soon. If we strike before they've prepared, we may still accomplish what we need."

Samdon's massive frame straightened, his face held no expression as he offered a curt nod. Approval was implied, but Kael doubted the man would ever voice disagreement.

With a sudden, thunderous motion, Samdon slammed a hand to his chest, the sound reverberating through the chamber like the thud of a war drum. Even Tyland flinched at the intensity of it. "I'll ready the armies immediately," Samdon declared. He inclined his head in a formal bow and stood waiting, silent and steady.

Kael gestured with a flick of his hand, dismissing them both. "Go. We have no time to waste."

The monks departed, their footsteps echoing down the corridor until silence settled once more. Alone now, Kael turned his gaze back to the table. The scattered remnants of his earlier outburst lay before him—books askew, candles sputtering.

This complicates things. The plan had been carefully laid, each piece moving into position with sureness. He'd intended a larger force, a calculated approach, the inevitability of an encroaching storm. But Fate had seen fit to hasten his hand.

Time was no longer an ally. Victory, once a certainty, now teetered on the edge of chance. But hesitation was a luxury Kael could not bear. He would press forward, without remorse. If sacrifices were required, then so be it. Better to burn the world in shadow than let his ambitions falter.

Chapter 13:
Morning Reflection

Ash awoke early, dragged from the grasp of restless sleep. The dream clung to his mind with unsettling clarity—a writhing sphere of shadowy strands, swirling in unpleasant darkness. Even after slipping back into uneasy slumber, its ominous presence lingered, threading through his dreams like a malignant whisper he couldn't escape.

Sliding from his makeshift bed, he rose to his knees, his body protesting with groans and the sharp crack of stiff joints. "I'm too old for this," he muttered under his breath, his voice thick with weariness. With a grunt, Ash pushed himself upright and cast a glance at his sleeping companions. They lay sprawled in a discordant display of snoring, their ragged chorus no doubt audible throughout the inn.

Suppressing a smirk, Ash stretched the tightness from his muscles, the familiar ache settling into him like an old companion. He dressed in silence, moving with care to avoid waking the others. Grabbing his staff, he slipped through the door and descended the creaking steps, each one groaning under his weight.

The hallway was steeped in darkness, thick and unbroken. Ash doubted the innkeepers were awake yet—

not that it surprised him. If he had any choice in the matter, he'd still be asleep himself, lost in the kind of deep rest his body craved. But fate, it seemed, had other plans.

The common room lay shrouded in dimness, the dying embers in the hearth offering little more than a whisper of warmth. The faint, acrid scent of smoke hung in the air, a reminder of the fire that once crackled there. Moving through the shadows, Ash found an empty table in the far corner and sank into the chair with a sigh, letting the quiet settle around him like a heavy cloak.

The early morning silence, heavy and sombre, offered no solace from the haunting dream that had plagued him. It had been too vivid, too visceral to dismiss as a mere product of sleep. The echoes of its revelation gnawed at his mind, as relentless as the vision from days earlier. He would have to share it with the others—this much he knew.

Soft footsteps from the kitchen broke him from his daydream, faint but enough to stir him from his brooding. Soon, the others would wake as well. He could only hope they had found some true rest, for the road ahead would demand all their strength.

Ash heard the distant clatter of pots, followed by a muffled curse. He smirked to himself, guessing the inn's kitchen had just suffered an unfortunate accident. Moments later, the door behind the counter creaked open, and the innkeeper's wife stepped into the room, her expression one of tired focus.

She moved with quiet efficiency, stacking clean mugs behind the bar with experienced ease. A brief pause, a swipe of her cloth across the worn surface of the counter, and then—her gaze lifted.

She started violently at the sight of him sitting there in the dark.

"Oh!" she gasped, a hand flying to her chest. "I hadn't expected anyone to be up yet. I was just going to tend the fire before the guests stirred." Despite her surprise, she recovered quickly, offering him a warm, if slightly modest, smile.

Ash rose from his chair, the legs scraping softly against the wooden floor. He moved toward her consciously, making sure his footsteps sounded against the planks so as not to startle her further.

"Here," he said, his voice low, steady. "Allow me. I'm sure you have enough to worry about this morning." He offered her a small, reassuring smile, his posture open, nonthreatening.

Without waiting for her reply, he crouched to retrieve a pair of logs and a handful of kindling from the box beside the hearth.

"Oh, no—no, I can't have you doing that," she protested, stepping forward as though to take the wood from his arms. "You're my guest!"

Ash turned to her, offering a warm smile that softened the edges of his sharp features. "My dear lady, your kindness has been a balm to our weary souls. Please, allow me to repay it in this small way."

She hesitated, the resistance in her expression faltering against the sincerity in his words. Finally, she nodded, returning his smile. "Fine, if you insist," she said. Then, as if to excuse her concession, she added, "Let me head back and fix you something warm. How about some eggs and a bit of pork? I've still got some bread from last night; I'll toast it up with butter. Should set you right for the morning."

Her words trailed off as she disappeared back into the kitchen, leaving Ash alone once more. He knelt before the hearth, arranging the kindling atop the glowing embers, coaxing the dying coals with gentle breaths. The dry wood caught after a few moments, sparks blooming into small, eager flames. Satisfied, he laid the logs onto the fire and stood back to admire the renewed blaze.

The warmth spread quickly, the crackling fire banishing the last shadows clinging to the room. Ash returned to the table and sank into his chair, the silence broken only by the fire's steady song and the faint sounds of movement from the kitchen beyond.

From the other room, Ash caught the faint sound of

the cook singing a tune. The melody threading through the quiet inn like a ghost of memory. He almost recognized it—some tavern song he'd heard before, perhaps during one of his many nights spent in places just like this. Inns had a way of blurring together after a while, their songs, their faces, all fading into the same half-forgotten haze. Bards were common fare, hired to fill the air with music, to keep tempers from boiling over into drunken brawls.

The door creaked open, drawing Ash from his thoughts. The innkeeper's wife stepped inside, balancing a plate piled high with food in one hand, a mug in the other. She moved with careful grace, weaving past the bar and toward his table, her expression one of quiet pride. Clearly, she considered the meal a job well done.

"Here you are, love," she said, setting the meal before him with a skilled ease, her smile warm, her nod firm. "Brought you a fresh cup of milk, too."

The rich aroma curled up from the plate, warm and inviting, carrying the promise of satisfaction. Even the monastery's finest offerings couldn't compare to the bounty placed before him now. A true feast—one that might even rouse his slumbering companions from their dreams.

Ash picked up his fork, his lips curling into an appreciative smile. "This smells incredible," he said. "Thank you, truly."

The woman gave a small nod, already half-turned

toward the kitchen. “Plenty of hungry mouths to feed soon,” she said over her shoulder before vanishing through the door once more, leaving Ash alone with his meal.

As he ate, the telltale creak of footsteps from above signaled the awakening of his companions. The boards groaned under their shifting weight, a sound both familiar and comforting in its way. A door opened down the hall, and shortly afterwards Kiran emerged, arms stretched overhead as she yawned. Her ebony hair caught the light of the fire as she wandered into the common room, her eyes bright despite the early hour.

Spotting Ash at the table, she broke into a radiant smile and crossed the room to join him. “You’re up early,” she said cheerfully, dropping into the seat beside him.

Ash looked up from his plate and returned her smile, the weight of the morning’s solitude lifting slightly. “Couldn’t sleep,” he replied simply. Though his tone was light, the shadow of his dream lingered behind his eyes.

“How was your night?” Ash asked, his tone light but laced with the weight of unspoken thoughts. He suspected they had carried on well after he’d seen himself to bed, seizing the rare chance to set aside their burdens, if only for a while. A fleeting respite before the storm he felt was coming.

Kiran’s lips curled into a soft smile, and Ash caught the glint of fond recollection in her eyes. “It was wonderful," she said, her voice carrying the warmth of the memory. "Seanne and I danced for quite some time, then we rested. A couple of others asked for a dance as well." She paused, the smile deepening. "Even Rowan got up once to join in."

Ash blinked, the notion of Rowan—grim, practical Rowan—dancing of all things, seemed to catch Ash off guard. He had always assumed the old man to be too grounded, too serious for such indulgences. Then again, Ash reflected, wasn't that what people thought of him as well? The realization gnawed at him. Perhaps, if he let his guard down, it might ease the weight pressing on his shoulders, even if just for a moment.

He frowned slightly, pushing the thought aside. It had been too long since he'd allowed himself to simply *relax*, and the idea of it now felt almost foreign.

Celest emerged from the hall, her steps unhurried but sure as she crossed the dimly lit room and eased into a chair beside Kiran. The two women slipped effortlessly into conversation, their laughter soft yet vibrant, like the lingering echoes of last night's festivities. They spoke of the dancing, the music, their words weaving a tapestry of fleeting joy against the ever-present shadow of their journey.

Celest's cheeks were still flushed, and there was a spark in her eyes as she leaned in, a conspiratorial smile tugging at her lips. "I swear," she murmured, her voice touched with amusement, "one of those young men was completely taken with me."

Their quiet giggles rippled through the room, light and warm, like the first touch of dawn after a long, restless night. For a brief, stolen moment, the weight they all carried seemed a little easier to bear.

"Someone's in high spirits this morning," Rowan remarked as he strode into the room, Seanne trailing close behind him. The two men dropped heavily into chairs across from the women, their presence shifting the mood. Kiran and Celest exchanged amused glances but let Rowan's comment hang unanswered, their giggles subsiding into knowing smiles.

Ash couldn't help but notice the quiet smile tugging at Seanne's lips. The young man had clearly enjoyed himself. "Had a good time last night?" Ash asked, reaching out to tap Seanne's hand, drawing his attention.

Seanne's grin widened, bright and unguarded. "Yes, sir. It's been far too long since I last danced—I'd nearly forgotten the steps." He cast a teasing glance at Kiran. "Lucky for me, she fumbled around enough to make me look good."

Kiran scoffed, feigning indignation. "Oh no, you don't! I spent half the night tripping over *your* floppy feet."

Laughter rippled between them, Celest joining in

with a chuckle of her own. It was a rare, fleeting moment of levity, and Ash found himself reluctant to let it go. These moments—simple, unguarded, *human*—felt like something precious. Something distant.

But he knew it wouldn't last. It never did.

Rowan rubbed his beard with the back of his knuckles, his expression grim. "We should eat quickly and then get moving. We've wasted enough time already," he said, the edge in his voice unmistakable. The lines of worry etched into his face spoke volumes about the urgency weighing on him.

Ash, seated quietly at the end of the table, leaned forward. "Before we leave, there's something I need to tell you," he said, his voice low but firm. The seriousness in his tone drained the levity from the room. All eyes turned to him, the air thick with expectation.

He hesitated, his fingers tracing the grain of the wooden table as he gathered his thoughts. Not all monks were blessed with the prescient gift when they received the Divine Mother's touch, but those who were often spoke of visions that carried grave importance. Ash could only hope his companions would believe him.

"Last night," Ash began, his voice low. He cleared his throat, the weight of his words pressing against him. "I dreamed—no, *saw*—something. It was no ordinary dream. Too vivid. Too... *real* to ignore. A nightmare, yes, but one laced with truths that cut deeper than they should."

He ran a hand through his hair, pulling it back and securing it with a tie, the motion slow, but with the intention of grounding his thought in his memory.

The others leaned in, their eyes fixed on him, the idle noise of the common room slipping into the background. Ash kept his voice steady but quiet, his gaze flicking to the patrons drifting in and out of the inn. This was not something meant for idle ears.

"It was a vision," he said, the word carrying weight, *meaning*. "A glimpse of something... old. Forgotten." He paused, letting the silence stretch, before continuing. "At first, I thought it was just another nightmare, something born of exhaustion and fear. But there were details—fragments—too precise, too sharp to be dismissed."

His eyes darkened, and for a moment, the firelight flickering in the hearth seemed colder. "No, this was no mere dream. It was something else. Something real."

Ash recounted the experience with meticulous precision, sparing no detail. He spoke of the beginning—how he had found himself in a chamber cluttered with strange, unfamiliar objects, each one exuding an unsettling aura of function that was beyond his understanding. He described the way he had wandered deeper, drawn inexorably toward a room where a sphere of writhing shadow strands spun in a frenzied, chaotic dance.

His voice grew quieter as he spoke of the men—figures clad in garments unlike any he had ever seen—gathered around the orb, their voices rising in a ritualistic cadence, thick with intent. Then came the explosion. The shadowy mass burst forth, consuming all in its path, swallowing the room, the men, and reality itself in its hungry void. He told them how, when the darkness cleared, the men who had once stood proud now lay twisted and lifeless, their forms eerily reminiscent of the nárgrim they had fought before.

Finally, he described the landscape—the ruin that stretched endlessly beneath him as he stood atop the place where the Dawn's End monastery would one day rise. The desolation was absolute.

Ash watched his companions closely as he spoke, their expressions shifting from quiet intrigue to something graver—unease settling in the lines of their faces. The lightness of their earlier conversation had vanished, replaced by the heavy weight of something far more ominous.

When Ash finished, silence settled over the table like a shroud, thick and suffocating. It was Celest who finally shattered it, her voice low, thoughtful, and laced with unease. "Some sort of weapon?" she asked, her gaze drifting from face to face, seeking confirmation—or perhaps reassurance.

"I don't think that it was intended as a weapon."

Ash said as he rubbed the back of his knuckles against his cheek. "When I heard the voice of the woman within the orb, and saw the face manifesting in the ooze… It seemed more like some sort of gateway. Like they were trying to open a door to somewhere else." Ash looked down at the table trying hard to recollect that point in the dream with more clarity.

"I can't even guess at what their original intentions were with the orb, but it was clear that they were using it to bring something through to here. Perhaps that dark power." Ash let the silence linger in the room a little longer before speaking up again.

"What bothers me, is that when the voice came through, it talked to me." He shook his head at the thought, as though trying to shake the dust from the image. "The whole dream, I was just a spectator to the actions that were unfolding. I was just a silent witness. Then, she manifested in the orb and talked to me as though I was there." This bothered him the most about the dream, but he could not put his finger on the reason why.

"None of the… Ancients seemed to notice her there." The idea of seeing the Ancients first hand still sat uneasy with him. He just shook his head at the thought. "It was as if time did not influence the owner of that voice." He did not know what else to say on the subject, so he just looked up at them and remained silent, watching there expressions for any signs of what they may be thinking.

Ash exhaled slowly, dragging the back of his knuckles across his cheek in thought. “I don’t think it was meant to be a weapon,” he said at last. His voice carried an edge of uncertainty, as though speaking the words aloud forced him to confront a truth he hadn't yet fully grasped. "When I heard the woman's voice inside the orb, when I saw her face forming in the ooze… it felt more like a gateway. Like they were trying to pry open a door to something beyond."

Rowan nodded, his expression grim, the muscle in his jaw flexing with restrained tension. “It must be what your… old friend is after.” His words were thoughtful, but the import behind them was unmistakable. The intentional choice of “friend” at Ash’s heart, carrying with it the unspoken blame that lingered, unacknowledged but present.

Seanne, fidgeting with the edge of his cloak, leaned forward. “Then we have to stop him. If this... thing is as powerful as your vision suggests—” He let the thought hang unfinished, the implication clear enough. No one needed him to elaborate; the horror in their minds spoke for itself.

Rowan’s voice cut through the tension like steel. “Then we leave. No more delays.” His tone brooked no argument, and none was offered. The gravity of their situation pressed against them all, a shared burden that no one dared question.

They finished their meals in silence, the innkeeper's wife offering them kind words and a warm smile that felt distant—out of place against the shadow that now loomed over them. Soon enough, they were on the road again, their thoughts weighed down by the grim certainty of what lay ahead.

The path stretched before them, long and uncertain, winding through a land indifferent to their burdens. No promises lay at its end—only the trials yet to come.

Chapter 14:
Ambush

The morning air outside the inn bit at their skin, sharp and unforgiving, as they stepped out from the shelter of the canopy into the frost-laden yard. A brittle silence hung in the air, not even the morning songbirds could be heard singing their tunes. The delicate ice clung to every surface, glinting like shards of broken glass in the pale light, and each breath they exhaled drifted in thin, white trails before dissipating into the chill.

Kiran tugged her cloak tighter around her shoulders, so tightly it seemed as though she might burst free from the top under the strain. Her expression twisted into one of discomfort, lips pressed thin and brows knit as the cold dug deep. Disappointment settled visibly on all their faces, the unrelenting bite of the frost unwelcome even by those accustomed to harsher climates.

"Blessed Mother..." she muttered through chattering teeth, her voice a stammering mix of complaint and disbelief. Her cheeks flushed deeper than the frost-bitten morning warranted, and whatever else she intended to say was swallowed in her embarrassment. She turned her face away quickly, but Ash caught the moment and smirked, a soft laugh rumbling in his chest.

"When the sun crests the hills, it'll warm you up a bit," Ash said with an easy smile, his voice warm against the cold air. He added a quick wink for good measure, a gesture that only deepened the colour in Kiran's cheeks. "If it helps, you can take my cloak for a while. I've gotten used to weather like this."

For a moment, she hesitated, her pride warring with her obvious need for warmth. She was convinced by a cold wind which was stronger than her stubbornness. "Yes, please," she finally admitted, her teeth still chattering. Ash shrugged off his cloak and draped it over her shoulders as she was seized by a visible shiver.

"Thank you," she said, her voice quiet but sincere. The relief was instant, her shivers calming as she pulled the cloak tightly around herself. Her grateful smile was radiant, cutting through the frost like a beam of sunlight.

The sound of Rowan's quarterstaff striking the gravel path snapped their attention back to the task at hand. The sharp crack of wood against stone echoed through the brisk morning. "Well," he said, his voice carrying an edge of impatience, "shall we get going?"

Nods of agreement rippled through the group. Together, they turned toward the street, their cloaks stirring gently in the breeze. Each step was accompanied by the rhythmic tap of their staves hitting the stones in harmony, a sound that seemed almost musical in the morning stillness.

Around them, the village slept, its houses dark and quiet save for the occasional puff of smoke spiralling lazily from their chimneys. Near the end of the street, one house had a faint light glowing within. As they passed, a curtain shifted, and a nosy neighbour peeked out, their curious eyes tracking the group as they moved toward the edge of town.

The road ended at a modest wooden bridge spanning a rushing creek. The water below sang a restless tune, tumbling over stones in its hurried journey. Kiran paused, leaning over the rail to gaze at the frothing currents. Ash stopped beside her, watching her with quiet amusement. There was something about her fascination—whether it was with water or bridges, he wasn't sure—that seemed almost childlike in its wonder. For a moment, he joined her, leaning over the rail to share in her view.

When Kiran looked up at him, her smile was soft and unguarded. It carried a warmth that eased the cold gnawing at his skin, if only for a fleeting moment. Without a word, they fell into step together, trailing slightly behind the others as the group pressed onward.

As the village receded behind them, the trees began to thicken, their towering trunks and interwoven branches offering some protection from the cutting breeze. The road grew steeper, and Ash felt the subtle strain in his legs as the incline became more pronounced. His breath quickened with the effort. The silence between the companions remained unbroken, save for the sound of their steps and the occasional rustle of leaves stirred by the wind.

After a while, Kiran slowed her pace and shrugged off Ash's cloak, handing it back to him with a sheepish but grateful smile. "Thank you," she said, a light laugh escaping her lips. "One moment I'm freezing, the next I feel like I'm sweating from the inside out."

Ash took the cloak from her without a word, but the faint smile he gave her spoke volumes. He threw it back over his shoulders, feeling her warmth clinging to the fabric. He wasn't cold yet, but the creeping chill was beginning to claw its way into his bones. The road ahead promised more trials, but for now, he was content to march forward, the warmth of Kiran's smile lingering in his mind.

The first rays of sunlight pierced the canopy above, shafts of golden light breaking through the leaves and scattering across the forest floor. Ash marvelled at the exquisite beauty of the scene, the mist rising from the melting frost turning the air into a shimmering haze. Celest, too, seemed captivated, running her fingers through one of the beams, her hand illuminated like something out of a dream.

A sudden crack echoed from deep within the woods, sharp and unexplained. The group froze, crouching low with their staffs gripped tightly. Eyes darted through the dense foliage, searching for the source of the sound.

Anticipation coiled in their muscles like a spring, ready to unleash. But the threat never materialized. Instead, a deer emerged from the shadows, its delicate frame slipping between the trunks. Two more followed, their movements graceful and unhurried.

The tension eased, and the companions exchanged quick glances before straightening and resuming their trek. The quiet was broken by Seanne's playful antics as he tried to convince Celest of his superior dancing skills witnessed the night before. He paused mid-step to demonstrate, performing a clumsy little jig on the road before darting after her. Celest laughed, swatting him on the shoulder, her amusement clear. Kiran covered her mouth to muffle her giggles, and even Ash allowed himself a brief snicker, though he quickly masked it with a shake of his head.

Another crack rang out, this one sharper, more unnatural. It carried easily through the crisp morning air, stirring unease among the group. Still, they pressed on, telling themselves it was nothing more than the forest's natural symphony. But then it came again—closer this time. A series of cracks erupted all around them, the sound snapping like brittle bones.

The attack came without warning. Shadows erupted from the treeline, a blur of movement that resolved into shambling forms. Nárgrim. Their grotesque, decayed bodies wielded crude weapons, stabbing and slashing as they charged. The monks moved instinctively, falling into a tight formation, backs pressed against one another as they readied themselves for the onslaught.

The first wave came crashing in. Ash met them head-on, his staff a blur of movement as he deflected blows and retaliated with powerful strikes. The nárgrim fell, one after another, but for every one that dropped, two more seemed to take its place. Kiran fought fiercely beside him, her staff connecting with a sickening crack against a nárgrim's skull, but even as it collapsed, another lunged at her. She twisted away just in time, her movements sharper and more skilled than Ash had ever seen before.

Grunts and sharp exhales punctuated the air as the monks fought desperately to hold their ground. Ash could feel the occasional bump of a companion's back against his, a grim reminder of how little space they had left to retreat. The nárgrim pressed in, relentless, their decayed faces twisted in silent snarls. Bodies began to pile at their feet, turning the ground into a treacherous obstacle course of rotting flesh and broken limbs.

Ash's focus wavered for a moment as he glanced toward Kiran. She moved with a speed and ferocity that bordered on desperation, sweat streaking her face as she parried and struck with almost reckless abandon. Whether it was fear or newfound determination driving her, but she held her ground with unyielding resolve.

His own breaths came fast and shallow, his muscles burning with exertion. The nárgrim's numbers were overwhelming, their assault unending. Ash knew they couldn't keep this up much longer. He felt the familiar energy stir within him, coiling at the base of his spine, waiting. Without hesitation, he opened himself to it, allowing the force to surge through him like wildfire. It roared up his spine, filling his body with raw, unrelenting power, and his vision sharpened as he prepared to unleash it against the unholy tide.

As the energy surged through him, Ash unleashed a barrage of strikes with his quarterstaff, each impact detonating like loud cracks of thunder through the cold morning air. His staff connected with the nárgrim in a series of violent arcs, shattering bone and rending decayed flesh. Behind him, the sound of similar impacts echoed, a clear sign the others had also embraced the fury of the Divine Mother's power.

"Press forward. Harder," came a voice from beyond the throng of nárgrim. It was commanding, and unfamiliar. Ash's gaze flicked toward the source, but the press of undead bodies forced his attention back to the fight. The nárgrim, galvanized by the command, surged with renewed ferocity. Their relentless assault pushed the monks to the edge of their endurance.

A piercing scream broke through the cacophony.

Ash knew it was Kiran. The sound made Ash falter for a heartbeat before he recovered, spinning to locate her. What he saw stopped him cold. Kiran moved in a frenzied blur, her strikes wild yet devastating. Her lithe form was wreathed in flickering blue flames, an sublime glow that danced along her limbs, ignited by the same power that coursed through him. But her movements were raw, untempered by control.

"Don't fight it, Kiran!" Ash shouted, his voice cutting through the chaos. "Surrender to it—let it flow through you!" It was all he could offer her before another nárgrim came crashing toward him. His muscles burned, his breath coming in ragged gasps, but he pushed forward, carving a path through the unholy swarm.

Ash knew this was far from the ideal moment for Kiran to experience the flow of the Divine Mother's power for the first time. He had hoped—prayed—that her awakening would come in a smaller skirmish, under circumstances where he could guide her through it, steady her before the raw force overwhelmed her. But fate, as always, had little regard for such hopes.

The power surged through her now, wild and unchecked, a torrent barely held at bay by her inexperience. He could see it in her eyes—the widening pupils, the tremor in her fingers as they curled into fists. She was young, but not the youngest to bear this gift. Others before her had stood at this threshold, had learned to master it... she would too.

As the ranks of the nárgrim thinned, Ash finally caught sight of the man who had issued the command. He stood at the rear of the horde, a dark figure wreathed in ebony wisps that clung to him like living threads of silk. His hair hung in damp, matted strands, but it was his eyes that held Ash's attention—dark, piercing black orbs which were utterly devoid of the light of the Divine Mother. Instead of the radiant blue glow of a monk's power, the man's aura was tainted, a writhing miasma of black energy that radiated malice.

What corruption has he embraced? Ash wondered, his grip tightening on his staff. He moved with intention now, driving toward the darkened figure.

The man saw him coming and stepped forward to meet him, his presence commanding the nárgrim to part and make way. They scattered like leaves on the wind, leaving the two men alone in the center of the battlefield.

Their staves clashed in a blur of motion, each strike echoing like drums being beaten at a fall festival. The man's strength was staggering, his blows carrying a ferocity that rivalled a wild beast. Even with the Divine Mother's power coursing through him, Ash found himself straining against the onslaught. His muscles screamed in protest, and he felt his energy draining faster than it should. It wasn't natural.

He's siphoning my strength, Ash realized, his jaw clenching with the effort of fending off another powerful strike.

The revelation fuelled his resolve. Gritting his teeth, he lashed out with renewed intensity, but the man met him blow for blow, his movements unnaturally fast, his strikes unrelenting. Kiran appeared at Ash's side, her staff a blur as she joined the fray. Together, they pressed the vile monk, their combined assault forcing him to give ground.

Yet, even as the man stumbled, his speed and precision never faltered. Each of his counters came dangerously close to landing, his attacks pushing both Ash and Kiran to their limits. Sweat dripped from his brow stinging his eyes, his breath coming in short, controlled bursts, but Ash could see the strain beginning to take its toll. The man wasn't invincible—he was being stretched thin.

"Kiran," Ash shouted through clenched teeth, "go wide! Force his focus!" She nodded, stepping to the side to flank the man. The movement forced him to split his attention, and in doing so, his defence faltered. Ash seized the opportunity, delivering two precise strikes to the man's chest. The tainted monk staggered, his footing slipping as he tripped over the body of a fallen nárgrim.

Kiran capitalized on the moment, sweeping her staff low to catch the back of his knees. The man crumpled to the ground, landing hard on his back. Ash didn't hesitate.

He was on him in an instant, his staff raised high. Their eyes met—Ash saw no fear in the man's gaze, only cold defiance.

The monk raised a hand toward Ash, a final, futile gesture, as the staff came down with devastating force. The impact erupted in a blinding explosion of light and darkness. The blast hurled Ash and Kiran backward, their bodies crashing to the ground in a tangle of limbs.

Dazed, Ash struggled to sit up, his vision swimming. He froze as black tendrils of obsidian threads crawled along his skin, sinking into his flesh like serpents. Panic surged through him as he fought to resist, but the darkness was insidious, weaving itself into his very being.

He turned his head, searching for Kiran. She flailed on the ground, swatting at the tendrils that clung to her like a swarm of angry bees. The black threads twisted around her, sinking into her skin despite her desperate efforts to repel it.

"Kiran..." Ash rasped, his voice barely above a whisper. He could do nothing but watch as the black tendrils claimed her, just as they had claimed him. Helplessness settled over him like a shroud as the darkness seeped deeper, binding them both to its terrible will.

Ash clawed at the gravel beneath him, his fingers scraping against the rough ground as he tried to drag himself forward. His body refused to cooperate, collapsing under extreme fatigue, so profound it threatened to swallow him whole. He strained toward her, his vision swimming, until he saw Celest drop to her knees beside Kiran. She pulled the writhing, screaming girl into her arms, holding her tight against her chest, whispering soothing words Ash couldn't hear over the pounding in his ears.

The others… The thought struck him like a hammer, and he turned his head, his eyes scanning the carnage around him. The road was littered with the broken forms of nárgrim, their twisted bodies sprawled like discarded refuse. But where were the others?

He forced himself onto his elbows, the effort drawing a sharp groan from his lips. His gaze landed on Rowan, kneeling in the disturbed dirt of battle, his head bowed low. Grief was etched into the man's face, his shoulders trembling as though under the weight of the world. Ash followed Rowan's line of sight—and froze.

Seanne's body lay before him, crumpled and lifeless. Rowan's hand rested gently on the young monk's chest, a silent farewell. The realization hit Ash like a blow to the gut, and he lowered his head, the strength draining from him once more. A bitter ache welled up inside him, twisting his stomach into knots. *Seanne…* The name echoed in his mind, heavy with guilt and sorrow.

Ash tried to push himself closer, to reach Rowan, to offer some fragment of comfort, but his body refused to obey. His arms trembled, and he collapsed back to the ground, gasping for air. He flinched as hands wrapped around him from behind, but Celest's soft voice cut through his panic.

"Easy, Ash. Just breathe," she murmured, her tone firm yet tender as she pulled him upright. She bore much of his weight as she guided him toward the massive trunk of a nearby tree where Kiran rested, her back slumped against the bark. Ash stumbled, nearly falling, before collapsing beside her with a grunt of relief. His muscles burned, his breaths coming in shallow gasps, but at least Kiran was alive.

He turned toward Celest, words forming on his cracked lips, but she was already moving, her steps steady despite her obvious fatigue. She crossed the body littered road to kneel beside Rowan. Ash watched as the two monks bowed their heads over Seanne's body, their voices low and reverent. The faint murmurs of a prayer reached his ears, the familiar words stirring something deep within him. He closed his eyes and let the sacred lines spill softly from his own lips, barely more than a whisper.

Beside him, Kiran's voice joined his, trembling and raw with grief. Tears streaked her face as she stared at the solemn scene before them, her disbelief etched in every line of her expression. Ash placed a hand on her shoulder, a small offering of comfort, though it felt inadequate. He, too, was hollowed out, his spirit battered by the strain of loss.

As the prayer concluded, Celest leaned forward, wrapping her arms around Rowan in a gesture of solidarity. They remained like that for a moment, the silence between them heavy but shared. Then, without a word, they both rose and began the arduous task of lifting Seanne's body. Exhaustion clung to them like a second skin, but they bore his weight with grim determination, carrying him toward the edge of the forest.

Ash watched them disappear into the trees, his heart sinking further with each step they took. His fists clenched at his sides, frustration warring with sorrow. He wanted to be there with them, to help carry the burden, but his body betrayed him. All he could do was sit there, useless and broken.

Kiran's quiet sobs pulled him from his thoughts. She clung to his arm, her grief spilling over in ragged cries. Ash wrapped an arm around her, drawing her close as she buried her face in his chest. Her tears soaked through his tattered robes, but he didn't care. He stroked her hair gently, murmuring words of solace he wasn't sure he believed himself.

The toll of exhaustion bore down on him, heavier with each passing moment. His eyelids drooped, his will to remain conscious crumbling beneath the crushing fatigue.

He felt Kiran's grip on his arm slacken as she succumbed to her own weariness, her body growing limp against him.

Ash exhaled a long, shuddering breath and allowed his eyes to close. Just for a moment, he told himself, as the world around him dissolved into a haze of grief and blackness.

Chapter 15: Down The Road

Ash stirred at the gentle nudges of Celest. Blinking away the haze of sleep, he looked up to find her smiling down at him. It wasn't real—not entirely. He could see the sadness lingering just beneath the surface, the cracks in the mask she wore for his sake. It wasn't just Seanne's death that weighed on her, though that loss alone would have been enough. The relentless barrage of trials, the unyielding weather, and the fatigue of the last few days hung over all of them like a dark cloud.

His gaze drifted to Kiran, who sat nearby, her movements were slow and careless as she drank from a waterskin handed to her by Rowan. Her face was pale, her shoulders slumped, and Ash knew she must feel the same weakness as he did. Still, she was alive. That was what mattered most. He exhaled in relief, grateful that she had survived the explosion, though the mystery of it lingered in his mind. *What was that blast?*

He tried to recall the moment it had happened, but his thoughts swam in a murky fog. Pain throbbed behind his eyes, and his memory fractured when he tried to piece it together. He remembered the other monk, his shadowed hand reaching out, and then—the explosion. He had been thrown through the air like a child's doll, the impact rattling his body and mind. Beyond that, it was all a blur.

Celest interrupted his ruminations by thrusting a waterskin toward him. "You should drink." she said softly. Her voice was calm, almost soothing, though it rang in his ears like a thunderclap. Ash winced at the sound. *Another souvenir from the blast?* He added the thought to his growing list of discomforts to endure.

He took the waterskin and drank deeply, the cool liquid offering some relief from the dryness in his throat. When Celest let go of it, however, the waterskin felt unnaturally heavy in his grip, like a sack of stones instead of a simple container. He nearly dropped it before catching himself.

"Thank you," he muttered, managing a weak smile as she sat down beside him. Celest studied him, tilting her head this way and that as if searching for something. Finally, she nodded.

"You may have knocked your head pretty good," she said, the hint of laughter in her voice an odd but welcome balm, "but I think you'll live."

Ash attempted to return Celest's laugh, but the effort pulled a sharp pain through his chest, forcing a wet, rattling cough. Celest caught him before he could topple over, her grip steadying him. He grimaced, the ache radiating like fire. Cracked ribs, maybe worse. He pushed the thought aside—there was no time for weakness, not now.

"What happened while we fought the monk?" he asked, his voice low. It wasn't the right moment, he knew that, but the question burned in his chest as fiercely as the pain. They had just laid Seanne to rest, his body now returned to the Divine Mother's embrace. Ash had thought, for one terrible moment in the fight, that they all might join him.

"There were too many," Celest began, her voice wavering. She lowered herself to the ground beside him, her hands trembling slightly as she clasped them together. Kiran, who had been quietly nursing a drink from Rowan's waterskin, turned to lean against Ash, her head resting on his shoulder. Rowan moved slowly, setting his waterskin aside before sitting cross-legged on the ground in front of them.

"At first, we were holding our ground," Celest said, shaking her head. A tear traced its way down her cheek, carving a path of grief through the grime of battle. "We were keeping them at bay. I thought..." Her voice faltered, the memory too raw to give words to.

"It was the flank," Rowan said, his tone hard. There was an edge of reproach in his words, though not entirely directed at anyone present. Celest reached out, her hand gripping his knee in silent reproach.

"It wasn't their fault," she said firmly, her voice steadier now. "None of us could see what was happening behind us."

Ash stiffened, the unspoken accusation sharp enough to cut. His mind struggled to piece together the fragmented flashes of the battle—the nárgrim, the chaos, the dark monk who had seemed to command the undead like pawns on a chessboard. Had Rowan meant to blame him and Kiran?

Rowan's expression softened, the fight bleeding out of him. "You're right," he murmured, glancing at Celest. "I know it wasn't your fault." He looked back to Ash and Kiran, his face carved with grief. "You were facing the monk. One of the nárgrim must have slipped past."

Ash's memory stirred at the mention of the monk. He had seen it—the moment when the nárgrim had parted like shadowy waves, giving the dark monk space to step forward and engage. His gut churned at the realization. "He was commanding them," Ash said, his voice breaking Rowan's train of thought. "When he came into play, the nárgrim stopped attacking us directly. They parted for him, and then—"

"I just kept fighting," Kiran interrupted, her voice shaking. Tears streamed down her face as she buried it into Ash's sleeve, her sobs vibrating against his arm. "I thought—I thought I got them all before I came to help you…"

"It wasn't your fault, dear girl," Rowan said, his voice as gentle as his battle-worn demeanour allowed. He reached out, resting a comforting hand on her shoulder. "None of this was your fault. There were too many of them, too much chaos. No one could have accounted for it all."

Kiran's sobs quieted, though her shoulders still trembled. Ash's gaze shifted to Rowan, catching the pain buried behind the man's resolute expression. He'd lost someone he loved—someone he saw as a son. The gravity of that grief was palpable, an ache penetrated the tightness in Ash's chest. And yet, as much as the blame had been outwardly dismissed, Ash couldn't help but feel it lingering in the background.

"One must have slipped through our defences," Celest said softly, her voice trembling yet laced with sympathy. "I didn't see it happen... I just heard Seanne scream." Her voice cracked, and she buried her face in her hands. "When I turned, the spear was already through him, protruding straight through his chest from behind." The memory seemed to take the air from her lungs, and her shoulders sagged under the impact of it.

The words struck Kiran like a blow, and she dissolved into sobs, clutching at her knees as if to ground herself. Even Ash felt the emotional ache ripple through the group, a shared grief that filled the silence like smoke in a room.

Ash moved instinctively, putting an arm around Celest and pulling her close. It wasn't a gesture he was accustomed to—comforting others felt like walking blindfolded through a maze—but he didn't know what else to do. She leaned into him, her tears soaking the fabric of his tunic. For a while, no one spoke. They simply sat with their pain, letting the silence do what words could not.

Rowan was the first to break it. "What happened?" he asked, his voice low and gravelly. "One moment we were battling the nárgrim, barely holding our ground. Then there was... something. A blast behind us. And suddenly, they all collapsed—like their life had been torn out of them."

Ash nodded, his brow furrowed as he pulled at the fragments of his memory. "I think their lives were tied to the powers of their master, the one who was responsible for their resurrection." he said, his voice heavy with thought. He shook his head. "The monk fought like a storm. Relentless. And more than that—he was drawing strength from me. I could feel it. The more I struck at him, the weaker I became." His gaze flickered to Rowan, and he saw the unease tightening the older man's jaw.

"I thought I was finished," Ash admitted, closing his eyes as he pieced the memory together. "I could feel the end creeping in. But then Kiran was there. She came to my side, and together we managed to gain the upper hand." He tapped the back of his knuckles against his forehead, as though trying to dislodge the memories from the fog they were trapped in.

"We had him down. He was on the ground, and I raised my staff to deliver the final blow," Ash continued, his expression darkening as his voice dropped. He looked Rowan directly in the eye, his words laced with bewilderment. "But he didn't care. He just grinned up at me. Like he'd already won."

Ash shook his head, as though trying to shake off the image. "The dark threads—*his* dark threads—they moved like living things, coiling toward his outstretched hand. I swear, it was like strands of darkness weaving together, forming... something." He hesitated, the realization hitting him even as he spoke. "A sphere. A small orb of writhing black threads."

The group exchanged uneasy glances, the significance of his words tying itself to other, darker truths they'd uncovered regarding Ash's dream. Ash let the silence stretch as the memory crept over him, sharp and vivid now. "The orb... it exploded. I don't know how… I just remember the force of it sent me flying." He let his voice trail off, his mind turning over the image of the monk's twisted grin and the darkness that seemed to heed his call.

Celest, ever pragmatic despite her grief, broke the heavy quiet. "Come," she said, rising to her feet with a resolute steadiness that belied the tears still shining on her cheeks. "We need to keep moving. If we're going to make any difference in how this unfolds, we can't linger here." She brushed the dust from her robes, stepping behind Ash to help him to his feet.

For a moment, Ash hesitated. The impact of the monk's actions, the grief for Seanne, and the uncertain road ahead threatened to anchor him in place. But then he looked at Kiran, still leaning against him, and Rowan, who carried his sorrow like armour. They would move forward, together. It was the only choice they had.

Without so much as a warning, Celest's hands gripped him like iron, and with a bear-like strength, she hauled him to his feet. His legs wobbled dangerously as they took his weight, and for a moment, he thought they might betray him. A pain from his rib shot across him as she released her hold on his body.

"Steady now," she said, her grip firm on his shoulders as he swayed. "We don't want you toppling over."

Ash stood motionless for a few breaths, forcing his body to comply. The first tentative steps felt like walking on uneven ground, but after a few shaky strides, confidence returned to his limbs. He gave Celest a grateful nod before turning his attention to Rowan.

The other monk stood close with Kiran leaning heavily against him for support. She clung to his arm as if afraid to let go, her gaze fixed downward on her feet, as though sheer focus might keep them from giving out beneath her. Kiran lifted her head and smiled faintly. The expression was strained, her dirt-streaked face etched with exhaustion and grief. The trails of dried tears marked her cheeks like scars.

Ash felt a pang of sorrow at the sight. He knew the pain that haunted her now, the hollow ache of losing a friend for the first time. It was a wound that cut deep and took time to heal. Yet, in his heart, he also knew the terrible truth: it would grow easier with time—not because the loss became less significant, but because repetition numbed the soul.

That realization hurt more than he cared to admit. Was that why he preferred solitude these days? Why he wandered the world alone, avoiding bonds that could be severed by death? The thought left a bitter taste in his mouth, one he couldn't shake as he looked at Kiran's fragile form and the sorrow etched into Rowan's face.

He forced the thoughts aside and steadied himself. There would be time for reflection later—if they survived long enough to have it. For now, there were other battles ahead, and no amount of grief would stop their march forward.

The four remaining companions resumed their march down the trail, each step slow and unsteady at first. Ash and Kiran staggered, their legs heavy and uncertain beneath them, but with each step, their footing grew surer. Kiran gnawed on an apple handed to her by Celest, who now lingered at the rear of the group. Ash suspected her position wasn't by chance—she was there to catch either of them if they faltered.

As they worked their way down the winding road, Ash noticed it narrowing as the forest thickened, the evergreens pressing close on either side. Their dense needles choked the ground beneath, leaving it barren and lifeless, while the lower branches, stripped of needles and sunlight, jutted like skeletal limbs. Ash's eyes scanned the treeline, noting the interplay of concealment and obstruction. The terrain offered ideal cover for an ambush—both to set one and to suffer one.

Rocks jutted through the surface of the road, and deep grooves carved by rushing rainwater snaked across its length, creating treacherous footing. Every step demanded care, the path's jagged nature a test of balance and patience. Ash wondered how a wagon could possibly traverse this trail without shattering its axles.

When they finally stopped for a midday meal, Ash felt a pang of gratitude. His body still bore the echoes of the battle—muscles sore, energy drained. He glanced at Kiran, whose paleness suggested she fared no better. They ate in silence, chewing on dry rations.

Rowan broke the stillness first, his voice low but deliberate. "We haven't talked about those... shadows. The ones we saw enter you and Kiran." He tossed the gnawed remains of his apple into the underbrush, his gaze fixed on Ash.

Ash met the older man's gaze but had no answers to offer. He chose honesty. "I don't know," he said, shaking his head. "I didn't feel anything enter me. When I tried to force it off of me, I couldn't even touch it." He glanced at Kiran, who visibly recoiled at the mention, her face tightening as if reliving the moment.

"But something is happening," Ash admitted, his brow furrowing. "I can feel it. I don't know what, but it's... there."

Rowan leaned forward, concern etched into his features. "How so?" His tone was cautious, and Ash could read the unspoken worry in his eyes. Rowan feared the possibility that Ash—or Kiran—might become a threat. Ash didn't blame him. He would've thought the same.

"Earlier, when I fell," Ash began, "I was sure I'd cracked a rib. Maybe broken it. The pain was..." He paused, searching for the words. "It was unbearable." He noticed Celest nodding, likely recalling his earlier grimaces and laboured movements. “But now—” he slapped the side of his ribs, testing the spot—“it’s gone. No pain. It feels like it’s healed completely.”

Rowan and Celest exchanged glances, their expressions betraying more fear than astonishment. Ash understood. It unsettled him, too. “Maybe that’s why I feel so weak right now,” he offered, the thought forming as he spoke. “Whatever it is—it must be using everything I’ve got to repair the damage.”

A heavy silence fell over the group. No one spoke, but Ash could sense their unease, mirroring his own. He understood the implications as clearly as Rowan did: if the shadows were altering him in ways he couldn’t control, he might eventually become a liability—a danger.

Rowan’s voice broke the quiet, his tone firm. “If either of you notice any other changes, you tell me immediately. Understood?”

The command carried a heaviness of responsibility and concern, and Ash respected that. He nodded, as did Kiran. They both understood what Rowan wasn’t saying out loud—that any threat to the group, no matter the source, would be dealt with.

Without another word, they rose and began packing their gear, the tension palpable. Ash adjusted his pack and glanced at Rowan, whose watchful eyes lingered on him. Whatever was happening, Ash knew one thing with certainty: the road ahead wouldn't just test their strength. It would test their trust.

The road stretched on, unyielding beneath the fading light, as the chill of the wind began to snake through the trees, biting at exposed flesh. Ash pulled his cloak tighter around his shoulders, and the others followed suit, instinctively moving closer to share what little warmth their collective presence could offer.

With each step, exhaustion sank deeper into Ash's bones. His boots, once supple leather, now felt like iron weights dragging at his feet. Ahead of him, Kiran faltered, her movements betraying the same creeping fatigue. She masked it better than he did, but it was there—in the subtle stumble of her steps and the hunch in her shoulders.

"We have to stop soon," Ash said at last, his voice low, almost ashamed. "My body... I can't keep going like this."

The admission stung worse than the cold wind. He hated the weakness in his voice, hated even more the thought of being a burden. The words "leave me behind" hovered on his tongue, but he swallowed them, knowing they'd never comply.

Rowan studied him with sharp eyes, his jaw tightening before he gave a curt nod. Disappointment etched lines into his weathered face. It wasn't anger—just the burden of knowing they were losing precious time. The unspoken regret only deepened Ash's guilt.

"Thank the gods," Kiran exhaled, her knees buckling as she practically dropped to the ground. "I couldn't stand much longer." She shuffled off the road, finding a seat beside the bleached skeleton of a fallen pine.

"Why didn't you say something earlier, sweetheart?" Celest asked, moving to Kiran's side with concern softening her voice. She crouched beside the younger woman and pulled her into a gentle embrace.

"I didn't want to hold everyone back," Kiran murmured, her head dipping. Her gaze found Ash's, and he caught the sadness lingering in her eyes. "I didn't want to let you down."

"Oh, sweetie, don't think like that," Celest said, her voice kind as she wrapped an arm around Kiran's shoulders. Kiran smiled faintly at the gesture, but Ash knew the truth behind it. He felt it too—that gnawing sense of inadequacy.

Ash lowered himself heavily to the ground beside them, his legs trembling with relief and defeat. He looked up at Rowan, whose tense posture betrayed his frustration. "I'm sorry, Rowan, but we can't go any farther today," Ash said, the words coming out hollow. "If Kiran and I don't rest—if we're attacked again—we won't survive it."

The declaration hung in the air like a storm cloud, and for a long moment, Rowan said nothing. Then, with a sigh that spoke of reluctant acceptance, he nodded.

"Off the road, then," Rowan ordered. "I'll gather firewood. We'll make camp here."

Ash didn't miss the way Rowan's eyes lingered on the road ahead, as though willing it to yield to his resolve. But reason had tempered his determination, and the group set to work, finding a spot just over a small rise to shield themselves from view.

By the time the fire flickered to life, its warmth felt like a small blessing against the creeping cold. They huddled around it, eating the last of their rations in silence, the weariness of the day pressing down on them like a physical mass.

Ash leaned back against the rough bark of a tree, the only thing keeping him upright as his body succumbed to weakness. He barely noticed when Kiran moved closer, curling into his side. Her presence was a comfort, and he draped the edge of his cloak over her as she nestled against him.

Within minutes, her soft snores broke the silence, a sound that brought an unexpected smile to his face. Across the fire, Celest and Rowan exchanged quiet words, their conversation too low for Ash to make out. He could guess the topic, though—the journey ahead, the dangers waiting for them.

Ash's eyelids grew heavy, his thoughts slipping into a fog. The warmth of the fire, Kiran's weight against him, and the quiet murmurs of his companions blurred together into a soft lullaby. Sleep claimed him swiftly, pulling him down into its dark embrace.

Chapter 16:
Morrathis

Ash found himself engulfed in absolute darkness, a suffocating void stretching endlessly in every direction. He turned his head, straining for any sign of light, but there was none. If not for the firmness beneath his feet, he might have believed he was adrift in an empty abyss. Without it, vertigo would have surely consumed him.

He took a tentative step forward, his movements cautious. His boots scuffing softly against the unseen ground. The silence pressed in on him, amplifying the sound of his breath and the soft shuffle of his steps. After a few paces, the disorientation clawed at him, and he sank to one knee, pressing a hand against the surface beneath him to steady himself.

Sand. Coarse, gritty, and cold. It wasn't the fine, smooth grains of a sunlit beach—it was rougher, heavier, with a texture that made his fingers curl instinctively.

Ash rose slowly, spreading his arms wide for balance, feeling like a tightrope walker from one of those travelling bands, traversing an invisible line. The darkness seemed alive as though it clung to him, wrapping around his body and thoughts alike. *Why is there no light in this damned place?* he thought bitterly.

As if in answer, a torch sputtered to life to his left, its flame a flickering beacon in the sea of black. The fire danced wildly, exposing the surrounding walls, yet its light barely extended, as though the darkness swallowed it whole just beyond its reach.

Ash turned toward the flame, squinting as his surroundings revealed themselves in fragments. He stood in a long corridor. The walls were smooth and black, their polished surfaces reflecting the weak torchlight like fractured glass. Beneath him, the sand crunched faintly underfoot, its inky grains a stark contrast to the vivid orange of the firelight.

Reaching for the torch, Ash pried it from its cold, iron sconce. Its weight was reassuring in his hand, and the faint warmth of the flame offered a meagre comfort against the chill that seemed to seep from the very air. Two choices presented themselves: forward or back. There was no sign of where either direction might lead, but standing still wasn't an option.

Silently, he moved forward. The corridor curved subtly to the left, and as he walked, a faint sound began to creep into his awareness. At first, it was barely discernible, a noise that could have been mistaken for his own imagination. But as he progressed, it grew—a whispering chorus of voices, too soft to make out the words, if words they even were.

"Is someone there?" Ash called, his voice cutting through the silence.

The whispers didn't answer. Or maybe they did, their response tangled in the unintelligible murmur. He couldn't be certain if the voices spoke a language he didn't know, or if they existed at all outside his own mind. He pressed on, the whispers growing in intensity, joined now by a low, resonant moan. Or was it a hum? The sound vibrated through the corridor, setting his teeth on edge.

A sudden scream shattered the ambient noise, piercing and inhuman. Ash froze, dropping instinctively into a crouch, holding the torch aloft in a defensive posture. Its flame flickered wildly, but it revealed nothing ahead—only the endless stretch of the corridor. But no. Something *was* there.

He squinted, straining his eyes to see further into the darkness. At first, it was only a shadow, a faint distortion at the edge of his vision. Then it became clearer—a jagged opening, a break in the unending black walls.

Hope surged in his chest. He straightened, tightening his grip on the torch, and started forward, his steps quickening. Whatever lay ahead, it was better than this endless corridor. Or so he told himself.

Ash moved toward the jagged opening he had seen in the distance, the weak torchlight revealing the fractured edges of stone and a mound of debris. It was no archway crafted by a mason's hands—this was a wound in the corridor, a collapse or something forced open with violence. The scattered rubble on the far side only confirmed his suspicions.

Climbing over the debris, his boots slipping on loose shards of stone, Ash stepped through and found himself… in yet another hallway. Identical black walls stretched endlessly before him, the same coarse sand beneath his feet. The overwhelming monotony gnawed at him, and for a fleeting moment, he felt despair take hold.

What madness is this? he thought, his fingers tightening around the torch as if it were a lifeline. The walls, the sand, the endless dark—they pressed against his mind, threatening to unravel it. Was this some cruel design, a labyrinth meant not to kill him but to grind away his sanity piece by piece?

He exhaled slowly, forcing the thought aside, and glanced down the hallway. There, far ahead, two small red orbs hovered in the air. They were new, different, something that broke the monotony of this accursed place.

Ash stepped forward cautiously, his breath slow and rhythmic. The orbs seemed to move as he moved, gliding closer whenever he advanced, halting when he paused. The realization chilled him.

"You failed them."

The words came from the dark ahead, deep and ethereal, like a voice shaped from the shadows themselves. The sound resonated in his chest, sending a shiver down his spine.

Ash's jaw tightened as his eyes narrowed. The orbs weren't just floating lights—they were *eyes*.

"Who are you?" he demanded, his voice echoing faintly against the walls. He raised the torch higher, the flame flickering as if in protest. "Speak, or face the consequences!"

The thing didn't answer. Instead, it began to move toward him, gliding with an haunting smoothness.

"Last chance!" Ash shouted, his words a defiant edge against the encroaching dread.

It ignored him, the distance between them shrinking rapidly. When it was no more than fifteen feet away, the entity charged. Its movement was sudden, violent. Ash thrust the torch forward instinctively, its flame licking the air in defence, but the creature passed straight through him as if he were no more than mist.

A cold wave crashed over him, leaving him momentarily breathless. He spun, clutching the torch tightly, but the entity was gone, swallowed by the darkness as though it had never existed.

A wraith. He recognized the nature of it now—ghostly remnants of restless souls. Normally harmless, little more than taunting phantoms, wraiths played games with the minds of their prey. But here, in this place, nothing could be trusted. Rules bent, truths twisted. Certainty was as scarce as light.

He turned back to face the direction he had been heading, his grip firm on the torch. His chest still heaved as he scanned the corridor—and froze. Another pair of red eyes glowed in the distance. This time, he didn't stop.

He marched forward, determined to push through whatever trick or terror awaited him. The eyes began their slow approach again, the voice hissing from the shadows. "You are a failure, and you know it. They all know it."

The creature charged once more, its shadowy form rushing at him with a terrible speed. Ash raised the torch and swiped at the thing as it passed through him again, sending another wave of icy dread surging through his body. He didn't flinch this time, didn't even turn to look for it. Whether it was the same wraith or another, he didn't care.

He pressed on, his steps steady. The hallway seemed endless, the darkness eternal, and for all he knew, he was walking in circles. Or perhaps this was the true nature of the place—to stretch on forever, a maze designed to trap him in futility.

"You killed Seanne."

The words stopped him cold.

The voice came again, sharp and venomous, curling around him like a serpent. "You let the enemy pass your defences. It killed the boy. It's your fault. They all know it."

Ahead, the red eyes hovered once more, watching. Waiting.

Ash felt the words burrow deep this time, striking at a wound he had buried but never healed. His grip on the torch faltered, and for a moment, the stress of those words crushed his defiance. He clenched his jaw against the sorrow welling up within him, forcing himself to breathe, forcing himself to move forward. But the truth, cold and unrelenting, whispered alongside him.

He remembered Seanne. The young man who had joined them on their journey, and their fight on the road, eager and determined, only to fall because of Ash's failure. A nárgrim had slipped past him, its weapon finding its way into the boy's back. It was his fault—there was no escaping that truth—but there was no undoing it now. The past was as immutable as stone.

They had fought, then moved on. Down the road. Toward... *where?*

Dawn's End. That was it. He scratched at his head, as though he could dig the memory loose, force it to surface from the haze clouding his mind. Dawn's End, the monastery they'd been trying to reach. Kiran, Celest, and Rowan—they were with him. Or they had been. *Where were they now?*

Ash turned, his torchlight spinning with him, the flames diminished temporarily and then sparked back to life. The hallway stretched endlessly in both directions. He turned again, disoriented, and the movement made his head swim.

The eyes—those red, infernal orbs—hovered in the distance, unblinking, unmoving. A voice drifted toward him from the darkness, low and malicious, its tone like the scurry of critters across a field of dried leaves. "You are not strong enough here. The light cannot save you."

Ash ignored it. The voice, the eyes—they no longer held any power over him. They were background noise to the growing desperation in his mind. He needed to understand. Where was this place? How could he escape it?

He tried piecing together the fragments of memory, searching for something solid. They had stopped to make camp. Yes, he remembered now—he'd been tired. Exhausted. He'd fallen asleep by the fire.

Asleep. He froze as the realization hit him. This wasn't real. None of it was. "I'm dreaming!" he shouted, his voice echoing down the endless hall.

Laughter answered him. It came from everywhere and nowhere, a sound that resonated through the stone like an earthquake. It was a woman's laughter, sharp and cruel, each note a dagger that pierced his resolve. The walls trembled with its power, the floor buckled beneath his feet, and Ash stumbled, falling to his knees as the entire hallway seemed to groan and shudder.

Dust rained down from the ceiling. A crack split the wall across from him, thin at first, but it widened as the laughter grew louder, more piercing. Stones broke away, crumbling into dust, until the wall in front of him collapsed partially, revealing a hole just large enough to crawl through.

Ash didn't hesitate. He surged forward, diving through the opening and tumbling onto the other side, landing hard on coarse, black sand. He lay there for a moment, his breath ragged, before pushing himself to his feet. The torch lay extinguished on the ground not far from him.

He turned back to see what he had escaped. The hole gaped in the side of a tower, a structure so vast it defied comprehension. Its walls stretched upward into the sky, vanishing into the gloom above. The stones glistened like obsidian, sharp and angular, as if the tower had been carved from a mountain of darkness itself.

What kind of society could have built such a monstrosity? he wondered. And who would willingly live here?

He turned away from the tower, but the landscape offered no comfort. The world around him was barren, bleak. Black hills rose in jagged shapes, their slopes broken by rivers of molten lava that oozed sluggishly toward unseen destinations. The air stank of sulphur and decay, thick and suffocating, coating his lungs with each breath. Above, the sky churned with chaos—maroon and indigo clashed with roiling clouds of deepest grey, broken only by the occasional jagged tear of crimson lightning. It was a vision of despair given form.

"Don't you like what you see?"

The voice was right behind him, sharp and lilting, carrying a mocking edge that made his heart lurch. He spun, nearly tripping over himself, and froze at the sight before him.

She was colossal, standing nearly twenty feet tall, her figure pale and commanding. Her skin was the colour of ash, smooth yet unnatural, as if it had been sculpted from moonlight. Her eyes, orbs of black so polished they seemed to devour light, fixed on him with an intensity that made his blood run cold.

Her garments flowed around her, a seamless cascade of shifting folds, whispering softly as they moved. Atop her head sat a crown, twisted and grotesque, fashioned from bleached bones that seemed to glow faintly in the dim, unnatural light.

Ash felt the weight of her presence press down on him, an almost physical force that made his knees weak.

She was beautiful in the way that storms are beautiful—terrifying, destructive, unstoppable.

He wanted to run, to flee into the endless gloom and lose himself in the hills. But he stood frozen, unable to move, his body betraying him as her dark gaze bore into his very soul.

Who is she?

"Mmm, my sweet, sweet boy. Don't you recognize me?" Her voice rolled through the air like thunder across the distant hills, deep and resonant, shaking him to his core. Her black, abyssal eyes burned into his. "I am Morrathis."

The name struck Ash like a blow to the face. The sound of it reverberated through his mind, burrowing into his very being. He staggered under its magnitude, the truth of it gnawing at the edges of his sanity. This towering, terrifying creature—this *magnificence*—claimed to be the goddess of death.

She threw her head back and laughed, a sound that pierced the silence. Her polished white teeth gleamed in the gloom, sharp and predatory. The sight of her fangs—long, wolf-like—only deepened Ash's dread. The laugh rolled over him, a crushing wave that drove him to his knees. His hands clawed at the black sand as if it might somehow anchor him.

"You doubt me." Her voice carried an edge now, a

subtle twist that made Ash's chest tighten. She could see that the look on his face said otherwise. Her lips curled into a smile, cruel and knowing. "You see the truth in my words. I am Morrathis. And in time, you *will* serve me."

Her words clawed at his mind, prying, digging, trying to splinter his thoughts.

"Why would I ever serve you?" The words came through gritted teeth, his voice trembling with defiance. "You bring death and despair to all of existence. You are everything I fight against." His words lingered in the stale air, defiant yet brittle.

Her shadowed form shifted, the darkness around her seeming to coil and writhe as she spoke. "Misunderstood, as always." Her voice carried a mocking sadness, vibrating through the ground beneath him. "All souls go to their rightful place in the end. I do not choose their fate. I am the keeper of the forgotten. I take the souls the world discards—the ones no gods claim, the ones no prayers reach. This place, this realm you see as bleak and lifeless, is their sanctuary."

Her words stung more than Ash wanted to admit. He hated the way they crawled beneath his skin, planting seeds of doubt. Could there be truth in her claim? He clenched his fists against the thought, yet it lingered, undeniable. Morrathis was the goddess who ended all things. It was a tenet he had always held as absolute. Yet her words cast shadows on that certainty, and he loathed her for it.

"You're lying," he spat, though even he could hear the wavering in his voice.

She tilted her head, her grin widening. "Am I?" Her voice was silk now, smooth and insidious. "I bring an end to all things because all things must end. That is the way of existence. I give value to life, Ash. *We cherish only what we fear to lose.*"

Her words hit him like a dagger to the chest. He thought of Seanne—his eager grin, his untested skill, and the way his body had lay there still in the dirt. The memory burned, but it burned hotter alongside the creeping suspicion that Morrathis was using it to twist his heart, to weaken his defences.

She watched him, her black eyes glittering with cruel amusement, as if she could read his every thought.

"You're wrong," he said, though his voice was hoarse and unconvincing. He didn't know if he was trying to convince her or himself.

She laughed again, the sound sending ripples through the air. It struck him like a physical force, almost sending him sprawling once more. But this time, Ash fought it. Gritting his teeth, he forced himself to his feet, his body trembling with the effort. He wanted to run, to crawl into the black sand and vanish, but he would not give her the satisfaction.

The laughter stopped abruptly. Morrathis regarded him in silence, her head tilted as if in thought. The corners of her lips quirked upward in the faintest hint of amusement.

“Interesting,” she mused, her voice softer now, though it carried no less weight. “Perhaps there’s more to you than I thought.”

"Your defiance is commendable," she said, smiling down at him, her teeth gleaming like polished ivory. "It’s why I chose you. You will serve me, Ash. You will help me reclaim what is mine. You will be my champion."

Ash’s jaw tightened. “I will not serve you,” he said, his voice firm, though doubt twisted in his gut. Then, a thought struck him, sharp and sudden. “Besides, I thought Kael was your champion.” The name left a bitter taste in his mouth. Could it be that Kael had stood where he now stood, ensnared by this same creature, this goddess?

Her laughter erupted like a thunderclap, cold and cruel, echoing through the sweltering air. “That *fool*?” Her tone was venomous, and her smile soured into a sneer. “Kael and the others he serves? They are no followers of mine.” She spat the words like poison. “They stole my power. Twisted it. And now they wield it against my will. That is why I need *you*, Ash. To take it back.”

Ash hesitated, her words clawing at his thoughts,

demanding to be dissected. Kael serves others. He hadn't considered that. The dark magic Kael wielded—the dark power that clung to him like an unholy aura—had been stolen from Morrathis. She stood opposed to his plans.

"Why don't you stop him yourself?" he asked, staring up at her towering form, his voice sharper than he intended.

Her eyes narrowed, and her tone shifted, softer but no less intense. "My place is here," she said, her voice dipping into a whisper that resembled a breeze forcing itself through the leaves of autumn trees. "The world bends to my rules, but my true power is bound to this realm. That is why I need *you*."

"And if I refuse?" he asked, though the burden of her presence made the question feel hollow. He already knew the answer, but some part of him still clung to defiance.

She tilted her head, her smirk cutting deep into him. "If you refuse, I'll turn to the other one," she said, her tone laced with cruel amusement. "Kiran, I believe you call her? She, too, bears the mark of my void. She will do my bidding if you won't."

The threat struck him like a blow. His stomach churned, and his fists clenched. He had almost forgotten—Kiran had been touched by the same shadowy blast. She carried the taint as well. He couldn't let Morrathis sink her claws into her.

Ash forced himself to meet her gaze, resistance flickering in his eyes. “I will do your bidding,” he said at last. “But you will leave Kiran alone.” The words tasted of ash, and regret surged through him even as they left his lips.

Her smile widened, cruel and triumphant. “You presume to make demands of me?” she said, her voice coiling around him like a serpent. “You have no power here, mortal. She will play her part, as will you. The only choice you have is to obey.” Her words dug into his mind, tearing at his resolve.

Ash stood rigid, his fists trembling at his sides. He hated the truth of her words. Hated that he was powerless to stop her. All he could do was try to protect Kiran, to shield her from whatever dark designs Morrathis had in store.

“I'll do it,” he said finally, his voice strained.

“Of course you will,” she said, her tone brimming with satisfaction. “That's why I chose you.” Her laughter followed, booming and unrelenting, carrying across the expansive valley. It echoed long after she fell silent, as though the land itself mocked him for what he had become.

Chapter 17:
The North Road

A scream—raw, piercing—tore through the night. The sudden thrashing of limbs sent Ash jolting awake. His pulse pounded as he fought through the haze of sleep, scanning the darkness.

Kiran sat three paces from him, curled into herself, shoulders shaking. She sobbed into her knees, her body trembling with something beyond cold or fear.

Rowan was already up, his staff raised, sweeping the perimeter with sharp, assessing eyes. Celest had risen as well, stepping closer to Ash and Kiran, concern etched across her face. But when Ash turned toward her, she stopped dead in her tracks, her breath hitching.

Ash's gaze snapped back to Kiran. It had been her scream. Was she hurt?

He approached cautiously, kneeling beside her, his touch light as he placed a hand on her arm. She flinched. Then she looked up, and his breath caught. Her eyes—black as the void. Just like the monk they had fought.

She recoiled from him, panic flickering in her expression.

Ash turned to Celest, searching for understanding, but she just stood there, silent, eyes locked on him. There was something wrong. Something *else.*

Rowan returned to the fire, lowering his staff as he observed there was no threat beyond the camp. But as soon as he saw Ash and Kiran staring up at him, his stance shifted. His fingers flexed around the wood. He raised the staff again, his expression darkening.

"Ash," Rowan said, voice steady, but edged with wariness. "You alright?"

The question sent a prickle of unease down Ash's spine. *Why was he asking about me? Kiran's the one who screamed.*

"Of course I am," Ash replied, frowning. But as he turned back to Kiran, he saw the way she refused to meet his gaze. The way she shrank from him.

The realization struck him in the gut. His eyes. His eyes had changed too.

He exhaled, then leaned back against the gnarled tree he had perched against the night before. A smirk tugged at his lips, bitter and humourless. He turned to Kiran.

"Don't be afraid of me," he said. "Your eyes have turned black too."

She froze, her breath wrenching. Confusion flickered across her face. Slowly, she turned to Celest, then Rowan, searching for confirmation.

Celest only gave a slow, hesitant nod. Rowan said

nothing.

Ash exhaled. "It seems the dark's touch has… left its mark," he said, breaking the silence. His voice was quieter now. "You can relax, Rowan." He looked up at the older monk, who still held his quarterstaff like a weapon, his body coiled with tension. "It's still me in here. That won't change."

Rowan studied him for a long, quiet moment before finally, cautiously, lowering his staff. He tossed it onto the ground and sank onto a fallen log, though the uncertainty didn't quite leave his gaze.

Celest, too, seemed to ease, settling onto a patch of grass near what was left of the smouldering fire.

Kiran, though—Kiran still sat rigid, her head shaking, disbelief and confusion still carved into her features.

Ash met her gaze, his own uncertainty mirrored in her darkened eyes. Whatever had happened to them… it was only beginning.

"It was just a dream," Kiran murmured, her voice barely more than a breath. She sat stiffly, arms wrapped around her knees, as if trying to shrink into herself. "A nightmare, that's all."

Ash studied her. The uncertainty in her voice, the way her hands clenched against her sleeves—she didn't believe her own words. Neither did he.

"A dream…" he said, shifting closer. "What dream?"

She tensed at first, but when he settled across from her, she exhaled, some of the fear in her posture easing.

"I was trapped," she whispered. "I couldn't see anything. It was just… darkness. And then the whispers started." Her voice faltered. "They were blaming me. Blaming me for Seanne's death."

Her words broke into quiet sobs. Ash placed a steadying hand on her back, rubbing slow circles between her shoulders.

"It wasn't your fault," he said, voice firm. "They said the same things to me."

Rowan and Celest both turned, their attention now fully on him. Celest's lips parted, but no words came. Rowan, however, was not so easily shaken.

"You're saying you had the same dream?" His tone was edged with skepticism, though something deeper—concern, maybe—lurked beneath it.

Ash hesitated. "I… I don't know for certain," he admitted. "But my dream started the same way."

Kiran lifted her head slightly, her blackened eyes locking onto his. He would have expected relief at the shared experience, but instead, he saw something else. A quiet kind of dread.

"Did a torch finally light up?" he asked.

She shook her head. "No," she said, and for the first time, her voice was steady. "No torch. I just kept moving forward, feeling my way through the dark. The whispers—" she swallowed, "—they taunted me. And the red eyes… they watched. I tried to fight them, but I couldn't touch them."

"Wraiths," Celest said suddenly, the word slipping from her lips like an instinct. When the others turned toward her, she flushed slightly but held her ground.

Ash gave a slow nod. "I saw them too," he admitted. "But I had a torch. I saw them for what they were." He looked back to Kiran. "Go on."

"I found a hole in the wall," she continued. "I squeezed through, but I tripped. I fell on something sharp—I swear, I felt my skin tear." She glanced down at herself, as if expecting to see fresh wounds.

Ash listened, something uneasy settling in his gut. *She was in the same place I was. But she wasn't in my dream.* Before he could dwell on it, Kiran pressed on.

"I kept walking, my hand on the wall. The whispers got louder. Harsher." She closed her eyes, as if trying to push the memory away. "Then I felt a crack in the stone. Deep enough to get my fingers in. I started pulling at it, breaking the wall apart, stone by stone, until I made an opening big enough to crawl through."

Ash braced himself. He thought he knew what was

coming next. But she surprised him.

"I climbed through… and I fell. Just—fell. Into nothingness." Her voice dropped to a whisper. "I kept falling and falling. And then I woke up screaming."

Silence stretched between them. That was not how his dream had ended. One by one, they turned to Ash, their eyes heavy with expectation. Waiting. He forced a nod, but said nothing. He couldn't tell them. Not what he had seen. Not what he had *done.* Because his dream hadn't ended in a fall. His had ended with a goddess. And a promise.

They sat in silence, each lost in their own thoughts. The fire had burned down to little more than smouldering embers, and Celest idly prodded at them with a stick, watching as tiny sparks flared and died. Rowan sat apart, his jaw tight, knuckles dragging absently across his cheek.

Ash shifted closer to Kiran and wrapped an arm around her shoulders. She didn't resist. He understood the significance of those whispers, the scars they could leave. He had his own. And he knew she bore hers just as deeply.

At last, Rowan exhaled and pushed to his feet. "There's nothing we can do with this right now," he said, his tone firm. "The only thing that matters is whether it happens again. If either of you experience… changes, you tell us. Immediately."

Ash caught the meaning beneath the words. Rowan was watching them. Waiting to see if the darkness they'd touched would twist them into something else. Ash couldn't blame him. He was watching for the same thing.

He met Rowan's gaze and gave a slow nod. "Of course," he said. "We do what must be done." A silent understanding passed between them. Rowan acknowledged it with a curt nod of his own before stooping to retrieve his quarterstaff.

"Come," he said. "We need to move before we lose more ground."

One by one, they rose, shouldering their packs, stamping out the last traces of the fire. As Ash bent to gather his own gear, Kiran's voice brushed against his ear.

"Thank you." For what, he wasn't sure. But he gave her a small nod, and when he offered her a faint smile, she returned it. They turned toward the road, and soon the camp was behind them.

***

The day felt warmer than before, Ash realized. Or maybe it was just that the cold no longer bit at him the way it once had. He wasn't sure which was the truth. Yet another question to haunt his steps as they walked onward.

They kept a steady pace along the road, eating as they walked. Conversation was scarce—just the occasional cough breaking the quiet. For the first time in what felt like ages, Ash noticed birdsong threading through the air. It was a small thing, but it set him at ease. Wildlife meant no immediate predators.

“We shouldn’t be far from the North Road now,” Rowan said, glancing back over his shoulder. “Once we reach the crossroads, we’ll stop and rest.” He didn’t wait for a response, simply turned forward again, his stride unbroken.

Kiran drifted closer to Ash, her voice low. “The North Road?” Curiosity flickered in her expression, momentarily overriding her fatigue. The shift in focus nearly cost her balance, and she stumbled before catching herself.

Ash had to remind himself that not everyone had travelled as much as he had. To him, the roads and trade routes were as familiar as the back of his hand, but for someone like Kiran, who had spent most of her life in one place, the world was still full of unknowns.

“It’s a trade route,” he explained, meeting those unsettling black eyes of hers. He still wasn’t used to them. “It stretches across the northern edge of the land, just south of the mountains. Merchants use it, and during the great war, it was vital for moving armies west.” He considered saying more but decided against it. The explanation seemed to satisfy her. She nodded and turned her attention back to the road.

Before long, as Rowan had predicted, they reached a fork in the path. The crossroads was unremarkable—just another dusty trail cutting through their own, blending into the barren landscape. No markers, no signs. No indication of what lay ahead. Just another choice to make in a world that offered few clear answers.

Rowan shrugged off his pack and let it drop to the ground, then followed, stretching out beside it. Dust swirled in the air from the impact. Ash took in the scenery—sparse vegetation, mostly evergreens and half-withered shrubs, which struggled against the encroaching cold. The mountains loomed close now, jagged and impassive. A breathtaking sight. He had missed this view from his time at Dawn's End. He had not missed the cold.

"Rest while you can," Rowan murmured from his makeshift nest. "We won't be staying long. I want to get a good distance up the pass before we stop for the night."

Ash scanned the area, noting Celest and Kiran seated across from Rowan. He made his way over and dropped down beside them, letting out a quiet breath as he pulled his pack around himself and dropped it between his legs.

Rummaging through the worn leather satchel, his fingers brushed against the last remnants of his supplies. A single piece of jerky, crumbling at the edges, coated in dust and stray crumbs. He frowned. The next few days were going to be rough.

They had taken longer than expected to reach this

point, and now the food was gone. Hunger would set in soon, but there was nothing to be done about it. They would endure. And once they reached the monastery, there would be a real meal prepared for them. That, at least, was something to look forward to.

Ash tore into the dried meat with sharp bites, the salt drawing more saliva than the leathery scrap deserved. It had little flavour left—just a hint of what it once was—but he devoured it anyway. Every scrap of energy mattered.

The sound of approaching footsteps shattered the quiet. Ash swallowed hard and sprang to his feet, his body moving before his mind caught up. The others did the same, staves in hand, slipping into defensive stances. Instinct spread them out along the edges of the trail, using what little cover the terrain provided. For a breath, silence reigned—taut, waiting. Then voices carried toward them, distant but unmistakably human. Tension eased, but only slightly.

Six men emerged from the bend in the road, clad in worn leathers, swords at their hips. They spoke in low tones, unaware of the monks watching from the shadows. Then one of them—the leader, by his bearing—caught sight of Rowan and halted. His abrupt stop sent the others stumbling into him, confusion rippling through their ranks. His hand drifted to his sword hilt but hesitated there, fingers flexing over the grip. The others mirrored his unease, waiting for his command.

Rowan stepped forward, his expression warm, open.

"The Divine Mother's blessing upon you," he said, spreading his arms wide, his quarterstaff loose in his left hand—a deliberate show of peace.

The lead soldier studied him, then exhaled and eased his grip from his weapon. He raised a hand, signalling his men to stand down. A few hesitated, but they obeyed.

"Greetings, monks," the man said, his words for Rowan, though his gaze swept across the others. Celest kept her staff at the ready, but Ash let his rest against the ground. Kiran, though, edged behind him, shifting subtly out of view. Only then did Ash remember their eyes. How would the soldiers react to that unnatural sight?

"I am Doran," the man continued, "and these are my men from Vaelthorne's North Watch Point." He spoke as though expecting recognition.

Ash had heard of it. A military post along the trade routes, known for its rigid hierarchy. He'd always steered clear—men with rank were often men led by pride, and pride was just another kind of trap.

Rowan nodded. "A pleasure, Captain?"

Doran stiffened, shoulders squaring with a trace of self-satisfaction. "Aye," he confirmed, the title sitting comfortably with him.

"I am Rowan, and these are my companions—

Celest, Ash, and Kiran," Rowan said, motioning to each in turn. "We've just come up from the Maiden's Haven monastery, heading for Dawn's End."

Something flickered in Doran's eyes. Surprise.

"I assumed you'd come down from the mountains," he admitted. "A long journey from the south, no doubt…" He let the thought hang, unspoken questions evident in his expression.

Rowan met his gaze evenly. "We've been chasing tales of nárgrim."

Doran's brow lifted at that. He took a slow step forward, his men following, though at ease. Not a threat. Not yet.

"It seems," Doran said, "we've been chasing the same ghosts."

The words hung in the air, and for a fleeting moment, Rowan and Ash exchanged a glance—surprised, perhaps, though by now, little should surprise them.

"We've received word of nárgrim sightings to the west," Doran said, his gaze flicking past Rowan, searching for something—or someone—at the back of the group. "Three merchant parties travelling that way reported the same. One swore the creatures pursued them. Orders came down for us to investigate."

His men nodded in silent confirmation, their earlier ease giving way to something warier.

"There are nárgrim" Rowan said simply. "Many."

The validity of his words settled over them like a shroud. The soldiers' confident stances wavered, their hands shifting closer to their sword hilts. Eyes darted toward the tree line, as though expecting the undead to lurch from the underbrush at any moment.

"Then we should move at once," Doran declared, but there was a hesitation in his voice now, a slight crack in his certainty.

His men instinctively formed ranks, but their motions lacked their previous crispness.

"Don't bother heading west," Rowan said, halting them with a glance. "We know where they're going. We're just hoping to get there first."

Silence hung between them, thick with unspoken dread. Even Kiran, who had kept to the shadows behind Ash, tensed. Ash could feel her presence behind him, the slight shift of her weight as she clenched her hands. Perhaps, until now, she hadn't truly considered that they might be too late.

Doran frowned. "How could you possibly know where these abominations are headed? Are they not mindless things, drawn only by hunger for destruction?"

"They are not acting on their own," Rowan said. His tone was steady, but there was a steel edge beneath it. "They are being resurrected and directed. Their will is being directed by others. They're to march on Dawn's End."

The words struck like a hammer. Every soldier turned, eyes locking onto the northern road, their breath a little heavier than before.

"My pardon, sir monk," Doran muttered, scanning the trail, as though he might spot the first shambling forms through the distant trees.

"There's no sign of an army having passed this way," Ash said, stepping forward. He felt Kiran relax slightly behind him, but the unease remained, a phantom weight in the air. "That doesn't mean they aren't already on their way."

The soldiers stirred, shifting uneasily. Their hands hovered near their weapons once more as they finally noticed Ash's eyes. And Kiran's.

Doran stiffened. "What's wrong with them?"

Rowan exhaled slowly, his voice calm but firm. "They've endured something none of us understand. But they are not your enemy." His gaze swept the group, a silent command. "The nárgrim are."

Doran studied Ash's face, then Kiran's. He wasn't convinced, not entirely. But he let his hand fall away from his sword.

Ash stepped beside Rowan, his voice low and cutting. "You should come with us."

Doran's mouth opened, but Ash didn't let him object.

"If you march west, you'll die in open ground against an army of the dead. You'll be torn apart. Your best chance is behind stone walls."

A muscle in Doran's jaw tightened. Pride and pragmatism warred across his face. Finally, he exhaled sharply and nodded. "We will join you." His eyes locked onto Rowan. "But I remain in command of my men."

Rowan inclined his head. "Of course."

The matter settled, they gathered their gear and pressed northward. The path wound between jagged rock faces, the sun dipping lower in the sky, stretching long shadows across the trail. The stress of what lay ahead pressed down on them all, heavy and inescapable.

Chapter 18:
The Mountain Pass

The incline grew steeper as they wound through jagged rocks, the path tightening like a noose. Barren stone stretched in all directions, broken only by the occasional, withered plant clinging stubbornly to life amid the gravel and dust.

A sharp wind cut through them, burrowing into exposed flesh, relentless in its bite. Cloaks were pulled tight, heads bowed against the chill. Kiran had drawn her hood up, shielding her face—not just from the cold, Ash suspected, but from the wary eyes of the soldiers trailing behind.

They kept their distance. All but Doran, who walked near Rowan at the front. The rest lagged, deliberately keeping clear of the monks. Superstitious fools, Ash thought. And yet, could he blame them? They had never seen anything like this before. Few had, perhaps only the gods.

Ash cast a glance over his shoulder, scanning the slope for any sign of nárgrim marching in their wake. Nothing. Not yet. But that meant little. The undead could be moving through the trees, staying out of sight to avoid giving away their location. The sun burned high above, offering light but little warmth, its heat absorbed by the dark stone beneath their feet.

The air shimmered where sunlight struck the rock, warmth bleeding from the surface in waves. Fog was coming. Ash knew this terrain well enough—when the heat pulled moisture from the stones, mist would rise. It would grant them cover. It would also blind them.

As if summoned by his thoughts, thin wisps of fog curled through the crevices, ghostly tendrils weaving through the crags. At first, they hung low in the shadows, barely noticeable. But with each step upward, the mist thickened, creeping into the spaces between them.

Tension built among the soldiers. Ash could feel it in the way they moved—tight, wary steps, hands too near their sword hilts. They had been on edge before, but the fog would only make it worse. He prayed none of them were fool enough to lash out at empty shadows or the wind's low wail as it howled through the pass.

Celest drifted closer, placing a hand on Kiran's back. Ash saw her flinch before she realized who it was. A quick, tight smile passed between them. Celest murmured something low, reassuring, though Ash couldn't make out the words. Likely an attempt to steady the girl's nerves.

Higher they climbed, and with each step, a strange sensation prickled at Ash's skin. The thinning air, perhaps. Or something else. He wasn't sure. But doubt made him cautious. Ever since the darkness had touched him, every shift in his body—every flicker of unease—felt like something more. He suspected Kiran felt the same.

Soon, the mist thickened into an opaque wall, swallowing the landscape. Beyond ten paces, there was only blank whiteness. Their formation tightened by necessity, though Ash saw the reluctance in the soldiers' movements. They wanted no part of him or Kiran, but orders were orders, and their captain had given the command.

So they moved forward as one—upward into the unknown, into the mist, toward the monastery waiting at the edge of the world.

The tension in the group thickened like the fog around them. A stone clattered somewhere in the distance, sharp against the silence. Kiran flinched. Ash didn't look back, but he had no doubt the trailing soldiers had tensed at the sound as well.

Another rock tumbled loose, this one closer. Kiran's gaze snapped upward, scanning the cliffs above.

"Mountain goats," Ash murmured, keeping his tone light. "This place is full of them." She exhaled, just a little. "Quite the spectacle, watching them climb. No hands, no fingers, and yet they move like the cliffs were built for them." He allowed himself the ghost of a smile.

The party pressed on, silence settling over them once more. Cold crept into their garments, into their bones.

Wind moaned through the narrowing pass, its echoes twisting in the mist. More stones cracked loose, tumbling unseen, their impacts sharp against the stillness.

Rowan raised a hand, signalling a halt. Ash watched as the monk moved forward, Doran at his side. Their figures faded to silhouettes, then ghosts, then shadows swallowed whole by the fog.

Ash hesitated, then turned to Kiran and Celest. "Wait here. I'll see what's going on."

He stepped into the mist, closing the distance to Rowan and Doran. As their shapes solidified, Ash saw what had drawn their attention. A carcass lay at their feet. Torn fur, the bare remains of a skull—what little was left identified it as a mountain goat. But its body had been stripped nearly to the bone, shreds of flesh and sinew clinging in tatters.

Doran glanced at Ash as he approached. "Think it fell from a height?" His tone made it clear he wanted the answer to be yes.

Ash shook his head. "Too much meat is missing. It's been eaten."

Rowan nodded grimly. Doran exhaled through his nose, shifting his weight. "Carrion birds, then? Or raptors?" A flicker of doubt coloured his voice.

Ash knelt, running a finger along deep grooves carved into the ribs. Doran and Rowan saw it, too.

"No," Ash said, rising. His eyes flicked up the path ahead, though the fog veiled whatever lay beyond. "These are claw marks, fangs." He paused. "Mountain lion."

Doran shook his head, but Ash saw the understanding settle behind his eyes. Rowan simply nodded.

"We stay close," Rowan said at last. "We stay vigilant."

Doran let out a breath. "It's likely moved on."

"Likely," Ash agreed, but he wasn't convinced.

Ash turned to rejoin the others, but found the rest of the group had crept forward, drawn in by curiosity. Their eyes flicked from the carcass to him, waiting.

"You heard," Ash said, meeting their gazes. "There's a mountain lion in the area. Stay tight. Stay aware." He let the words settle. A few of the soldiers glanced toward their captain, searching for confirmation, but when none came, they turned back to Ash and nodded.

As they worked their way up the pass, Ash heard the unmistakable hiss of steel leaving a scabbard. He tensed. A blade at his back—even one wielded by an ally—was never comforting. He couldn't fault the soldiers for wanting their weapons ready, but he didn't have to like it.

More swords were drawn behind him, their edges whispering against worn leather. He exhaled through his nose, uneasy. These men were young, untested, their hands likely steadier on a plow than a blade. He had no desire to see one of them panic and drive a sword into an ally when chaos struck. Shaking his head, he pressed on.

A scream tore through the fog, raw and desperate. The group wheeled around, weapons drawn, every eye scanning the swirling mist that smothered the path behind them. The sound did not linger. It faded fast, swallowed by distance, yanked away as though the mountain itself had reached out and claimed the source. Ash did not like the implications.

"Rylin," one of the soldiers whispered, his voice tight with dread. His gaze darted around, searching the shifting gloom for a figure that would never reappear. The others caught his urgency, their own heads snapping back and forth, frantic, desperate.

Ash stepped toward the cliff's edge, peering over into the abyss. The fog was a wall, thick and unyielding, but he already knew what he would—or wouldn't—find. The soldiers rushed to his side, each taking a turn, leaning forward as if sheer will alone could pierce the veil of mist. When they turned to Ash, waiting for direction, he only shook his head.

A hunting beast had been stalking them. Ash had felt it earlier, sensed the unseen eyes lingering at their backs. The lion had waited for an opportunity, for a moment when the last man in line strayed too far, when vigilance dulled just enough. One well-placed strike. A single lunge. The weight of the beast alone would have been enough to send Rylin over the edge, down into the maw of the valley below. The cat wouldn't need to chase its meal—gravity had done the work for it.

"We have to go after him," one of the soldiers said, his voice shaking. His fingers clenched around the hilt of his sword, knuckles white with urgency. He kept looking from the cliff to Ash, waiting, pleading for confirmation. Ash would not give it.

"I'm sorry, friend." His voice was quiet, firm. "Your companion is either dead from the fall, or he will be before we can ever reach him."

It was the truth. A hard, merciless truth, but truth nonetheless. He saw it hit them, watched the dread settle over their expressions as reality sank in. Some opened their mouths as if to argue, but no words came. Even if Rylin had survived the fall, even if bones had not shattered on the way down, there was no hope of retrieving him now.

Ash did not say the other truth—that the mountain lion had its meal, and at least they would not be the ones being hunted now. Some truths had no place here.

Doran studied his men, his silence heavy. He was a man of experience, Ash could tell that much. It was in his bearing, the burden of command pressing down on his shoulders. He let the moment stretch, gave his men time to absorb what had happened. When he finally spoke, his voice was steel-wrapped exhaustion.

"We move on." His tone brooked no argument. "We mourn when we can, but not here. Not now. The nárgrim are still coming."

That struck them hard. As if, for a moment, they had forgotten why they were here, what waited just beyond the fog. Death did not come only in the form of beasts lurking in the dark. A greater horror pressed in from behind, shambling, relentless. The walls of the monastery were their only hope of sanctuary.

Doran placed a firm hand on each of his men's shoulders, a silent condolence, a wordless command to keep moving. Then, without another glance at the cliff, he turned and strode forward, leading them once more up the mountain path.

"Come," he said, his voice heavy but steady. "We press on."

As they pressed onward, the stony path winding ever higher, Ash could feel Kiran's unease as keenly as the mist curling around them. Her gaze flicked through the fog, searching for shapes that did not belong. He waited until the silence stretched between them before speaking. "You alright?" His voice was low, meant only for her.

She glanced up at him, a half-smile tugging at the corner of her lips. For a moment, he thought she would simply nod and let the question pass. Instead, she hesitated, her expression shifting.

"Will there be more?" she asked. "More lions?"

Her voice carried no fear, only concern. It was that restraint, that quiet steadiness, that reminded him how much she had changed. He shook his head.

"I doubt it. Mountain lions are territorial. They don't compete for food if they can avoid it." He exhaled, glancing toward the ledge as they walked. "There's always the chance of it being a female with cubs, but if it was, she'd be keeping them close, not hunting us."

She considered this, then gave a small nod, content for now. The two of them fell into step once more, their silence companionable but heavy with unspoken thoughts.

When the path twisted, cutting a gentler incline up the mountainside, Kiran turned to him again. This time, there was something else behind her eyes, a question that had been clawing at her from within.

"What if we're in battle," she said, her words slow, deliberate, "and we try to—" she hesitated, searching for the right phrasing "—draw on the Divine Mother's power… but it doesn't come? Not for you. Not for me. Because we've become… tainted."

The same thought had been gnawing at him, lingering in the edges of his mind where doubt took root. He kept his face neutral, forcing confidence into his tone.

"I don't think it works that way, but in truth… I don't know." He met her gaze, holding it steady. "When the time comes, we'll stay close. If the Divine Mother graces us with her power, we'll be fine. If she doesn't, we'll still have each other. Either way, things will be as they are meant to be."

That earned a faint smile from her, and she nodded. But Ash saw the uncertainty lingering in her eyes, the same uncertainty he fought to keep buried within himself.

He leaned in, lowering his voice so the others wouldn't hear. "Besides," he murmured, "I think there might be… another watching over us."

She cocked her head, confusion flickering across her features. She hadn't seen Morrathis in her vision. She hadn't felt the presence of the shadowed goddess or the strange, inexorable pull of that power. The others, too, hadn't yet pieced together what Ash had known.

"We don't know how this power works," he continued, choosing his words carefully. "Or where it comes from." That was a lie. He knew exactly where it came from. Unlike Kael and the others, this power had been granted to him. Morrathis had given her blessing. "But maybe, just maybe, we can use it to help ourselves."

Kiran's reaction was instant. She shook her head, her black eyes wide, edged with something he hadn't seen before—fear. "I don't want to use anything evil," she whispered fiercely. "I just want this taint gone."

Ash studied her, wondering how alien his own gaze must seem now, the same darkness pooling in his irises. He had never considered how it might look through another's eyes.

"I don't believe it's evil," he said gently, meeting her stare with quiet conviction. "A knife is just a tool. One man uses it to slice bread, another uses it to take a life. The knife itself isn't evil. It's how it is used."

A poor analogy. The thought of fresh bread made his stomach tighten with hunger, but he pushed the distraction aside.

"I think this shadowy essence… this power… is the same. It's a tool. How we use it, how we choose to wield it, determines if it is good or evil." He let that settle, let her wrestle with the idea. "You and I—we are good people," he added, allowing a rare smile. "If we have to use it, I know we'll use it to do good."

For a moment, she said nothing, her gaze searching his. Then, slowly, her expression softened, and the smile returned.

The ascent through the mountains was a trial in silence, each of them too preoccupied with the demands of the climb to waste breath on idle talk. Ash doubted it was mere exhaustion that stilled their tongues—something about the thinning air and the strain of the journey pressed down on them like an unseen hand. He felt it in his lungs, in the burn of his muscles, in the way the mist coiled around them, thick and sappy, as if the mountain itself sought to slow their passage.

His own panting was loud in his ears, at first an embarrassment he attributed to age and wear, but then he heard the others. Kiran, Rowan, even the younger soldiers—all of them exhaling in quick, misty gasps, their breath curling into the fog like fleeting spirits. The realization offered little comfort. Whatever natural force worked upon them, it did not discriminate.

They pressed on, step by weary step, their boots scuffing against loose stones as the path narrowed and twisted higher. Then, at last, they reached a bend that Ash recognized instantly. Relief flickered through him, dull but undeniable.

Rounding the curve, the path gave way to a plateau, stretching wide and flat beneath a dense veil of fog. The world beyond was obscured, but Ash didn't need to see it to know what lay ahead. Dawn's End. They had made it.

Chapter 19: Dawn's End

As the group pressed onward across the plateau, the fog thinned, unravelling in wisps to reveal the towering stone wall at the far end. The sight of it sent a ripple of relief through Ash's weary limbs, though he did not let it slow his pace. The high wooden gates stood open, yawning wide in welcome—common practice during the daylight hours. At night, those doors would be sealed, a deterrent against the beasts that prowled the mountains.

He felt the shift in his companions as well. The tension in their shoulders unwound, their steps quickened with a renewed sense of purpose. Even the most exhausted among them seemed to find a second wind, fuelled not by strength but by sheer relief. The sight of sanctuary had that effect on men who had spent too long on the road, at the edge of battle.

Two monks stood at the gateway, their robes still against the windless air. At first, they remained at their post, impassive observers, but as the party drew closer, they stepped forward in greeting. Ash knew that if it had been only the monks returning, there would have been no hesitation—passage would have been granted without question. But the presence of the soldiers trailing in their wake would complicate things.

"The Divine Mother's blessings be upon you," one of the monks intoned, his voice calm as he blocked the threshold. His gaze flicked first to Rowan and Doran, leading the group forward, but then his attention settled on Ash. There it lingered, his expression tightening almost imperceptibly. He did not speak the question that burned behind his eyes, did not name the thing he was witnessing, but Ash saw the worry etched in his features.

Rowan, unwilling to waste time on formalities, pushed forward. "We need to get inside and bar these doors. Now." His words carried an urgency that left no room for debate.

The monks hesitated, exchanging uncertain glances. Their eyes darted past the group, scanning the fog-laden pass behind them, but the thick mist revealed nothing. They saw no pursuers, no immediate threat, only weary travellers asking for entry.

Still, Rowan did not wait for their approval. He moved past them, ushering his men through the gate. Every second wasted was a second closer to disaster. He had no way of knowing how much time remained before Kael's forces arrived—if they arrived at all. It was possible Kael had altered his plans after realizing his secrecy had been compromised, but Rowan would not gamble on that chance.

The monks, bound more by routine than authority, made no move to physically stop them. Their hesitation, however, came with protest. "Sir, we can't simply close the doors without cause," one began, his tone wavering between protocol and concern. "There are—"

Ash cut him off. "An army of nárgrim marches here as we speak." His voice was steady, carrying the heir of certainty. "We need to see the headmaster. Now."

Shock flickered across the monks' faces, disbelief warring with instinct. They turned again to the open doors, their expressions uncertain, then back to Ash. He could see the doubt tightening their features, but they could also see the fear in the eyes of those who stood behind him. The truth settled over them like a slow-moving chill.

With a reluctant nod, the monks turned back to the doors. The massive wooden slabs groaned as they were pulled inward, closing with a deep, resonant thud. Without hesitation, they moved to either side, retrieving a thick timber beam and dropping it into the iron brackets that secured the gates in place. The sound echoed through the monastery grounds.

"What is the meaning of this?"

The voice carried across the courtyard, cutting through the thick air of unease. The companions turned as one, their gazes settling on the figure moving toward them—a monk, older than the others, his expression set in hard lines. The two guards who had barred the gates straightened instinctively, their heads bowing in respect, but Ash and his group remained still, waiting.

The monk came to a halt before Rowan and Doran, arms folded within the sleeves of his robes. He said nothing at first, but his silence was not empty. It was a demand more pressing than any spoken challenge. Doran looked ready to step forward, words forming on his lips, but Rowan raised a hand, cutting him off before he could speak.

"We bring grim tidings, I'm afraid." Rowan's voice was steady, but pressing. "A fallen monk of this very monastery has raised an army of nárgrim. Even now, they march upon us, intent on seizing Dawn's End."

The elder monk's face remained impassive, but his eyes betrayed the stirrings of disbelief. "Why would anyone seek to besiege a monastery? We have nothing to offer marauders, nothing here to plunder." The question was unmistakable, but Ash could hear something beneath it—a reluctance, a wish for the world to be as simple as the old monk wanted it to be.

"There's more to Dawn's End than you pretend," Ash said, his voice quiet but firm. He watched as the old monk's attention snapped to him, eyes narrowing in scrutiny. "Kael isn't coming for silver or for scripture. He seeks the ruins beneath your feet."

The monk's breath hitched, barely perceptible, but Ash saw it—the slight stiffening of his shoulders, the way his hands curled just a little tighter within his sleeves. He did not ask what ruins Ash spoke of. He already knew.

Ash pressed on. "He believes something lies buried beneath this monastery. Something that will strengthen his corruption."

The monk turned then towards Ash, as if to rebuke him, but the moment his gaze met Ash's, his expression faltered. His lips parted in a sharp inhale, his composure cracking like ice beneath sudden weight. Ash had seen this reaction before—had felt it, even, the first time Kiran and the others caught sight of his gaze after the change. The monk had not expected to find something looking back at him with blackened eyes. Ash wasn't sure if he had glimpsed Kiran's as well. She had kept close behind him, tilting her head to let her hair obscure her gaze—but the damage had been done. Silence stretched between them.

"We need to see the headmaster," Rowan said at last, breaking the quiet like a hammer against glass.

The monk did not answer immediately, but when he did, it was with a slow, reluctant nod. "Come," he said, turning away and heading down the stone path.

Before he had gone more than a few steps, Rowan spoke again. "Our people need food." His tone held no room for negotiation. "It's been more than a day since any of us have had a proper meal." He glanced over his shoulder at the weary faces behind him, exhaustion evident in every slouched shoulder, every hollowed cheek.

The elder monk regarded them for a moment, then gestured to a structure off to the left. "You will find warm meals there," he said. Then his gaze returned to Rowan, Doran, and Ash. "Those of you in command, follow me."

Doran and Rowan fell in behind him without hesitation. Ash moved to follow, unsurprised when Kiran did the same. He expected no less. Whatever silent war she fought within herself, she had no interest in the pitying glances of strangers. The judgment, the suspicion—it was already weighing on her, as it was with him.

Ash understood. It was one thing to feel yourself changing. It was another to endure the stares of those who feared what you might become. People did not like the unknown.

The four companions followed the elder monk along the worn cobblestone path, their footsteps muffled beneath the burden of expectation. The monastery grounds stretched around them in solemn quiet, the air thick with the scent of crisp mountain air, incense, and damp stone. Monks clad in simple robes moved through the cloisters and courtyards, tending to their tasks with quiet efficiency. Yet as the group passed, their presence did not go unnoticed. Conversations stilled. Movements slowed.

Dozens of heads turned, watchful eyes lingering on Ash and his companions.

It wasn't difficult to understand why. Dawn's End was a sanctuary, a place of seclusion high in the mountain heights. Strangers were a rarity, aside from the occasional merchant braving the treacherous ascent to barter goods for alms. A small party of armed travellers, ushered by an elder monk, would only deepen the mystery. The hush that followed them was heavy with speculation.

Ahead, their guide ascended a short flight of stone steps, his movement as fluid as drifting parchment. He reached for the great wooden door before him and pushed it open without ceremony, revealing the dimly lit corridor beyond. Without a word, he held the door wide, waiting as the group stepped inside. Shadows swallowed them as they crossed the threshold. The scent of aged wood and smouldering candle wax filled the air, the distant flicker of their lantern light casting wavering silhouettes along the walls.

The monk stepped in behind them and shut the door, sealing out the view of the curious onlookers. Resuming his place at the front of the group, he led them down the corridor, the edge of his robes whispering against the flagstones. At the far end, he came to a stop before a heavy door bearing the brass sign with 'Headmaster' etched into its surface. Without hesitation, he raised a hand and delivered two firm knocks. The sound echoed down the corridor like the tolling of a distant bell, reverberating in the silence that followed.

A rasping voice answered from within. "Enter."

The monk pushed open the door and stepped aside. Ash moved in first, his eyes adjusting to the dim glow of candlelight. Behind the desk at the center of the chamber sat the oldest man Ash had ever seen. The headmaster's features were carved by the passage of time, deep lines tracing the contours of his face. His skin, like aged parchment, stretched over fragile bones, and yet his eyes—clear and sharp—held an awareness that belied his years.

Ash hesitated. He knew that those who devoted their lives to the Divine Mother were graced with a gift that slowed the ravages of time. Yet the headmaster looked impossibly ancient, a relic of another age. How long had he presided over this place?

The old monk shifted, gripping the edge of the desk as he rose to his feet, his frail frame swaying with the effort. A kind smile touched his lips, and he bowed his head slightly in greeting. "The Mother's blessing be upon you all." His voice, though rasped by years, carried warmth. With careful movements, he lowered himself back into his chair. "Please, sit. Rennick, fetch another chair for our guests."

The monk named Rennick gave a curt nod before

slipping out of the room. Rowan and Doran seated themselves at once, but Kiran hesitated, her hands hovering near the back of the remaining chair. She cast a glance at Ash, who gave a subtle nod before she sank into it.

Ash remained standing until Rennick returned, a wooden chair balanced in his arms. Without a word, the monk placed it beside the others and stepped back, retreating to a spot against the wall where he leaned, arms crossed, watching in silence. Ash lowered himself into the chair, keenly aware of the unspoken questions, the scrutiny, the expectancy hanging between them all.

The headmaster studied them for a long moment before exhaling a quiet breath. "I assume you've come with questions about Ash and the young woman." His gaze flicked to Kiran, then back to Ash. "Their eyes, I mean."

Ash stiffened, caught off guard. The headmaster knew his name. Recognition dawned too slowly, his mind scrambling to piece together the memory. He searched the old man's face, peeling back the layers of time.

"Master Calder," he murmured at last.

A name from another life, it seemed. His old instructor in ancient scripture, a figure of quiet authority from his time at Dawn's End. Calder had aged beyond recognition, yet somehow, impossibly, he had recognized Ash.

Before Ash could process the revelation, Rowan

leaned forward, his expression darkening. "Ash and Kiran's eyes are the least of our concerns." His voice carried the seriousness of urgency.

The subtle shift in Calder's demeanour betrayed his surprise. He leaned back slightly, his fingers resting against the surface of the desk. "Then tell me," he said, his voice lowering. "What has brought you to my door?"

Rowan recounted their journey with considered accuracy, his voice steady as he wove the tale from their departure at Maiden's Haven to the harrowing trials that had brought them to the gates of Dawn's End. Sitting next to Rowan, Doran listened with unwavering attention, absorbing the details of the nárgrim's emergence, the cryptic omens, and the grim necessity that had driven them north. Though he had journeyed with them since they had made it to the mountains, much of the deeper story had remained untold until now.

Ash, though largely silent, interjected on occasion to clarify a point or expand upon a crucial moment. Kiran, seated beside him, reminded them all of the dream Ash had experienced about the ruins beneath Dawn's End, the one that had felt too real to dismiss as mere illusion. That led naturally to the other vision—the one they had shared after being struck by the shadow's blast. At this, Calder's expression tightened, his brow lifting in the flickering candlelight. Was it curiosity? Or was he weighing the significance of what they revealed against knowledge he had long held in silence?

The mention of an invading force of nárgrim soured the conversation further. The old master did not try to hide his unease, though he spoke not a word. The tension in his features, the way his fingers curled slightly against the worn wood of his desk, betrayed his thoughts. Behind them, Rennick shifted where he stood, the scrape of his boot against the stone floor betraying his own disquiet. These were men who had seen much, but this—this unsettled them.

For a time, silence loomed between them, stretching long enough to feel like an unspoken prayer. Then, at last, Calder exhaled, and when he spoke, his voice carried the acknowledgement of inevitability. "It seems we have no choice but to prepare for battle" His gaze flicked to Rennick, who answered with a solemn nod before turning sharply on his heel and striding from the room. The door's closure was a quiet but certain punctuation, the first movement in a course now set.

A beat passed, and then Calder's focus returned, sharpening upon Rowan and Doran. "I would speak with Ash and the young woman alone, if you don't mind." His tone was even, but there was no mistaking the command within it. "You would both do well to take a hot meal while you still can. You'll need your strength before long."

Rowan exchanged a glance with Doran, then nodded, rising from his seat. Without protest, the two of them departed, leaving only the three behind. The latch clicked into place, sealing them in seclusion.

"Now," Calder said, his fingers interlocking atop the desk. "Let us speak of your eyes." His gaze lingered on them, searching. "You have been void-touched. I have read of this."

Ash was not surprised. Calder had been more than a scholar of scripture—he had been the monastery's chief translator, the steward of countless ancient texts, some of which had likely spoken of such afflictions. The old master leaned forward, eyes narrowing as he scrutinized Kiran. "Let me see them properly."

Ash half-expected her to flinch away, but she held steady beneath his inspection, unblinking. His study was meticulous, searching for something beyond the obvious stain left upon them by shadow's touch. When at last he pulled away, his expression was unreadable. He laced his fingers again, considering. "Have you noticed any other changes?"

Kiran hesitated, but Ash spoke first. "I was certain my ribs were broken in the blast, yet by nightfall, I felt whole again."

Calder's lips curled into a knowing smile as he reclined, fingers tapping absently against his jaw.

"Fascinating," he murmured, rubbing his palm against his cheek. "It seems she has granted her approval."

Ash did not need to ask who 'she' was. The assumption was obvious, yet something in him resisted certainty. The moment stretched, heavy with implication. Then, with the sharpness of a blade slipping between ribs, Calder asked, "And what did you trade Morrathis in exchange for these gifts?"

Kiran stiffened. Confusion flickered across her face, a silent question unspoken. Ash, however, understood at once. He should not have been surprised—of course the old man knew more than he let on.

Calder's smirk deepened. "It is unlikely that the Lady of Death would grant such power freely. In all written accounts, her gifts come at a price."

"I don't know who you are talking about," Kiran said, shaking her head vigorously. Her eyes darted to Ash, searching for answers. He exhaled, resigned. If there was ever a time to withhold the truth, it had passed.

"There are those who have stolen aspects of her power," he admitted. "She has tasked me with eradicating them so she may reclaim what was taken."

Kiran inhaled sharply, reeling from his words. The unspoken accusation hung between them—that he had not told her this before, that he had kept hidden something of grave importance. And yet, before she could speak, Ash pressed forward, recounting his dark dream, the moment he had stood before the goddess of death herself. He spared no detail, not even the moment of his choice—the deal struck in the black abyss, the whispered bargain meant to spare Kiran from the taint even as it bound him to the will of something vast and unknowable.

As he finished, silence claimed the chamber once more. Only the distant howl of the wind beyond the monastery walls bore witness to what had just been revealed.

Calder pushed himself up from his chair, the effort visible in the slow, careful way he moved. His joints creaked like the wood beneath his feet, but he ignored the protest of his body and made his way to the far side of the chamber, where a small bookshelf stood, its shelves half-filled with worn tomes. He leaned in, scanning the cracked spines with a discerning eye, his fingers hovering over the faded lettering as if searching for something just out of reach. At last, he pulled a thick volume from its resting place, the weight of it making his arm tremble slightly. Without a word, he returned to his chair, lowering himself with a quiet exhale before setting the tome down between them. The old leather cover, embossed with an intricate but faded sigil, seemed to drink in the dim light of the room.

“I have seen this dark aspect before," Calder said at last, his voice grave. "Once. A long time ago.” He ran a hand over the book's surface as if contemplating whether he should continue. “The woman afflicted by it… she was not the same when it took hold. In time, it twisted her mind. She lost herself.” He looked up then, his sharp gaze settling on Ash and Kiran. “I don’t know if that will be your fate. But you need to understand what you carry.”

He pushed the tome across the desk with the gradual, careful finality of a man handing over a weapon, though his fingers lingered on the edge, reluctant to let go. "Over the years, I found traces of this condition in multiple texts, scattered references hidden in forgotten scriptures. It has always piqued my interest. This—" he tapped the cover with a bony knuckle, "—is everything I’ve gathered. My notes, translations, theories. You may find answers here… or only more questions."

Ash took the book in his hands, the weight of it heavier than expected. "This will be invaluable," he said, meaning it. “You have our deepest thanks, Master Calder. This will save us untold time searching in the dark.”

Calder inclined his head slightly, though the sombre expression on his face remained unchanged. His lips curled into something resembling a smile, but there was little warmth in it. “Now all you have to do is survive long enough to read it.” The man paused, considering his words, but then just shook his head. “Go. Eat something. Rest if you can. You'll need your strength soon enough.”

He rose once more, slower this time, and moved to the door, his presence heavy with unspoken thoughts. He opened it, gesturing for them to leave. Ash and Kiran stepped into the dimly lit corridor, the hush of the monastery settling around them.

The door closed behind them with a soft but final *click*, sealing Calder away with the flickering candlelight within. They stood in the darkened hallway, the weight of the book in Ash's hands matched only by the weight of their thoughts.

Chapter 20:
Before The Storm

At the end of the hallway, Ash stopped before the heavy wooden door, shifting the weight of his pack before pulling it off his shoulder. He handed Kiran his quarterstaff without a word, and she took it, watching in silence as he knelt and unfastened the straps of his bag. He flipped open the leather flap, and carefully slid the thick tome into the bottom, ensuring it lay flat, undamaged. The book's age alone made it fragile, but it carried something more than just old ink and parchment—knowledge of a subject most likely deemed taboo within the monastery walls. Kiran remained quiet as he secured the bag once more, only speaking when he rose to his feet.

"Do you think it holds the answers we seek?" Her voice was low, yet it carried in the empty corridor, the stone walls sending her words stretching into the darkness beyond them.

Ash tightened the straps on his pack before glancing at her, his expression pensive. "I have no doubt it contains stories—accounts of those who have witnessed the shadow's touch. But what are the odds that any of them truly understood it, let alone wielded it?" He exhaled, adjusting the weight on his shoulders. "I'm sure there's plenty of theory, speculation... but little in the way of true understanding. Books can illuminate, but they rarely instruct in the matters that demand experience."

Kiran nodded, though her expression remained unreadable. When Ash took back his quarterstaff, she fell into step beside him as he pushed through the door, holding it long enough for her to follow. The cool evening air greeted them as they stepped into the courtyard, the stone paths stretching out before them like veins leading into the monastery's heart. Their steps were steady but unhurried as they turned toward the kitchens. Before they made it halfway, a familiar figure approached from the other direction.

Celest emerged from the shadow of the building, a deep tray balanced in her hands. Two bowls rested upon it, steam curling into the air, as well as a woven basket beside them carrying the unmistakable scent of fresh bread. She halted in front of them, offering a small, knowing smile.

"I wasn't sure you'd make it to the kitchens before we had to run to the walls," she said, holding the tray out. "So I brought you something."

Ash barely had time to react before Kiran took the tray, her face brightening at the sight of the meal. The scent of herbs and roasted vegetables mingled with the crisp air, a comforting reminder of simpler things.

"Thank you," Kiran said, sincerity thick in her

voice.

Ash dipped his head in gratitude as well. "You have our thanks, Celest."

Celest acknowledged them with a nod, though there was little time for pleasantries. "I'm heading to the wall. We're setting wards—precautions against the nárgrim. If we're fortunate, they may serve as a deterrent." She shifted her grip on her satchel before glancing toward the distant monastery gates. "Scouts have already been sent ahead. Now that the fog has lifted, we should have plenty of warning before anything reaches us."

She paused as if considering saying more but merely smiled instead, turning back toward her destination. "Eat well," she called over her shoulder before disappearing down the path.

Ash turned to Kiran, eyeing the tray she now held. "Come," he said. "I know a quiet place where we can eat. The view is worth the walk."

Kiran raised an eyebrow but said nothing. She followed as he led them along the winding pathways, past training yards and meditation alcoves, until they reached the rear of one of the taller buildings. Behind it, a narrow staircase spiralled up toward the roof, its steep stone steps worn smooth by years of use.

Without hesitation, Ash ascended first, moving with proficient grace, but Kiran followed just as deftly despite the tray in her arms. He glanced back at her in mild amusement, half expecting to see her struggling to keep the bowls steady, but her balance was flawless. He supposed he shouldn't have been surprised—her footwork in battle had always been as precise as his own.

At the top, the roof sloped gently downward before levelling off into a broad, flat surface. The two of them settled there, setting the tray between them as dusk deepened around them. The sky stretched wide, streaked in deep purples and burning oranges, the last remnants of the sun bleeding out from beneath the horizon. A cool breeze stirred the air, carrying with it the faintest traces of pine and earth, the scent of the burning incense from the monastery blending with the vast wilderness beyond.

They ate in silence, the only sounds the occasional scrape of a spoon against a bowl and the whisper of wind curling over the rooftop. The stew was simple but hearty, the warmth of it warding off the evening chill. Kiran tore off chunks of her freshly baked bun, stuffing them into her mouth with unconcealed satisfaction. Ash smirked at the sight, though he understood the comfort of a good meal after long days of strain. He took his own leasurely bites, savouring the rare moment of stillness.

Beyond them, the sky deepened into a shifting expanse of crimson and violet, the last vestiges of daylight surrendering to night. Ash found his gaze drawn not only to the horizon but to the monastery grounds below. The front gate stood stark in the growing dusk, flanked by robed figures moving with hasty intention. Monks scurried through the courtyard, their arms wreathed in tongues of blue flame as they wove protective enchantments into the air. Doran's soldiers worked tirelessly, erecting barricades just inside the walls, layering obstacles in a desperate attempt to slow the inevitable breach.

Kiran followed his gaze, the same intensity in her expression. "Celest said she was going to help with the wards." She turned to look up at him, curiosity shadowing her face. "I read about them at Maiden's Haven, but I was never shown how they're crafted."

There was more to her words than idle interest; Ash could sense the silent question that lingered beneath them. He set his empty bowl aside and rested his hands on his knees. "The Divine Mother's gift doesn't just strengthen our bodies or sharpen our skills—it can be wielded externally, shaped and projected beyond us." He lifted his quarterstaff slightly, turning it over in his hands as if to illustrate his point. "That same power can be woven into objects, reinforcing them, binding force to them. A staff, for instance, can be imbued with energy—made stronger, or even enhanced with a spectral edge, an added weapon unseen but no less deadly."

Kiran listened with rapt attention, absorbing his

words as she so often did, her brow furrowed in thought.

"Wards work much the same way," Ash continued. "They're crafted with a different function, laid like traps infused with the Divine Mother's essence. Their intention depends on the wielder's will—whether to repel, ensnare, or annihilate. They linger in the air or upon the earth, dormant until triggered."

Kiran leaned forward, peering down at the distant figures below as if she might glimpse the secrets of their work. But with the fading light and the sheer distance, the details remained obscured. She exhaled, sitting back again without complaint, her gaze shifting upward to the sky now thick with twilight. Streaks of deep blue melded into wisps of violet, the heavens darkening with the promise of night.

A long silence stretched between them before Kiran finally spoke again. "How do you think this will unfold?"

Ash let out a slow breath, considering the question. He wanted to shake his head, to say nothing, but the truth pressed against the back of his teeth, demanding to be spoken.

"The nárgrim have only one path up the mountain," he said at last. "The same pass we took. That bottleneck works in our favour, but they'll concentrate their assault on the weakest point— the front gate." He imagined it, the relentless tide of corpses battering against the stone, pressing forward with single-minded goal. "They won't tire.

They won't retreat. They'll keep coming until the walls fall, or they do."

Kiran's face darkened, but she said nothing. She didn't need to.

"Eventually," Ash continued, "they will break through. And we will have to fight." There was no point in softening the words, no comfort to be found in false hope. He studied Kiran's expression, watching as she absorbed the truth of its inevitability.

"If we're lucky," he went on, "they'll funnel in through a single breach, and we'll be able to hold them off in smaller numbers at a time." His jaw tightened as he considered their odds. "That's our best hope."

The words hung in the air between them, heavy with unspoken fears. Ash exhaled and ran a hand over his face, the quiet moment they had stolen already slipping away, replaced by the grim certainty of the battle ahead.

"If we're in the thick of battle and we can't draw on the Divine Mother's power, you'll still have my back, right?" Kiran's voice was steady, but Ash could see the worry behind her eyes. The way she watched him, waiting for reassurance, made it clear she had been carrying the thought for some time.

Ash answered her with a smirk, nodding as he swallowed the last of his stew. "As long as you promise you've got mine." His tone was light, teasing, though they both knew the magnitude of the question.

Kiran's grin stretched wide, her earlier apprehension melting away as she nodded vigorously. The tension that had been pressing against them loosened, just a little.

The sound of footsteps crunching over stone drew their attention. They turned in unison to see Celest cresting the ridge, moving with the confident stride of a seasoned warrior. Her silhouette cut against the twilight, as she swayed back and forth with each step. Without hesitation, she made her way toward them, and as she reached the edge where they sat, Ash turned back toward the monastery below, watching the steady churn of preparation unfold.

Kiran, ever the polite one, nudged the tray aside to make room. Celest, however, wasted no time with formalities—she dropped onto the cedar shake roof between them, slinging an arm around each of their shoulders with a theatrical sigh.

"How are my two new best friends handling the hour before our possible demise?" She grinned, squeezing them both in a fierce embrace before pulling back just enough to glance between them. "Come on now, lighten up. We've got this."

Kiran hesitated before speaking, her earlier confidence faltering. "What if we start fighting, and we can't reach any kind of power?" She turned to Celest as she spoke, her voice quieter this time. Ash didn't need to look at her to know the fear was creeping back in. He had felt it himself, gnawing at the edges of his resolve.

Celest, however, simply shrugged. “Well, let’s go find out.” She stretched her legs out in front of her and tilted her head toward Ash, as if it were the most obvious answer in the world. “Why wait for battle to test it? Let’s head to the training grounds, see if you two can summon whatever it is you need.”

Ash hadn’t considered that. He had assumed they would learn the truth when the fight began—when there would be no second chances. The idea of testing their connection to power beforehand seemed so simple, so practical, that he almost felt foolish for not thinking of it first.

He exhaled and pushed himself to his feet, nodding his approval. “It’s a brilliant idea.” He extended a hand to each of them in an unnecessary but instinctive gesture of companionship. Neither of them needed the assistance, yet both accepted it.

Together, they made their way across the roof, Ash carrying the tray of empty dishes while Kiran retrieved his staff. The air grew cooler as they descended into the dark embrace of the building. By the time they reached the training yard, the monastery’s towering walls cast long shadows across the open space.

Ash set the tray down on a bench at the perimeter,

gesturing toward Kiran to drop the staves. "Leave them here," he said. "We won't need them for this."

Kiran hesitated, gripping the weapon a moment longer before laying it gently beside the bench.

Celest took a seat on the bench, arms crossed, while watching as Ash led Kiran to the center of the clearing.

"Reach for the source," Ash instructed, his voice steady but firm. "I know you've only felt it once, so it won't come easily. But don't think of it as something distant. The dark threads—the ones that entered you when we fought that monk—they're still inside you. Find them."

Kiran's brows furrowed, but she said nothing. She exhaled slowly, closed her eyes, and lowered her head in concentration. The night was silent save for the occasional flicker of torchlight. Ash watched, waiting.

At first, nothing. Just the stillness of the monastery, the quiet sounds of distant movement from the soldiers and the monks working at the gate.

Then, the first trace of darkness began to slither around her forearm. Wisps of darkness curled from her skin, subtle at first, then growing in presence, swirling in slow, conscious motion.

Ash felt the tight knot of unease in his chest. Hope was a fragile thing, but in that moment, he grasped at it.

Ash felt the pull of his own darkness within as he watched Kiran weave them into being. It was instinct, a silent call that he could no longer ignore. He reached inward, feeling for the dark force coiled at the edges of his soul, no longer an alien corruption but something intrinsic, something that had always been there—merely veiled from his sight.

Now, taking ownership of it, the power surged forward, not stolen or commanded, but welcomed. It spread through him, saturating his being like ink dissolving in water, dark tendrils curling through his veins. It did not resist. It did not burn. It did not sear his conscience the way he had once feared. Instead, it was intoxicating, seamless, as if he had merely removed a blindfold to glimpse his truest self for the first time.

A breath later, he opened his eyes and found Kiran watching him. Dark threads coiled around her like a living thing, ribbons of black tendrils shifting and twisting as though caught in a storm. He did not need to look at himself to know he was the same. He could feel it—ebony threads wrapping his frame, not as an external force to be wielded but as an extension of his own existence. It was unlike the blue flame of the Divine Mother, which had always felt like something borrowed, something manipulated and controlled. This was different. This was *his*.

The power whispered of endless potential. He could shape it, stretch it, let it consume more of him if he wished.

And yet, somewhere deep within, caution coiled like a serpent. He craved more, but he knew—*knew*—that taking too much would be dangerous. Kiran felt it too. He could see it in her eyes, the precarious balance of awe and restraint, the hunger for control battling against the instinctive fear of overstepping.

He turned toward Celest. She was no longer seated. She stood rigid, her stance wide, shoulders squared, her gaze fixed on them. Even in the dim light, Ash saw the tightness in her jaw, the tension in her hands. Shock was written plainly across her face, but there was something else beneath it. Not just awe. Not just unease. *Fear.* Ash understood. This was unknown, and people feared the unknown.

Before any of them could speak, a shout rang out from the front gates. A sentry called for the doors to be opened, and three monks were hurried inside before the heavy wooden doors slammed shut again. The scouts had returned. News of the enemy.

The dark threads around Ash snapped inward at his command. He was surprised by how easily he could will them back into himself, as though he had been wielding them his entire life. He turned to Kiran and saw her struggle, her hands clenched, her breaths focused. But, inch by inch, the writhing darkness receded, sinking back beneath her skin. Almost. Not completely. He watched as the last wisps hesitated, curling at her fingertips before finally vanishing. She exhaled and met his gaze.

"Come," he said, voice steady, the command effortless. "We need to hear what they've found." She nodded, and together they strode back toward Celest, who was still watching them as if she didn't quite recognize them anymore.

They retrieved their packs and staves, their grip familiar, grounding. Then, without another word, they turned and made their way toward the gates, toward whatever grim tidings awaited them.

Chapter 21:
The Battle Begins

As they neared the barred gate, Ash took in the sight of Rennick speaking with Rowan, a loose circle of warriors and monks gathered around them. Doran stood nearby with a pair of his men, their expressions set in grim lines. Rowan glanced up, his sharp gaze finding Ash and the others moving toward the assembled crowd. He murmured a word to Rennick before breaking away to intercept them.

A few paces from the others, the monks came to a halt. Rowan did not hesitate to speak.

"Their sentinels have returned," he said, his voice steady, though his eyes remained fixed on Ash. "The army of nárgrim has begun its ascent up the pass."

Ash caught the way the older monk scrutinized him, the unspoken dread behind that lingering stare. No doubt it was difficult for Rowan to look into his eyes now, knowing what had seeped into them—the abyssal black sheen that reflected no light, only the hunger of this Shadow Weave that lay beneath their depth. But Rowan did not flinch, did not avert his gaze. That, at least, Ash respected.

"There is one advantage," Rowan continued, a wry smile ghosting across his lips. "The watchmen report that the nárgrim struggle with the terrain. The narrow paths slow them. A few have even been shoved off the cliffs by their own in the press forward. It seems they don't concern themselves much with the survival of their own ranks."

Kiran and Ash exchanged a glance. It was something, but not enough. A few mindless dead tumbling into the abyss did little to change the overwhelming numbers still pressing onward. Whatever delay the terrain provided would only last so long.

Beyond them, the monastery was a flurry of motion. Men and women moved with determination, assembling into formations, reinforcing the defences. Archers climbed to the wooden platforms along the walls, bows in hand, quivers stuffed with arrows slung across their backs. Ash doubted those arrows would do much good. A direct hit to the head, perhaps. But even then, how many shots would it take to bring one down? Two? Three? Against a horde, the odds were bleak.

"The doors will hold for a time," Rennick said as he strode toward them, but his gaze flicking once toward the gate. "They're sturdy enough, but not indestructible. Eventually, the nárgrim will break through. They have weapons. They'll carve their way through if given time."

Kiran was the first to respond, her voice firm, edged with the quiet confidence of someone who had seen battle before. "What kind of weapons?"

Rennick turned to her, his gaze weighing her in that brief pause before he answered. Ash noted the shift. Even Rennick, a man of experience, had begun regarding Kiran as an equal. She carried herself differently now—no longer the uncertain girl he had met at the Maiden's Haven monastery's threshold. The last few days had changed her.

"Mostly crude," Rennick said at last. "Farm tools turned to war—clubs, sticks. But some have proper blades. Swords, axes. It's a mixed lot, but enough to be dangerous."

Doran scoffed. "Sounds more like an inconvenience than an actual fight."

Rowan shifted slightly, his stance unreadable, but the weight of his presence alone was enough to quiet the man.

"It's their numbers," Rennick said, levelling his gaze at the soldier. "That's what will wear us down. They don't tire. We do." He exhaled, his eyes scanning the faces gathered. "If we can keep them contained, we stand a chance. We'll rotate the fighters—one line holds the front, and when fatigue sets in, the next shifts forward to take their place while the first withdraws to recover."

His voice rose, carrying across the courtyard now, addressing not just them but everyone within earshot. "When the doors fall, we hold our ground. We let them enter. Let the wards do their work first—*then* we strike. Keep them contained. Keep them behind our barriers. Do not let them spread unchecked."

A murmur of acknowledgement rippled through those assembled. Eyes hardened. Hands tightened on weapons. The waiting would not last much longer.

Ash and his company took their places within the second formation of monks, a step removed from the front lines. He would have preferred to stand at the vanguard when the battle began, but Rennick's orders had been clear. The old monk had seen fit to distribute their strength evenly between the ranks. A practical decision, that Ash had to agree with. Many of those standing in formation now were barely more than novices, untested in the field. The rawness of their inexperience was written plainly across their faces, the tight-set jaws, the fingers clenching and unclenching around weapons they had likely trained with more in ritual than in true combat.

He had forgotten how many students were here at Dawn's End. For a fleeting moment, a pang of unease stirred in his gut. It was an echo of that first battle against the nárgrim, Kiran at his side, fear riding on the edges of his every thought. He had fought then not just to survive, but to protect her. And now, looking at these novices, he felt that same impulse creeping in. He would do what he could to shield them, but they would have to find their own footing in the assault to come. No one could fight their battles for them.

His gaze flicked to Kiran, and for the first time, he recognized the shift in himself. That old need to shield her, to stand between her and the worst of the world, had faded. He no longer felt responsible for her safety. She had grown beyond it. Strength radiated from her, the ease of her stance, the readiness in her grip. She was still young by a warrior's measure, but in the span of days, she had gathered the kind of experience that shaped survivors. If fate chose to sever their paths, Ash no longer feared for her. She would hold her own.

The torches along the wall sputtered to life, casting long, shifting shadows against the monastery's stone. Their glow did little to cut through the gathering dark. The night pressed in, thick and heavy, wrapping around the monastery like the hush before a storm. Ash tilted his gaze skyward. The full moon would rise soon, perhaps within the hour. Its light would bring some aid to assist with their lack of visibility. The battle would be waged beneath open sky, and the dead had no fear of what lurked in the shadows.

The first sound of the advancing nárgrim did not come as the measured cadence of soldiers marching to war, but as something far more primal. It began as a murmur—a discordant whisper against the night—then swelled into a seething, chaotic rhythm. It was not the stomp of boots in unison, but a clatter, an avalanche of footfalls tumbling over one another in a relentless surge forward. It was the sound of a landslide that did not know how to stop.

A ripple of movement passed through the novices. Heads turned, wide-eyed, searching for reassurance in their elders. But the elder monks did not waver. Their focus remained locked forward, their discipline unshaken. They knew what was coming. They had prepared for it.

The young man beside Ash shifted uneasily, his breath shallow. When he finally dared to glance toward Ash, his eyes held the silent question that many of them shared: *Would they survive this?* Ash met his gaze, steady, unwavering. The boy looked away.

"Hey." Ash kept his voice low but firm, drawing the novice's attention back to him. "We've got this. You watch my back, and I'll watch yours."

The boy hesitated, then nodded. His grip on his weapon tightened, his shoulders squaring just slightly. It wasn't much, but it was something.

A slight tug at his sleeve made Ash turn. Kiran stood beside him, grinning ear to ear, eyes alight with something dangerously close to amusement.

"You're a good man, Master Stormrider," she said, laughter woven into her voice.

Ash snorted, shaking his head as he gave her a light tap on the shoulder. She had no business smiling like that before a battle. But then again, neither did he. She deserved a better fate than this war. He knew that. And yet, selfish as it was, he was glad she was here.

Above them, the first volley of arrows loosed from the walls. The monks were not archers by trade, but they knew enough to send a volley of demise into the ranks below. Ash knew that it would not be enough. The nárgrim would come, and they would keep coming. All they could do now was hold the entrance.

A thunderous crash shattered the night, reverberating through the monastery grounds as the nárgrim slammed into the thick wooden gates. The sheer force of the impact sent vibrations through the stone beneath Ash's feet, a tremor that promised ruin. As expected, the grating sound of metal biting into wood followed—a relentless scraping, the gradual and meticulous carving of destruction. They would chip away at the barricade, tearing it apart splinter by splinter, until the doors inevitably gave way.

Above, the sky rained death. The monks atop the walls loosed arrows in a constant, unrelenting volley. At first, they had aimed with precision, selecting their targets, but that discipline had long since crumbled. Now they fired with raw desperation, pouring shafts into the mass below with little thought beyond keeping the enemy at bay. The supply would dwindle soon. Ash knew it. They all did.

A voice cut through the chaos, raw with urgency.

"They're climbing! Using their dead as a ramp!"

Ash's eyes snapped to the wall just as Rennick barked orders to the monks at his side. Without hesitation, they sprinted toward the battlements, staves gripped tight. Above, the monks struck downward with practised force, hammering the abominations trying to scale their own dead. The nárgrim, heedless of pain or reason, clawed their way up the writhing pile, their bodies forming an ever-rising ramp toward the monastery's walls.

Ash had not anticipated this. He had envisioned the undead breaking through by sheer force, tearing down the doors with brute persistence. But this? This was something else. A grotesque, mindless determination. They did not need to breach the gate; they would simply rise over it, an unrelenting tide cresting the walls.

Rennick must have reached the same conclusion at the same moment. His voice rang out, sharp and commanding. "Unbar the doors! Now!"

The monks closest to the entrance hesitated for only a heartbeat before rushing forward. With hurried hands, they wrestled the heavy wooden beam from its iron latches and cast it aside. The doors groaned, straining under the weight of bodies pressed against them, before they burst inward, carried by the momentum of the horde.

Nárgrim poured through.

At first, only a handful staggered in, but more

surged behind them, pressing forward in a relentless flood. The monks stood firm behind the barricades, waiting. Then the first of the wards ignited.

A brilliant flare of blue fire seared the darkness, cascading over the entryway like an explosion of lightning. The blast consumed the nearest undead, their rotting forms torn apart in the eruption of energy. The air cracked with the force of it, the shockwave sending body parts flying, severed limbs tumbling end over end before crashing to the ground.

The young monk beside Ash gasped, his eyes lighting with something dangerously close to hope. He thought they had turned the tide. That the wards had broken the enemy's charge. Ash knew better. The damage was not enough. The gaps the explosions created were instantly filled. The undead did not hesitate. They did not feel fear. The wards had bought them seconds, nothing more.

The monks braced as the nárgrim surged forward, slamming into their defences. Staves cracked against bone and decayed flesh, striking true, but the horde did not falter. The sheer volume of bodies pressed against them. It was overwhelming to witness, an unceasing wave of dead flesh driven by something unnatural, something beyond the grave.

And then the senior monks stepped forward. Their

staves ignited with divine fire, burning with the unmistakable radiance of the Divine Mother's blessing. Each strike landed with devastating force, blue flames erupting on impact, searing through the undead with concussive bursts of light. Every motion was exact, controlled, honed through years of experience. They fought not with desperation, but with the certainty of warriors who had devoted their lives to this moment.

The monastery had not yet fallen. But the dead did not tire. And they would keep coming.

The novices fought from behind the barricades, their staves striking out in quick, practised jabs, battering the nárgrim wherever they could reach. The head was the best target—a sharp blow to the temple or crown sent the undead staggering, if not crumpling outright. The young monks had held their ground longer than Ash expected. He watched them work in disciplined tandem, their strikes calculated, their resolve unbroken.

Above, the monks atop the wall must have sensed that their arrows were of little use now. They abandoned their posts, snatching up their staves before rushing down to reinforce the ranks below. Most slid into formation just behind the novices, waiting, poised to replace the weary when the time came. Their stance was firm, their grip steady. They knew what was coming.

The battle pressed on. The clash of wood and bone

echoed through the monastery grounds, a rhythmic, merciless cadence. Staves blurred in motion, cutting through the dim light in sweeping arcs. Grunts of exertion, the sharp crack of impact, the dull thud of bodies hitting the ground—each sound wove into the brutal symphony of war.

Ash caught sight of a novice ahead of him staggering, his breath forced from his lungs in a ragged gasp. A pitchfork had found his shoulder, the crude weapon driven deep. The boy crumpled, sent reeling backward, but his hands did not loosen around his staff. He sucked in a breath, gritted his teeth, and surged forward once more, driving his weapon into the nearest nárgrim's skull. His strike landed, but the strength behind it had waned.

Ash fought the urge to move to his aid, knowing the moment he broke formation, another gap would open. The monk ahead of him would falter soon, and Ash had to be ready to step in.

Then, through the open gates, something new entered the fray. A monk, or something that had once been a monk, strode forward with eerie calm, stepping over the twisted remains of fallen nárgrim. His eyes were pools of utter blackness, the faint glow of torchlight reflecting in them like distant stars swallowed by the void. Black threads curled and writhed along his arms, dancing like living things, coiling around his staff in serpentine waves. He lifted it, extending the tip toward the monks still locked in combat. A gesture of command. Or a warning.

Ash tensed, watching the darkness slither up the corrupted monk's staff, gathering, concentrating. The air thickened, heavy with something unnatural. The dark threads at the staff's tip twisted, spiralling faster, a storm about to break. Instinct screamed in Ash's veins.

"Down!" he bellowed, but he knew it was already too late.

The corrupted monk released the gathered power in a pulse of pure darkness, a blast of threaded void that screamed across the battlefield in front of him. Ash barely had time to react. His arm shot out, and with a thought, a barrier of black ooze coalesced before him, stretching outward in a sweeping arc. The impact struck like a hammer, rattling his bones and shoving him back a step, but the shield held.

The monks caught in the blast were not so fortunate. They collapsed to the ground, writhing in agony, clutching at themselves as though something unseen gnawed at their flesh. Yet they lived.

Ash let the shield dissipate, the lingering threads of darkness slithering back into his hand before vanishing entirely. He turned. To his left, the young monk—the one he had tried to bolster earlier—was crouched, arm raised in a feeble attempt at defence. Behind him, Kiran stared, her expression torn between awe and a touch of glee. But it was the black-eyed monk's reaction that caught Ash's attention. Surprise flickered across his face, the barest crack in his controlled veneer.

Ash did not hesitate. He stepped over his fallen brethren, closing the distance with intent. Behind him, he heard Kiran shift into position, her presence a steady reassurance at his back.

The corrupted monk did not wait for Ash to reach him. He moved first, launching into a whirlwind of motion, his quarterstaff a blur as he spun it through the air in a display of practised skill. He struck out with ruthless precision, each blow aimed to disarm, to break, to kill.

Ash met him strike for strike. Their staves collided in a rapid series of impacts, each clash sending shudders down Ash's arms. He gritted his teeth, forcing himself forward, refusing to give ground. His opponent was fast. Too fast. The blows carried the unnatural strength of something no longer entirely human.

Ash pressed harder, his muscles burning with exertion. This was no mindless nárgrim. This was something else. And if he faltered, if he gave even an inch, it would be the last mistake he ever made.

Nárgrim pressed in from Ash's flanks, their fetid breath thick with rot, but Kiran was there—quick, efficient, relentless. Her staff blurred through the air, striking with brutal precision, but Ash knew she couldn't cover both sides for long. The tide would overwhelm her.

Then another monk appeared at her side, a figure Ash barely recognized, wielding his stave with proficient ease. Together, they held the line, their movements synchronized in desperate defiance of the creatures closing in. Ash had no time to dwell on it. His focus was locked on the tainted monk before him.

Exhaustion had begun to gnaw at his limbs, his every movement a strain against the slow creep of fatigue. The other monk struck again, his quarterstaff a whirling blur of ironwood, each impact jarring down Ash's arms. His defences wavered. If he faltered now, if he hesitated for even a breath, he would fall.

Instinct took over. He didn't counter with his staff, but with something deeper, something darker. The darkness stirred within him, coiling down his arms, thickening with substance. He felt them stretch outward, slithering toward his enemy, not in thought but in need.

The monk's expression flickered—first confusion, then fear. He stepped back, sensing the unseen threads curling toward him, reaching. Ash advanced. With each step forward, the death-tendrils lengthened, closing the distance between them until they were mere inches apart. Then they struck.

The monk shuddered as the darkness latched onto

him, siphoning the strength from his body. Ash felt it—felt the rush of stolen energy surging into him, the exhaustion melting away, replaced by raw power. His limbs no longer ached. His muscles no longer burned. He drove forward, pressing the attack, forcing the monk onto his heels. Then pain—sharp, searing, real.

The world staggered sideways as Ash felt the wound tear into his ribs, white-hot agony stealing his breath. His connection to the void snapped. A quick glance downward revealed the gash, blood seeping into his robes, the blade's work clean and deep. He jerked his gaze to the side, searching for the source, and saw the monk who had defended his right crumpled on the ground, throat torn open. Dead.

Ash staggered back, struggling to regain his footing. The nárgrim lunged at his exposed side, their rusted weapon dimly lit by the flickering torchlight. He twisted, barely deflecting their blows, each movement sending a fresh wave of pain through his side. Blood slicked his robes. The wound was bad. He had to end this. Now.

Kiran shifted, her back pressing against his. She was still fighting, her every strike laced with a savagery he hadn't seen before. She moved ruthlessly, her attacks unrelenting. Ash tried to match her, but the wound drained him, slowing him, weakening him.

The enemy monk stepped forward, darkness

swirling around his staff once more. He was preparing another blast. Ash saw it in the way the dark threads coiled tighter, how the air itself seemed to tremble with anticipation. He knew they wouldn't survive another.

He would have no chance at defending himself. There would be no opportunity to brace himself for impact, or raise another shield of black void. He knew that it wouldn't be enough. This wasn't about defence. This was about ending it.

Ash exhaled, emptying himself of thought, of hesitation. He reached beyond instinct, beyond training, beyond the limitations of flesh. He reached into the abyss within. It answered.

The darkness within him did not simply erupt—it lashed out, a tide of murderous intent that cracked the air like a thunderclap. Even the monks pressing toward him faltered, instinct recoiling at the malevolent aura that bled from his form. The force of it sent Kiran to one knee, her breath stolen by the sheer violence of its release.

Ash saw nothing but blackness before him. The world had been swallowed whole. The monk who had once gained the upper hand, who had threatened to break him, now ceased to exist, blasted apart in a burst of writhing blackness. Limbs and scraps of cloth scattered into the gloom, consumed by the same force that had undone him.

Then the power drained from Ash's limbs, leaving

them hollow, useless. He collapsed, the impact jarring through his body as he barely caught himself on one trembling arm. A hand seized his shoulder, dragging him back from the fray. The monks surged forward to take his place, their ranks shifting seamlessly to close the gap he left behind.

Ash fought to steady himself as he was hauled away, his boots scraping against loose gravel. His side still burned where the blade had cut deep, but the pain was no longer the raw agony it had been. Something was changing, something was... knitting. He planted a foot behind him, wrenching his arm free, and stopped his retreat.

"Relax, we've got this," a monk muttered, pressing him against the barricade. Ash barely heard him. He exhaled sharply, steadying himself, and forced his body upright. His balance wavered, but the unnatural stitching of his wound held. He refused to look. Some part of him already knew what wove the flesh back together, and he did not want to see it. Strength, slow but undeniable, returned to his limbs.

A nárgrim broke through the monks' line, slipping past their defences with a snarl, its milky eyes fixed on him. Ash's staff was already in motion. The impact was final, the creature collapsing in a heap at his feet. He stumbled back against the barricade, breath heavy, body trembling but still standing. That was all he could do now—stand and watch.

The monastery gates remained open, and through them, the dead poured in. The ground beyond was choked with bodies, twisted and piled, an indistinguishable mass of the fallen. Most wore the tattered remnants of their former lives, but among them, Ash caught glimpses of crimson and brown—the robes of his brothers, his kin. The loss gnawed at him, but they were holding. That was more than he had dared hope.

Kiran peeled away from the melee, weaving through the chaos until she reached him. The cut on her forehead ran deep, yet it no longer bled. As Ash focused, he saw the strands—thin, black, writhing—stitching the wound closed.

"Are you alright?" she asked, scanning him with sharp intent. Her gaze flicked to the gash in his robes, to the blood drying along his side. She reached for it, but Ash caught her wrist before she could touch.

"I'm okay," he said. The words carried more importance than their simplicity suggested. His eyes locked onto hers, and she understood. Whatever had mended him, whatever had answered his unspoken need, was not something to be acknowledged here. Not yet.

She nodded once, pressing two fingers against her own temple where the wound had been. Whatever she felt, she did not speak of it.

A groan sounded behind them. Kiran turned in an

instant, staff already in motion. The nárgrim barely had time to lurch forward before she struck—three rapid, brutal blows, her movements instinctive, lethal. Ash couldn't help the small smile that curved his lips. She was no longer the girl from the monastery. She had become something far more deadly.

She turned back to him, clasping his shoulder with a firm grip, her gaze steady. Then, with a final nod, she was gone, diving back into the fray. Ash watched her go, watched the way she fought without hesitation. A formidable warrior, indeed.

The tide of nárgrim that had once poured through the open gates had finally ceased. The flow of the dead was spent, their numbers dwindling to what remained inside the monastery's walls. Yet the battle had not ended. Weapons still clashed against the tangled forms of the undead. The monks fought on, cutting down the last of the nárgrim with grim determination, while others had abandoned the front line to drag the wounded to whatever semblance of safety the buildings behind them could provide.

Ash stood amid the wreckage of the battle, his breath heavy, his body aching, but it was the weight in his chest that threatened to break him. The monastery's courtyard, once a place of quiet contemplation, had become a graveyard. The dead lay in heaps, some twisted and broken, others motionless yet eerily intact, as if merely waiting for some unseen command to rise again. And among them, the robes of the fallen monks stood out in stark contrast to the lifeless husks of their enemy.

Near the gate, Doran fought along side one of his soldiers. The others—those who had followed them up the pass—were nowhere to be seen. Perhaps they were among the wounded, pulled back from the carnage to be tended in the dim lamplight of the monastery halls. But Ash knew better. Inexperience had been a fatal burden tonight. The men who had put their faith in this fight, who had stood alongside the monks in their defence, now lay scattered among the fallen.

The clash of weapons still rang through the night, the snarls of the nárgrim mixing with the grunts and cries of those who fought to outlast them. Ash clenched his fists, a deep frustration burning through his limbs. He wanted to fight. Every part of him screamed to throw himself back into the fray, to cut down whatever remained of the enemy, to make this slaughter mean something. But his body betrayed him. He remained where he was, back braced against the wooden barricade, his breath slow, controlled, waiting for the strength to return.

The thought came suddenly, a cold rush of panic that sent his gaze snapping across the battlefield. He turned sharply, scanning the monks, the wounded, the fallen. His pulse hammered in his ears, drowning out the monotonous clash of weapons.

Where was Kacl?

Chapter 22:
Kael

Ash seized the arm of a young monk rushing past, his grip firm but not unkind. The boy startled, wide-eyed, the flicker of fear unmistakable in his expression. It took Ash a moment to understand—how he must look to them, battered, bloodied, his eyes shadowed with something darker than exhaustion.

He forced a smile, a projected attempt to soften the tension knotting the monk's shoulders. The boy hesitated, his stance loosening ever so slightly, then stepped closer. Ash pushed himself upright, using the barricade for support, his movements heavy, cautious. The monk instinctively reached to help him, but Ash shook his head, a silent refusal that sent the boy stepping back.

"The ruins they uncovered here," Ash said, his voice rough, laced with the remnants of battle. "Where is the entrance?"

The monk's expression froze, his face suddenly blank. His gaze darted left, then right, as though searching for an escape. When he finally turned back to Ash, his lips parted, but no words came. Silence stretched between them, awkward and uncertain, before he finally found his voice.

"I—I'm sorry, sir," he stammered, the words

tumbling out in a rush. "We were told not to speak of them. To anyone."

His fingers fidgeted with the hem of his sleeve, his discomfort laid bare in every small, nervous gesture. Ash didn't have time for it.

"This is important," he said, the edge in his tone sharpening. "Tell me where the entrance is."

The monk hesitated. Ash exhaled, his patience thinning. He locked eyes with the boy, silently asserting his authority. The monk swallowed hard, then nodded quickly, caving under the unspoken pressure.

"It's behind the library," he said, his voice shaking. "They were planning to expand the building, but when they started clearing the stone, they found an entrance."

Ash barely acknowledged the response before he pushed off from the barricade, staggering in the direction the monk had indicated. The wound in his side still throbbed, but it was no longer the searing agony it had been before. He stumbled, caught himself, then moved on, taking every opportunity to brace against the walls of the buildings that lined his path. Each step sent fresh fire through his ribs, but he clenched his jaw and pressed forward.

The library came into view at last. He knew it well—had known it since he was a boy, when he had spent more time lost in its tomes than listening to the droning voices of his teachers. The memory struck him as strangely ironic now. He hadn't picked up a book in years.

Rounding the back of the building, he found the entrance. A crude rope barricade had been erected around the site, and scattered chunks of stone lay strewn across the ground. A simple wooden sign leaned against the wall just inside the opening, the words *KEEP OUT* hastily painted across its surface. Ash ignored it.

He stepped past the rope, picking his way over the rubble with care. As he reached the threshold, he paused, turning to glance back at the monastery. The buildings blocked much of his view, making it impossible to know for certain whether this was the same place he had exited in his dream. But in his gut, he knew. This was it.

Without another thought, he turned and descended into the darkness below.

Ash reached for the nearest torch hanging from the wall, yanked it from its sconce, and let it drop to the floor at his feet. The iron handle clattered against stone, the sound swallowed by the heavy silence of the underground. Shrugging off his pack, he rifled through its contents, fingers brushing past the weight of the book nestled inside. He had nearly forgotten about it.

Finding his flint and steel, he worked quickly, striking until a shower of sparks caught the resin on the torch. Flames licked up the wood, casting flickering shadows that stretched and danced across the walls. He slung the pack back over his shoulder, seized the torch, and pressed forward. There was no certainty that Kael was here, but his intuition told him otherwise.

After the battle, when Ash realized Kael was missing, the truth had struck him with humiliating clarity. The attack on the monastery had never been meant to conquer—it had been a diversion. A well-orchestrated misdirection to grant Kael the time he needed to slip inside unnoticed, to do whatever he had come here to do.

Ash clenched his jaw at the thought, at his own failure to see it sooner. He only prayed he wasn't too late.

What was Kael after? What could possibly be worth all of this—the blood spilled, the chaos sown? The question gnawed at Ash as he moved deeper into the ruinous corridor, the torchlight exposing the layers of time and decay that had settled over the place.

The passage opened into a chamber he recognized. An entrance hall, perhaps, once meant to welcome guests in some long-forgotten age. Now, overturned tables lay scattered like the corpses of broken beasts, chairs strewn in careless disarray. He scanned the room, searching for anything out of place, but as expected, the monastery officials had long since stripped it of anything of value.

So why had Kael come down here? Ash frowned. If the monks had already scoured these ruins, then Kael wouldn't have wasted his time searching for scraps. Either he knew of something they had missed, or he was after something too large to be removed—something still waiting in the dark.

His fingers tightened around the torch as he pressed on, following the path burned into his mind from his dream. Another corridor. Another room, its skeletal remains familiar. He was getting close. He needed to find the chamber where he had seen the explosion. That had to be where Kael was.

At last, he entered the hallway where his dream had first begun. The familiarity sent a cold tremor down his spine. He passed an open doorway, catching a glimpse inside—a room where once there had been treasures, books, a map. Now, stripped bare. Exactly as he had expected.

He moved on. He knew he was close now. The air thickened with the strain of anticipation as he neared the grand chamber—the place where, in his dream, he had witnessed the world unravel. He stepped inside, his torchlight spilling across the vast expanse. Towering pillars stood like sentinels, the melted remains of the decorative filigree that once lined the walls now glinted in the flickering glow as globular masses at the base of the walls. The floor, the walls, every detail mirrored what he had seen before. But there was no Kael.

Ash turned in place, scanning every shadow, every

corner. The room was empty. Where was he, Ash thought to himself.

Ash crossed the chamber, his boots scuffing against the dust-laden stone, making for the arched passage at the far side. Other hallways veered off in competing directions, each a yawning maw leading deeper into the ruin, but he ignored them. This one stood directly in his path, as though waiting for him. Perhaps it was intuition, or perhaps simple haste. He had no time for deliberation. He had to move.

Corridors twisted into rooms, which fed into more hallways, splitting and shifting like veins in the corpse of some long-dead beast. Ash pressed forward, forcing speed over caution, his breath steady but his pulse quickening. The layout made no sense, and it wasn't long before he realized he was lost. That wasn't the concern. The others would come for him eventually. What gnawed at him was the fear that he wouldn't find Kael in time. That whatever foul design his old companion was enacting would reach its conclusion before Ash could stop it.

Then, a voice—distant, barely more than a whisper, slipping through the meandering corridors like a wraith. It shivered against the walls, stretching and warping as it echoed through the hollows of the forgotten city that lay within the mountain beneath the monastery. The words were indiscernible, but the direction was clear enough.

Ash pivoted left, crossing the chamber in long, quick strides. A stairwell yawned open before him, descending into darkness. His fingers tightened around the torch as he moved downward, the flame casting wild shadows against the walls, his staff clicking against the stairs as he descended. He had hoped Kael would be easy to find, that this pursuit would end in swift confrontation. But that hope had already begun to crumble.

At the base of the stairs, a corridor split into three separate paths. He slowed, glancing down each one. No clues. No signposts. He lifted the torch, pressing its burning end to the wall and drawing a crude arrow in soot, marking the path to his right before proceeding down it.

The voice returned. Louder now. Clearer. Curses, spat into the dark with the sharp edge of frustration.

A small smirk tugged at Ash's lips. So Kael had encountered an obstacle. Good. Whatever he was trying to accomplish wasn't going as smoothly as he had hoped. Ash picked up his pace, following the voice, stepping lightly to avoid the loose stones scattered along the floor.

The corridor bent sharply. A glow seeped from beyond its final stretch, illuminating the entrance to a vast chamber ahead. Ash tossed his torch to the ground, letting the fire sputter out against the stone. No need for unnecessary light now. His grip tightened around his staff as he crept forward, keeping close to the wall, folding himself into the shadows.

He reached the threshold and peered inside. What he saw stole the breath from his lungs.

The chamber stretched far beneath him, stairs spiralling downward along the walls to his left, leading to a massive, hovering sphere of glass that pulsed with eerie energy. The orb hung just above the stone floor, rising at least thirty feet high, its smooth surface veined with cracks of flickering light. Inside, a thick, slithering ooze coiled upon itself, writhing like a thing alive, a slow, sinuous dance of darkness. Ash barely had a moment to take it in before the orb surged to life.

The ooze within churned violently, twisting into ever-darkening tendrils. The floor trembled. A low hum filled the air, reverberating through Ash's bones. He caught himself against the wall, bracing as the vibrations deepened into a low, shuddering quake.

"Yes!"

The exultant cry rang out from beyond the orb. This had to be Kael. Ash squinted through the haze of torchlight and flickering threads of darkness. Kael was speaking again, lost in fevered murmurs, but the words refused to carry to Ash's ears. He didn't need to hear them.

His gaze remained fixed on the orb, on the writhing mass inside. The strands of darkness were shifting, merging, forming shapes he recognized. Not just silken threads, not just ebony tendrils, but something more—something alive. Ash had seen this before.

The darkened tendrils from his vision. The swirling core of malice from his dream. But here, now, it was something far greater, something real. Something monstrous.

Ash slipped from the shadow of the entrance, his movements careful, gauged. He descended down the staircase. Every step carried the risk of revealing his position, but waiting was no longer an option. He kept his gaze locked on the chamber, searching for Kael. He had come too far to be caught unprepared.

The massive orb churned with a violence that sent tremors through the air. The blackness within it thrashed like a caged beast, battering against unseen barriers, straining to break free. The very air pulsed in rhythm with its rage, hammering against Ash's skull with an unbearable force. A sudden spike of agony sent him to one knee, a strangled cry rising to his lips. But as quickly as it had come, the force receded, drawn inward. The dark tendrils slowed, dissipating once more into the swirling mist.

Kael's voice sliced through the silence, raw with frustration. "No, no, no!"

Ash forced himself to his feet and moved swiftly down the remaining steps. Reaching the floor, he spotted Kael at the far end of the chamber, hunched over a stone pedestal. A heavy tome lay open before him, his fingers delicately shifting black crystals across a strange contraption Ash couldn't immediately place.

Then Kael stilled. His eyes flicked up, catching movement. He set the crystal down with an almost reverent care and straightened. For a moment, confusion flickered across his face.

"The battle is over already? I had hoped for more time." His voice was calm, but there was an edge beneath it. He studied Ash, his expression shifting. "Shall we make this simple? You let me kill you, and we spare ourselves the trouble—" His words faltered as Ash advanced, his staff held at the ready.

Kael's eyes narrowed, then widened slightly. He lifted a finger, pointing at Ash's face. "She has touched you with her gift, I see." His voice carried something new—curiosity. He took a step forward, his lips curling into something that was almost a smile. "If you have tasted her power, perhaps you might be of use to me yet." He extended a hand, fingers splayed, a silent command to halt. "You will serve me, I think."

Ash scoffed, his grip tightening on his staff. "What madness is this, Kael?"

The name landed like a hammer. Kael's head tilted, his brow furrowing, as if he were sifting through memories long buried. Finally, he exhaled sharply and shook his head.

“Who are you, monk?”

Ash forced a smile, trying to ease the coiled tension in the room. “It’s me, Kael. Don’t you remember?” He loosened his hold on the quarterstaff just enough to lift an open palm, a gesture of peace.

Kael's eyes darkened. "Ashram Stormrider," he murmured, the name rolling off his tongue like a forgotten tale. He took a step back. “So, you've finally come to join my cause?” He let the question hang for only a moment before shaking his head. “No, I doubt that. You were always the obedient one, weren’t you? The loyal student. The follower.”

Ash remained silent, his instincts sharpening as tendrils of darkness began to coil around Kael’s arms.

“What are you doing, Kael?” Ash’s voice was firm but lacked anger. There was still a sliver of hope, a chance to pull him back from whatever abyss he had stepped into. “This thing is dangerous. I believe it was responsible for the fall of the Ancients.”

Kael's lips twitched into a smirk, cold and knowing. “Of course it was.” His fingers flexed, and the darkness around him pulsed. “That is what I intend to do here.”

Ash stared at him, horrified. He had expected arrogance, perhaps even delusion. But this? This was something else.

“You want to destroy everything?” The words tasted

bitter as he spoke them.

Kael tilted his head, amused. "Everything? No, not everything. Just the world as it is."

Ash exhaled slowly, his mind sharpening. There would be no reasoning with him. Whatever man he had once known was gone. He had tried for words. Now, it would come to something far older, something more primal.

Ash reached inward, drawing upon the power coiled within him. Dark threads slithered at the edges of his vision, drawn to his will.

Kael watched him, smiling. "Ah. There it is."

Ash's voice was edged with urgency. "I watched a group of men lose control of this thing, Kael. How do you plan to harness it alone?" He had no real interest in the answer. His words were meant as a blade, not an inquiry—an attempt to cut through Kael's delusions and reason him out of this madness.

Kael twitched at that, his head cocking slightly. The reaction was slight, but Ash caught it. His mention of the men from the vision had unsettled Kael. Confusion flickered across his face, though only for an instant. Then, just as quickly, he smoothed it over with a smirk.

"This glass prison is what they fashioned to contain and manipulate the Void Weave," Kael said, his voice dripping with condescension. "It slipped from their grasp, unruly, indomitable—too vast for them to hold. But they lacked what I possess." He reached to the podium and plucked one of the black crystals between two fingers, holding it up as if displaying a sacred relic. "Taken from the Shattered Lands of the West. Not of this world, they say. The remnants of the god Vorrakoth, after his betrayal and murder."

The name meant nothing to Ash. No such deity had been mentioned in the monastery's teachings, nor in the dusty tomes he had studied in the archives. Another thing to investigate—if he survived this encounter.

Kael placed the crystal back with care. When he turned again, darkness clung to him. Wisps of shadowy threads curled from his blackened eyes, writhing like hungry things in the air.

"Once I have gathered enough of Marrathis' power in this vessel," Kael continued, "I will bind it—lock it within the orb using the essence of these crystals. The Ancients attempted the same, but with mundane crystals, flawed materials. It was not enough. The power slipped free. These, however… these will hold." His hand gestured to the crystals with a confidence that sent a cold shudder through Ash.

Ash's fingers tightened around his quarterstaff. "You would end all life to achieve your goal." His voice was quiet, yet filled with understanding. A truth he wished he had not uncovered.

Kael exhaled a soft laugh, shaking his head. "Life always ends, Ashram. The Ancients? Merely the last chapter of an old story. Before them, there were others, and before them, still more. The cycle is inevitable." He spread his arms in a mockery of enlightenment. "I do not seek to end it, only to control it. To dictate the shape of the next age. To craft a world in my image."

There was no hesitation. Kael moved like a striking serpent, black threads whipping from his arms, rods of darkness lancing toward Ash. Instinct took hold. Ash's staff snapped up, and before he could consciously will it, the void within him responded. The darkness coiled up his weapon, spread outward, and deflected Kael's onslaught with a twisting arc.

Kael halted, blinking as though seeing Ash for the first time. Then, a slow smile crept across his lips, hungry and full of something like admiration. "You've learned to wield it," he murmured, head tilting in contemplation. "And with such ease. That is… unexpected."

Ash remained silent, unwilling to give Kael even a sliver of insight into his own ignorance. The truth was, he had no idea how he had done it. The power had simply answered, moving to his will without his command. Was it Marrathis? Was she guiding him? He reached inward but felt no trace of the goddess, no whisper of her presence.

Kael did not wait for an answer. He summoned a staff from the very void within him, its shape flickering at the edges as though struggling to decide whether it was real. And then he lunged.

Their weapons met in a thunderous crack, tendrils of darkness bursting outward only to recoil, slithering back to their masters. Blow after blow, their staves blurred in motion, striking with inhuman speed. They moved in a confined, deadly dance, circling, twisting, each attack answered with equal ferocity. The chamber rang with the piercing echoes of their clash, the darkness pulsing with the rhythm of their battle. And Ash knew, with a certainty that chilled him, that only one of them would leave this room alive.

The dance of combat wove a deadly rhythm through the chamber, each step dictated by the clash of a quarterstaff. One of hardened wood against one of a void-forged material. Ash and Kael moved in precise arcs around the perimeter, the glass orb standing silent and unyielding at the chamber's heart. Every impact sent shivering ripples across its surface, warping the reflections within. It wasn't glass, Ash realized. It had the appearance of glass, but something in the way it pulsed, in the way it drank the light rather than refracted it, told him otherwise. The revelation cost him.

Pain lanced through his thigh as Kael's staff struck

home. Ash staggered, barely catching himself before he crumpled, breath hissing through clenched teeth. He forced himself upright, but his leg throbbed, already threatening to betray him. A foolish lapse in concentration. He would not survive another. Kael fought like a man accustomed to winning, his strikes sharp and relentless, his stance one of absolute control. Ash had not faced an opponent of his calibre in years.

Blow after blow, each strike Ash delivered met Kael's defences with effortless precision. A kick aimed at the ribs—blocked. A swift sweep of the quarterstaff—parried with a flick of the wrist. The contest should have felt like a battle of equals, but it wasn't. Kael was toying with him. The realization settled in Ash's gut like a stone.

Kael's amusement was plain, his smirk barely concealed between attacks. Then, without warning, the darkness itself struck. A tendril of black ooze lashed from Kael's form, slamming into Ash's ribs. It was not physical, yet it sent a deep, twisting ache through him, sapping his breath. He recoiled, barely keeping his stance as Kael laughed. Another tendril struck, catching him across the temple, sending stars bursting behind his eyes. Then another—his hip. A fourth—his shoulder. The barrage drove him backward, his balance crumbling. Ash was losing. Worse, he was outmatched in every way.

He gritted his teeth and forced himself forward.

Losing did not mean surrender. He moved with desperate speed, pressing the attack, but no matter how swift, Kael was faster. No matter how unpredictable, Kael anticipated each move. Ash tried to retaliate in kind, summoning the darkness within him, but Kael met it with ease, swatting his void-born attacks aside as though they were nothing.

Fatigue set in, creeping through his limbs like a slow, insidious poison. But it was not natural. The realization dawned too late—Kael was leeching his strength, draining him with every exchange. The darkness that clung to Ash, the ones he had barely begun to understand, were being unravelled, siphoned into his foe. He fought against it, shoving Kael's influence away, but the effort cost him. His body wavered, and then he fell.

He raised his staff in defence, expecting the final blow. It never came.

Kael loomed over him, smiling. "Come now, Ashram," he murmured. "Join me. Help me shape this world into something beautiful." His voice was a serpent's whisper, insidious, inviting.

Ash forced himself to his feet. Before he could respond, a flicker of movement behind Kael caught his eye.

A sharp crack split the air as Kael lurched forward, his breath hitching. He spun, reacting with a jab of his staff, but his strike met another weapon in a resounding clash. The moment of distraction was all Ash needed. He surged forward and drove his staff into Kael's ribs with all his remaining strength. He felt the impact shudder through bone, felt something give beneath the force of his strike. Kael staggered, turning to face Ash, revealing Kael's other opponent. Kiran.

She was relentless, her strikes swift and exact, but Kael deflected each one, his defences near impenetrable. Ash did not waste the opportunity. He pressed in from the flank, landing blow after punishing blow against Kael's legs, his back, his shoulder—driving him toward the wall. Kael snarled, whipping his staff around in a vicious arc, but Ash met the strike and turned it aside with ease.

Kiran was unyielding. She struck the moment Kael faltered, her attacks coming in rapid succession, giving him no chance to recover. Kael retaliated, but she was quicker. Ash saw his opening and took it. He fought with renewed fury, forcing Kael to split his focus.

Kael faltered. His staff wavered, the darkness unravelling. Then, with a sharp breath, he collapsed to the floor. The weapon in his hands dissipated into nothingness, fading into the very darkness he had commanded. He raised his arms in weak defence, his breath ragged.

Kiran stood over him, her stance poised for another strike. Kael flinched, shying away. For the first time, there was a look of fear in his eyes.

Kiran raised her staff, her breath steady, her grip

unyielding. One final strike, and it would be over. But before she could bring the weapon down, Ash lifted a hand, staying the execution. Kael had answers—answers they needed.

Kiran hesitated only a moment before lowering her staff, her fingers tightening around the wood with barely restrained fury. She shook her head, her expression grim, her gaze burning with something Ash had never seen in her before.

"He is too dangerous to be allowed to live," she said, her voice low, steady. "We can't imprison him. He'll escape, and we'll be right back where we started." Disappointment flickered in her eyes, sharpening the edges of her features. "You know this as well as I do."

She wasn't wrong. Ash knew it the moment she said it. They could bind Kael, shackle him in iron, wrap him in wards—but it wouldn't hold. Even now, weakened, bleeding, Kael was beyond them, and given time, he would slip his chains like a phantom in the night. He would return, stronger, deadlier, and the cycle would begin again. But Ash needed answers.

He gripped his quarterstaff, stepped forward, and raised it high. Kael, half-collapsed against the stone, only laughed. Blood painted his lips, trailing in thin rivulets down his chin. The sound was hollow, mirthless, yet it carried a promise—a promise that sent a slow, crawling dread through Ash's spine. Then the change began.

Kael's flesh darkened, his edges fraying like ink spilled into water. His form grew transparent, dissolving into twisting tendrils of darkness. Ash struck without hesitation, his quarterstaff slicing through the dissipating figure, but his weapon met nothing but the stone below. No resistance, no impact—only mist, unravelling like breath on a winter morning. In seconds, Kael was gone, his body breaking apart into spectral strands that slithered along the chamber walls, slipping into the cracks, vanishing into the darkness beyond. All that remained were his bloodied robes, crumpled on the cold stone floor.

Kiran lunged, her own dark threads coiling in pursuit, but Ash called her back. There was no point in chasing him. The fight was over, for now.

"He's gone," Ash said.

Kiran spun toward him, eyes blazing. "And we're letting him go?" Her anger was raw and unfiltered.

"There's no 'letting' about it." Ash exhaled, his grip tightening on his staff. "We can't fight him like this. Not yet. He won't come for us here, not after this. This has been a set back for him. That's a victory."

Kiran stared at him as if seeing him for the first time, searching his face for something—certainty, perhaps, or resolve. She found neither.

Ash turned, moving across the chamber toward the

pedestal on the far side of the room. He dropped his pack to the floor, flipping it open. The book Kael had been using was still there, its darkened pages thick with the aura of old power. He slipped it inside, then reached for the obsidian crystals embedded in the grooves of the pedestal's surface. The moment his fingers closed around them, a pulse of something ancient and malignant shuddered through him. Not a weapon. A conduit. He pocketed them anyway.

Kiran followed but said nothing, her frustration simmering beneath her silence. He knew the questions would come later, but for now, she let the subject rest.

"You're angry with me," Ash said, fastening the pack shut. He didn't need to look at her to know she was nodding. "I made a mistake. I underestimated him."

"He should be dead," she said, her voice quiet but firm. She wasn't looking at him now; her gaze was fixed on the bloodied robes left behind, her jaw tight. "He's responsible for so many deaths, Ash. He should have paid for them." A pause.

"Seanne is dead because of him." The words hit like a hammer bringing pangs of guilt, but before Ash could respond, she grabbed his shoulder and wrenched him around to face her."And now Rowan is, too."

For a moment, Ash said nothing. Rowan. The deep sorrow of it pressed against him, heavy and suffocating. Rowan had been a warrior. A veteran. A man who had survived more battles than Ash could count. And yet, he had fallen.

Ash exhaled sharply, slumping against the wall behind him. He rubbed a hand across his face, feeling the grime, the sweat, the exhaustion pressing in. Too many losses. Too many deaths. And yet, he had spared the one responsible.

"I know," Ash said, barely above a whisper. "But this isn't over. We'll find him. And when we do, he will pay."

Kiran stood over him for a long moment, searching his face again. This time, he met her gaze, and for the first time since the battle ended, he truly saw the grief in her eyes. She was hurting, but so was he. His own pain was just quieter, dulled by the barriers of time, by the weight of all the other deaths before this one.

Finally, she reached out, offering him a hand. He took it.

"I'll hold you to that promise," she said, voice steady but laced with something deeper. She turned and strode toward the stairs, back toward the surface. Ash followed, struggling to keep pace, his steps heavy with exhaustion.

They moved in silence through the ruined halls, through shadowed corridors. The stone beneath their feet was cold, the air stale, but ahead, beyond the threshold, the first light of dawn bled through the cracks, waiting to greet them. Neither of them spoke. There was nothing left to say. Not yet.

Chapter 23: All That Remains

Ash stepped out of the ruins into the pale light of morning, blinking against the sudden brightness. The cool air bit at his skin as a damp mist clung to his form. Kiran walked ahead, her steps brisk, her silence deeper than the ruins they'd left behind. She was angry, though she didn't say it aloud. He couldn't blame her. He wasn't particularly pleased with how things had unfolded either. But there was nothing to be done about it now—except press forward.

Kael had escaped, but Ash had taken something from him. The book. The black crystals. Artifacts the fallen monk had carried with him into the ruins. Whatever their purpose, they were vital to his plans, and now they were in Ash's possession. That had to count for something. He could only hope it was enough to throw Kael off balance, to delay whatever horror he intended to unleash.

They rounded the back of the monastery grounds, and the battlefield stretched before them. The rising sun cast long shadows over the carnage, its light struggling to burn away the thick morning mist. The few torches that remained flickering from the night's battle barely illuminated the grim scene—bodies strewn in tangled heaps, the dead indistinguishable at first glance from the abominations they had fought. Here and there, survivors moved among the fallen, separating their own from the twisted remains of the nárgrim, laying them in neat rows.

Ash exhaled slowly. Too many had died.

Most of them had likely been novices, young and untested, barely prepared for a fight of this magnitude. He had known that even before the battle began, but the reality of it now lay in front of him in blood and broken bodies. He felt the pang in his chest tighten. No one was guaranteed a long life, but that did little to dull the sorrow of seeing one ended too soon.

Ahead, Celest was dragging a body across the damp earth, her movements sluggish, her limbs trembling with exhaustion. When she saw them approach, she straightened, though it was clear the effort cost her. She swayed slightly, as if only now remembering how heavy her own body had become.

"You're alive," she breathed, relief breaking through the weariness in her face. A smile tugged at her lips, but it was thin, stretched too tight. "I didn't see you after the fighting. I was afraid I'd find you buried under the bodies somewhere."

"We should have told you," Kiran admitted. "I saw Ash disappear behind the buildings and went after him."

Celest said nothing at first. She simply stepped forward and pulled Kiran into a firm embrace.

Kiran stiffened, clearly unprepared for the gesture. For all her fire in battle, she had never been one for open displays of affection. But after a beat, she relented, resting her chin lightly on Celest's shoulder before pulling away.

"We found Kael," she said, her voice quiet but edged with frustration. "We fought him. He was powerful—too powerful. We almost had him, but..." She hesitated, her gaze flickering toward Ash for the briefest of moments before she looked away. "He slipped through our fingers." She had left something out.

Ash said nothing. He didn't need to. Kiran hadn't told Celest the part where Kael could have been finished, the moment when Ash hesitated.

Celest studied them both for a long moment, then nodded. "I'm just glad you're alive," she said. "We've lost too many friends already."

This time, Kiran was the one who reached out. She wrapped her arms around Celest, and they stood there in the growing light, sharing a grief that words could not mend.

Ash let them be. His gaze drifted downward to the body Celest had been carrying. A young man, barely more than a boy. Blood crusted his robes, dark against pale, lifeless skin. The recognition pained him.

It was the nervous novice who had stood beside him before the battle, the one who had barely been able to hold his weapon steady. The one Ash had promised to watch over.

A slow, hollow guilt settled in his bones. He had no memory of the boy after the fighting started. Had he fallen early? Had he even stood a chance?

Ash clenched his jaw, but the tension remained, pressing down, dragging his breath shallow. He had promised to watch his back. But the boy had died alone. And there was nothing he could do to change that.

Ash forced himself to look away from the fallen novice, trying to silence the quiet voice of guilt gnawing at the edges of his thoughts. Casualties were a part of war. He had seen far worse during the Great War against the western kingdoms—entire companies slaughtered, comrades turned to corpses in the space of a breath. Many of them had been young, just like the monks lying motionless on the battlefield now. But he had never promised them he would watch their backs. That was the difference.

He exhaled sharply, dragging his focus forward, scanning the shifting remnants of the battlefield until his gaze settled on a familiar figure. Rennick stood near the monastery's edge, speaking with Headmaster Calder, the older monk leaning subtly against a young attendant who braced his arm for support.

Ash reached out, tapping Kiran and Celest on their

arms before nodding toward the monks. "I need to speak with them." He didn't wait for a response.

As he strode across the bloodied field, another monk passed him, struggling under the weight of a young woman's lifeless body. The sight twisted something in his chest. Too many fallen. The words came unbidden, low under his breath.

Rennick's conversation faltered as he noticed Ash approaching. The monk's face, drawn with exhaustion, held an unspoken question. Ash inclined his head in brief acknowledgement before speaking, his tone sharper than intended.

"We need to talk about the device in the ruins." His voice carried an edge, the burden of everything that had transpired pressing into the words. "That's what Kael came here for. That's why all these people died."

Calder and Rennick exchanged uneasy glances, their expressions shifting from confusion to grim realization.

"That's impossible," Rennick said. "How would Kael even know about it? We only discovered it recently."

Ash folded his arms, his brow furrowing. "I don't know. Maybe a loose tongue. A novice mentioning it to a visitor. A rumour that spread beyond these walls." He was speculating, but it didn't matter. The damage had been done.

Shrugging his pack from his shoulders, Ash set it on

the ground and placed his staff beside it. He dug through its contents before pulling free the tome Kael had carried into the ruins. The leather binding was stiff beneath his fingers, old but well-preserved. He held it out to Calder.

"Maybe this has the answers." He met the Headmaster's gaze. "Kael had it with him while he was inside."

Rennick's expression darkened as he glanced at the book, then back to Ash. "Kael was in the ruins?" He hesitated, his gaze shifting toward the monastery gates where the remains of the fallen monk still lay. "I thought the one you fought—"

Ash cut him off with a shake of his head. "No. The monk we fought was not him. The entire battle was just a diversion. A ruse to keep us occupied while Kael slipped in unnoticed. He activated the device while we were too busy fighting to stop him."

Rennick's shoulders tensed. "He activated it?" His disbelief was echoed in Calder's expression, the older monk gripping the book as though it might crumble under his touch.

"We've tried everything to determine its function," Calder admitted. "Nothing we've done has had any effect."

Whatever Kael had learned, whatever he had awakened, the monastery scholars had never come close to understanding it. That alone was unsettling.

Calder handed the book back, and Ash carefully tucked it into his pack, mindful of the delicate pages. The knowledge inside was priceless, but he suspected it was also dangerous.

Straightening, he locked eyes with Rennick. "That device needs to be destroyed," he said, his voice quiet but firm. "It's too dangerous to keep here. We've reason to believe Kael isn't working alone. There are others who want it just as badly as he does."

Rennick's expression hardened. He understood what Ash was implying.

"We can't afford to wait," Ash continued. "If it remains, more will come for it. And next time, we might not be able to stop them."

"We don't believe it can be destroyed," Rennick admitted, his voice heavy with resignation. He lowered his gaze, deep in thought, as though searching for an answer in the stones beneath his feet. "We tested the Divine Mother's power against it—threw everything we had at the damn thing—but no matter what we hurled at it, it absorbed the force like it was nothing. It didn't crack, didn't weaken. Just stood there, untouched, as if mocking us."

Calder, standing beside him, nodded in solemn agreement. The dim morning light deepened the lines on his face, the brunt of years and knowledge pressing into his frame. "I've read everything I could find on the Void

Weave," he said, his voice unsteady. "Compiled what I learned in that book I gave you earlier. But nothing—nothing—mentions this device." His gaze drifted toward the sky, as if he might find guidance in the heavens. If he did, none was forthcoming.

Ash exhaled sharply, his frustration mounting. "Then we bury it," he said, turning to where the ruins lay in the shadow of the buildings at the far end of the monastery's grounds. "If we can't destroy it, we make sure no one else can get to it. Collapse the entire structure if we have to." His thoughts turned to Kael. The bastard had already slipped away once. Ash wouldn't risk him coming back for whatever dark task he had in mind. "And we spread a rumour—a cave-in, an accident, something to make anyone looking for it believe it's lost." He wasn't sure if that was how Kael had learned of it in the first place, but if deception could keep him away, then they'd use it.

Rennick considered that, then let out a slow breath. "It could work," he admitted, but his expression darkened as his gaze swept across the field of the dead. "But we have another problem—these bodies. We always build a pyre for our fallen, but there are too many this time. If we burn them, we'll use up every last reserve of dried wood we have. And without it, we won't survive the winter."

Ash didn't need to be told that the ground here was too hard to dig graves. He had lived at Dawn's End long enough to know that the frozen rock of the mountains didn't yield to shovels. Burials had never been an option. He remembered the last funeral pyre he had attended here as a novice—a monk lost to an accident, the entire monastery gathered in solemn silence as the flames carried him to the next life. Ash hadn't known the man well, but he had watched, and he had remembered.

He let his gaze drift across the battlefield once more. The bodies of the fallen were scattered in grotesque heaps—monks, novices, nárgrim alike. A sight that should never have stained these sacred grounds. Then, beyond them, he saw Doran moving toward Celest and Kiran, and something in the moment reminded him of Doran's own fallen soldiers, men who had followed them into battle only to be left behind on the ground, in the carnage.

"We take the bodies," Ash said, the words coming as certainty settled in him, "and we move them into the ruins. All of them. Then we bring the ruins down. Let them rest together, sealed away from the world." He turned to Calder, meeting the old man's weary gaze. "And when it's done, we build a monument. Something to honour them. Those who fought and fell here deserve to be remembered."

Calder studied him for a long moment, then nodded. It was a slow movement, filled with grief, but also acceptance. He turned to Rennick. "See that it's done."

Rennick gave a curt nod, already shifting his focus

to the grim task ahead, and Calder, saying nothing more, turned and made his way back toward his quarters, his gait heavy with exhaustion.

Ash watched him go, then turned back to Rennick. He reached out, grasping the monk's shoulder in a firm hold. There was something he wanted to say—thanks for standing beside him in the fight, sorrow for the losses they had suffered—but the words wouldn't come. There were too many, or maybe too few.

Rennick seemed to understand. He pressed a firm hand to Ash's shoulder in return, holding it there for a moment before nodding. Then, without a word, he turned back to the bodies, and Ash left him to his duty, heading off to find Celest and Kiran once more.

Ash found Kiran and Celest still speaking with Doran and the lone soldier who remained at his side. The immensity of the night's losses hung over them all, unspoken but understood. Ash approached, his expression solemn, and offered his condolences to the two surviving soldiers. Words felt insufficient, but they were all he had to give.

Turning, he gestured toward the ruins at the back of the monastery grounds. "We're moving all the bodies inside, nárgrim and monks." he said. "We'll bury them within the remains of the structure, and once it's done, Headmaster Calder has agreed to erect a monument in their honour. A reminder of their sacrifice, so it won't be forgotten." His gaze settled on Doran. "If it's acceptable to you, I'd like to see that your soldiers are laid to rest alongside ours. They stood with us. They bled with us. That makes them kin in this, and they should be honoured here as well."

Doran's voice cut through the cold morning air, sharp with unexpected anger. "I don't want my soldiers buried with those creatures!" His jaw tightened, his gaze hard. "Why would anyone want to spend eternity lying next to the enemy?" Disappointment and something close to disgust flickered across his face as he looked to Ash for an answer.

Ash met his stare without flinching. "You're thinking of them as monsters," he said, his tone was even. "But those nárgrim weren't our enemy. Not truly. They were the remains of the Ancients, twisted and reanimated by dark powers. Puppets, nothing more. Whatever honour they once held in life was stolen from them." He let the words settle, watching as the hardness in Doran's face wavered.

"If the souls of the Ancients had any awareness left," Ash continued, "they would loathe what was done to them. They would fight against it if they could. We aren't laying your men to rest beside monsters—we're returning them to the earth with warriors who, in another time, might have fought beside us."

Doran exhaled, his anger cooling, but he said nothing. He didn't have to. Ash could see the shift in his expression—the understanding, reluctant but real.

Doran glanced at his remaining man, seeking silent confirmation. The soldier gave the barest nod, and Doran turned back to Ash. "Agreed," he said. His voice was firm, but there was a thread of grief woven through it. "And what of our fallen soldier on the path up the mountain?"

Ash considered that for a moment. "I'll speak with Rennick. He'll see to it that your man's remains are found and brought back to the monastery." He reached out, clasping Doran's shoulder with a firm grip, offering what little comfort he could. Doran held his gaze for a moment, then nodded in quiet acceptance.

Ash exhaled and turned toward the gate, where Rennick was already issuing new orders to the monks. "Let's move," he said, steel creeping into his tone. "I want the bodies inside the ruins as quickly as possible. The sooner we have them sealed away, the better." Without waiting for confirmation, he strode toward the nearest of the fallen monks and crouched, taking hold of the lifeless form. The cold weight of the body pressed into his arms, but he lifted without hesitation. There would be time for rest later. For now, there was still work to do.

Chapter 24:
The Night Came

Calder stepped up beside Ash and Rennick, the young novice at his side steadying him as he leaned forward, peering into the gaping maw of the ruins. His silence carried the misery of a man standing at the edge of something he wished he could understand, something already slipping beyond his grasp. Ash and Rennick both acknowledged his presence with a nod, but no words were exchanged at first. They all simply stood there, staring into the darkness.

“It seems a shame to bury that device,” Rennick said at last, his voice quiet, almost uncertain. "We don’t even understand its potential." His gaze remained fixed on the ruins, as if he might glimpse some answer in the void.

Calder exhaled, his expression drawn with the burden of hard choices. "Ash is right. It’s too dangerous to leave exposed." He hesitated, his fingers tightening around the novice’s arm. "If Ash’s vision of the device is true, if the Ancients truly brought about their own extinction by misusing it…" He trailed off, letting the thought hang in the cold air between them. "No. I wouldn’t risk being responsible for that. Even if someone intended to use it for good—intentions don’t always dictate outcomes."

Sorrow etched itself into the old man's features. Ash understood. Calder had likely nurtured the same hope as Rennick, that the device might hold some forgotten power, some knowledge worth preserving. People always assumed the Ancients were far more advanced than the present age, that they had unlocked wonders lost to time. Was it possible this relic of theirs could be turned toward something other than destruction? Ash had no answer, and he doubted anyone else did either.

Rennick said nothing, though Ash could sense the hesitancy in him. The decision had been made, and he would follow it without protest. His silence spoke volumes. Should Calder pass in the days ahead, would Rennick leave the device buried? Ash hoped so. The alternative was unthinkable.

The sound of boots scuffing against stone drew Ash's attention. Kiran and Celest emerged from the ruins, speaking quietly to one another as they approached. Kiran dusted off her robes and gave Ash a slight nod. There was distance in her gaze, something unresolved still lingering between them. He could hardly blame her. In time, perhaps, they would find a way through it.

"That was the last of them," Celest announced, breaking the heavy silence. "A crew of senior monks are already inside, preparing wards to be detonated. Shouldn't be much longer now."

Calder gave her a solemn nod of appreciation before turning back to Ash. "If not for you and your crew, we would have been caught entirely off guard. Our losses would have been far greater—we might not have survived at all." He shook his head, his gaze dropping to the earth as though he could see the cost of the battle written in the soil beneath his feet. "And if Kael had succeeded… gods only know what ruin he would have unleashed."

A chill ran through Ash, and he wasn't sure whether it was the value of Calder's words or the creeping cold of the setting sun behind the walls. Celest shivered as well, though she said nothing. They had been at this for hours, pausing only once to eat when Rennick had given the order. Now, with night closing in, exhaustion gnawed at Ash's edges.

Before he had a chance to express his need for sleep, Ash watched a group of monks glide out from the darkness of the ruins entrance. One of the monks spotted them and moved towards where they stood, while the other monks headed off into the heart of the monastery. No doubt they sought the comfort of a bed, just as Ash now did.

"Sir, all the wards are in place, just as you asked." the monk said as he came to a halt in front of Ash and his companions. Ash could see the weariness written all across the man's face. It had been a long couple days for everyone at Dawn's End.

"Wonderful, that will be all." Calder said to the exhausted looking monk, then placed a gentle hand on the man's shoulder and gave him a nod. The younger monk returned the nod then headed off in the direction of the other group of monks who had left the ruins with him.

Celest and Kiran both looked a little confused at the Head Master. Ash could see the question that dominated their thought. The wards are set, but now how do they detonate them? Ash was pretty sure he knew what the Head Master was planning at that moment.

"Ash, if you don't mind..." the Head Master said, turning his attention to Ash.

Ash looked towards the opening of the ruins, its dark secrets calling out to him. He knew that the device inside had to be locked away for ever, that it was far too dangerous for anyone to be messing around with.

The wards were set and Ash knew that this dark power that he now wielded would become the catalyst that could trigger the explosions that would be needed to cave in the ruins. As soon as Calder had suggested placing wards within the ruins to be detonated, Ash had come to the conclusion that his dark threads could potentially set off the wards.

He felt for the dark weaves that lay within him. He could feel its desire to be used, to be released. He reached for the darkness that now clung to his very being and let it wrap around his hands and arms. The threads began spinning around in a ball between his open hands, raging with a force that seemed to taint the air around them. Ash let the ball of darkness rise to its energetic peak, with its threads thrashing about in front of him.

The others must have felt uneasy about what was happening. They all stepped back from him, except for Kiran, who continued watching intently on what he had been manifesting. When he finally felt that he had forced enough of the darkness into that small orb of destruction, he forced it forward, into the entrance of the ruins.

He could feel it moving at such a rapid pace through the halls of the ruins, as though still connected to him somehow. Explosions sounded within that sent vibrations through the ground at their feet. Ash kept his focus on the movement of his creation though, forcing its direction down towards the device that lay below.

As Ash could sense the dark force approach the chamber where the device rested, he felt a change. The device lashed out at his dark intrusion and sucked it into its own mass, absorbing it within itself. Ash felt the connection with his creation sever.

The others looked to him as though expecting more, but he could only shrug his shoulders in response. "The device absorbed my attempt to detonate the wards that were in the chamber." He looked just as confused as they did.

"The rest of the ruins are sealed up, and now there are wards in place around the device." Rennick said, looking towards the Head Master for confirmation of agreement. "That should be enough to deter anyone from trying to go after the device." The Head Master did nod towards Rennick, but Ash could sense the hesitation in the gesture.

Ash considered the nod as meaning that the task was complete. He rubbed his weary hands against the side of his face, as though to wipe the exhaustion from his mind. They would rest at the monastery tonight. Come morning, they would have to decide what came next.

It was as if Rennick had plucked the thought straight from Ash's mind. "I'll see to it that you all have beds tonight. You've more than earned a well-deserved rest." Without waiting for a reply, he turned and strode toward the main monastery buildings.

Calder exhaled, his breath a thin mist in the cooling air. "I must get inside as well," he said, offering a tired smile to the monks. "These old bones have their own mind about the cold, and they protest louder with each passing year. Wisdom may come with age, but so do aches, pains, and the memories of battles best left behind." His words trailed off into something quieter, almost muttered to himself, as he shuffled down the path, his novice attendant keeping a careful pace at his side.

Celest glanced toward Ash. "Perhaps we can get something light to eat before turning in," she suggested, though she hardly needed his approval. He was no commander issuing orders, no grand figure of authority—just another monk who had completing a mission like any other. Even so, he placed a steadying hand against her back and nodded.

"A little food in the belly sounds like a good idea," he agreed, and together, the three of them followed the path after Calder, their steps slow, the strain of exhaustion pressing down at last.

"Ash?" Kiran's voice was quieter, almost hesitant, as she moved to his side. "Would you mind if I stayed in your room tonight? I don't want to be alone. And… there are some things I'd like to talk to you about."

He turned to her, catching the sorrow in her dark eyes. She had been through much in the past few days, more than she should have had to endure. And there had been no time to talk, no moment to process the things they had seen, the things they had done. He understood that she needed someone—not just to listen, but to understand.

"I'll make sure we get a room with two beds," he said, offering her a small smile as he draped an arm around her shoulders. She leaned into it, just slightly, as though drawing some comfort from the gesture.

She was a good kid. Strong. Capable. But the world had forced her to grow up faster than she should have. And there was no undoing that now.

As they wound their way through the monastery's quiet paths, the cool night air settling in around them, Ash caught sight of a young novice emerging from the kitchens. Without breaking stride, he gestured for her attention. The girl halted, eyes wide with silent deference, and Ash wasted no time.

"Would you send word to Brother Rennick? Let him know we'll need an extra bed in my quarters for Kiran."

She nodded without hesitation and disappeared into the night, her sandaled feet whispering against the stone as she made her way toward the sleeping quarters.

Inside the kitchen, the warmth of the fire greeted them, carrying the rich scent of soup still warming in the pot. A basket of fresh buns rested on the counter beside it, a simple yet welcome sight. Celest, never one to stand on ceremony, grabbed a bowl and filled it without waiting for invitation. Ash and Kiran followed her lead, each taking their portion in silence. Their fatigue pressed against them, muting any inclination toward conversation.

They ate, the occasional scrape of a spoon against a bowl the only sound between them. When the meal was finished, they left the comfort of the fire behind, stepping out into the darkened courtyard. The path to the sleeping quarters was dimly lit by flickering torches, their light casting restless shadows against the monastery's stone walls. The air had turned bitter now that the sun had slipped beneath the horizon, and Kiran exhaled a long breath, watching the vapour curl and dissipate in the cold.

When they reached the two-story dormitory, a young woman awaited them at the entrance. Her long blonde hair was pulled back into a loose braid, and she held herself with the quiet discipline of one accustomed to the monastery's ways.

"I am Sister Vaelin," she introduced herself with a polite nod. "I will take you to your rooms."

They murmured their thanks and followed her inside. The halls were dim, the glow of lanterns casting soft pools of light along the stone corridors. At the far end, they reached a staircase leading to the upper level, their footfalls echoing through the silence. The noise must have disturbed one of the younger monks, for a door creaked open, and a weary face peered out. Celest offered a quiet apology, and the young man merely nodded before retreating back into the dark.

At last, Vaelin came to a stop before a wooden door. She rested her palm lightly against it and turned toward them. "This is the room with two beds, as requested."

Kiran stepped forward, pausing just long enough to

give Celest a quick embrace. "Rest well," she murmured.

"You too," Celest said, her voice carrying the lingering strain of the day.

Ash offered Celest a firm pat on the shoulder before following Kiran inside. Vaelin hesitated for the briefest moment, her expression betraying a flicker of curiosity as Ash passed her, but she said nothing. He closed the door behind them with a quiet thud.

The room was simple, built for function rather than comfort. Two beds stretched across from one another, framing a narrow window on the far wall. A small wooden table sat beneath it, holding an empty water basin and a flickering lantern that bathed the room in golden light. Near the door, three pegs jutted from the wall, bare save for a single, forgotten scrap of cloth left by some previous occupant.

Ash moved with silent ease, propping his quarterstaff in the corner and hanging his cloak on one of the pegs. With a sigh, he shrugged off his pack, letting it drop beside the bed opposite Kiran's. She had already settled onto the mattress, silent and pensive, her fingers tracing the fabric of the blanket absently. It had been a long day. And it was not over yet.

Ash kicked off his boots, rubbing at the soreness in his feet, though the ache ran deeper than muscle and bone. The burden of the past days pressed on him like a stone, and exhaustion made his limbs heavy. Across the room, Kiran sat motionless, her gaze fixed on the flickering candle in the lantern. The warm light cast restless shadows over her face, but it did nothing to soften the tension in her features. She looked as if she were unravelling some thought too vast to be contained, something raw and unsettling.

He watched her for a long moment before finally breaking the silence. "What is it?"

She turned to him then, her dark eyes meeting his, and in their depths, he saw something that made his stomach twist. Doubt. Fear. The kind of questions that could rot a person from the inside out.

"When we fought the nárgrim at the gates," she said, her voice quiet, "I reached for the Divine Mother's power. I prayed. I begged. But there was nothing. No warmth, no light—just emptiness." Her fingers curled in her lap, gripping at the edges of her robes as if she could hold herself together by sheer will. "Has she abandoned us, Ash? Or did we abandon her?"

Ash exhaled slowly, considering his answer. He should have asked himself the same question, but in the chaos of survival, faith had been the last thing on his mind. Yet now, forced to face it, he realized the unease had been festering beneath the surface, a quiet whisper in the back of his thoughts.

"The Divine Mother does not abandon those who

turn to her," he said at last, though even to his own ears, it sounded more like a hope than a certainty. "But I think… somehow, Morrathis has come between us and the Mother's power. She's intercepted it, replacing it with her own."

Kiran's eyes flickered with something unreadable—anger, perhaps, or grief. "What if I don't *want* Morrathis' power?" she asked, her voice sharper now, more urgent. "It doesn't feel right. It doesn't *belong* to me." Her hands clenched tighter around the fabric of her robes, her knuckles paling. "I just want to be *me.* But I don't think I am anymore. I feel—tainted."

Ash watched her carefully, choosing his words with care. "The Divine Mother would not place a burden upon us if she didn't believe we could bear it." He tried for a reassuring smile, but she saw through it. He could tell. The truth was, even he wasn't certain. Not anymore.

A forced smile crept onto her lips, brittle and hollow. She wanted to believe him, but belief alone was not enough.

After a moment, she spoke again, her voice softer. "Do you think Morrathis will release us when we fulfill our bargain?"

Ash had asked himself that same question too many times. The goddess of death was not known for her mercy. If they proved useful to her, why *would* she let them go?

"I don't know," he admitted. "But I'll fight to the death to free you from her grasp."

Her gaze lingered on him for a beat longer, and then, slowly, she loosened her grip on her robes. Ash reached out, resting his hand over her fist, and she let out a slow breath, her fingers uncurling beneath his touch.

She looked up at him, her expression searching. "If we aren't wielding the Divine Mother's power, if we're following the will of Morrathis... are we even monks anymore?"

Ash had no easy answer for that. How long had she dreamed of taking her vows, of serving the Divine Mother? And now, that dream was unravelling, slipping from her grasp like sand through her fingers.

He met her gaze and said, "We serve the Divine Mother. We follow Morrathis' direction *only* when it does not stray from that path." His voice steadied. "We are monks of the Divine Mother. Whatever this is, whatever we have agreed to—it is temporary. We will see this through, and then we will set it right."

For the first time that night, Kiran's expression softened. The worry was still there, but now, perhaps, there was something else beneath it. A sliver of hope.

The lantern's flame flickered, and the silence between them stretched long. Eventually, Kiran lay back, staring at the ceiling, while Ash leaned against the wall, lost

in his own thoughts.
"Ash?"

Kiran's voice barely disturbed the silence, a whisper carried by the dim glow of the lantern. She lay still on her bed, but her eyes, dark and searching, turned to focus on him. There was something in them—hesitation, uncertainty, a question she wasn't sure she wanted answered.

"If I start to turn…" she hesitated, fingers curling into the blanket at her side, her voice barely audible. "Dark. Evil. Will you guide me back? Will you remind me of who I was?"

The words struck harder than she probably intended, heavier than either of them were prepared for. The question burrowed into his mind, coiling there like something waiting to unfurl in the dark. What *would* he do if she started to change? If the power of Morrathis took root inside her, twisting her into something unrecognizable?

"Of course," he said, his own voice barely more than breath. "I've always got your back."

The promise came easily, instinctively, but the moment the words left his lips, his stomach knotted. He had spoken those same words before. To another young monk. To a youth-who now lay dead beneath the ruins. The memory of it was sudden and sharp, and guilt bled into his thoughts. He had promised to protect, to stand beside, to never let harm come. And yet—

He closed his eyes for a moment, swallowing down the ache in his chest.

The room settled into silence once more, save for the soft crackle of the lantern's flame. A moment later, Kiran's breathing slowed, deepened. Soon, the faint sound of her snoring reached him—gentle, almost peaceful. The edges of his mouth curled, though the weight pressing down on him did not lift.

He let himself sink back onto the pillow, staring at the ceiling, his mind unwilling to grant him rest. The past few days pressed in around him, a tangle of unanswered questions, of shifting certainties. His path had never felt so uncertain, the line between light and shadow never so thin.

Sleep would not come easy. But then, it never did.

Chapter 25:
Departure

Morning came too soon. Ash felt as if he had only just closed his eyes when the first hints of light spilled through the window, prodding him from restless sleep. He considered lying there a moment longer, savouring what little comfort remained in the warmth of his blankets, but the thought was fleeting. There was no time for lingering. Too many questions needed answering, too many things left undone.

With a sigh, he swung his legs over the edge of the bed, bracing for the usual stiffness—the deep aches earned from battle, the dull protest of overworked muscles. Yet, none came. That gave him pause. His body should have felt battered, worn down from the strain of yesterday's fight, but instead, he felt… restored. Energized, even. He flexed his fingers, testing the strength in them. Whatever exhaustion had nearly undone him the night before had vanished in the night. Strange.

His gaze flicked to Kiran's bed. Empty. She had risen before him and left without a sound. He hadn't even stirred. A part of him was glad—she deserved what rest she could get—but another part was wary. After last night's conversation, he hoped she had found sleep easier than he had.

Reaching down, he retrieved his worn boots and pulled them on with little ceremony, grimacing as his feet met the cold leather. He freed his hair from its tie, running his fingers through the tangled mess before pulling it back and binding it again.

A basin of water sat on the small table by the wall, half-filled, with a copper pitcher beside it. He poured some into the basin and splashed the water over his face, the cold liquid barely clinging to it. The chill was startling, but it served its purpose, clearing away the remnants of sleep and sharpening his thoughts.

He slung his pack over one shoulder, grasped his staff and cloak, and stepped out into the corridor. The monastery had already come to life around him, the quiet hum of morning routines drifting through the halls. He wasn't surprised. He had always been the last to rise. The others, younger and less burdened by years, took it upon themselves to let him sleep, assuming he needed the rest. It was one of the few benefits of being the so-called *old fellow.*

Outside, the cold greeted him like an old adversary, biting against his skin and drawing a sharp breath from his lungs. A thin veil of snow covered the monastery grounds, though the rising sun had already begun its slow work of erasing it. Winter was creeping closer. Soon, the real snows would come, and with them, new challenges. He traced a line through the frost-laced earth with the toe of his boot, thoughts already weighing the implications. Decisions would need to be made. Some of them, he would not like.

He followed the well-worn path toward the dining hall, his steps falling into the trail left by the monks who had risen before him. A few passed him on their way to their duties, offering polite nods. He returned them in kind. A young novice held the door open for him as he approached, bowing her head slightly in greeting.

"Morning, master monk," she said, voice warm and inviting.

Ash nodded, offering a brief smile. "And to you as well."

For a fleeting moment, he thought she might be the same novice who had shown them to their rooms last night, but he wasn't certain. He really should pay more attention to the details. It was a failing of his—faces, names, all too easily slipping through the cracks of his mind. It was a small thing, but small things mattered.

Stepping inside, the scent of warm food met him, filling the great hall with an air of momentary comfort. He scanned the room and quickly spotted Kiran and Celest seated at a table near the far wall, joined by Doran and the young soldier who had accompanied them. What was his name again? Ash frowned. The boy had been introduced when they first met, but the name eluded him. *Another reminder to pay better attention.*

Navigating through the rows of occupied tables, Ash approached and slid onto the bench beside his companions. They greeted him as he sat, their words light but carrying an underlying strain. There was an energy to them—heightened, restless—but beneath it lay the unmistakable shadows of grief. The battle had taken its toll. They had lost good men. Good friends.

Ash met their gazes in turn, noting the unspoken sorrow lingering behind their eyes. They had survived, but survival was not without cost.

"I trust everyone had an adequate rest," Ash said, his tone light but edged with expectation as his gaze swept over his companions.

A couple hesitant nods followed, though some were coupled with raised brows, subtle protests against his choice of words. The rest merely responded with grunts, the universal language of the battle-weary and sleep-deprived.

Doran leaned back, rubbing a hand over his unshaven chin before jerking a thumb toward the young soldier at his side. "Garron and I will be heading out shortly after we finish here. We need to get back to our post with news of what's transpired these past days." He punctuated the statement by tearing off a chunk of bread and tossing it into his mouth, chewing with the air of a man who had said his piece and was done with it.

Ash nodded, absorbing the words even as his own thoughts drifted elsewhere. "I'll be staying here a while," he said at last, drawing a few glances from the others, some curious, others mildly surprised. "Dawn's End isn't my first choice for wintering. Gods know, I've grown to despise the cold, and Dawn's End has more of it than I care for." A smirk ghosted across his lips before fading. "But there are things I need to look into—things I can't ignore."

He let the dismay of that statement settle over them before continuing. "This… *transition* that Kiran and I have endured—I need to understand it, to know if there's a way to undo it." He glanced briefly at Kiran, searching her face for any reaction, but she kept her gaze locked on the table. "Then there's Kael. He may not be a threat at this moment, but whatever he has planned, I doubt he's finished."

Celest, who had been listening in thoughtful silence, finally spoke. "I had hoped to return to Maiden's Haven, but if you need me to stay, I'd be happy to offer my services."

Ash met her gaze, appreciating the offer more than he could express. Having her experience and skill at his side would be invaluable, but he knew it was not her burden to bear. More importantly, there was something else he needed her to do. "I'd be honoured to have you with me, but your place is at the monastery," he said, his tone firm but not unkind. "Headmaster Mandor needs to know everything that's happened. He needs to hear it from you."

Celest studied him for a long moment before inclining her head. He didn't miss the quiet relief in her expression. She would not argue—because she had no desire to stay. The road had been long, the toll heavy. She had earned her reprieve.

"I'm not even going to respond to this conversation," Kiran muttered, crossing her arms over her chest in a defiant posture. "I'm stuck with you until this is figured out."

She still refused to meet his eyes, staring at a knot in surface of the heavy wooden table. There was no need for further discussion—her mind had been made up long before this moment. Ash had no intention of arguing. If anything, he wanted her there, needed her insight as much as she needed answers of her own. An extra set of hands and sharp eyes wouldn't hurt either.

"I wouldn't have it any other way," he said simply.

A smirk tugged at the corner of her lips, small but unmistakable. It was enough to make Ash grin in return.

"Well then," he said, rising from his seat and stretching his shoulders. "If that's settled, I think I'll see if there's any food left in the kitchen before the novices pick it clean."

Without waiting for a response, he turned and strode toward the kitchen, leaving the others to their conversations. He was sure that they would have plenty to discuss, plenty of plans to make for their days ahead.

When Ash returned to the dining hall, the room had nearly emptied. Only Kiran remained at their table, sitting on the same bench as before, her posture more at ease. Across the room, a pair of novices sat murmuring over their meal, their conversation low and unimportant. He made his way back to Kiran, but rather than sitting beside her, he took the seat opposite, forcing her to meet his gaze. She no longer seemed burdened by the same troubles from the night before. Instead, she offered him a small smile.

"I'm sorry about last night," she said, rubbing her palms absently against the worn wooden surface of the table. "I was in a heavy mood and just needed to share my concerns." She shrugged as if embarrassed by the admission.

Ash shook his head. "No need to apologize." His voice was steady, but there was something distant in his tone, an understanding carried in his words. "I've had the same concerns as you, I just—" He exhaled through his nose, half-nodding to himself. "I suppose I've just learned to bury them. Keep them locked away. Not because they don't trouble me, but because I assumed no one else would want to carry them." A faint, humourless smirk touched his lips. "Smile, go about your business, pretend none of it lingers."

She studied him, saying nothing, but he could see

in her expression that she understood all too well. After a beat of silence, he leaned forward slightly. "I'm glad to have you with me." Her eyes lifted to his, her smile warming just a little.

"Before I met you, I felt like just another washed-up monk," he admitted, his fingers drumming idly against the tabletop. "Someone who had served his purpose in his youth, but was now expected to spend his days tending gardens or buried in secluded reading." A short, self-deprecating laugh escaped him. "You've given me back my sense of meaning, or at least something close to it."

He paused, frowning slightly, as if reconsidering his choice of words. "It felt *right* to be fighting beside you," he finally said. "To be able to share what I know, to use it for something real again."

Kiran glanced away, her lips pressing together in discomfort. Compliments didn't sit well with her.

Ash let the moment pass before reaching into his pack. He hesitated for half a breath, then withdrew the two tomes he had stored away, setting them carefully on the table before pushing them toward her. She looked at him, then at the books, her expression shifting into something that hovered between curiosity and hesitation. He could see the silent question in her eyes—*You trust me with these?*

She ran a fingertip over the etchings on the top book's cover, tracing the intricate patterns. He understood the impulse. He had done the same when he first took the time to truly examine the craftsmanship, marvelling at the detail of the embossed sigils.

"I figured between the two of us, we might be able to extract something useful," he said, leaning back as he tore a piece of bread from a half-loaf and popped it into his mouth, chewing thoughtfully before spooning up some of his oatmeal. "Something that might help us gain some control over this condition—maybe even find a way to rid ourselves of it."

Kiran remained still, her fingers resting lightly on the tome's cover. Then, in a quiet voice, she asked, "I know I've asked you this before, but… do you really think we'll find an answer in these books?" There was no skepticism in her tone, only concern.

Ash wiped his mouth with the back of his hand before answering. "Kael knew more about this condition than we do," he said, tapping a finger against the tome closest to her. "I don't know if he ever looked for a way to *undo* it, but it's clear he studied it deeply. Maybe there's something in his writings that gives us an edge, something we can use." His gaze shifted briefly to the second book. "The other one is mostly lore—accounts of others who've experienced this before us. Not much in the way of practical application, but maybe… maybe there's something buried in the details."

His voice trailed off, and for a long moment, they sat in silence, uncertainty settling between them. Then, Kiran pulled the books closer, her expression hopeful.

"We should probably get moving. Celest was gathering supplies earlier, and I'd like to say goodbye before she heads out," Kiran said as she rose from her seat.

Ash gave a nod and stood as well. She handed him the two books, and he carefully slid them back into his pack before swinging it over his shoulder. Gripping his quarterstaff where it rested against the table's edge, he fell into step beside her.

"Ash?" Her voice cracked slightly as she spoke his name, hesitation flickering across her face. Whatever she meant to say was lost in the moment as she simply stepped forward and wrapped her arms around him. Surprised, Ash froze for the briefest of moments before sliding his free arm around her and pulling her in close.

"Thank you," she whispered, lingering just long enough for him to feel the tension ease from her shoulders before she pulled away.

He met her gaze and offered a quiet nod, the faintest trace of a smile on his lips.

They stepped out into the morning cold, and Ash immediately regretted leaving the warmth of the hall. The wind cut sharp, threading through his cloak like it had weight, seeping into his skin. He pulled the fabric tighter around him and noted Kiran doing the same. At least it wasn't just him—at least the chill wasn't another sign of his age creeping up on him.

The path before them was quiet save for the crunch of stone beneath their boots. A few monks passed on their way to morning duties, nodding in passing but saying nothing. Ash and Kiran made their way toward the monastery gates, now standing open, flanked by two vigilant guards, their breath curling in the cold air.

Kiran spotted Celest first, moving along one of the side paths. Her pack was slung over her shoulder, her quarterstaff repurposed as a walking stick. At the sight of them, she lifted her head, her face breaking into a grin. Without hesitation, she quickened her pace, striding toward them.

"Hey, I was hoping I'd run into you before I left," she said as she reached them. "Thought you two might be too preoccupied to come see me off."

"Nonsense," Kiran said, pulling Celest into a fierce embrace. "We would never allow you to leave without saying goodbye."

Celest held her at arm's length, studying her with something that hovered between pride and fondness. "You've come a long way, Kiran." Her voice was warm, steady. "Take care of yourself out there—and keep the old man out of trouble, yeah?"

Ash arched a brow at that, but the two women only laughed at his expense. He shook his head, exhaling a quiet chuckle as well.

Celest turned to him, extending a hand for a shake, but instead, she pulled him into a tight embrace. Her strength caught him off guard. He had known she was strong—her frame and skill had spoken for that—but underestimating it was a mistake. He patted her back, his own grip firm as they pulled apart.

"It was an honour fighting alongside you," he said, nodding. "I hope our paths cross again. Maybe under less dire circumstances, though I suspect that if fate did bring us back together it would not be under pleasant circumstances."

Celest smirked. "Well, I do hope your journey ahead isn't riddled with too many obstacles." She glanced at Kiran and smiled before they resumed walking toward the gates in silence.

Doran and Garron rounded the corner of a weathered stone building, their packs slung over their shoulders, swords swaying at their hips with each step. Their expressions brightened when they caught sight of the waiting companions, a shared grin passing between them. The exertion of their past battles still lingered on their faces, but there was a quiet ease in their demeanour, a soldier's acceptance of danger endured and survived.

Ash stepped forward, clasping each man's hand in turn, his grip firm with gratitude. "Your aid at the monastery was invaluable," he said. "Had you not been there, the outcome might have been far worse."

Kiran moved beside him, offering her own thanks as she shook their hands. "When I didn't see you at the gate, I assumed you'd already set off."

Doran chuckled, adjusting the strap of his pack. "We would have, but when we heard Celest was leaving today, we figured we'd walk with her down the mountain pass." His gaze flicked toward Celest, and though his voice remained light, there was an undertone of practicality in his words. "Still a mountain lion prowling somewhere out there, maybe even a lost nárgrim. Seems smarter to travel in numbers."

Ash nodded, stepping back to stand beside Kiran and Celest. "I'm glad you'll be travelling together. Celest is more than capable, but it eases my mind knowing the two of you will be with her. Watching each other's backs."

The soldiers gave him a respectful nod, their easy smiles never quite masking the readiness in their eyes. They were warriors, after all, and the road ahead—like every road in these uncertain times—was never without its dangers.

At the gate, Ash and Kiran shared one final embrace with Celest before she turned and joined the soldiers, slinging her pack higher on her shoulder, and strode down the path, leaving the monastery behind.

Ash considered retreating back inside to chase away the cold, but Kiran remained rooted in place, watching Celest and the soldiers until they disappeared from view. Only then did she exhale, glance once at Ash, and turn back toward the path leading deeper into the monastery's grounds. Without a word, he fell into step beside her.

Ash exhaled slowly, watching the faint mist of his breath dissipate in the crisp morning air. He adjusted the strap of his pack, glancing at Kiran before speaking.

"I think we should wait out the winter here," he said, his voice steady. "We can study the texts, make sense of what we've uncovered, and plan our next move." He let the words settle, then added, "Winters here tend to stretch longer than most, but we'll put that time to use."

Kiran met his gaze, searching for something in his expression before offering a quiet nod. There was no hesitation, no argument—just silent agreement.

Without another word, they turned toward the largest of the monastery's buildings, their steps heavier, yet wilful. The stone path stretched ahead of them, a road leading toward warmth and respite. Beyond that, the true path—the one that mattered—remained uncertain, waiting to be shaped by whatever they uncovered in the cold months to come.

Epilogue

Malakar moved through the darkened corridor, his steps a whisper against the ancient stone, a sound barely more than a breath in the stagnant air. The walls, slick with the damp weight of centuries, loomed close around him, but their chill did not touch him. It had been years—longer, perhaps—since such sensations had meant anything at all. The nerves that once carried the sharp bite of cold, the warmth of a fire, the thrill of pain, or the simple indulgence of touch had long since withered into useless relics of a past self. What remained was something less than life, yet more than death—a hollow existence animated by will alone, sustained not by breath or blood, but by something darker.

Even now, he could recall the ghost of sensation, a memory of what it was to feel. But that, too, was slipping away. Soon, there would be nothing left but purpose, sharpened into something cold and unrelenting. And that, he supposed, was fitting.

He had grown to loathe this body—this husk of a form he had bartered for power. His skin, papery and brittle, threatened to tear with even the simplest of movements. His hair, once thick and dark in his youth, now clung to his scalp in cobweb-thin strands. His flesh had become more like dust than anything living. He had become something else, something greater, something less. A creature of the undead, a being of will and magic, cursed by the choices he had made.

Stopping before a heavy wooden door at the hall's end, Malakar hesitated. His mind wandered, tracing the winding path that had led him here—the choices made, the power claimed, the price paid. Immortality and dominion, the twin lures that had drawn him to this fate. How many had dreamed of such gifts? How many would trade away their souls for even a fraction of what he possessed? Yet, in the long, quiet hours of contemplation, he often wondered—had he been given the choice again, would he have taken a different path?

He shook the thought aside and pushed open the door. Inside, the obsidian table gleamed beneath the flickering candlelight, its polished surface reflecting the figures of his companions, already seated, waiting. Neither spoke as he entered. They only acknowledged him with a nod, knowing better than to waste words on pleasantries—or to comment on his lateness. They had squabbled over such trivial matters before, but each had learned their lessons in turn.

Malakar moved past Thal'gorath and took his seat at the head of the table, the scrape of wood against stone echoing through the chamber. He exhaled a slow, rattling breath, a sound that might have once been a sigh, and lifted skeletal hands to the table, fingers interwoven. A hoarse cough rattled in his throat, but he made no attempt to speak. Instead, he turned his gaze to Valrath, who was all too eager to begin.

Valrath smiled, though there was no warmth in it. His lips peeled back, the cracked flesh splitting at the corners, revealing jagged teeth that barely clung to the desiccated remnants of his gums. Malakar did not shudder, though the urge pressed against him like a whisper of his former humanity.

"It is clear that this monk, Kael, has failed," Valrath said at last, his voice a dry rasp, as if spoken through ancient parchment. "Either he miscalculated or failed to anticipate certain... complications. I don't have the details of his defeat. Not yet."

He turned his gaze toward Thal'gorath, perhaps expecting an argument. After all, Thal'gorath had never fully supported entrusting the monk with such an important task. But the younger lich only nodded in acknowledgement, his long, claw-like fingernail tapping a slow, deliberate rhythm against the table's surface.

"We will have to wait for Kael's return before we learn more of the situation," Valrath continued, settling back into his chair. His brittle form crackled with the movement, dry bones and ancient sinew shifting as he sought a more comfortable position.

Malakar said nothing. He merely watched, listened, considered. The game was far from over, and Kael's failure—if indeed he had failed—was but a single move in a much greater contest.

Thal'gorath's black, sunken eyes narrowed, his skeletal fingers curling around the edge of the table as if it were the only thing anchoring him to the present. His voice came like a blade honed on old grievances, each syllable laced with venom. "You brought the monk to us," he spat, his words cracking through the stillness. "You swore he had potential. We should have ended him the moment he set foot in our presence. Now look where we are." His disappointment radiated like a storm held barely in check, each accusation a force meant to shift the course of what had already been set in motion.

Valrath's withered features tightened, though his response came thoughtful, tempered by centuries of restraint. His voice, though quiet, carried the weight of his conviction. "Kael would have come for us regardless. His thirst for knowledge, his need to understand the power that stirred within him—it was only a matter of time. We were never the architects of his path; we merely offered him a doorway. He followed the same echoes of the past that we did, and now, inevitably, he stands where we once stood."

The chamber was silent but for the rhythmic

tapping of Valrath's nails against the obsidian table, each impact a heavy, methodical beat that betrayed the irritation seething beneath his controlled exterior. He leaned back, his bones creaking, the desiccated remnants of his flesh stretching taut. When he spoke again, his tone had shifted, smoothing into something more calculated. "Kael's work is not yet finished. A single failure does not seal our fate. The Ancients were not fools. If one artifact existed, there may yet be another. They would not have placed all their knowledge, all their power, in a single vessel. We must consider the possibility that they prepared contingencies."

Thal'gorath's gaze dropped, his fingers tracing idle patterns against the polished stone. The fire behind his words dimmed, replaced by something quieter, heavier. "Hope alone will not carry us to our goal," he murmured, uncertainty creeping into his voice. "We lack the knowledge to recreate such a thing ourselves. We placed too much faith in Kael, assuming he could unravel what centuries have buried. Perhaps we should have guided him more, shaped his understanding instead of trusting him to find his own way." The admission sat thick between them, the certainty in his earlier defiance eroding, leaving only the bitter taste of doubt.

The three of them had set this plan in motion, and now, as cracks formed in its foundation, each was left to wonder whether the path they had chosen had been theirs at all—or if they, too, were merely playing a role in something far older, far more inevitable.

Malakar, who had remained silent until now, finally spoke, his voice carrying quiet authority. "There is nothing to be done at this moment." The words were cold, the finality in them unmistakable. "We will wait for Kael to return. When he does, we will learn what went wrong, and only then will we determine our next course of action." He lifted a hand to his face, absently rubbing at his cheek before recoiling, disgust flickering in his pale eyes. The sound of his flesh cracking under his touch—brittle, parchment-thin—sickened him. He placed his hand back on the table, the movement almost involuntary, a small but telling betrayal of his own distaste for what he had become.

Thal'gorath turned to him, disbelief sharp in his expression. "And if he does not return?" His voice was edged with suspicion, a current of barely contained frustration threading through it. "We have given him enough knowledge to make himself a power in his own right. Why should he come back at all? He could remain in the east, gather followers, carve out his own dominion. What need has he of us now?" The question hung in the air, laced with an unspoken accusation—one that suggested their reliance on Kael had been a mistake from the beginning.

Malakar exhaled slowly, shaking his head. A small,

almost imperceptible smile curled the corners of his lips, a glint of something knowing in his sunken gaze. "He will return." The certainty in his tone was unshakable, as cold as the grave. "Kael is hungry for answers. We have what he seeks, and as long as we keep those answers just beyond his reach, he will always come back. His curiosity, his thirst for knowledge, is his greatest weakness. It binds him to us more effectively than any spell."

Valrath gave a slow, considering nod, his expression shifting from skepticism to restrained understanding. Thal'gorath, however, remained unconvinced, his hollow gaze fixed on Malakar, searching for any flaw in his reasoning.

"There is no guarantee," Malakar admitted, his voice slicing cleanly through the lingering tension. "But Kael knows the truth. He understands that, for now, we are allies he cannot afford to lose. He also knows that, should he choose to betray us, we would become enemies he cannot afford to make." His gaze locked with Thal'gorath's, daring him to refute the point. The silence that followed was telling. For all Kael's growing power, he was still a fledgling compared to the three of them—his potential vast, but his experience lacking. That truth was undeniable.

For a long moment, the chamber was steeped in contemplation, each of them weighing the words spoken and the uncertain path ahead. In the end, there was no question. This was not over. The game had not yet been decided. And Kael, however weak he may be, had proven himself and *would* return.

"It is settled, then," Malakar finally said, as though sealing an unspoken pact. He leaned back, the creak of his chair cutting through the heavy stillness that had settled over them. "We wait for Kael. When he returns, we will reassess and decide how to proceed. Until then, our work continues. We will comb through the remnants of the past, sift through every whisper of lost knowledge until we find what we seek—a way to wield this power without limit." His gaze swept over the two figures seated across from him, the dim torchlight catching on the wasted remnants of their faces. Slowly, they nodded, silent in their agreement. The decision had been made.

Malakar did not rise immediately. He remained seated, his fingers curled loosely against the cold surface of the table, his gaze fixed on the empty space where his companions had stood only moments before. Their absence left a silence that pressed against him, thick with unspoken truths. His mind turned inward, cold and precise, sifting through the nuances of their exchange. There had been something in the way Valrath had spoken—something subtle yet unmistakable, a shadow beneath his words, a quiet, insidious shift of intent. Malakar could feel it, not in anything tangible, but in the very air, as if the room itself had recoiled from the undercurrent of unspoken ambition. Valrath hungered. Not for knowledge, not for power alone, but for control.

It was inevitable. In time, that hunger would surface in full. Malakar knew this as surely as he knew the paths of the stars, the cycles of the moon, the immutable truths that governed existence. The day would come when Valrath would tire of the pretense of obedience, when he would seek to claim what was not his to take. The thought did not unsettle Malakar, nor did it inspire anger. Instead, it stirred something deeper—something ancient and patient. He would be ready. When the time came, when Valrath made his move, Malakar would remind him who had been first among them, who had reached into the abyss and grasped what the others had only dared to glimpse.

A small, grim smile curled at the edge of his mouth. Outwardly, to those who stood at his side, he was an equal. His influence, his authority—these were things carefully measured, balanced in appearance. But the truth ran deeper, coiled beneath the surface like a serpent in the dark. Valrath and Thal'gorath wielded power, but they had only scraped at the edges of true understanding. They did not know, could not *comprehend*, what Malakar had taken into himself, the fragment of something vast and ineffable that burned within him like a silent, unquenchable fire.

There were nights when he almost wished he could

relinquish it, when the force of it pressed against his soul like iron. But such thoughts were fleeting, and he would never give voice to them. He had made his choice long ago, and there was no turning back.

About The Author

Syd Nault is an author of Dark Fantasy, Epic Fantasy, and Cosmic Horror fiction. He has been writing since he was very young.

Syd spends most of his time reading books on all topics of interest, though mostly spirituality, and religions, which he likes to incorporate into his writings. He also enjoys playing his guitar and sketching out his ideas on paper.

He and his wife live in a small, rural community in Ontario, Canada with their two dogs.

Manufactured by Amazon.ca
Bolton, ON

45417281R00232